QUEECHY.

BY

ELIZABETH WETHERELL,

AUTHOR OF "THE WIDE, WIDE WORLD."

"I hope I may speak of woman without offence to the ladies."
THE GUARDIAN.

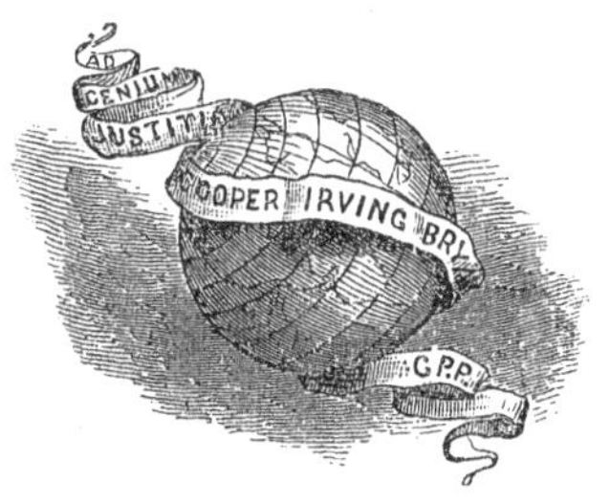

VOLUME I.

New York:
GEORGE P. PUTNAM, 10 PARK PLACE.
M.DCCC.LII.

STEREOTYPED BY
BILLIN & BROTHERS,
NO. 10 NORTH WILLIAM-ST., N. Y.

R. CRAIGHEAD, PRINTER,
VESEY-STREET.

CONTENTS OF VOL. I.

NOTE.

Whatever credit may be due to the bits of poetry in these volumes, it is not due to the writer of the rest. She has them only by gift—not the gift of nature.

QUEECHY.

CHAPTER I.

> A single cloud on a sunny day
> When all the rest of heaven is clear,
> A frown upon the atmosphere,
> That hath no business to appear,
> When skies are blue and earth is gay.
>
> BYRON.

"COME, dear grandpa!—the old mare and the wagon are at the gate—all ready."

"Well, dear!"— responded a cheerful hearty voice, "they must wait a bit; I haven't got my hat yet."

"O I'll get that."

And the little speaker, a girl of some ten or eleven years old, dashed past the old gentleman and running along the narrow passage which led to his room soon returned with the hat in her hand.

"Yes, dear,—but that ain't all. I must put on my great-coat—and I must look and see if I can find any money—"

"O yes—for the post-office. It's a beautiful day, grandpa. Cynthy!—won't you come and help grandpa on with his great-coat?—And I'll go out and keep watch of the old mare till you're ready."

A needless caution. For the old mare, though spirited enough for her years, had seen some fourteen or fifteen of them and was in no sort of danger of running away. She stood in what was called the back meadow, just without the little paling fence that enclosed a small courtyard round the house. Around this courtyard rich pasture-fields lay on every side, the high road cutting through them not more than a hundred or two feet from the house.

The little girl planted herself on the outside of the paling and setting her back to it eyed the old mare with great contentment; for besides other grounds for security as to her quiet behaviour, one of the men employed about the farm, who had harnessed the equipage, was at the moment busied in putting some clean straw in the bottom of the vehicle.

"Watkins," said the child presently to this person, "here is a strap that is just ready to come unbuckled."

"What do you know about straps and buckles?" said the man rather grumly. But he came round however to see what she meant, and while he drew the one and fastened the other took special good care not to let Fleda know that her watchful eyes had probably saved the whole riding party from ruin; as the loosing of the strap would of necessity have brought on a trial of the old mare's nerves which not all her philosophy could have been expected to meet. Fleda was satisfied to see the buckle made fast, and that Watkins, roused by her hint or by the cause of it, afterwards took a somewhat careful look over the whole establishment. In high glee then she climbed to her seat in the little wagon, and her grandfather coming out coated and hatted with some difficulty mounted to his place beside her.

"I think Watkins might have taken the trouble to wash the wagon, without hurting himself," said Fleda; "it is all speckled with mud since last time."

"Ha'n't he washed it!" said the old gentleman in a tone of displeasure. "Watkins!"—

"Well."—

"Why didn't you wash the wagon as I told you?"

"I did."

"It's all over slosh."

"That's Mr. Didenhover's work—he had it out day 'fore yesterday; and if you want it cleaned, Mr. Ringgan, you must speak to him about it. Mr. Didenhover may file his own doings; it's more than I'm a going to."

The old gentleman made no answer, except to acquaint the mare with the fact of his being in readiness to set out.

A shade of annoyance and displeasure for a moment was upon his face; but the gate opening from the meadow upon the high road had hardly swung back upon its hinges after letting them out when he recovered the calm sweetness of demeanour that was habitual with him, and seemed as well as his little granddaughter to have given care the go-by for the time. Fleda had before this found out another fault in the harness, or rather in Mr. Didenhover, which like a wise little child she kept to herself. A broken place which her grandfather had ordered to be properly mended was still tied up with the piece of rope which had offended her eyes the last time they had driven out. But she said not a word of it, because "it would only worry grandpa for nothing;" and forgetting it almost immediately she moved on with him in a state of joyous happiness that no mud-stained wagon nor untidy rope-bound harness could stir for an instant. Her spirit was like a clear still-running stream which quietly and surely deposits every defiling and obscuring admixture it may receive from its contact with the grosser elements around; the stream might for a moment be clouded; but a little while, and it would run as clear as ever. Neither Fleda nor her grandfather cared a jot for the want of elegancies which one despised, and the other if she had ever known had well nigh forgotten. What mattered it to her that the little old green wagon was rusty and worn, or that years and service had robbed the old mare of all the jauntiness she had ever possessed, so long as the sun shone and the birds sang? And Mr. Ringgan, in any imaginary comparison, might be pardoned for thinking that *he* was the proud man, and that his poor little equipage carried such a treasure as many a coach and four went without.

"Where are we going first, grandpa? to the post office?"

"Just there!"

"How pleasant it is to go there always, isn't it, grandpa? You have the paper to get, and I—I don't very often get a letter, but I have always the *hope* of getting one; and that's something. Maybe I'll have one to-day, grandpa?"

"We'll see. It's time those cousins of yours wrote to you."

"O *they* don't write to me—it's only Aunt Lucy; I never

had a letter from a single one of them, except once from little Hugh,—don't you remember, grandpa? I should think he must be a very nice little boy, shouldn't you?"

"Little boy? why I guess he is about as big as you are, Fleda—he is eleven years old, ain't he?"

"Yes, but I am past eleven, you know, grandpa, and I am a little girl."

This reasoning being unanswerable Mr. Ringgan only bade the old mare trot on.

It was a pleasant day in autumn. Fleda thought it particularly pleasant for riding, for the sun was veiled with thin hazy clouds. The air was mild and still, and the woods, like brave men, putting the best face upon falling fortunes. Some trees were already dropping their leaves; the greater part standing in all the varied splendour which the late frosts had given them. The road, an excellent one, sloped gently up and down across a wide arable country, in a state of high cultivation and now shewing all the rich variety of autumn. The reddish buckwheat patches, and fine wood-tints of the fields where other grain had been; the bright green of young rye or winter wheat, then soberer-coloured pasture or meadow lands, and ever and anon a tuft of gay woods crowning a rising ground, or a knot of the everlasting pines looking sedately and steadfastly upon the fleeting glories of the world around them; these were mingled and interchanged and succeeded each other in ever-varying fresh combinations. With its high picturesque beauty the whole scene had a look of thrift and plenty and promise which made it eminently cheerful. So Mr. Ringgan and his little granddaughter both felt it to be. For some distance the grounds on either hand the road were part of the old gentleman's farm; and many a remark was exchanged between him and Fleda as to the excellence or hopefulness of this or that crop or piece of soil; Fleda entering into all his enthusiasm, and reasoning of clover leys and cockle and the proper harvesting of Indian corn and other like matters, with no lack of interest or intelligence.

"O grandpa," she exclaimed suddenly, "won't you stop a minute and let me get out. I want to get some of that beautiful bittersweet."

"What do you want that for?" said he. "You can't get out very well."

"O yes I can—please, grandpa! I want some of it *very* much—just one minute!"

He stopped, and Fleda got out and went to the roadside, where a bittersweet vine had climbed into a young pine tree and hung it as it were with red coral. But her one minute was at least four before she had succeeded in breaking off as much as she could carry of the splendid creeper; for not until then could Fleda persuade herself to leave it. She came back and worked her way up into the wagon with one hand full as it could hold of her brilliant trophies.

"Now what good'll that do you?" inquired Mr. Ringgan good-humouredly, as he lent Fleda what help he could to her seat.

"Why grandpa, I want it to put with cedar and pine in a jar at home—it will keep for ever so long, and look beautiful. Isn't that handsome?—only it was a pity to break it."

"Why yes, it's handsome enough," said Mr. Ringgan, "but you've got something just by the front door there at home that would do just as well—what do you call it?—that flaming thing there?"

"What, my burning bush? O grandpa! I wouldn't cut that for any thing in the world! It's the only pretty thing about the house; and besides," said Fleda, looking up with a softened mien, "you said that it was planted by my mother. O grandpa! I wouldn't cut that for any thing."

Mr. Ringgan laughed a pleased laugh. "Well, dear!" said he, "it shall grow till it's as big as the house, if it will."

"It won't do that," said Fleda. "But I am very glad I have got this bittersweet—this is just what I wanted. Now if I can only find some holly—"

"We'll come across some, I guess, by and by," said Mr. Ringgan; and Fleda settled herself again to enjoy the trees, the fields, the roads, and all the small handiwork of nature, for which her eyes had a curious intelligence. But this was not fated to be a ride of unbroken pleasure.

"Why what are those bars down for?" she said as they came up with a field of winter grain. "Somebody's been in here with a wagon. O grandpa! Mr. Didenhover has let the Shakers have my butternuts!—the butternuts that you told him they mustn't have."

The old gentleman drew up his horse. "So he has!" said he.

Their eyes were upon the far end of the deep lot, where at the edge of one of the pieces of woodland spoken of, a picturesque group of men and boys in frocks and broad-brimmed white hats were busied in filling their wagon under a clump of the now thin and yellow leaved butternut trees.

"The scoundrel!" said Mr. Ringgan under his breath.

"Would it be any use, grandpa, for me to jump down and run and tell them you don't want them to take the butternuts?—I shall have so few."

"No, dear, no," said her grandfather, "they have got 'em about all by this time; the mischief's done. Didenhover meant to let 'em have 'em unknown to me, and pocket the pay himself. Get up!"

Fleda drew a long breath, and gave a hard look at the distant wagon where *her* butternuts were going in by handfuls. She said no more.

It was but a few fields further on that the old gentleman came to a sudden stop again.

"Ain't there some of my sheep over yonder there, Fleda,—along with Squire Thornton's?"

"I don't know, grandpa," said Fleda,—"I can't see—yes, I do see—yes, they are, grandpa; I see the mark."

"I thought so!" said Mr. Ringgan bitterly; "I told Didenhover, only three days ago, that if he didn't make up that fence the sheep would be out, or Squire Thornton's would be in;—only three days ago!—Ah well!" said he, shaking the reins to make the mare move on again,—"it's all of a piece.—Every thing goes—I can't help it."

"Why do you keep him, grandpa, if he don't behave right?" Fleda ventured to ask gently.

"'Cause I can't get rid of him, dear," Mr. Ringgan answered rather shortly.

And till they got to the post-office he seemed in a disagreeable kind of muse, which Fleda did not choose to break in upon. So the mile and a half was driven in sober silence.

"Shall I get out and go in, grandpa?" said Fleda when he drew up before the house.

"No, deary," said he in his usual kind tone; "you sit still. Holloa there!—Good-day, Mr. Sampion—have you got any thing for me?"

The man disappeared and came out again.

"There's your paper, grandpa," said Fleda.

"Ay, and something else," said Mr. Ringgan: "I declare! —'Miss Fleda Ringgan—care of E. Ringgan, Esq.'—There, dear, there it is."

"Paris!" exclaimed Fleda, as she clasped the letter and both her hands together. The butternuts and Mr. Didenhover were forgotten at last. The letter could not be read in the jolting of the wagon, but, as Fleda said, it was all the pleasanter, for she had the expectation of it the whole way home.

"Where are we going now, grandpa?"

"To Queechy Run."

"That will give us a nice long ride. I am very glad. This has been a good day. With my letter and my bitter-sweet I have got enough, haven't I, grandpa?"

Queechy Run was a little village, a very little village, about half a mile from Mr. Ringgan's house. It boasted however a decent brick church of some size, a school-house, a lawyer's office, a grocery store, a dozen or two of dwelling-houses, and a post-office; though for some reason or other Mr. Ringgan always chose to have his letters come through the Sattlersville post-office, a mile and a half further off. At the door of the lawyer's office Mr. Ringgan again stopped, and again shouted "Holloa!"—

"Good-day, sir. Is Mr. Jolly within?"

"He is, sir."

"Will you ask him to be so good as to step here a moment? I cannot very well get out."

Mr. Jolly was a comfortable-looking little man, smooth and sleek, pleasant and plausible, reasonable honest too, as the world goes; a nice man to have to do with, the world went so easy with his affairs that you were sure he would make no unnecessary rubs in your own. He came now fresh and brisk to the side of the wagon, with that uncommon hilarity which people sometimes assume when they have a disagreeable matter on hand that must be spoken of.

"Good-morning, sir! Fine day, Mr. Jolly."

"Beautiful day, sir! Splendid season! How do you do, Mr. Ringgan?"

"Why, sir, I never was better in my life, barring this lameness, that disables me very much. I can't go about and see to things any more as I used to. However—we must expect evils at my time of life. I don't complain. I have a great deal to be thankful for."

"Yes, sir,—we have a great deal to be thankful for," said Mr. Jolly rather abstractedly, and patting the old mare with kind attention.

"Have you seen that fellow McGowan?" said Mr. Ringgan abruptly, and in a lower tone.

"I have seen him," said Mr. Jolly, coming back from the old mare to business.

"He's a hard customer I guess, aint he?"

"He's as ugly a cur as ever was whelped!"

"What does he say?"

"Says he must have it."

"Did you tell him what I told you?"

"I told him, sir, that you had not got the returns from your farm that you expected this year, owing to one thing and 'nother; and that you couldn't make up the cash for him all at once; and that he would have to wait a spell, but that he'd be sure to get it in the long run. Nobody ever suffered by Mr. Ringgan yet, as I told him."

"Well?"

"Well, sir,—he was altogether refractible—he's as pig-headed a fellow as I ever see."

"What did he say?"

"He gave me names, and swore he wouldn't wait a day longer—said he'd waited already six months."

"He has so. I couldn't meet the last payment. There's a year's rent due now. I can't help it. There needn't have been an hour,—if I could go about and attend to things myself.—I have been altogether disappointed in that Didenhover."

"I expect you have."

"What do you suppose he'll do, Mr. Jolly?—McGowan, I mean."

"I expect he'll do what the law'll let him, Mr. Ringgan; I don't know what'll hinder him."

"It's a worse turn than I thought my infirmities would ever play me," said the old gentleman after a short pause,—"first to lose the property altogether, and then not to be permitted to wear out what is left of life in the old place—there won't be much."

"So I told him, Mr. Ringgan. I put it to him. Says I, 'Mr. McGowan, it's a cruel hard business; there ain't a man in town that wouldn't leave Mr. Ringgan the shelter of his own roof as long as he wants any, and think it a pleasure,—if the rent was anyhow.'"

"Well—well!" said the old gentleman, with a mixture of dignity and bitterness,—"it doesn't much matter. My head will find a shelter somehow, above ground or under it. The Lord will provide.—Whey! stand still, can't ye! what ails the fool? The creature's seen years enough to be steady," he added with a miserable attempt at his usual cheerful laugh.

Fleda had turned away her head and tried not to hear when the lowered tones of the speakers seemed to say that she was one too many in the company. But she could not help catching a few bits of the conversation, and a few bits were generally enough for Fleda's wit to work upon; she had a singular knack at putting loose ends of talk together. If more had been wanting, the tones of her grandfather's voice would have filled up every gap in the meaning of the scattered words that came to her ear. Her heart sank fast as the dialogue went on, and she needed no commentary or explanation to interpret the bitter little laugh with which it closed. It was a chill upon all the rosy joys and hopes of a most joyful and hopeful little nature.

The old mare was in motion again, but Fleda no longer cared or had the curiosity to ask where they were going. The bittersweet lay listlessly in her lap; her letter, clasped to her breast, was not thought of; and tears were quietly running one after the other down her cheeks and falling on her sleeve; she dared not lift her handkerchief nor turn her face towards her grandfather lest they should catch his eye.

Her grandfather?—could it be possible that he must be turned out of his old home in his old age? could it be possible? Mr. Jolly seemed to think it might be, and her grandfather seemed to think it must. Leave the old house! But where would he go?—Son or daughter he had none left; resources he could have none, or this need not happen. Work he could not; be dependent upon the charity of any kin or friend she knew he would never; she remembered hearing him once say he could better bear to go to the almshouse than do any such thing. And then, if they went, he would have his pleasant room no more where the sun shone in so cheerfully, and they must leave the dear old kitchen where they had been so happy, and the meadows and hills would belong to somebody else, and she would gather her stores of butternuts and chestnuts under the loved old trees never again. But these things were nothing, though the image of them made the tears come hot and fast, these were nothing in her mind to the knowledge or the dread of the effect the change would have upon Mr. Ringgan. Fleda knew him and knew it would not be slight. Whiter his head could not be, more bowed it well might, and her own bowed in anticipation as her childish fears and imaginings ran on into the possible future. Of McGowan's tender mercies she had no hope. She had seen him once, and being unconsciously even more of a physiognomist than most children are, that one sight of him was enough to verify all Mr. Jolly had said. The remembrance of his hard sinister face sealed her fears. Nothing but evil could come of having to do with such a man. It was however still not so much any foreboding of the future that moved Fleda's tears as the sense of her grandfather's present pain,—the quick answer of her gentle nature to every sorrow that touched him. His griefs were doubly hers. Both from his openness of character and her penetration, they could rarely be felt unshared; and she shared them always in more than due measure.

In beautiful harmony, while the child had forgotten herself in keen sympathy with her grandfather's sorrows, he on the other hand had half lost sight of them in caring for her. Again, and this time not before any house but in a wild piece of woodland, the little wagon came to a stop.

"Ain't there some holly berries that I see yonder?" said Mr. Ringgan,—"there, through those white birch stems? That's what you were wanting, Fleda, ain't it? Give your bittersweet to me while you go get some,—and here, take this knife dear, you can't break it. Don't cut yourself."

Fleda's eyes were too dim to see white birch or holly, and she had no longer the least desire to have the latter; but with that infallible tact which assuredly is the gift of nature and no other, she answered, in a voice that she forced to be clear, "O yes! thank you, grandpa;"—and stealthily dashing away the tears clambered down from the rickety little wagon and plunged with a cheerful *step* at least through trees and underbrush to the clump of holly. But if any body had seen Fleda's face!—while she seemed to be busied in cutting as large a quantity as possible of the rich shining leaves and bright berries. Her grandfather's kindness and her effort to meet it had wrung her heart; she hardly knew what she was doing, as she cut off sprig after sprig and threw them down at her feet; she was crying sadly, with even audible sobs. She made a long job of her bunch of holly. But when at last it must come to an end she choked back her tears, smoothed her face, and came back to Mr. Ringgan smiling and springing over the stones and shrubs in her way, and exclaiming at the beauty of her vegetable stores. If her cheeks were red he thought it was the flush of pleasure and exercise, and she did not let him get a good look at her eyes.

"Why you've got enough to dress up the front room chimney," said he. "That'll be the best thing you can do with 'em, won't it?"

"The front room chimney! No, indeed I won't, grandpa. I don't want 'em where nobody can see them, and you know we are never in there now it is cold weather."

"Well, dear! anyhow you like to have it. But you ha'n't a jar in the house big enough for them, have you?"

"O I'll manage—I've got an old broken pitcher without a handle, grandpa, that'll do very well."

"A broken pitcher! that isn't a very elegant vase," said he.

"O you wouldn't know it is a pitcher when I have fixed

it. I'll cover up all the broken part with green, you know. Are we going home now, grandpa?"

"No, I want to stop a minute at uncle Joshua's."

Uncle Joshua was a brother-in-law of Mr. Ringgan, a substantial farmer and very well to do in the world. He was found not in the house but abroad in the field with his men, loading an enormous basket-wagon with corn-stalks. At Mr. Ringgan's shout he got over the fence and came to the wagon-side. His face shewed sense and shrewdness, but nothing of the open nobility of mien which nature had stamped upon that of his brother.

"Fine morning, eh?" said he. "I'm getting in my corn-stalks."

"So I see," said Mr. Ringgan. "How do you find the new way of curing them answer?"

"Fine as ever you see. Sweet as a nut. The cattle are mad after them. How are you going to be off for fodder this winter?"

"It's more than I can tell you," said Mr. Ringgan. "There ought to be more than plenty; but Didenhover contrives to bring every thing out at the wrong end. I wish I was rid of him."

"He'll never get a berth with *me*, I can tell you," said uncle Joshua laughing.

"Brother," said Mr. Ringgan, lowering his tone again, "have you any loose cash you could let me have for six months or so?"

Uncle Joshua took a meditative look down the road, turned a quid of tobacco in his cheek, and finally brought his eyes again to Mr. Ringgan and answered.

"Well, I don't see as I can," said he. "You see, Josh is just a going to set up for himself at Kenton, and he'll want some help of me; and I expect that'll be about as much as I can manage to lay my hands on."

"Do you know who has any that he would be likely to lend?" said Mr. Ringgan.

"No, I don't. Money is rather scarce. For your rent, eh?"

"Yes, for my rent! The farm brings me in nothing but my living. That Didenhover is ruining me, brother Joshua."

"He's feathering his own nest, I reckon."

"You may swear to that. There wa'n't as many bushels of grain, by one fourth, when they were threshed out last year, as I had calculated there would be in the field. I don't know what on earth he could have done with it. I I suppose it'll be the same thing over this year."

"Maybe he has served you as Deacon Travis was served by one of his help last season—the rascal bored holes in the granary floor and let out the corn so, and Travis couldn't contrive how his grain went till the floor was empty next spring, and then he see how it was."

"Ha!—did he catch the fellow?"

"Not he—he had made tracks before that. A word in your ear—I wouldn't let Didenhover see much of his salary till you know how he will come out at the end."

"He has got it already!" said Mr. Ringgan, with a nervous twitch at the old mare's head; "he wheedled me out of several little sums on one pretence and another,—he had a brother in New York that he wanted to send some to, and goods that he wanted to get out of pawn, and so on,—and I let him have it! and then there was one of those fatting steers that he proposed to me to let him have on account, and I thought it was as good a way of paying him as any; and that made up pretty near the half of what was due to him."

"I warrant you his'n was the fattest of the whole lot. Well, keep a tight hold of the other half, brother Elzevir, that's my advice to you."

"The other half he was to make upon shares."

"Whew!—well—I wish you well rid of him; and don't make such another bargain again. Good-day to ye!"

It was with a keen pang that little Fleda saw the downhearted look of her grandfather as again he gave the old mare notice to move on. A few minutes passed in deep thought on both sides.

"Grandpa," said Fleda, "wouldn't Mr. Jolly perhaps know of somebody that might have some money to lend?"

"I declare!" said the old gentleman after a moment, "that's not a bad thought. I wonder I didn't have it myself."

They turned about, and without any more words measured back their way to Queechy Run. Mr. Jolly came out again, brisk and alert as ever; but after seeming to rack his brains in search of any actual or possible money-lender was obliged to confess that it was in vain; he could not think of one.

"But I'll tell you what, Mr. Ringgan," he concluded, "I'll turn it over in my mind to-night and see if I can think of any thing that'll do, and if I can I'll let you know. If we hadn't such a nether millstone to deal with, it would be easy enough to work it somehow."

So they set forth homewards again.

"Cheer up, dear!" said the old gentleman heartily, laying one hand on his little granddaughter's lap,—"it will be arranged somehow. Don't you worry your little head with business. God will take care of us."

"Yes, grandpa!" said the little girl, looking up with an instant sense of relief at these words; and then looking down again immediately to burst into tears.

CHAPTER II.

Have you seen but a bright lily grow,
  Before rude hands have touch'd it?
Ha' you mark'd but the fall o' the snow,
  Before the soil hath smutch'd it?

BEN JONSON.

WHERE a ray of light can enter the future, a child's hope can find a way—a way that nothing less airy and spiritual can travel. By the time they reached their own door Fleda's spirits were at par again.

"I am very glad we have got home, aren't you, grandpa?" she said as she jumped down; "I'm so hungry. I guess we are both of us ready for supper, don't you think so?"

She hurried up stairs to take off her wrappings and then came down to the kitchen, where standing on the broad hearth and warming herself at the blaze, with all the old associations of comfort settling upon her heart, it occurred to her that foundations so established *could not* be shaken. The blazing fire seemed to welcome her home and bid her dismiss fear; the kettle singing on its accustomed hook looked as if quietly ridiculing the idea that they could be parted company; her grandfather was in his cushioned chair at the corner of the hearth, reading the newspaper, as she had seen him a thousand times; just in the same position, with that collected air of grave enjoyment, one leg crossed over the other, settled back in his chair but upright, and scanning the columns with an intent but most un-careful face. A face it was that always had a rare union of fineness and placidness. The table stood spread in the usual place, warmth and comfort filled every corner of the room, and Fleda began to feel as if she had been in an uncomfortable dream, which was very absurd, but from which she was very glad she had awoke.

"What have you got in this pitcher, Cynthy?" said she. "Muffins!—O let me bake them, will you? I'll bake them."

"Now Flidda," said Cynthy, "just you be quiet. There ain't no place where you can bake 'em. I'm just going to clap 'em in the reflector—that's the shortest way I can take to do 'em. You keep yourself out o' muss."

"They won't be muffins if you bake 'em in the reflector, Cynthy; they aren't half so good. Ah, do let me! I won't make a bit of muss."

"Where'll you do 'em?"

"In grandpa's room—if you'll just clean off the top of the stove for me—now do, Cynthy! I'll do 'em beautifully, and you won't have a bit of trouble.—Come!"

"It'll make an awful smoke, Flidda; you'll fill your grandpa's room with the smoke, and he won't like that, I guess."

"O he won't mind it," said Fleda. "Will you, grandpa?"

"What, dear?"—said Mr. Ringgan, looking up at her from his paper with a relaxing face which indeed promised to take nothing amiss that she might do.

"Will you mind if I fill your room with smoke?"

"No, dear!" said he, the strong heartiness of his acquiescence almost reaching a laugh,—"No, dear!—fill it with anything you like!"

There was nothing more to be said; and while Fleda in triumph put on an apron and made her preparations, Cynthy on her part, and with a very good grace, went to get ready the stove; which being a wood stove, made of sheet iron, with a smooth even top, afforded in Fleda's opinion the very best possible field for muffins to come to their perfection. Now Fleda cared little in comparison for the eating part of the business; her delight was by the help of her own skill and the stove-top to bring the muffins to this state of perfection; her greatest pleasure in them was over when they were baked.

A little while had passed, Mr. Ringgan was still busy with his newspaper, Miss Cynthia Gall going in and out on various errands, Fleda shut up in the distant room with the muffins and the smoke; when there came a knock at the door, and Mr. Ringgan's "Come in!"—was followed by the entrance of two strangers, young, well-dressed, and comely. They wore the usual badges of seekers after game, but their guns were left outside.

The old gentleman's look of grave expectancy told his want of enlightening.

"I fear you do not remember me, Mr. Ringgan," said the foremost of the two coming up to him,—" my name is Rossitur—Charlton Rossitur—a cousin of your little granddaughter. I have only"—

"O I know you now!" said Mr. Ringgan, rising and grasping his hand heartily,—" you are very welcome, sir. How do you do? I recollect you perfectly, but you took me by surprise.—How do you do, sir? Sit down—sit down."

And the old gentleman had extended his frank welcome to the second of his visitors almost before the first had time to utter,

"My friend Mr. Carleton."

"I couldn't imagine what was coming upon me," said Mr. Ringgan cheerfully, "for you weren't anywhere very near my thoughts; and I don't often see much of the gay world that is passing by me. You have grown since I saw you last, Mr. Rossitur. You are studying at West Point, I believe."

"No sir; I *was* studying there, but I had the pleasure of bringing that to an end last June."

"Ah!—Well, what are you now? not a cadet any longer, I suppose."

"No sir—we hatch out of that shell lieutenants."

"Hum.—And do you intend to remain in the army?"

"Certainly sir, that is my purpose and hope."

"Your mother would not like that, I should judge. I do not understand how she ever made up her mind to let you become that thing which hatches out into a lieutenant. Gentle creatures she and her sister both were.—How was it Mr. Rossitur? were you a wild young gentleman that wanted training?"

"I have had it sir, whether I wanted it or no."

"Hum!—How is he, Mr. Carleton?—sober enough to command men?"

"I have not seen him tried, sir," said this gentleman smiling; "but from the inconsistency of the orders he issues to his dogs I doubt it exceedingly."

"Why Carleton would have no orders issued to them at all, I believe," said young Rossitur; "he has been saying 'hush' to me all day."

The old gentleman laughed in a way that indicated intelligence with one of the speakers,—which, appeared not.

"So you've been following the dogs to-day," said he. "Been successful?"

"Not a bit of it," said Rossitur. "Whether we got on the wrong grounds, or didn't get on the right ones, or the dogs didn't mind their business, or there was nothing to fire at, I don't know; but we lost our patience and got nothing in exchange."

"Speak for yourself," said the other. "I assure you I was sensible of no ground of impatience while going over such a superb country as this."

"It *is* a fine country," said Mr. Ringgan,—"all this tract; and I ought to know it, for I have hunted every mile of it for many a mile around. There used to be more game than partridges in these hills when I was a young man;—bears and wolves, and deer, and now and then a panther, to say nothing of rattlesnakes."

"That last-mentioned is an irregular sort of game, is it not?" said Mr. Carleton smiling.

"Well, game is what you choose to make it," said the old gentleman. "I have seen worse days' sport than I saw once when we were out after rattlesnakes and nothing else. There was a cave sir, down under a mountain a few miles to the south of this, right at the foot of a bluff some four or five hundred feet sheer down,—it was known to be a resort of those creatures; and a party of us went out,—it's many years ago now,—to see if we couldn't destroy the nest—exterminate the whole horde. We had one dog with us,—a little dog, a kind of spaniel; a little white and yellow fellow,—and he did the work! Well, sir,—how many of those vermin do you guess that little creature made a finish of that day?—of large and small, sir, there were two hundred and twelve."

"He must have been a gallant little fellow."

"You never saw a creature, sir, take to a sport better;

he just dashed in among them, from one to another,—he would catch a snake by the neck and give it a shake, and throw it down and rush at another;—poor fellow, it was his last day's sport,—he died almost as soon as it was over; he must have received a great many bites. The place is known as the rattlesnakes' den to this day, though there are none there now, I believe."

"My little cousin is well, I hope," said Mr. Rossitur.

"She? yes, bless her! she is always well. Where is she? Fairy, where are you?—Cynthy, just call Elfleda here."

"She's just in the thick of the muffins, Mr. Ringgan."

"Let the muffins burn! Call her."

Miss Cynthia accordingly opened a little way the door of the passage, from which a blue stifling smoke immediately made its way into the room, and called out to Fleda, whose little voice was heard faintly responding from the distance.

"It's a wonder she can hear through all that smoke," remarked Cynthia.

"She," said Mr. Ringgan laughing,—"she's playing cook or housekeeper in yonder, getting something ready for tea. She's a busy little spirit, if ever there was one. Ah! there she is. Come here, Fleda—here's your cousin Rossitur from West Point—and Mr. Carleton."

Fleda made her appearance flushed with the heat of the stove and the excitement of turning the muffins, and the little iron spatula she used for that purpose still in her hand; and a fresh and larger puff of the unsavoury blue smoke accompanied her entrance. She came forward however gravely and without the slightest embarrassment to receive her cousin's somewhat unceremonious "How do, Fleda?"—and keeping the spatula still in one hand shook hands with him with the other. But at the very different manner in which Mr. Carleton *rose* and greeted her, the flush on Fleda's cheek deepened, and she cast down her eyes and stepped back to her grandfather's side with the demureness of a young lady just undergoing the ceremony of presentation.

"You come upon us out of a cloud, Fleda," said her cousin. "Is that the way you have acquired a right to the name of Fairy?"

"I am sure, no," said Mr. Carleton.

Fleda did not lift up her eyes, but her mounting colour shewed that she understood both speeches.

"Because if you are in general such a misty personage," Mr. Rossitur went on half laughing, "I would humbly recommend a choice of incense."

"O I forgot to open the windows!" exclaimed Fleda ingenuously. "Cynthy, won't you please go and do it? And take this with you," said she, holding out the spatula.

"She is as good a fairy as *I* want to see," said her grandfather, passing his arm fondly round her. "She carries a ray of sunshine in her right hand; and that's as magic-working a wand as any fairy ever wielded,—hey, Mr. Carleton?"

Mr. Carleton bowed. But whether the sunshine of affection in Fleda's glance and smile at her grandfather made him feel that she was above a compliment, or whether it put the words out of his head, certain it is that he uttered none.

"So you've had bad success to-day," continued Mr. Ringgan. "Where have you been? and what after? partridges?"

"No sir," said Mr. Carleton, "my friend Rossitur promised me a rare bag of woodcock, which I understand to be the best of American feathered game; and in pursuance of his promise led me over a large extent of meadow and swamp land this morning, with which in the course of several hours I became extremely familiar, without flushing a single bird."

"Meadow and swamp land?" said the old gentleman. "Whereabouts?"

"A mile or more beyond the little village over here where we left our horses," said Rossitur. "We beat the ground well, but there were no signs of them even."

"We had not the right kind of dog," said Mr. Carleton.

"We had the kind that is always used here," said Rossitur; "nobody knows anything about a Cocker in America."

"Ah, it was too wet," said Mr. Ringgan. "I could have told you that. There has been too much rain. You wouldn't find a woodcock in that swamp after such a day as we had a few days ago. But speaking of game, Mr. Rossitur, I don't know anything in America equal to the grouse. It is far before woodcock. I emember, many years back, going a grouse shooting, I ana a friend, down in Pennsylvania,—we went two or three days running, and the birds we got were worth a whole season of woodcock.—But gentlemen, if you are not discouraged with your day's experience and want to try again, *I'll* put you in a way to get as many woodcock as will satisfy you—if you'll come here to-morrow morning I'll go out with you far enough to shew you the way to the best ground *I* know for shooting that game in all this country; you'll have a good chance for partridges too in the course of the day; and that ain't bad eating, when you can't get better—is it, Fairy?" he said, with a sudden smiling appeal to the little girl at his side. Her answer again was only an intelligent glance.

The young sportsmen both thanked him and promised to take advantage of his kind offer. Fleda seized the opportunity to steal another look at the strangers; but meeting Mr. Carleton's eyes fixed on her with a remarkably soft and gentle expression she withdrew her own again as fast as possible, and came to the conclusion that the only safe place for them was the floor.

"I wish I was a little younger and I'd take my gun and go along with you myself," said the old gentleman pleasantly; "but," he added sighing, "there is a time for every thing, and my time for sporting is past."

"You have no right to complain, sir," said Mr. Carleton, with a meaning glance and smile which the old gentleman took in excellent good part.

"Well," said he, looking half proudly, half tenderly, upon the little demure figure at his side, "I don't say that I have. I hope I thank God for his mercies, and am happy. But in this world, Mr. Carleton, there is hardly a blessing but what draws a care after it. Well—well—these things will all be arranged for us!"

It was plain, however, even to a stranger, that there was some subject of care not vague nor undefined pressing upon Mr. Ringgan's mind as he said this.

"Have you heard from my mother lately, Fleda?" said her cousin.

"Why yes," said Mr. Ringgan,—"she had a letter from her only to-day. You ha'n't read it yet, have you, Fleda?"

"No grandpa," said the little girl; "you know I've been busy."

"Ay," said the old gentleman; "why couldn't you let

Cynthia bake the cakes, and not roast yourself over the stove till you're as red as a turkey-cock?"

"This morning I was like a chicken," said Fleda laughing, "and now like a turkey-cock."

"Shall I tell mamma, Fleda," said young Rossitur, "that you put off reading her letter to bake muffins?"

Fleda answered without looking up, "Yes, if he pleased."

"What do you suppose she will think?"

"I don't know."

"She will think that you love muffins better than her."

"No," said Fleda, quietly but firmly,—"she will not think that, because it isn't true."

The gentlemen laughed, but Mr. Carleton declared that Fleda's reasoning was unanswerable.

"Well, I will see you to-morrow," said Mr. Rossitur, "after you have read the letter, for I suppose you will read it some time. You should have had it before,—it came enclosed to me,—but I forgot unaccountably to mail it to you till a few days ago."

"It will be just as good now, sir," said Mr. Ringgan.

"There is a matter in it though," said Rossitur, "about which my mother has given me a charge. We will see you to-morrow. It was for that partly we turned out of our way this evening."

"I am very glad you did," said Mr. Ringgan. "I hope your way will bring you here often. Won't you stay and try some of these same muffins before you go?"

But this was declined, and the gentlemen departed; Fleda, it must be confessed, seeing nothing in the whole leave-taking but Mr. Carleton's look and smile. The muffins were a very tame affair after it.

When supper was over she sat down fairly to her letter, and read it twice through before she folded it up. By this time the room was clear both of the tea equipage and of Cynthia's presence, and Fleda and her grandfather were alone in the darkening twilight with the blazing wood fire; he in his usual place at the side, and she on the hearth directly before it; both silent, both thinking, for some time. At length Mr. Ringgan spoke, breaking as it were the silence and his seriousness with the same effort.

"Well dear!" said he cheerfully,—"what does she say?"

"O she says a great many things, grandpa; shall I read you the letter?"

"No dear, I don't care to hear it; only tell me what she says."

"She says they are going to stay in Paris yet a good while longer."

"Hum!"—said Mr. Ringgan. "Well—that ain't the wisest thing I should like to hear of her doing."

"Oh but it's because uncle Rossitur likes to stay there, I suppose, isn't it, grandpa?"

"I don't know, dear. Maybe your aunt's caught the French fever. She used to be a good sensible woman; but when people will go into a whirligig, I think some of their wits get blown away before they come out. Well—what else?"

"I am sure she is very kind," said Fleda. "She wants to have me go out there and live with her very much. She says I shall have everything I like and do just as I please, and she will make a pet of me and give me all sorts of pleasant things. She says she will take as good care of me as ever I took of the kittens. And there's a long piece to you about it, that I'll give you to read as soon as we have a light. It is very good of her, isn't it, grandpa? I love aunt Lucy very much."

"Well," said Mr. Ringgan after a pause, "how does she propose to get you there?"

"Why," said Fleda,—"isn't it curious?—she says there is a Mrs. Carleton here who is a friend of hers, and she is going to Paris in a little while, and aunt Lucy asked her if she wouldn't bring me, if you would let me go, and she said she would with great pleasure, and aunt Lucy wants me to come out with her."

"Carleton!—Hum—" said Mr. Ringgan; "that must be this young man's mother?"

"Yes, aunt Lucy says she is here with her son,—at least she says they were coming."

"A very gentlemanly young man, indeed," said Mr. Ringgan.

There was a grave silence. The old gentleman sat looking on the floor; Fleda sat looking into the fire, with all her might.

"Well," said Mr. Ringgan after a little, "how would you like it, Fleda?"

"What, grandpa?"

"To go out to Paris to your aunt, with this Mrs. Carleton?"

"I shouldn't like it at all," said Fleda smiling, and letting her eyes go back to the fire. But looking after the pause of a minute or two again to her grandfather's face, she was struck with its expression of stern anxiety. She rose instantly, and coming to him and laying one hand gently on his knee, said in tones that fell as light on the ear as the touch of a moonbeam on the water, "*You* do not want me to go, do you, grandpa?"

"No dear!" said the old gentleman, letting his hand fall upon hers,—"no dear!—that is the last thing I want!"

But Fleda's keen ear discerned not only the deep affection but something of *regret* in the voice, which troubled her. She stood, anxious and fearing, while her grandfather lifting his hand again and again let it fall gently upon hers; and amid all the fondness of the action Fleda somehow seemed to feel in it the same regret.

"You'll not let aunt Lucy, nor anybody else, take me away from you, will you, grandpa?" said she after a little, leaning both arms affectionately on his knee and looking up into his face.

"No indeed, dear!" said he, with an attempt at his usual heartiness,—"not as long as I have a place to keep you. While I have a roof to put my head under, it shall cover yours."

To Fleda's hope that would have said enough; but her grandfather's face was so moved from its wonted expression of calm dignity that it was plain *his* hope was tasting bitter things. Fleda watched in silent grief and amazement the watering eye and unnerved lip; till her grandfather indignantly dashing away a tear or two drew her close to his breast and kissed her. But she well guessed that the reason why he did not for a minute or two say anything, was because he could not. Neither could she. She was fighting with her woman's nature to keep it down, —learning the lesson early!

"Ah well,"—said Mr. Ringgan at length, in a kind of

tone that might indicate the giving up a struggle which he had no means of carrying on, or the endeavour to conceal it from the too keen-wrought feelings of his little granddaughter,—"there will be a way opened for us somehow. We must let our Heavenly Father take care of us."

"And he will, grandpa," whispered Fleda.

"Yes dear!—We are selfish creatures. Your father's and your mother's child will not be forgotten."

"Nor you either, dear grandpa," said the little girl, laying her soft cheek alongside of his, and speaking by dint of a great effort.

"No," said he, clasping her more tenderly,—"no—it would be wicked in me to doubt it. He has blessed me all my life long with a great many more blessings than I deserved; and if he chooses to take away the sunshine of my last days I will bow my head to his will, and believe that he does all things well, though I cannot see it."

"Don't, dear grandpa," said Fleda, stealing her other arm round his neck and hiding her face there,—"please don't!—"

He very much regretted that he had said too much. He did not however know exactly how to mend it. He kissed her and stroked her soft hair, but that and the manner of it only made it more difficult for Fleda to recover herself, which she was struggling to do; and when he tried to speak in accents of cheering his voice trembled. Fleda's heart was breaking, but she felt that she was making matters worse, and she had already concluded on a mature review of circumstances that it was her duty to be cheerful. So after a few very heartfelt tears which she could not help, she raised her head and smiled, even while she wiped the traces of them away.

"After all, grandpa," said she, "perhaps Mr. Jolly will come here in the morning with some good news, and then we should be troubling ourselves just for nothing."

"Perhaps he will," said Mr. Ringgan, in a way that sounded much more like "Perhaps he won't!" But Fleda was determined now not to *seem* discouraged again. She thought the best way was to change the conversation.

"It is very kind in aunt Lucy, isn't it, grandpa, what she has written to me?"

"Why no," said Mr. Ringgan, decidedly, "I can't say I think it is any very extraordinary manifestation of kindness in anybody to want you."

Fleda smiled her thanks for this compliment.

"It might be a kindness in me to give you to her."

"It wouldn't be a kindness to me, grandpa."

"I don't know about that," said he gravely. They were getting back to the old subject. Fleda made another great effort at a diversion.

"Grandpa, was my father like my uncle Rossitur in any thing?"

The diversion was effected.

"Not he, dear!" said Mr. Ringgan. "Your father had ten times the man in him that ever your uncle was."

"Why what kind of a man is uncle Rossitur, grandpa?"

"Ho dear! I can't tell. I ha'n't seen much of him. I wouldn't judge a man without knowing more of him than I do of Mr. Rossitur. He seemed an amiable kind of man. But no one would ever have thought of looking at him, no more than at a shadow, when your father was by."

The diversion took effect on Fleda herself now. She looked up pleased.

"You remember your father, Fleda?"

"Yes grandpa, but not very well always;—I remember a great many things about him, but I can't remember exactly how he looked,—except once or twice."

"Ay, and he wa'n't well the last time you remember him. But he was a noble-looking man—in form and face too—and his looks were the worst part of him. He seemed made of different stuff from all the people around," said Mr. Ringgan sighing, "and they felt it too I used to notice, without knowing it. When his cousins were 'Sam' and 'Johnny' and 'Bill,' he was always, that is, after he grew up, '*Mr. Walter.*' I believe they were a little afeard of him. And with all his bravery and fire he could be as gentle as a woman."

"I know that," said Fleda, whose eyes were dropping soft tears and glittering at the same time with gratified feeling. "What made him be a soldier, grandpa?"

"Oh I don't know, dear!—he was too good to make a farmer of—or his high spirit wanted to rise in the world—

he couldn't rest without trying to be something more than other folks. I don't know whether people are any happier for it."

"Did *he* go to West Point, grandpa?"

"No dear!—he started without having so much of a push as that; but he was one of those that don't need any pushing; he would have worked his way up, put him anywhere you would, and he did,—over the heads of West Pointers and all, and would have gone to the top, I verily believe, if he had lived long enough. He was as fine a fellow as there was in all the army. *I* don't believe there's the like of him left in it."

"He had been a major a good while, hadn't he, grandpa?"

"Yes. It was just after he was made captain that he went to Albany, and there he saw your mother. She and her sister, your aunt Lucy, were wards of the patroon. I was in Albany, in the legislature, that winter, and I knew them both very well; but your aunt Lucy had been married some years before. She was staying there that winter without her husband—he was abroad somewhere."

Fleda was no stranger to these details and had learned long ago what was meant by 'wards' and 'the patroon.'

"Your father was made a major some years afterwards," Mr. Ringgan went on, "for his fine behaviour out here at the West—what's the name of the place?—I forget it just now—fighting the Indians. There never was anything finer done."

"He was brave, wasn't he, grandpa?"

"Brave!—he had a heart of iron sometimes, for as soft as it was at others. And he had an eye, when he was roused, that I never saw anything that would stand against. But your father had a better sort of courage than the common sort—he had enough of *that*—but this is a rarer thing—he never was afraid to do what in his conscience he thought was right. Moral courage I call it, and it is one of the very noblest qualities a man can have."

"That's a kind of courage a woman may have," said Fleda.

"Yes—you may have that; and I guess it's the only kind of courage *you*'ll ever be troubled with," said her grandfather looking laughingly at her. "However, any man may walk up to the cannon's mouth, but it is only one here and there that will walk out against men's opinions because he thinks it is right. That was one of the things I admired most in your father."

"Didn't my mother have it too?" said Fleda.

"I don't know—she had about everything that was good. A sweet, pretty creature she was, as ever I saw."

"Was she like aunt Lucy?"

"No, not much. She was a deal handsomer than your aunt is or ever could have been. She was the handsomest woman, I think, that ever I set eyes upon; and a sweet, gentle, lovely creature. *You*'ll never match her," said Mr. Ringgan, with a curious twist of his head and sly laughing twist of his eyes at Fleda;—"you may be as *good* as she was, but you'll never be as good-looking."

Fleda laughed, nowise displeased.

"You've got her hazel eyes though," remarked Mr. Ringgan, after a minute or two, viewing his little granddaughter with a sufficiently satisfied expression of countenance.

"Grandpa," said she, "don't you think Mr. Carleton has handsome eyes?"

"Mr. Carleton?—hum—I don't know; I didn't look at his eyes. A very well-looking young man though—very gentlemanly too."

Fleda had heard all this and much more about her parents some dozens of times before; but she and her grandfather were never tired of going it over. If the conversation that recalled his lost treasures had of necessity a character of sadness and tenderness, it yet bespoke not more regret that he had lost them than exulting pride and delight in what they had been,—perhaps not so much. And Fleda delighted to go back and feed her imagination with stories of the mother whom she could not remember, and of the father whose fair bright image stood in her memory as the embodiment of all that is high and noble and pure. A kind of guardian angel that image was to little Fleda. These ideal likenesses of her father and mother, the one drawn from history and recollection, the other from history only, had been her preservative from all the untoward influences and unfortunate examples which had surrounded her since her father's death some three or four years before had left her almost alone in her grandfather's house. They had created in her mind a standard of the true and beautiful in character, which nothing she saw around her, after of course her grandfather, and one other exception, seemed at all to meet; and partly from her own innate fineness of nature, and partly from this pure ideal always present with her, she had shrunk almost instinctively from the few varieties of human nature the country-side presented to her, and was in fact a very isolated little being, living in a world of her own, and clinging with all her strong out-goings of affection to her grandfather only; granting to but one other person any considerable share in her regard or esteem. Little Fleda was not in the least misanthropical; she gave her kindly sympathies to all who came in her way on whom they could possibly be bestowed; but these people were nothing to her; her spirit fell off from them, even in their presence; there was no affinity. She was in truth what her grandfather had affirmed of her father, made of different stuff from the rest of the world. There was no tincture of pride in all this; there was no conscious feeling of superiority; she could merely have told you that she did not care to hear these people talk, that she did not love to be with them; though she *would* have said so to no earthly creature but her grandfather, if even to him.

"It must be pleasant," said Fleda, after looking for some minutes thoughtfully into the fire,—"it must be a pleasant thing to have a father and mother."

"Yes dear!" said her grandfather, sighing,—"you have lost a great deal! But there is your aunt Lucy—you are not dependent altogether on me."

"Oh grandpa!" said the little girl laying one hand again pleadingly on his knee;—"I didn't mean—I mean—I was speaking in general—I wasn't thinking of myself in particular."

"I know, dear!" said he, as before taking the little hand in his own and moving it softly up and down on his knee. But the action was sad, and there was the same look of sorrowful stern anxiety. Fleda got up and put her arm over his shoulder, speaking from a heart filled too full.

"I don't want aunt Lucy—I don't care about aunt Lucy; I don't want anything but you, grandpa. I wish you wouldn't talk so."

"Ah well, dear," said he, without looking at her,—he couldn't bear to look at her,—"it's well it is so. I sha'n't last a great while—it isn't likely—and I am glad to know there is some one you can fall back upon when I am gone."

Fleda's next words were scarce audible, but they contained a reproach to him for speaking so.

"We may as well look at it, dear," said he gravely; "it must come to that—sooner or later—but you mustn't distress yourself about it beforehand. Don't cry—don't, dear!" said he, tenderly kissing her. "I didn't mean to trouble you so. There—there—look up, dear—let's take the good we have and be thankful for it. God will arrange the rest, in his own good way. Fleda!—I wouldn't have said a word if I had thought it would have worried you so."

He would not indeed. But he had spoken as men so often speak, out of the depths of their own passion or bitterness, forgetting that they are wringing the cords of a delicate harp, and not knowing what mischief they have done till they find the instrument all out of tune,—more often not knowing it ever. It is pity,—for how frequently a discord is left that jars all life long; and how much more frequently still the harp, though retaining its sweetness and truth of tone to the end, is gradually unstrung.

Poor Fleda could hardly hold up her head for a long time, and recalling bitterly her unlucky innocent remark which had led to all this trouble she almost made up her mind with a certain heroine of Miss Edgeworth's, that "it is best never to mention things." Mr. Ringgan, now thoroughly alive to the wounds he had been inflicting, held his little pet in his arms, pillowed her head on his breast, and by every tender and soothing action and word endeavoured to undo what he had done. And after a while the agony was over, the wet eyelashes were lifted up, and the meek sorrowful little face lay quietly upon Mr. Ringgan's breast, gazing out into the fire as gravely as if the Panorama of life were there. She little heeded at first her grandfather's cheering talk, she knew it was for a purpose.

"Ain't it most time for you to go to bed?" whispered Mr. Ringgan when he thought the purpose was effected.

"Shall I tell Cynthy to get you your milk, grandpa?" said the little girl rousing herself.

"Yes dear.—Stop,—what if you and me was to have some roast apples?—wouldn't you like it?"

"Well—yes, I should, grandpa," said Fleda, understanding perfectly why he wished it, and wishing it herself for that same reason and no other.

"Cynthy, let's have some of those roast apples," said Mr. Ringgan, "and a couple of bowls of milk here."

"No, I'll get the apples myself, Cynthy," said Fleda.

"And you needn't take any of the cream off, Cynthy," added Mr. Ringgan.

One corner of the kitchen table was hauled up to the fire, to be comfortable, Fleda said, and she and her grandfather sat down on the opposite sides of it to do honour to the apples and milk; each with the simple intent of keeping up appearances and cheating the other into cheerfulness. There is however, deny it who can, an exhilarating effect in good wholesome food taken when one is in some need of it; and Fleda at least found the supper relish exceeding well. Every one furthermore knows the relief of a hearty flow of tears when a secret weight has been pressing on the mind. She was just ready for anything reviving. After the third mouthful she began to talk, and before the bottom of the bowls was reached she had smiled more than once. So her grandfather thought no harm was done, and went to bed quite comforted; and Fleda climbed the steep stairs that led from his door to her little chamber just over his head. It was small and mean, immediately under the roof, with only one window. There were plenty of better rooms in the house, but Fleda liked this because it kept her near her grandfather; and indeed she had always had it ever since her father's death, and never thought of taking any other.

She had a fashion, this child, in whom the simplicity of practical life and the poetry of imaginative life were curiously blended,—she had a fashion of going to her window every night when the moon or stars were shining to look out for a minute or two before she went to bed; and sometimes the minutes were more than any good grandmother or aunt would have considered wholesome for little Fleda in the fresh night air. But there was no one to watch or reprimand; and whatever it was that Fleda read in earth or sky, the charm which held her one bright night was sure to bring her to her window the next. This evening a faint young moon lighted up but dimly the meadow and what was called the "east-hill," over-against which the window in question looked. The air was calm and mild; there was no frost to-night; the stillness was entire, and the stars shone in a cloudless sky. Fleda set open the window and looked out with a face that again bore tokens of the experiences of that day. She wanted the soothing speech of nature's voice; and child as she was she could hear it. She did not know, in her simplicity, what it was that comforted and soothed her, but she stood at her window enjoying.

It was so perfectly still, her fancy presently went to all those people who had hushed their various work and were now resting, or soon would be, in the unconsciousness and the helplessness of sleep. The *helplessness*,—and then that Eye that never sleeps; that Hand that keeps them all, that is never idle, that is the safety and the strength alike of all the earth and of them that wake or sleep upon it,—

"And if he takes care of them all, will he not take care of poor little me?" thought Fleda. "Oh how glad I am I know there is a God!—How glad I am I know he is such a God! and that I can trust in him; and he will make everything go right. How I forget this sometimes! But Jesus does not forget his children. Oh I am a happy little girl!—Grandpa's saying what he did don't make it so—perhaps I shall die the first—but I hope not, for what would become of him!—But this and everything will all be arranged right, and I have nothing to do with it but to obey God and please him, and he will take care of the rest. He has forbidden *us* to be careful about it too."

With grateful tears of relief Fleda shut the window and began to undress herself, her heart so lightened of its burden that her thoughts presently took leave to go out again upon pleasure excursions in various directions; and one of the last things in Fleda's mind before sleep surprised her was, what a nice thing it was for any one to bow and smile so as Mr. Carleton did!

CHAPTER III.

I know each lane, and every alley green,
Dingle or bushy dell of this wild wood,
And every bosky bourn from side to side;
My daily walks and ancient neighbourhood.
MILTON.

FLEDA and her grandfather had but just risen from a tolerably early breakfast the next morning, when the two young sportsmen entered the room.

"Ha!" said Mr. Ringgan,—"I declare! you're stirring betimes. Come five or six miles this morning a'ready. Well—that's the stuff to make sportsmen of. Off for the woodcock, hey?—And I was to go with you and shew you the ground.—I declare I don't know how in the world I can do it this morning, I'am so very stiff—ten times as bad as I was yesterday. I had a window open in my room last night, I expect that must have been the cause. I don't see how I could have overlooked it, but I never gave it a thought, till this morning I found myself so lame I could hardly get out of bed.—I am very sorry, upon my word!"

"I am very sorry we must lose your company, sir," said the young Englishman, "and for such a cause; but as to the rest!—I dare say your directions will guide us sufficiently."

"I don't know about that," said the old gentleman. "It is pretty hard to steer by a chart that is only laid down in the imagination. I set out once to go in New York from one side of the city over into the other, and the first thing I knew I found myself travelling along half a mile out of town. I had to get in a stage and ride back and take a fresh start. Out at the West they say when you are in the woods you can tell which is north by the moss growing on that side of the trees; but if you're lost you'll be pretty apt to find the moss grows on *all* sides of the trees. I couldn't make out any waymarks at all, in such a labyrinth of brick corners. Well, let us see—if I tell you now it is so easy to mistake one hill for another—Fleda, child, you put on your sun-bonnet and take these gentlemen back to the twenty-acre lot, and from there you can tell 'em how to go so I guess they won't mistake it."

"By no means!" said Mr. Carleton; "we cannot give her so much trouble; it would be buying our pleasure at much too dear a rate."

"Tut, tut," said the old gentleman; "she thinks nothing of trouble, and the walk'll do her good. She'd like to be out all day, I believe, if she had any one to go along with, but I'm rather a stupid companion for such a spry little pair of feet. Fleda, look here,—when they get to the lot they can find their own way after that. You know where the place is—where your cousin Seth shot so many woodcock last year, over in Mr. Hurlbut's land,—when you get to the big lot you must tell these gentlemen to go straight over the hill, not Squire Thornton's hill, but mine, at the back of the lot,—they must go straight over it till they come to cleared land on the other side; then they must keep along by the edge of the wood, to the right, till they come to the brook; they must *cross the brook*, and follow up the opposite bank, and they'll know the ground when they come to it, or they don't deserve to. Do you understand?—now run and get your hat for they ought to be off."

Fleda went, but neither her step nor her look shewed any great willingness to the business.

"I am sure, Mr. Ringgan," said Mr. Carleton, "your little granddaughter has some reason for not wishing to take such a long walk this morning. Pray allow us to go without her."

"Pho, pho," said the old gentleman, "she wants to go."

"I guess she's skeered o' the guns," said Cynthy, happy to get a chance to edge in a word before such company;—"it's that ails her."

"Well, well,—she must get used to it," said Mr. Ringgan. "Here she is!"

Fleda had it in her mind to whisper to him a word of hope about Mr. Jolly; but she recollected that it was at best an uncertain hope, and that if her grandfather's thoughts were off the subject it was better to leave them so. She only kissed him for good-by, and went out with the two gentlemen.

As they took up their guns Mr. Carleton caught the timid shunning glance her eye gave at them.

"Do you dislike the company of these noisy friends of ours, Miss Fleda?" said he.

Fleda hesitated, and finally said "she didn't much like to be very near them when they were fired."

"Put that fear away then," said he, "for they shall keep a respectful silence so long as they have the honour to be in your company. If the woodcock come about us as tame as quails our guns shall not be provoked to say anything till your departure gives them leave."

Fleda smiled her thanks and set forward, privately much confirmed in her opinion that Mr. Carleton had handsome eyes.

At a little distance from the house Fleda left the meadow for an old apple-orchard at the left, lying on a steep side hill. Up this hill-side they toiled; and then found themselves on a ridge of table-land, stretching back for some distance along the edge of a little valley or bottom of perfectly flat smooth pasture-ground. The valley was very narrow, only divided into fields by fences running from side to side. The table-land might be a hundred feet or more above the level of the bottom, with a steep face towards it. A little way back from the edge the woods began; between them and the brow of the hill the ground was smooth and green, planted as if by art with flourishing young silver pines and once in a while a hemlock, some standing in all their luxuriance alone, and some in groups. With now and then a smooth grey rock, or large boulder-stone which had somehow inexplicably stopped on the brow of the hill instead of rolling down into what at some former time no doubt was a bed of water,—all this open strip of the table-land might have stood with very little coaxing for a piece of a gentleman's pleasure-ground. On the opposite side of the little valley was a low rocky height, covered with wood, now in the splendour of varied red and green and purple and brown and gold; between, at their feet, lay the soft quiet green meadow; and off to the left, beyond the far end of the valley, was the glory of the autumn woods again, softened in the distance. A true October sky seemed to pervade all, mildly blue, transparently pure, with that clearness of atmosphere that no other month gives us; a sky that would have conferred a patent of nobility on any landscape. The scene was certainly contracted and nowise remarkable in any of its features, but Nature had shaken out all her colours over the land, and drawn a veil from the sky, and breathed through the woods and over the hill-side the very breath of health, enjoyment, and vigour.

When they were about over-against the middle of the valley, Mr. Carleton suddenly made a pause and stood for some minutes silently looking. His two companions came to a halt on either side of him, one not a little pleased, the other a little impatient.

"Beautiful!" Mr. Carleton said at length.

"Yes," said Fleda gravely, "I think it's a pretty place. I like it up here."

"We sha'n't catch many woodcock among these pines," said young Rossitur.

"I wonder," said Mr. Carleton presently, "how any one should have called these 'melancholy days.'"

"Who has?" said Rossitur.

"A countryman of yours," said his friend glancing at him. "If he had been a countryman of mine there would have been less marvel. But here is none of the sadness of decay—none of the withering—if the tokens of old age are seen at all it is in the majestic honours that crown a glorious life—the graces of a matured and ripened character. This has nothing in common, Rossitur, with those dull moralists who are always dinning decay and death into one's ears;—this speaks of Life. Instead of freezing all one's hopes and energies, it quickens the pulse with the desire to *do*.—'The saddest of the year'—Bryant was wrong."

"Bryant?—oh!"—said young Rossitur; "I didn't know who you were speaking of."

"I believe, now I think of it, he was writing of a somewhat later time of the year,—I don't know how all this will look in November."

"I think it is very pleasant in November," said little Fleda sedately.

"Don't you know Bryant's 'Death of the Flowers,' Rossitur?" said his friend smiling. "What have you been doing all your life?"

"Not studying the fine arts at West Point, Mr. Carleton."

"Then sit down here, and let me mend that place in your education. Sit down! and I'll give you something better than woodcock. You keep a game-bag for thoughts, don't you?"

Mr. Rossitur wished Mr. Carleton didn't. But he sat down however, and listened with an unedified face; while his friend, more to please himself it must be confessed than for any other reason, and perhaps with half a notion to try Fleda, repeated the beautiful words. He presently saw they were not lost upon one of his hearers; she listened intently.

"It is very pretty," said Rossitur when he had done. "I believe I have seen it before somewhere."

"There is no 'smoky light' to-day," said Fleda.

"No," said Mr. Carleton, smiling to himself. "Nothing but that could improve the beauty of all this, Miss Fleda."

"*I* like it better as it is," said Fleda.

"I am surprised at that," said young Rossitur. "I thought you lived on smoke."

There was nothing in the words, but the tone was not exactly polite. Fleda granted him neither smile nor look.

"I am glad you like it up here," she went on, gravely doing the honours of the place. "I came this way because we shouldn't have so many fences to climb."

"You are the best little guide possible, and I have no doubt would always lead one the right way," said Mr. Carleton.

Again the same gentle, kind, *appreciating* look. Fleda unconsciously drew a step nearer. There was a certain undefined confidence established between them.

"There's a little brook down there in spring," said she, pointing to a small grass-grown water-course in the meadow, hardly discernible from the height,—"but there's no water in it now. It runs quite full for a while after the snow breaks up; but it dries away by June or July."

"What are those trees so beautifully tinged with red and orange?—down there by the fence in the meadow."

"I am not woodsman enough to inform you," replied Rossitur.

"Those are maples," said Fleda, "sugar maples. The one all orange is a hickory."

"How do you know?" said Mr. Carleton, turning to her. "By your wit as a fairy?"

"I know by the colour," said Fleda modestly,—"and by the shape too."

"Fairy," said Mr. Rossitur, "if you have any of the stuff about you, I wish you would knock this gentleman over the head with your wand and put the spirit of moving into him. He is going to sit dreaming here all day."

"Not at all," said his friend springing up,—"I am ready for you—but I want other game than woodcock just now I confess."

They walked along in silence, and had near reached the extremity of the table-land, which towards the end of the valley descended into ground of a lower level covered with woods; when Mr. Carleton who was a little ahead was startled by Fleda's voice exclaiming in a tone of distress, "Oh not the robins!"—and turning about perceived Mr. Rossitur standing still with levelled gun and just in the act to shoot. Fleda had stopped her ears. In the same instant Mr. Carleton had thrown up the gun, demanding of Rossitur with a singular change of expression—"what he meant!"

"Mean?" said the young gentleman, meeting with an astonished face the indignant fire of his companion's eyes,—"why I mean not to meddle with other people's guns, Mr. Carleton. What do *you* mean?"

"Nothing but to protect myself."

"Protect yourself!" said Rossitur, heating as the other cooled,—"from what, in the name of wonder?"

"Only from having my word blown away by your fire," said Carleton, smiling. "Come Rossitur, recollect yourself—remember our compact."

"Compact! one isn't bound to keep compacts with unearthly personages," said Rossitur, half sulkily and half angrily; "and besides I made none."

Mr. Carleton turned from him very coolly and walked on.

They left the table-land and the wood, entered the valley again, and passed through a large orchard, the last of the succession of fields which stretched along it. Beyond this orchard the ground rose suddenly, and on the steep hill-side there had been a large plantation of Indian corn. The corn was harvested, but the ground was still covered with numberless little stacks of the cornstalks. Half way up the hill stood three ancient chestnut trees; veritable patriarchs of the nut tribe they were, and respected and esteemed as patriarchs should be.

"There are no 'dropping nuts' to-day, either," said Fleda, to whom the sight of her forest friends in the distance probably suggested the thought, for she had not spoken for some time. "I suppose there hasn't been frost enough yet."

"Why you have a good memory, Fairy," said Mr. Carleton. "Do you give the nuts leave to fall of themselves?"

"O sometimes grandpa and I go a nutting," said the little girl getting lightly over the fence,—"but we haven't been this year."

"Then it is a pleasure to come yet?"

"No," said Fleda quietly, "the trees near the house have been stripped; and the only other nice place there is for us to go to, Mr. Didenhover let the Shakers have the nuts. I sha'n't get any this year."

"Live in the woods and not get any nuts! that won't do, Fairy. Here are some fine chestnuts we are coming to—what should hinder our reaping a good harvest from these?"

"I don't think there will be any on them," said Fleda; "Mr. Didenhover has been here lately with the men getting in the corn,—I guess they have cleared the trees."

"Who is Mr. Didenhover?"

"He is grandpa's man."

"Why didn't you bid Mr. Didenhover let the nuts alone?"

"O he wouldn't mind if he was told," said Fleda. "He does everything just as he has a mind to, and nobody can hinder him. Yes—they've cleared the trees—I thought so."

"Don't you know of any other trees that are out of this Mr. Didenhover's way?"

"Yes," said Fleda,—"I know a place where there used to be beautiful hickory trees, and some chestnuts too, I think; but it is too far off for grandpa, and I couldn't go there alone. This is the twenty-acre lot," said she, looking though she did not say it, "Here I leave you."

"I am glad to hear it," said her cousin. "Now give us our directions, Fleda, and thank you for your services."

"Stop a minute," said Mr. Carleton. "What if you and I should try to find those same hickory trees, Miss Fleda? Will you take me with you?—or is it too long a walk?"

"For me?—oh no!" said Fleda with a face of awakening hope; "but," she added timidly, "you were going a shooting, sir?"

"What on earth are you thinking of, Carleton?" said young Rossitur. "Let the nuts and Fleda alone, do!"

"By your leave, Mr. Rossitur," said Carleton. "My murderous intents have all left me, Miss Fleda,—I suppose your wand has been playing about me—and I should like nothing better than to go with you over the hills this morning. I have been a nutting many a time in my own woods at home, and I want to try it for once in the New World. Will you take me?"

"Oh thank you, sir!" said Fleda,—"but we have passed the turning a long way—we must go back ever so far the same way we came to get to the place where we turn off to go up the mountain."

"I don't wish for a prettier way,—if it isn't so far as to tire you, Fairy?"

"Oh it won't tire me!" said Fleda overjoyed.

"Carleton!" exclaimed young Rossitur. "Can you be so absurd! Lose this splendid day for the woodcock, when we may not have another while we are here!"

"You are not a true sportsman, Mr. Rossitur," said the other coolly, "or you would know what it is to have some sympathy with the sports of others. But *you* will have the day for the woodcock, and bring us home a great many I hope. Miss Fleda, suppose we give this impatient young gentleman his orders and despatch him."

"I thought you were more of a sportsman," said the vexed West Pointer,—"or your sympathy would be with me."

"I tell you the sporting mania was never stronger on me," said the other carelessly. "Something less than a rifle however will do to bring down the game I am after. We will rendezvous at the little village over yonder, unless I go home before you, which I think is more probable. Au revoir!"

With careless gracefulness he saluted his disconcerted companion, who moved off with ungraceful displeasure. Fleda and Mr. Carleton then began to follow back the road they had come, in the highest good humour both. Her sparkling face told him with even greater emphasis than her words,

"I am so much obliged to you, sir."

"How you go over fences!" said he,—"like a sprite, as you are."

"O I have climbed a great many," said Fleda, accepting however, again with that infallible instinct, the help which she did not need.—"I shall be so glad to get some nuts, for I thought I wasn't going to have any this year; and it is so pleasant to have them to crack in the long winter evenings."

"You must find them long evenings indeed, I should think."

"O no we don't," said Fleda. "I didn't mean they were long in *that* way. Grandpa cracks the nuts, and I pick them out, and he tells me stories; and then you know he likes to go to bed early. The evenings never seem long."

"But you are not always cracking nuts."

"O no, to be sure not; but there are plenty of other pleasant things to do. I dare say grandpa would have bought some nuts, but I had a great deal rather have those we get ourselves, and then the fun of getting them, besides, is the best part."

Fleda was tramping over the ground at a furious rate.

"How many do you count upon securing to-day?" said Mr. Carleton gravely.

"I don't know," said Fleda with a business face,—"there are a good many trees, and fine large ones, and I don't believe anybody has found them out—they are so far out of the way; there ought to be a good parcel of nuts."

"But," said Mr. Carleton with perfect gravity, "if we should be lucky enough to find a supply for your winter's store, it would be too much for you and me to bring home, Miss Fleda, unless you have a broomstick in the service of fairydom."

"A broomstick!" said Fleda.

"Yes,—did you never hear of the man who had a broomstick that would fetch pails of water at his bidding?"

"No," said Fleda laughing. "What a convenient broomstick! I wish we had one. But I know what I can do, Mr. Carleton,—if there should be too many nuts for us to bring home I can take Cynthy afterwards and get the rest of them. Cynthy and I could go—grandpa couldn't, even if he was as well as usual, for the trees are in a hollow away over on the other side of the mountain. It's a beautiful place."

"Well," said Mr. Carleton smiling curiously to himself, "in that case I shall be even of more use than I had hoped. But sha'n't we want a basket, Miss Fleda?"

"Yes indeed," said Fleda,—"a good large one—I am going to run down to the house for it as soon as we get to the turning-off place, if you'll be so good as to sit down and wait for me, sir,—I won't be long after it."

"No," said he; "I will walk with you and leave my gun in safe quarters. You had better not travel so fast, or I am afraid you will never reach the hickory trees."

Fleda smiled and said there was no danger, but she slackened her pace, and they proceeded at a more reasonable rate till they reached the house.

Mr. Carleton would not go in, placing his gun in an outer shelter. Fleda dashed into the kitchen, and after a few minutes' delay came out again with a huge basket, which Mr. Carleton took from her without suffering his inward amusement to reach his face, and a little tin pail which she kept under her own guardianship. In vain Mr. Carleton offered to take it with the basket or even to put it in the basket, where he shewed her it would go very well; it must go nowhere but in Fleda's own hand.

Fleda was in restless haste till they had passed over the already twice-trodden ground and entered upon the mountain road. It was hardly a road; in some places a beaten track was visible, in others Mr. Carleton wondered how his little companion found her way, where nothing but fresh-fallen leaves and scattered rocks and stones could be seen, covering the whole surface. But her foot never faltered, her eye read way-marks where his saw none, she went on, he did not doubt unerringly, over the leaf-strewn and rock-strewn way, over ridge and hollow, with a steady light swiftness that he could not help admiring. Once they came to a little brawling stream of spring water, hardly three inches deep anywhere but making quite a wide bed for itself in its bright way to the lowlands. Mr. Carleton was considering how he should contrive to get his little guide over it in safety, when quick,—over the little round stones which lifted their heads above the surface of the water, on the tips of her toes, Fleda tripped across before he had done thinking about it. He told her he had no doubt now that she was a fairy and had powers of walking that did not belong to other people. Fleda laughed, and on her little demure figure went picking out the way, always with that little tin pail hanging at her side, like—Mr. Carleton busied himself in finding out similes for her. It wasn't very easy.

For a long distance their way was through a thick woodland, clear of underbrush and very pleasant walking, but permitting no look at the distant country. They wound about, now up hill and now down, till at last they began to ascend in good earnest; the road became better marked, and Mr. Carleton came up with his guide again. Both were obliged to walk more slowly. He had overcome a good deal of Fleda's reserve and she talked to him now quite freely, without however losing the grace of a most exquisite modesty in everything she said or did.

"What do you suppose I have been amusing myself with all this while, Miss Fleda?" said he, after walking for some time alongside of her in silence. "I have been trying to fancy what you looked like as you travelled on before me with that mysterious tin pail."

"Well what *did* I look like?" said Fleda laughing.

"Little Red Riding-Hood, the first thing, carrying her grandmother the pot of butter."

"Ah but I haven't got any butter in this as it happens," said Fleda, "and I hope you are not anything like the wolf, Mr. Carleton?"

"I hope not," said he laughing. "Well, then I thought you might be one of those young ladies the fairy-stories tell of, who set out over the world to seek their fortune. That might hold, you know, a little provision to last for a day or two till you found it."

"No," said Fleda,—"I should never go to seek my fortune."

"Why not, pray?"

"I don't think I should find it any the sooner."

Mr. Carleton looked at her and could not make up his mind whether or not she spoke wittingly.

"Well, but after all are we not seeking our fortune?" said he. "We are doing something very like it. Now up here on the mountain top perhaps we shall find only empty trees—perhaps trees with a harvest of nuts on them."

"Yes, but that wouldn't be like finding a fortune," said Fleda;—"if we were to come to a great heap of nuts all picked out ready for us to carry away, *that* would be a fortune; but now if we find the trees full we have got to knock them down and gather them up and shuck them."

"Make our own fortunes, eh?" said Mr. Carleton smiling. "Well people do say those are the sweetest nuts. I don't know how it may be. Ha! that is fine. What an atmosphere!"

They had reached a height of the mountain that cleared them a view, and over the tops of the trees they looked abroad to a very wide extent of country undulating with hill and vale,—hill and valley alike far below at their feet. Fair and rich,—the gently swelling hills, one beyond another, in the patchwork dress of their many-coloured fields,—the gay hues of the woodland softened and melted into a rich autumn glow,—and far away, beyond even where this glow was sobered and lost in the distance, the faint blue line of the Catskill; faint, but clear and distinct through the transparent air. Such a sky!—of such etherialized purity as if made for spirits to travel in and tempting them to rise and free themselves from the soil; and the stillness,—like nature's hand laid upon the soul, bidding it think. In view of all that vastness and grandeur, man's littleness does bespeak itself. And yet, for every one, the voice of the scene is not more humbling to pride than rousing to all that is really noble and strong in character. Not only "What thou art,"—but "What thou mayest be!" What place thou oughtest to fill—what work thou hast to do,—in this magnificent world. A very extended landscape however genial is also sober in its effect on the mind. One seems to emerge from the narrowness of individual existence, and take a larger view of Life as well as of Creation.

Perhaps Mr. Carleton felt it so, for after his first expression of pleasure he stood silently and gravely looking for a long time. Little Fleda's eye loved it too, but she looked her fill and then sat down on a stone to await her companion's pleasure, glancing now and then up at his face which gave her no encouragement to interrupt him. It was gravely and even gloomily thoughtful. He stood so long without stirring that poor Fleda began to have sad thoughts of the possibility of gathering all the nuts from the hickory trees, and she heaved a very gentle sigh once or twice; but the dark blue eye which she with reason admired remained fixed on the broad scene below, as if it were reading or trying to read there a difficult lesson. And when at last he turned and began to go up the path again he kept the same face, and went moodily swinging his arm up and down, as if in disturbed thought. Fleda was too happy to be moving to care for her companion's silence; she would have compounded for no more conversation so they might but reach the nut trees. But before they had got quite so far Mr. Carleton broke the silence, speaking in precisely the same tone and manner he had used the last time.

"Look here, Fairy," said he, pointing to a small heap of chestnut burs piled at the foot of a tree,—"here's a little fortune for you already."

"That's a squirrel!" said Fleda, looking at the place very attentively. "There has been nobody else here. He has put them together, ready to be carried off to his nest."

"We'll save him that trouble," said Mr. Carleton. "Little rascal! he's a Didenhover in miniature."

"Oh no!" said Fleda; "he had as good a right to the nuts I am sure as we have, poor fellow.—Mr. Carleton—"

Mr. Carleton was throwing the nuts into the basket. At the anxious and undecided tone in which his name was pronounced he stopped and looked up, at a very wistful face.

"Mightn't we leave these nuts till we come back? If we find the trees over here full we sha'n't want them; and if we don't, these would be only a handful—"

"And the squirrel would be disappointed?" said Mr. Carleton smiling. "You would rather we should leave them to him?"

Fleda said yes, with a relieved face, and Mr. Carleton still smiling emptied his basket of the few nuts he had put in, and they walked on.

In a hollow, rather a deep hollow, behind the crest of the hill, as Fleda had said, they came at last to a noble group of large hickory trees, with one or two chestnuts standing in attendance on the outskirts. And also as Fleda had said, or hoped, the place was so far from convenient access that nobody had visited them; they were thick hung with fruit. If the spirit of the game had been wanting or failing in Mr. Carleton, it must have roused again into full life at the joyous heartiness of Fleda's exclamations. At any rate no boy could have taken to the business better. He cut, with her permission, a stout long pole in the woods; and swinging himself lightly into one of the trees shewed that he was a master in the art of whipping them. Fleda was delighted but not surprised; for from the first moment of Mr. Carleton's proposing to go with her she had been privately sure that he would not prove an inactive or inefficient ally. By whatever slight tokens she might read this, in whatsoever fine characters of the eye, or speech, or manner, she knew it; and knew it just as well before they reached the hickory trees as she did afterwards.

When one of the trees was well stripped the young gentleman mounted into another, while Fleda set herself to hull and gather up the nuts under the one first beaten. She could make but little headway however compared with her companion; the nuts fell a great deal faster than she could put them in her basket. The trees were heavy laden and Mr. Carleton seemed determined to have the whole crop; from the second tree he went to the third. Fleda was bewildered with her happiness; this was doing business in style. She tried to calculate what the whole quantity would be, but it went beyond her; one basketful would not take it, nor two, nor three,—it wouldn't *begin to*, Fleda said to herself. She went on hulling and gathering with all possible industry.

After the third tree was finished Mr. Carleton threw down his pole, and resting himself upon the ground at the foot told Fleda he would wait a few moments before he began again. Fleda thereupon left off her work too, and going for her little tin pail presently offered it to him temptingly stocked with pieces of apple-pie. When he had smilingly taken one, she next brought him a sheet of white paper with slices of young cheese.

"No, thank you," said he.

"Cheese is very good with apple-pie," said Fleda competently.

"Is it?" said he laughing. "Well—upon that—I think you would teach me a good many things, Miss Fleda, if I were to stay here long enough."

"I wish you would stay and try, sir," said Fleda, who did not know exactly what to make of the shade of seriousness which crossed his face. It was gone almost instantly.

"I think anything is better eaten out in the woods than it is at home," said Fleda.

"Well I don't know," said her friend. "I have no doubt that is the case with cheese and apple-pie, and especially under hickory trees which one has been contending with pretty sharply. If a touch of your wand, Fairy, could transform one of these shells into a goblet of Lafitte or Amontillado we should have nothing to wish for."

'Amontillado' was Hebrew to Fleda, but 'goblet' was intelligible.

"I am sorry!" she said,—"I don't know where there is

any spring up here,—but we shall come to one going down the mountain."

"Do you know where all the springs are?"

"No, not all, I suppose," said Fleda, "but I know a good many. I have gone about through the woods so much, and I always look for the springs."

"And who roams about through the woods with you?"

"Oh nobody but grandpa," said Fleda. "He used to be out with me a great deal, but he can't go much now,—this year or two."

"Don't you go to school?"

"O no!" said Fleda smiling.

"Then your grandfather teaches you at home?"

"No,"—said Fleda,—"father used to teach me;—grandpa doesn't teach me much."

"What do you do with yourself all day long?"

"O plenty of things," said Fleda, smiling again. "I read, and talk to grandpa, and go riding, and do a great many things."

"Has your home always been here, Fairy?" said Mr. Carleton after a few minutes' pause.

Fleda said "No sir," and there stopped; and then seeming to think that politeness called upon her to say more, she added,

"I have lived with grandpa ever since father left me here when he was going away among the Indians,—I used to be always with him before."

"And how long ago is that?"

"It is—four years, sir;—more, I believe. He was sick when he came back, and we never went away from Queechy again."

Mr. Carleton looked again silently at the child, who had given him these pieces of information with a singular grave propriety of manner, and even as it were reluctantly.

"And what do you read, Fairy?" he said after a minute; —"stories of fairy-land?"

"No," said Fleda, "I haven't any. We haven't a great many books—there are only a few up in the cupboard, and the Encyclopædia; father had some books, but they are locked up in a chest. But there is a great deal in the Encyclopædia."

"The Encyclopædia!" said Mr. Carleton;—"what do you read in that? what can you find to like there?"

"I like all about the insects, and birds and animals; and about flowers,—and lives of people, and curious things. There are a great many in it."

"And what are the other books in the cupboard, which you read?"

"There's Quentin Durward," said Fleda,—"and Rob Roy, and Guy Mannering in two little bits of volumes; and the Knickerbocker, and the Christian's Magazine, and an odd volume of Redgauntlet, and the Beauties of Scotland."

"And have you read all these, Miss Fleda?" said her companion, commanding his countenance with difficulty.

"I haven't read quite all of the Christian's Magazine, nor all of the Beauties of Scotland."

"All the rest?"

"O yes," said Fleda,—"and two or three times over. And there are three great red volumes besides, Robertson's history of something, I believe. I haven't read that either."

"And which of them all do you like the best?"

"I don't know," said Fleda,—"I don't know but I like to read the Encyclopædia as well as any of them. And then I have the newspapers to read too."

"I think, Miss Fleda," said Mr. Carleton a minute after, "you had better let me take you with my mother over the sea, when we go back again,—to Paris."

"Why, sir?"

"You know," said he half smiling, "your aunt wants you, and has engaged my mother to bring you with her if she can."

"I know it," said Fleda. "But I am not going."

It was spoken not rudely but in a tone of quiet determination.

"Aren't you too tired, sir?" said she gently, when she saw Mr. Carleton preparing to launch into the remaining hickory trees.

"Not I!" said he. "I am not tired till I have done, Fairy. And besides, cheese is working man's fare, you know, isn't it?"

"No," said Fleda gravely,—"I don't think it is."

"What then?" said Mr. Carleton, stopping as he was

about to spring into the tree, and looking at her with a face of comical amusement.

"It isn't what *our* men live on," said Fleda, demurely eying the fallen nuts, with a head full of business.

They set both to work again with renewed energy, and rested not till the treasures of the trees had been all brought to the ground, and as large a portion of them as could be coaxed and shaken into Fleda's basket had been cleared from the hulls and bestowed there. But there remained a vast quantity. These with a good deal of labour Mr. Carleton and Fleda gathered into a large heap in rather a sheltered place by the side of a rock, and took what measures they might to conceal them. This was entirely at Fleda's instance.

"You and your maid Cynthia will have to make a good many journeys, Miss Fleda, to get all these home, unless you can muster a larger basket."

"O *that's* nothing," said Fleda. "It will be all fun. I don't care how many times we have to come. You are *very* good, Mr. Carleton."

"Do you think so?" said he. "I wish I did. I wish you would make your wand rest on me, Fairy."

"My wand?" said Fleda.

"Yes—you know your grandfather says you are a fairy and carry a wand. What does he say that for, Miss Fleda?"

Fleda said she supposed it was because he loved her so much; but the rosy smile with which she said it would have let her hearer, if he had needed enlightening, far more into the secret than she was herself. And if the simplicity in her face had not been equal to the wit, Mr. Carleton would never have ventured the look of admiration he bestowed on her. He knew it was safe. *Approbation* she saw, and it made her smile the rosier; but the admiration was a step beyond her; Fleda could make nothing of it.

They descended the mountain now with a hasty step, for the day was wearing well on. At the spot where he had stood so long when they went up, Mr. Carleton paused again for a minute. In mountain scenery every hour makes a change. The sun was lower now, the lights and shadows more strongly contrasted, the sky of a yet calmer blue, cool and clear towards the horizon. The scene said still the same that it had said a few hours before, with a touch more of sadness; it seemed to whisper, "All things have an end —thy time may not be for ever—do what thou wouldest do—'while ye have light believe in the light that ye may be children of the light.'"

Whether Mr. Carleton read it so or not, he stood for a minute motionless and went down the mountain looking so grave that Fleda did not venture to speak to him, till they reached the neighbourhood of the spring.

"What are you searching for, Miss Fleda?" said her friend.

She was making a busy quest here and there by the side of the little stream.

"I was looking to see if I could find a mullein leaf," said Fleda.

"A mullein leaf? what do you want it for?"

"I want it—to make a drinking-cup of," said Fleda, her intent bright eyes peering keenly about in every direction.

"A mullein leaf! that is too rough; one of these golden leaves—what are they?—will do better, won't it?"

"That is hickory," said Fleda. "No; the mullein leaf is the best because it holds the water so nicely.—Here it is!—"

And folding up one of the largest leaves into a most artist-like cup, she presented it to Mr. Carleton.

"For me, was all that trouble?" said he. "I don't deserve it."

"You wanted something, sir," said Fleda. "The water is very cold and nice."

He stooped to the bright little stream and filled his rural goblet several times.

"I never knew what it was to have a fairy for my cup-bearer before," said he. "That was better than anything Bordeaux or Xeres ever sent forth."

He seemed to have swallowed his seriousness, or thrown it away with the mullein leaf. It was quite gone.

"This is the best spring in all grandpa's ground," said Fleda. "The water is as good as can be."

"How come you to be such a wood and water spirit?

you must live out of doors. Do the trees ever talk to you? I sometimes think they do to me."

"I don't know—I think *I* talk to *them*," said Fleda.

"It's the same thing," said her companion smiling. "Such beautiful woods!"

"Were you never in the country before in the fall, sir?"

"Not here—in my own country often enough—but the woods in England do not put on such a gay face, Miss Fleda, when they are going to be stripped of their summer dress—they look sober upon it—the leaves wither and grow brown and the woods have a dull russet colour. Your trees are true Yankees—they 'never say die!'"

"Why, are the Americans more obstinate than the English?" said Fleda.

"It is difficult to compare unknown quantities," said Mr. Carleton laughing and shaking his head. "I see you have good ears for the key-note of patriotism."

Fleda looked a little hard at him, but he did not explain; and indeed they were hurrying along too much for talking; leaping from stone to stone, and running down the smooth orchard slope. When they reached the last fence, but a little way from the house, Fleda made a resolute pause.

"Mr. Carleton—" said she.

Mr. Carleton put down his basket, and looked in some surprise at the hesitating anxious little face that looked up at him.

"Won't you please not say anything to grandpa about my going away?"

"Why not, Fairy?" said he kindly.

"Because I don't think I ought to go."

"But may it not be possible," said he, "that your grandfather can judge better in the matter than you can do?"

"No," said Fleda, "I don't think he can. He would do anything he thought would be most for my happiness; but it wouldn't be for my happiness," she said with an unsteady lip,—"I don't know what he would do if I went!"

"You think he would have no sunshine if your wand didn't touch him?" said Mr. Carleton smiling.

"No sir," said Fleda gravely,—"I don't think that,—but won't you please, Mr. Carleton, not to speak about it?"

"But are you sure," he said, sitting down on a stone

hard by and taking one of her hands, "are you sure that you would not like to go with us? I wish you would change your mind about it. My mother will love you very much, and I will take the especial charge of you till we give you to your aunt in Paris;—if the wind blows a little too rough I will always put myself between it and you," he added smiling.

Fleda smiled faintly, but immediately begged Mr. Carleton "not to say anything to put it into her grandfather's head."

"It must be there already, I think, Miss Fleda; but at any rate you know my mother must perform her promise to your aunt Mrs. Rossitur; and she would not do that without letting your grandfather know how glad she would be to take you."

Fleda stood silent a moment, and then with a touching look of waiting patience in her sweet face suffered Mr. Carleton to help her over the fence; and they went home.

To Fleda's unspeakable surprise it was found to be past four o'clock, and Cynthy had supper ready. Mr. Ringgan with great cordiality invited Mr. Carleton to stay with them, but he could not; his mother would expect him to dinner.

"Where is your mother?"

"At Montepoole, sir; we have been to Niagara, and came this way on our return; partly that my mother might fulfil the promise she made Mrs. Rossitur—to let you know, sir, with how much pleasure she will take charge of your little granddaughter and convey her to her friends in Paris, if you can think it best to let her go."

"Hum!—she is very kind," said Mr. Ringgan, with a look of grave and not unmoved consideration which Fleda did not in the least like;—"How long will you stay at Montepoole, sir?"

It might be several days, Mr. Carleton said.

"Hum—You have given up this day to Fleda, Mr. Carleton,—suppose you take to-morrow for the game, and come here and try our country fare when you have got through shooting?—you and young Mr. Rossitur?—and I'll think over this question and let you know about it."

Fleda was delighted to see that her friend accepted this invitation with apparent pleasure.

"You will be kind enough to give my respects to your mother," Mr. Ringgan went on, "and thanks for her kind offer. I may perhaps—I don't know—avail myself of it. If anything should bring Mrs. Carleton this way we should like to see her. I am glad to see my friends," he said, shaking the young gentleman's hand,—"as long as I have a house to ask 'em to!"

"That will be for many years, I trust," said Mr. Carleton respectfully, struck with something in the old gentleman's manner.

"I don't know sir!" said Mr. Ringgan, with again the dignified look of trouble;—"it may not be!—I wish you good day, sir."

CHAPTER IV.

> A mind that in a calm angelic mood
> Of happy wisdom, meditating good,
> Beholds, of all from her high powers required,
> Much done, and much designed, and more desired,—
>
> WORDSWORTH.

"I'VE had such a delicious day, dear grandpa,"—said little Fleda as they sat at supper;—"you can't think how kind Mr. Carleton has been."

"Has he?—Well dear—I'm glad on't,—he seems a very nice young man."

"He's a smart-lookin' feller," said Cynthy, who was pouring out the tea.

"And we have got the greatest quantity of nuts!" Fleda went on,—"enough for all winter. Cynthy and I will have to make ever so many journeys to fetch 'em all; and they are splendid big ones. Don't you say anything to Mr. Didenhover, Cynthy."

"I don't desire to meddle with Mr. Didenhover unless I've got to," said Cynthy with an expression of considerable disgust. "You needn't give no charges to me."

"But you'll go with me, Cynthy?"

"I s'pose I'll have to," said Miss Gall dryly, after a short interval of sipping tea and helping herself to sweetmeats.

This lady had a pervading acidity of face and temper, but it was no more. To take her name as standing for a fair setting forth of her character would be highly injurious to a really respectable composition, which the world's neglect (there was no other imaginable cause) had soured a little.

Almost Fleda's first thought on coming home had been about Mr. Jolly. But she knew very well, without asking, that he had not been there; she would not touch the subject.

"I haven't had such a fine day of nutting in a great while, grandpa," she said again; "and you never saw such a good hand as Mr. Carleton is at whipping the trees."

"How came he to go with you?"

"I don't know,—I suppose it was to please me, in the first place; but I am sure he enjoyed it himself; and he liked the pie and cheese, too, Cynthy."

"Where did your cousin go?"

"O he went off after the woodcock. I hope he didn't find any."

"What do you think of those two young men, Fairy?"

"In what way, grandpa?"

"I mean, which of them do you like the best?"

"Mr. Carleton."

"But t'other one's your cousin," said Mr. Ringgan, bending forward and examining his little granddaughter's face with a curious pleased look, as he often did when expecting an answer from her.

"Yes," said Fleda, "but he isn't so much of a gentleman."

"How do you know that?"

"I don't think he is," said Fleda quietly.

"But why, Fairy?"

"He doesn't know how to keep his word as well, grandpa."

"Ay, ay? let's hear about that," said Mr. Ringgan.

A little reluctantly, for Cynthia was present, Fleda told the story of the robins, and how Mr. Carleton would not let the gun be fired.

"Wa'n't your cousin a little put out by that?"

"They were both put out," said Fleda; "Mr. Carleton was very angry for a minute, and then Mr. Rossitur was angry, but I think he could have been angrier if he had chosen."

Mr. Ringgan laughed, and then seemed in a sort of amused triumph about something.

"Well dear!" he remarked after a while,—"you'll never buy wooden nutmegs, I expect."

Fleda laughed and hoped not, and asked him why he said so. But he didn't tell her.

"Mr. Ringgan," said Cynthy, "hadn't I better run up

the hill after supper, and ask Mis' Plumfield to come down and help to-morrow? I s'pose you'll want considerable of a set-out; and if both them young men comes you'll want some more help to entertain 'em than I can give you, it's likely."

"Do so—do so," said the old gentleman. "Tell her who I expect, and ask her if she can come and help you, and me too."

"O and I'll go with you, Cynthy," said Fleda. "I'll get aunt Miriam to come, I know."

"I should think you'd be run off your legs already, Flidda," said Miss Cynthia; "what ails you to want to be going again?"

But this remonstrance availed nothing. Supper was hurried through, and leaving the table standing Cynthia and Fleda set off to "run up the hill."

They were hardly a few steps from the gate when they heard the clatter of horses' hoofs behind them, and the two young gentlemen came riding hurriedly past, having joined company and taken their horses at Queechy Run. Rossitur did not seem to see his little cousin and her companion; but the doffed cap and low inclination of the other rider as they flew by called up a smile and blush of pleasure to Fleda's face; and the sound of their horses' hoofs had died away in the distance before the light had faded from her cheeks or she was quite at home to Cynthia's observations. She was possessed with the feeling, what a delightful thing it was to have people do things in such a manner.

"That was your cousin, wa'n't it?" said Cynthy, when the spell was off.

"No," said Fleda, "the other one was my cousin."

"Well—I mean one of them fellers that went by. He's a soldier, ain't he?"

"An officer," said Fleda.

"Well, it does give a man an elegant look to be in the militie, don't it? I should admire to have a cousin like that. It's dreadful becoming to have that—what is it they call it?—to let the beard grow over the mouth. I s'pose they can't do that without they be in the army, can they?"

"I don't know," said Fleda. "I hope not. I think it is very ugly."

"Do you? Oh!—I admire it. It makes a man look so spry!"

A few hundred yards from Mr. Ringgan's gate the road began to wind up a very long heavy hill. Just at the hill's foot it crossed by a rude bridge the bed of a noisy brook that came roaring down from the higher grounds, turning sundry mill and factory wheels in its way. About half way up the hill one of these was placed, belonging to a mill for sawing boards. The little building stood alone, no other in sight, with a dark background of wood rising behind it on the other side of the brook; the stream itself running smoothly for a small space above the mill, and leaping down madly below, as if it disdained its bed and would clear at a bound every impediment in its way to the sea. When the mill was not going the quantity of water that found its way down the hill was indeed very small, enough only to keep up a pleasant chattering with the stones; but as soon as the stream was allowed to gather all its force and run free its loquacity was such that it would prevent a traveller from suspecting his approach to the mill, until, very near, the monotonous hum of its saw could be heard. This was a place Fleda dearly loved. The wild sound of the waters, and the lonely keeping of the scene, with the delicious smell of the new-sawn boards, and the fascination of seeing the great logs of wood walk up to the relentless tireless up-and-down-going steel; as the generations of men in turn present themselves to the course of those sharp events which are the teeth of Time's saw; until all of a sudden the master spirit, the man-regulator of this machinery, would perform some conjuration on lever and wheel,—and at once, as at the touch of an enchanter, the log would be still and the saw stay its work;—the business of life came to a stand, and the romance of the little brook sprang up again. Fleda never tired of it—never. She would watch the saw play and stop, and go on again; she would have her ears dinned with the hoarse clang of the machinery, and then listen to the laugh of the mill-stream; she would see with untiring patience one board after another cut and cast aside, and log succeed to log; and never turned weary away from that mysterious image of Time's doings. Fleda had besides, without knowing it, the eye of a painter. In the lonely hill-side, the odd-shaped little mill with its accompaniments of wood and water, and the great logs of timber lying about the ground in all directions and varieties of position, there was a picturesque charm for her, where the country people saw nothing but business and a place fit for it. Their hands grew hard where her mind was refining. Where they made dollars and cents, she was growing rich in stores of thought and associations of beauty. How many purposes the same thing serves!

"That had ought to be your grandpa's mill this minute," observed Cynthy.

"I wish it was!" sighed Fleda. "Who's got it now, Cynthy?"

"O it's that chap Mc Gowan, I expect;—he's got pretty much the hull of everything. I told Mr. Ringgan I wouldn't let him have it if it was me, at the time. Your grandpa'd be glad to get it back now, I guess."

Fleda guessed so too; but also guessed that Miss Gall was probably very far from being possessed of the whole rationale of the matter. So she made her no answer.

After reaching the brow of the hill the road continued on a very gentle ascent towards a little settlement half a quarter of a mile off; passing now and then a few scattered cottages or an occasional mill or turner's shop. Several mills and factories, with a store and a very few dwelling-houses were all the settlement; not enough to entitle it to the name of a village. Beyond these and the mill-ponds, of which in the course of the road there were three or four, and with a brief intervening space of cultivated fields, a single farm-house stood alone; just upon the borders of a large and very fair sheet of water from which all the others had their supply.—So large and fair that nobody cavilled at its taking the style of a lake and giving its own pretty name of Deepwater both to the settlement and the farm that half embraced it. This farm was Seth Plumfield's.

At the garden gate Fleda quitted Cynthy and rushed forward to meet her aunt, whom she saw coming round the corner of the house with her gown pinned up behind her, from attending to some domestic concern among the pigs, the cows, or the poultry.

"O aunt Miriam," said Fleda eagerly, "we are going to have company to tea to-morrow—won't you come and help us?"

Aunt Miriam laid her hands upon Fleda's shoulders and looked at Cynthy.

"I came up to see if you wouldn't come down to-morrow, Mis' Plumfield," said that personage, with her usual dry business tone, always a little on the wrong side of sweet;—"your brother has taken a notion to ask two young fellers from the Pool to supper, and they're grand folks I s'pose, and have got to have a fuss made for 'em. I don't know what Mr. Ringgan was thinkin' of, or whether he thinks I have got anything to do or not; but anyhow they're a comin', I s'pose, and must have somethin' to eat; and I thought the best thing I could do would be to come and get you into the works, if I could. I should feel a little queer to have nobody but me to say nothin' to them at the table."

"Ah do come, aunt Miriam!" said Fleda; "it will be twice as pleasant if you do; and besides, we want to have everything very nice, you know."

Aunt Miriam smiled at Fleda, and inquired of Miss Gall what she had in the house.

"Why I don't know, Mis' Plumfield," said the lady, while Fleda threw her arms round her aunt and thanked her,—"there ain't nothin' particler—pork and beef and the old story. I've got some first-rate pickles. I calculated to make some sort o' cake in the morning."

"Any of those small hams left?"

"Not a bone of 'em—these six weeks. *I* don't see how they've gone, for my part. I'd lay any wager there were two in the smoke-house when I took the last one out. If Mr. Didenhover was a little more like a weasel I should think he'd been in."

"Have you cooked that roaster I sent down?"

"No, Mis' Plumfield, I ha'n't—it's such a plaguy sight of trouble!" said Cynthy with a little apologetic giggle;—"I was keepin' it for some day when I hadn't much to do."

"I'll take the trouble of it. I'll be down bright and

early in the morning, and we'll see what's best to do. How's your last churning, Cynthy?"

"Well—I guess it's pretty middlin', Mis' Plumfield."

"'Tisn't anything very remarkable, aunt Miriam," said Fleda shaking her head.

"Well, well," said Mrs. Plumfield smiling, "run away down home now, and I'll come to-morrow, and I guess we'll fix it. But who is it that grandpa has asked?"

Fleda and Cynthy both opened at once.

"One of them is my cousin, aunt Miriam, that was at West Point, and the other is the nicest English gentleman you ever saw—you will like him very much—he has been with me getting nuts all to-day."

"They're a smart enough couple of chaps," said Cynthia; "they look as if they lived where money was plenty."

"Well I'll come to-morrow," repeated Mrs. Plumfield, "and we'll see about it. Good night, dear!"

She took Fleda's head in both her hands and gave her a most affectionate kiss; and the two petitioners set off homewards again.

Aunt Miriam was not at all like her brother, in feature, though the moral characteristics suited the relationship sufficiently well. There was the expression of strong sense and great benevolence; the unbending uprightness, of mind and body at once; and the dignity of an essentially noble character, not the same as Mr. Ringgan's, but such as well became his sister. She had been brought up among the Quakers, and though now and for many years a staunch Presbyterian, she still retained a tincture of the calm efficient gentleness of mind and manner that belongs so inexplicably to them. More womanly sweetness than was in Mr. Ringgan's blue eye a woman need not wish to have; and perhaps his sister's had not so much. There was no want of it in her heart, nor in her manner, but the many and singular excellencies of her character were a little overshadowed by super-excellent housekeeping. Not a taint of the littleness that sometimes grows therefrom,—not a trace of the narrowness of mind that over-attention to such pursuits is too apt to bring;—on every important occasion aunt Miriam would come out free and unshackled from all the cobweb entanglements of housewifery; she would have tossed housewifery to the winds if need were (but it never was, for in a new sense she always contrived to make both ends meet.) It was only in the unbroken everyday course of affairs that aunt Miriam's face shewed any tokens of that incessant train of *small cares* which had never left their impertinent footprints upon the broad high brow of her brother. Mr. Ringgan had no affinity with small cares; deep serious matters received his deep and serious consideration; but he had as dignified a disdain of trifling annoyances or concernments as any great mastiff or Newfoundlander ever had for the yelping of a little cur.

CHAPTER V.

Ynne London citye was I borne,
Of parents of grete note;
My fadre dydd a nobile arms
Emblazon onne hys cote.
CHATTERTON.

IN the snuggest and best private room of the House at Montepoole a party of ladies and gentlemen were gathered, awaiting the return of the sportsmen. The room had been made as comfortable as any place could be in a house built for "the season," after the season was past. A splendid fire of hickory logs was burning brilliantly and making amends for many deficiencies; the closed wooden shutters gave the reality if not the look of warmth, for though the days might be fine and mild the mornings and evenings were always very cool up there among the mountains; and a table stood at the last point of readiness for having dinner served. They only waited for the lingering woodcock-hunters.

It was rather an elderly party, with the exception of one young man whose age might match that of the absent two. He was walking up and down the room with somewhat the air of having nothing to do with himself. Another gentleman, much older, stood warming his back at the fire, feeling about his jaws and chin with one hand and looking at the dinner-table in a sort of expectant reverie. The rest, three ladies, sat quietly chatting. All these persons were extremely different from one another in individual characteristics, and all had the unmistakeable mark of the habit of good society; as difficult to locate and as easy to recognise as the sense of *freshness* which some ladies have the secret of diffusing around themselves;—no definable sweetness, nothing in particular, but making a very agreeable impression.

One of these ladies, the mother of the perambulating young officer, (he was a class-mate of Rossitur's) was extremely plain in feature, even more than *ordinary*. This plainness was not however devoid of sense, and it was relieved by an uncommon amount of good-nature and kindness of heart. In her son the sense deepened into acuteness, and the kindness of heart retreated, it is to be hoped, into some hidden recess of his nature; for it very rarely shewed itself in open expression. That is, to an eye keen in reading the natural signs of emotion; for it cannot be said that his manner had any want of amenity or politeness.

The second lady, the wife of the gentleman on the hearth-rug, or rather on the spot where the hearth-rug should have been, was a strong contrast to this mother and son; remarkably pretty, delicate and even lovely; with a black eye however that though in general soft could shew a mischievous sparkle upon occasion; still young, and one of those women who always were and always will be pretty and delicate at any age.

The third had been very handsome, and was still a very elegant woman, but her face had seen more of the world's wear and tear. It had never known placidity of expression beyond what the habitual command of good-breeding imposed. She looked exactly what she was, a perfect woman of the world. A very good specimen,—for Mrs. Carleton had sense and cultivation and even feeling enough to play the part very gracefully; yet her mind was bound in the shackles of "the world's" tyrannical forging and had never been free; and her heart bowed submissively to the same authority.

"Here they are! Welcome home," exclaimed this lady, as her son and his friend at length made their appearance;—"Welcome home—we are all famishing; and I don't know why in the world we waited for you for I am sure you don't deserve it. What success? What success, Mr. Rossitur?"

"'Faith ma'am, there's little enough to boast of, as far as I am concerned. Mr. Carleton may speak for himself."

"I am very sorry, ma'am, you waited for me," said that gentleman. "I am a delinquent I acknowledge. The day came to an end before I was at all aware of it."

"It would not do to flatter you so far as to tell you why we waited," said Mrs. Evelyn's soft voice. And then perceiving that the gentleman at whom she was looking gave her no answer she turned to the other. "How many woodcock, Mr. Rossitur?"

"Nothing to shew, ma'am," he replied. "Didn't see a solitary one. I heard some partridges, but I didn't mean to have room in my bag for them."

"Did you find the right ground, Rossitur?"

"I had a confounded long tramp after it if I didn't," said the discomfited sportsman, who did not seem to have yet recovered his good humour.

"Were you not together?" said Mrs. Carleton. "Where were you, Guy?"

"Following the sport another way, ma'am; I had very good success too."

"What's the total?" said Mr. Evelyn. "How much game did you bag?"

"Really sir, I didn't count. I can only answer for a bag full."

"Ladies and gentlemen!" cried Rossitur, bursting forth,—"What will you say when I tell you that Mr. Carleton deserted me and the sport in a most unceremonious manner, and that he,—the cynical philosopher, the reserved English gentleman, the gay man of the world,—you are all of 'em by turns, aren't you, Carleton?—*he!*—has gone and made a very cavaliero servante of himself to a piece of rusticity, and spent all to-day in helping a little girl pick up chestnuts!"

"Mr. Carleton would be a better man if he were to spend a good many more days in the same manner," said that gentleman, dryly enough. But the entrance of dinner put a stop to both laughter and questioning for a time, all of the party being well disposed to their meat.

When the pickerel from the lakes, and the poultry and half-kept joints had had their share of attention, and a pair of fine wild ducks were set on the table, the tongues of the party found something to do besides eating.

"We have had a very satisfactory day among the Shakers, Guy," said Mrs. Carleton; "and we have arranged to drive to Kenton to-morrow—I suppose you will go with us?"

"With pleasure, mother, but that I am engaged to dinner about five or six miles in the opposite direction."

"Engaged to dinner!—what with this old gentleman where you went last night? And you too, Mr. Rossitur?"

"I have made no promise, ma'am, but I take it I must go."

"Vexatious! Is the little girl going with us, Guy?"

"I don't know yet—I half apprehend, yes; there seems to be a doubt in her grandfather's mind, not whether he can let her go, but whether he can keep her, and that looks like it."

"Is it your little cousin who proved the successful rival of the woodcock to-day, Charlton?" said Mrs. Evelyn. "What is she?"

"I don't know, ma'am, upon my word. I presume Carleton will tell you she is something uncommon and quite remarkable."

"Is she, Mr. Carleton?"

"What, ma'am?"

"Uncommon?"

"Very."

"Come! That *is* something, from *you*," said Rossitur's brother officer, Lieut. Thorn.

"What's the uncommonness?" said Mrs. Thorn, addressing herself rather to Mr. Rossitur as she saw Mr. Carleton's averted eye;—"Is she handsome, Mr. Rossitur?"

"I can't tell you, I am sure, ma'am. I saw nothing but a nice child enough in a calico frock, just such as one would see in any farm-house. She rushed into the room when she was first called to see us, from somewhere in distant regions, with an immense iron ladle a foot and a half long in her hand with which she had been performing unknown feats of housewifery; and they had left her head still encircled with a halo of kitchen-smoke. If as they say 'coming events cast their shadows before,' she was the shadow of supper."

"Oh Charlton, Charlton!" said Mrs. Evelyn, but in a tone

of very gentle and laughing reproof,—"for shame! What a picture! and of your cousin!"

"Is she a pretty child, Guy?" said Mrs. Carleton, who did not relish her son's grave face.

"No ma'am—something more than that."

"How old?"

"About ten or eleven."

"That's an ugly age."

"She will never be at an ugly age."

"What style of beauty?"

"The highest—that degree of mould and finish which belongs only to the finest material."

"That is hardly the kind of beauty one would expect to see in such a place," said Mrs. Carleton. "From one side of her family to be sure she has a right to it."

"I have seen very few examples of it anywhere," said her son.

"Who were her parents?" said Mrs. Evelyn.

"Her mother was Mrs. Rossitur's sister,—her father"—

"Amy Charlton!" exclaimed Mrs. Evelyn,—"O I knew her! Was Amy Charlton her mother? O I didn't know whom you were talking of. She was one of my dearest friends. Her daughter may well be handsome—she was one of the most lovely persons I ever knew; in body and mind both. O I loved Amy Charlton very much. I must see this child."

"I don't know who her father was," Mrs. Carleton went on.

"O her father was Major Ringgan," said Mrs. Evelyn. "I never saw him, but I have heard him spoken of in very high terms. I always heard that Amy married very well."

"Major Ringgan!" said Mrs. Thorn;—"his name is very well known; he was very distinguished."

"He was a self-made man entirely," said Mrs. Evelyn, in a tone that conveyed a good deal more than the simple fact.

"Yes, he was a self-made man," said Mrs. Thorn, "but I should never think of that where a man distinguishes himself so much; he was very distinguished."

"Yes, and for more than officer-like qualities," said Mrs.

Evelyn. "I have heard his personal accomplishments as a gentleman highly praised."

"So that little Miss Ringgan's right to be a beauty may be considered clearly made out," said Mr. Thorn.

"It is one of those singular cases," said Mr. Carleton, "where purity of blood proves itself, and one has no need to go back to past generations to make any inquiry concerning it."

"Hear him!" cried Rossitur;—"and for the life of me I could see nothing of all this wonder. Her face is not at all striking."

"The wonder is not so much in what it *is* as in what it indicates," said Mr. Carleton.

"What does it indicate?" said his mother.

"Suppose you were to ask me to count the shades of colour in a rainbow," answered he.

"Hear him!" cried Thorn again.

"Well I hope she will go with us and we shall have a chance of seeing her," said Mrs. Carleton.

"If she were only a few years older it is my belief you would see enough of her, ma'am," said young Rossitur.

The haughty coldness of Mr. Carleton's look at this speech could not be surpassed.

"But she has beauty of feature too, has she not?" Mrs. Carleton asked again of her son.

"Yes, in very high degree. The contour of the eye and brow I never saw finer."

"It is a little odd," said Mrs. Evelyn with the slightest touch of a piqued air, (she had some daughters at home)—"that is a kind of beauty one is apt to associate with high breeding, and certainly you very rarely see it anywhere else; and Major Ringgan, however distinguished and estimable, as I have no doubt he was,—And this child must have been brought up with no advantages, here in the country."

"My dear madam," said Mr. Carleton smiling a little, "this high breeding is a very fine thing, but it can neither be given nor bequeathed; and we cannot entail it."

"But it can be taught, can't it?"

"If it could be taught it is to be hoped it would be oftener learned," said the young man dryly.

"But what do we mean, then, when we talk of the high breeding of certain classes—and families? and why are we not disappointed when we look to find it in connection with certain names and positions in society?"

"I do not know," said Mr. Carleton.

"You don't mean to say, I suppose, Mr. Carleton," said Thorn bridling a little, "that it is a thing independent of circumstances, and that there is no value in blood?"

"Very nearly—answering the question as you understand it."

"May I ask how you understand it?"

"As you do, sir."

"Is there no high breeding then in the world?" asked good-natured Mrs. Thorn, who could be touched on this point of family.

"There is very little of it. What is commonly current under the name is merely counterfeit notes which pass from hand to hand of those who are bankrupt in the article."

"And to what serve then," said Mrs. Evelyn colouring, "the long lists of good old names which even you, Mr. Carleton, I know, do not disdain?"

"To endorse the counterfeit notes," said Mr. Carleton smiling.

"Guy you are absurd!" said his mother. "I will not sit at the table and listen to you if you talk such stuff. What do you mean?"

"I beg your pardon, mother, you have misunderstood me," said he seriously. "Mind, I have been talking, not of ordinary conformity to what the world requires, but of that fine perfection of mental and moral constitution which in its own natural necessary acting leaves nothing to be desired, in every occasion or circumstance of life. It is the pure gold, and it knows no tarnish; it is the true coin, and it gives what it proffers to give; it is the living plant ever-blossoming, and not the cut and art-arranged flowers. It is a thing of the mind altogether; and where nature has not curiously prepared the soil it is in vain to try to make it grow. *This* is not very often met with?"

"No indeed," said Mrs. Carleton;—"but you are so fastidiously nice in all your notions!—at this rate nothing will ever satisfy you."

"I don't think it is so very uncommon," said Mrs. Thorn. "It seems to me one sees as much of it as can be expected, Mr. Carleton."

Mr. Carleton pared his apple with an engrossed air.

"O no, Mrs. Thorn," said Mrs. Evelyn, "I don't agree with you—I don't think you often see such a combination as Mr. Carleton has been speaking of—very rarely!—but, Mr. Carleton, don't you think it is generally found in that class of society where the habits of life are constantly the most polished and refined?"

"Possibly," answered he, diving into the core of his apple.

"No, but tell me;—I want to know what you think."

"Cultivation and refinement have taught people to recognise and analyze and imitate it; the counterfeits are most current in that society,—but as to the reality I don't know—It is nature's work and she is a little freaky about it."

"But Guy!" said his mother impatiently;—"this is not selling but giving away one's birthright. Where is the advantage of birth if breeding is not supposed to go along with it. Where the parents have had intelligence and refinement do we not constantly see them inherited by the children? and in an increasing degree from generation to generation?"

"Very extraordinary!" said Mrs. Thorn.

"I do not undervalue the blessings of inheritance, mother, believe me, nor deny the general doctrine; though intelligence does not always descend, and manners die out, and that invaluable legacy, *a name*, may be thrown away. But this delicate thing we are speaking of is not intelligence nor refinement, but comes rather from a happy combination of qualities, together with a peculiarly fine nervous constitution;—the *essence* of it may consist with an omission, even with an awkwardness, and with a sad ignorance of conventionalities."

"But even if that be so, do you think it can ever reach its full development but in the circumstances that are favourable to it?" said Mrs. Evelyn.

"Probably not often; the diamond in some instances wants the graver;—but it is the diamond. Nature seems now and then to have taken a princess's child and dropped it in some odd corner of the kingdom, while she has left the clown in the palace."

"From all which I understand," said Mr. Thorn, "that this little chestnut girl is a princess in disguise."

"Really, Carleton!"—Rossitur began.

Mrs. Evelyn leaned back in her chair and quietly eating a piece of apple eyed Mr. Carleton with a look half amused and half discontented, and behind all that, keenly attentive.

"Take for example those two miniatures you were looking at last night, Mrs. Evelyn," the young man went on;—"Louis XVI. and Marie Antoinette—what would you have more unrefined, more heavy, more *animal*, than the face of that descendant of a line of kings?"

Mrs. Evelyn bowed her head acquiescingly and seemed to enjoy her apple.

"*He* had a pretty bad lot of an inheritance sure enough, take it all together," said Rossitur.

"Well," said Thorn,—"is this little stray princess as well-looking as t'other miniature?"

"Better, in some respects," said Mr. Carleton coolly.

"Better!" cried Mrs. Carleton.

"Not in the brilliancy of her beauty, but in some of its characteristics;—better in its promise."

"Make yourself intelligible, for the sake of my nerves, Guy," said his mother. "Better looking than Marie Antoinette!"

"My unhappy cousin is said to be a fairy, ma'am," said Mr. Rossitur; "and I presume all this may be referred to enchantment."

"That face of Marie Antoinette's," said Mr. Carleton smiling, "is an undisciplined one—uneducated."

"Uneducated!" exclaimed Mrs. Carleton.

"Don't mistake me, mother,—I do not mean that it shows any want of reading or writing, but it does indicate an untrained character—a mind unprepared for the exigencies of life."

"She met those exigencies indifferent well too," observed Mr. Thorn.

"Ay—but pride, and the dignity of rank, and undoubtedly some of the finer qualities of a woman's nature, might suffice for that, and yet leave her utterly unfitted to play wisely and gracefully a part in ordinary life."

"Well, she had no such part to play," said Mrs. Carleton.

"Certainly, mother—but I am comparing faces."

"Well—the other face?"

"It has the same style of refined beauty of feature, but—to compare them in a word, Marie Antoinette looks to me like a superb exotic that has come to its brilliant perfection of bloom in a hothouse—it would lose its beauty in the strong free air—it would change and droop if it lacked careful waiting upon and constant artificial excitement;—the other," said Mr Carleton musingly,—"is a flower of the woods, raising its head above frost and snow and the rugged soil where fortune has placed it, with an air of quiet patient endurance;—a storm wind may bring it to the ground, easily,—but if its gentle nature be not broken, it will look up again, unchanged, and bide its time in unrequited beauty and sweetness to the end."

"The exotic for me!" cried Rossitur,—"if I only had a place for her. I don't like pale elegancies."

"I'd make a piece of poetry of that if I was you, Carleton," said Mr. Thorn.

"Mr. Carleton has done that already," said Mrs. Evelyn smoothly.

"I never heard you talk so before, Guy," said his mother looking at him. His eyes had grown dark with intensity of expression while he was speaking, gazing at visionary flowers or beauties through the dinner-table mahogany. He looked up and laughed as she addressed him, and rising turned off lightly with his usual air.

"I congratulate you, Mrs. Carleton," Mrs. Evelyn whispered as they went from the table, "that this little beauty is not a few years older."

"Why?" said Mrs. Carleton. "If she is all that Guy says. I would give anything in the world to see him married."

"Time enough," said Mrs. Evelyn with a knowing smile.

"I don't know," said Mrs. Carleton,—"I think he would be happier. He is a restless spirit—nothing satisfies him—nothing fixes him. He cannot rest at home—he abhors politics—he flits away from country to country and doesn't remain long anywhere."

"And you with him."

"And I with him. I should like to see if a wife could not persuade him to stay at home."

"I guess you have petted him too much," said Mrs. Evelyn slyly.

"I cannot have petted him too much, for he has never disappointed me."

"No—of course not; but it seems you find it difficult to lead him."

"No one ever succeeded in doing that," said Mrs. Carleton, with a smile that was anything but an ungratified one. "He never wanted driving, and to lead him is impossible. You may try it, and while you think you are going to gain your end, if he thinks it worth while, you will suddenly find that he is leading you. It is so with everybody—in some inexplicable way."

Mrs. Evelyn thought the mystery was very easily explicable as far as the mother was concerned; and changed the conversation.

CHAPTER VI.

To them life was a simple art
  Of duties to be done,
A game where each man took his part,
  A race where all must run;
A battle whose great scheme and scope
  They little cared to know,
Content, as men-at-arms, to cope
  Each with his fronting foe.

MILNES.

ON so great and uncommon an occasion as Mr. Ringgan's giving a dinner-party the disused front parlour was opened and set in order; the women-folks, as he called them, wanting the whole back part of the house for their operations. So when the visiters arrived, in good time, they were ushered into a large square bare-looking room—a strong contrast even to their dining-room at the Pool—which gave them nothing of the welcome of the pleasant farm-house kitchen, and where nothing of the comfort of the kitchen found its way but a very strong smell of roast pig. There was the cheerless air of a place where nobody lives, or thinks of living. The very chairs looked as if they had made up their minds to be forsaken for a term of months; it was impossible to imagine that a cheerful supper had ever been laid upon the stiff cold-looking table that stood with its leaves down so primly against the wall. All that a blazing fire could do to make amends for deficiencies, it did; but the wintry wind that swept round the house shook the paper window-shades in a remorseless way; and the utmost efforts of said fire could not prevent it from coming in and giving disagreeable impertinent whispers at the ears of everybody.

Mr. Ringgan's welcome however, was and would have been the same thing anywhere—genial, frank, and dignified;

neither he nor it could be changed by circumstances. Mr. Carleton admired anew, as he came forward, the fine presence and noble look of his old host; a look that it was plain had never needed to seek the ground; a brow that in large or small things had never been crossed by a shadow of shame. And to a discerning eye the face was not a surer index of a lofty than of a peaceful and pure mind; too peace-loving and pure perhaps for the best good of his affairs in the conflict with a selfish and unscrupulous world. At least now, in the time of his old age and infirmity; in former days his straightforward wisdom backed by an indomitable courage and strength had made Mr. Ringgan no safe subject for either braving or overreaching.

Fleda's keen-sighted affection was heartily gratified by the manner in which her grandfather was greeted by at least one of his guests, and that the one about whose opinion she cared the most. Mr. Carleton seemed as little sensible of the cold room as Mr. Ringgan himself. Fleda felt sure that her grandfather was appreciated; and she would have sat delightedly listening to what the one and the other were presently saying, if she had not taken notice that her cousin looked *astray*. He was eyeing the fire with a profound air and she fancied he thought it poor amusement. Little as Fleda in secret really cared about that, with an instant sacrifice of her own pleasure she quietly changed her position for one from which she could more readily bring to bear upon Mr. Rossitur's distraction the very light artillery of her conversation; and attacked him on the subject of the game he had brought home. Her motive and her manner both must have been lost upon the young gentleman. He forthwith set about amusing himself in a way his little entertainer had not counted upon, namely, with giving a chase to her wits; partly to pass away the time, and partly to gratify his curiosity, as he said, "to see what Fleda was made of." By a curious system of involved, startling, or absurd questions, he endeavoured to puzzle or confound or entrap her. Fleda however steadily presented a grave front to the enemy, and would every now and then surprise him with an unexpected turn or clever doubling, and sometimes when he thought he had her in a corner, jump over the fence and laugh at him from the other side. Mr. Rossitur's respect for his little adversary gradually increased, and finding that she had rather the best of the game he at last gave it up, just as Mr. Ringgan was asking Mr. Carleton if he was a judge of stock? Mr. Carleton saying with a smile "No, but he hoped Mr. Ringgan would give him his first lesson,"—the old gentleman immediately arose with that alacrity of manner he always wore when he had a visiter that pleased him, and taking his hat and cane led the way out; choosing, with a man's true carelessness of housewifery etiquette, the kitchen route, of all others. Not even admonished by the sight of the bright Dutch oven before the fire that he was introducing his visiters somewhat too early to the pig, he led the whole party through, Cynthia scuttling away in haste across the kitchen with something that must not be seen, while aunt Miriam looked out at the company through the crack of the pantry door, at which Fleda ventured a sly glance of intelligence.

It was a fine though a windy and cold afternoon; the lights and shadows were driving across the broad upland and meadows.

"This is a fine arable country," remarked Mr. Carleton.

"Capital, sir,—capital, for many miles round, if we were not so far from a market. I was one of the first that broke ground in this township,—one of the very first settlers—I've seen the rough and the smooth of it, and I never had but one mind about it from the first. All this—as far as you can see—I cleared myself; most of it with my own hand."

"That recollection must attach you strongly to the place, I should think, sir."

"Hum—perhaps I cared too much for it," he replied, "for it is taken away from me. Well—it don't matter now."

"It is not yours?"

"No sir!—it *was* mine, a great many years; but I was obliged to part with it, two years ago, to a scoundrel of a fellow—McGowan up here—he got an advantage over me. I can't take care of myself any more as I used to do, and I don't find that other people deal by me just as I could wish—"

He was silent for a moment and then went on,—

"Yes sir! when I first set myself down here, or a little further that way my first house was,—a pretty rough house too,—there wa'n't two settlers beside within something like ten miles round.—I've seen the whole of it cleared, from the cutting of the first forest trees till this day."

"You have seen the nation itself spring up within that time," remarked his guest.

"Not exactly—that question of our nationality was settled a little before I came here. I was born rather too late to see the whole of that play—I saw the best of it though—boys were men in those days. My father was in the thick of it from beginning to end."

"In the army, was he?"

"Ho yes, sir! he and every child he had that wasn't a girl—there wasn't a man of the name that wa'n't on the right side. I was in the army myself when I was fifteen. I was nothing but a fifer—but I tell you sir! there wasn't a general officer in the country that played his part with a prouder heart than I did mine!"

"And was that the general spirit of the ranks?"

"Not altogether," replied the old gentleman, passing his hand several times abstractedly over his white hair, a favourite gesture with him,—"not exactly that—there was a good deal of mixture of different materials, especially in this state; and where the feeling wasn't pretty strong it was no wonder if it got tired out; but the real stuff, the true Yankee blood, was pretty firm! Ay, and some of the rest! There was a good deal to try men in those days. Sir, I have seen many a time when I had nothing to dine upon but my fife, and it was more than that could do to keep me from feeling very empty!"

"But was this a common case? did this happen often?" said Mr. Carleton.

"Pretty often—pretty often, sometimes," answered the old gentleman. "Things were very much out of order, you see, and in some parts of the country it was almost impossible to get the supplies the men needed. Nothing would have kept them together,—nothing under heaven—but the love and confidence they had in one name. Their love of right and independence wouldn't have been strong enough, and besides a good many of them got disheartened.

A hungry stomach is a pretty stout arguer against abstract questions. I have seen my father crying like a child for the wants and sufferings he was obliged to see and couldn't relieve."

"And then you used to relieve yourselves, grandpa," said Fleda.

"How was that, Fairy?"

Fleda looked at her grandfather, who gave a little preparatory laugh and passed his hand over his head again.

"Why yes," said he,—"we used to think the tories, King George's men you know, were fair game; and when we happened to be in the neighbourhood of some of them that we knew were giving all the help they could to the enemy, we used to let them cook our dinners for us once in a while."

"How did you manage that, sir?"

"Why, they used to have little bake-ovens to cook their meats and so on, standing some way out from the house,—did you never see one of them?—raised on four little heaps of stone; the bottom of the oven is one large flat stone, and the arch built over it;—they look like a great beehive. Well—we used to watch till we saw the good woman of the house get her oven cleverly heated, and put in her batch of bread, or her meat pie, or her pumpkin and apple pies!—whichever it was—there didn't any of 'em come much amiss—and when we guessed they were pretty nigh done, three or four of us would creep in and whip off the whole—oven and all!—to a safe place. I tell you," said he with a knowing nod of his head at the laughing Fleda,—"those were first-rate pies!"

"And then did you put the oven back again afterwards, grandpa?"

"I guess not often, dear!" replied the old gentleman.

"What do you think of such lawless proceedings, Miss Fleda?" said Mr. Carleton, laughing at or with her.

"O I like it," said Fleda. "You liked those pies all the better, didn't you, grandpa, because you had got them from the tories?"

"That we did! If we hadn't got them maybe King George's men would, in some shape. But we weren't always so lucky as to get hold of an oven full. I remember one time several of us had been out on a foraging expedition——there, sir, what do you think of that for a two and a half year old?"

They had come up with the chief favourite of his barnyard, a fine deep-coloured Devon bull.

"I don't know what one might see in Devonshire," he remarked presently, "but I know *this* county can't shew the like of him!"

A discussion followed of the various beauties and excellencies of the animal; a discussion in which Mr. Carleton certainly took little part, while Mr. Ringgan descanted enthusiastically upon 'hide' and 'brisket' and 'bone,' and Rossitur stood in an abstraction, it might be scornful, it might be mazed. Little Fleda quietly listening and looking at the beautiful creature, which from being such a treasure to her grandfather was in a sort one to her, more than half understood them all; but Mr. Ringgan was too well satisfied with the attention of one of his guests to miss that of the other.

"That fellow don't look as if *he* had ever known short commons," was Rossitur's single remark as they turned away.

"You did not give us the result of your foraging expedition, sir," said Mr. Carleton in a different manner.

"Do, grandpa," said Fleda softly.

"Ha!—Oh it is not worth telling," said the old gentleman, looking gratified;—"Fleda has heard my stories till she knows them by heart—she could tell it as well herself. What was it?—about the pig?—We had been out, several of us, one afternoon to try to get up a supper—or a dinner, for we had had none—and we had caught a pig. It happened that I was the only one of the party that had a cloak, and so the pig was given to me to carry home, because I could hide it the best. Well sir!—we were coming home, and had set our mouths for a prime supper, when just as we were within a few rods of our shanty who should come along but our captain! My heart sank as it never has done at the thought of a supper before or since, I believe! I held my cloak together as well as I could, and kept myself back a little, so that if the pig shewed a cloven foot behind me, the captain might not see it. But I almost gave up all for lost when I saw the captain going into the hut with us. There was a kind of a rude bedstead standing there; and I set myself down upon the side of it, and gently worked and eased my pig off under my cloak till I got him to roll down behind the bed. I knew," said Mr. Ringgan laughing, "I knew by the captain's eye as well as I knew anything, that he smelt a rat; but he kept our counsel, as well as his own; and when he was gone we took the pig out into the woods behind the shanty and roasted him finely, and we sent and asked Capt. Sears to supper; and he came and helped us eat the pig with a great deal of appetite, and never asked no questions how we came by him!"

"I wonder your stout-heartedness did not fail, in the course of so long a time," said Mr. Carleton.

"Never sir!" said the old gentleman. "I never doubted for a moment what the end would be. My father never doubted for a moment. We trusted in God and in Washington!"

"Did you see actual service yourself?"

"No sir—I never did. I wish I had. I should like to have had the honour of striking one blow at the rascals. However they were hit pretty well. I ought to be contented. My father saw enough of fighting—he was colonel of a regiment—he was at the affair of Burgoyne. *That* gave us a lift in good time. What rejoicing there was everywhere when that news came! I could have fifed all day upon an empty stomach and felt satisfied. People reckoned everywhere that the matter was settled when that great piece of good fortune was given us. And so it was! —wa'n't it, dear?" said the old gentleman, with one of those fond, pleased, sympathetic looks to Fleda with which he often brought up what he was saying.

"General Gates commanded there?" said Mr. Carleton.

"Yes sir—Gates was a poor stick—I never thought much of him. That fellow Arnold distinguished himself in the actions before Burgoyne's surrender. He fought like a brave man. It seems strange that so mean a scamp should have had so much blood in him?"

"Why, are great fighters generally good men, grandpa?" said Fleda.

"Not exactly, dear!" replied her grandfather;—"but such little-minded rascality is not just the vice one would expect to find in a gallant soldier."

"Those were times that made men," said Mr. Carleton musingly.

"Yes," answered the old gentleman gravely,—"they were times that called for men, and God raised them up. But Washington was the soul of the country, sir!"

"Well, the time made him," said Mr. Carleton.

"I beg your pardon," said the old gentleman with a very decided little turn of his head,—"I think he made the time. I don't know what it would have been, sir, or what it would have come to, but for him, After all, it is rather that the things which try people shew what is in them;—I hope there are men enough in the country yet, though they haven't as good a chance to shew what they are."

"Either way," said his guest smiling; "it is a happiness, Mr. Ringgan, to have lived at a time when there was something worth living for."

"Well—I don't know—" said the old gentleman;—"those times would make the prettiest figure in a story or a ro'mance, I suppose; but I've tried both, and on the whole," said he with another of his looks at Fleda,—"I think I like these times the best!"

Fleda smiled her acquiescence. His guest could not help thinking to himself that however pacific might be Mr. Ringgan's temper, no man in those days that tried men could have brought to the issue more stern inflexibility and gallant fortitude of bearing. His frame bore evidence of great personal strength, and his eye, with all its mildness, had an unflinching dignity that *could* never have quailed before danger or duty. And now, while he was recalling with great animation and pleasure the scenes of his more active life, and his blue eye was shining with the fire of other days, his manner had the self-possession and quiet sedateness of triumph that bespeak a man always more ready to do than to say. Perhaps the contemplation of the noble Roman-like old figure before him did not tend to lessen the feeling, even the sigh of regret, with which the young man said,

"There was something then for a man to do!"

"There is always that," said the old gentleman quietly. "God has given every man his work to do; and 'tain't difficult for him to find out what. No man is put here to be idle."

"But," said his companion, with a look in which not a little haughty reserve was mingled with a desire to speak out his thoughts, "half the world are busy about hum-drum concerns and the other half doing nothing, or worse."

"I don't know about that," said Mr. Ringgan;—"that depends upon the way you take things. 'Tain't always the men that make the most noise that are the most good in the world. Hum-drum affairs needn't be hum-drum in the doing of 'em. It is my maxim," said the old gentleman looking at his companion with a singularly open pleasant smile,—"that a man may be great about a'most anything —chopping wood, if he happens to be in that line. I used to go upon that plan, sir. Whatever I have set my hand to do, I have done it as well as I knew how to; and if you follow that rule out you'll not be idle, nor hum-drum neither. Many's the time that I have mowed what would be a day's work for another man, before breakfast."

Rossitur's smile was not meant to be seen. But Mr. Carleton's, to the credit of his politeness and his understanding both, was frank as the old gentleman's own, as he answered with a good-humoured shake of his head,

"I can readily believe it, sir, and honour both your maxim and your practice. But I am not exactly in that line."

"Why don't you try the army?" said Mr. Ringgan with a look of interest.

"There is not a cause worth fighting for," said the young man, his brow changing again. "It is only to add weight to the oppressor's hand, or throw away life in the vain endeavour to avert it. I will do neither."

"But all the world is open before such a young man as you," said Mr. Ringgan.

"A large world," said Mr. Carleton with his former mixture of expression,—"but there isn't much in it."

"Politics?" said Mr. Ringgan.

"It is to lose oneself in a seething-pot, where the scum is the most apparent thing."

"But there is society?" said Rossitur.

"Nothing better or more noble than the succession of motes that flit through a sunbeam into oblivion."

"Well, why not then sit down quietly on one's estates and enjoy them, one who has enough?"

"And be a worm in the heart of an apple."

"Well then," said Rossitur laughing, though not knowing exactly how far he might venture, "there is nothing left for you, as I don't suppose you would take to any of the learned professions, but to strike out some new path for yourself—hit upon some grand invention for benefiting the human race and distinguishing your own name at once."

But while he spoke his companion's face had gone back to its usual look of imperturbable coolness; the dark eye was even haughtily unmoved, till it met Fleda's inquiring and somewhat anxious glance. He smiled.

"The nearest approach I ever made to that," said he, "was when I went chestnuting the other day. Can't you find some more work for me, Fairy?"

Taking Fleda's hand with his wonted graceful lightness of manner he walked on with her, leaving the other two to follow together.

"You would like to know, perhaps," observed Mr. Rossitur in rather a low tone,—"that Mr. Carleton is an Englishman."

"Ay, ay?" said Mr. Ringgan. "An Englishman, is he?—Well sir,—what is it that I would like to know?"

"*That*," said Rossitur. "I would have told you before if I could. I supposed you might not choose to speak quite so freely, perhaps, on American affairs before him."

"I haven't two ways of speaking, sir, on anything," said the old gentleman a little dryly. "Is your friend very tender on that chapter?"

"O not that I know of at all," said Rossitur; "but you know there is a great deal of feeling still among the English about it—they have never forgiven us heartily for whipping them; and I know Carleton is related to the nobility and all that, you know; so I thought—"

"Ah well!" said the old gentleman,—"we don't know much about nobility and such gimcracks in this country. I'm not much of a courtier. I am pretty much accustomed to speak my mind as I think it.—He's wealthy, I suppose?"

"He's more than that, sir. Enormous estates! He's the finest fellow in the world—one of the first young men in England."

"You have been there yourself and know?" said Mr. Ringgan, glancing at his companion.

"If I have not, sir, others have told me that do."

"Ah well," said Mr. Ringgan placidly,—"we sha'n't quarrel, I guess. What did he come out here for, eh?"

"Only to amuse himself. They are going back again in a few weeks, and I intend accompanying them to join my mother in Paris. Will my little cousin be of the party?"

They were sauntering along towards the house. A loud calling of her name the minute before had summoned Fleda thither at the top of her speed; and Mr. Carleton turned to repeat the same question.

The old gentleman stopped, and striking his stick two or three times against the ground looked sorrowfully undetermined.

"Well, I don't know!—" he said at last,—"It's a pretty hard matter—she'd break her heart about it, I suppose,—"

"I dare urge nothing, sir," said Mr. Carleton. "I will only assure you that if you entrust your treasure to us she shall be cherished as you would wish, till we place her in the hands of her aunt."

"I know that, sir,—I do not doubt it," said Mr. Ringgan, "but—I'll tell you by and by what I conclude upon," he said with evident relief of manner as Fleda came bounding back to them. "Mr. Rossitur, have you made your peace with Fleda?"

"I was not aware that I had any to make, sir," replied the young gentleman. "I will do it with pleasure if my little cousin will tell me how. But she looks as if she needed enlightening as much as myself."

"She has something against you, I can tell you," said the old gentleman, looking amused, and speaking as if Fleda were a curious little piece of human mechanism which could hear its performances talked of with all the insensibility of any other toy. "She gives it as her judgment that Mr. Carleton is the most of a gentleman, because he keeps his promise."

"Oh grandpa!"—

Poor Fleda's cheek was hot with a distressful blush. Rossitur coloured with anger. Mr. Carleton's smile had a very different expression.

"If Fleda will have the goodness to recollect," said Rossitur, "I cannot be charged with breaking a promise for I made none."

"But Mr. Carleton did," said Fleda.

"She is right, Mr. Rossitur, she is right," said that gentleman; "a fallacy might as well elude Ithuriel's spear as the sense of a pure spirit—there is no need of written codes. Make your apologies, man, and confess yourself in the wrong."

"Pho, pho," said the old gentleman,—"she don't take it very much to heart. I guess *I* ought to be the one to make the apologies," he added, looking at Fleda's face.

But Fleda commanded herself, with difficulty, and announced that dinner was ready.

"Mr. Rossitur tells me, Mr. Carleton, you are an Englishman," said his host. "I have some notion of that's passing through my head before, but somehow I had entirely lost sight of it when I was speaking so freely to you a little while ago—about our national quarrel—I know some of your countrymen owe us a grudge yet."

"Not I, I assure you," said the young Englishman. "I am ashamed of them for it. I congratulate you on being Washington's countryman and a sharer in his grand struggle for the right against the wrong."

Mr. Ringgan shook his guest's hand, looking very much pleased; and having by this time arrived at the house the young gentlemen were formally introduced at once to the kitchen, their dinner, and aunt Miriam.

It is not too much to say that the entertainment gave perfect satisfaction to everybody—better fate than attends most entertainments. Even Mr. Rossitur's ruffled spirit felt the soothing influence of good cheer, to which he happened to be peculiarly sensible, and came back to its average condition of amenity.

Doubtless that was a most informal table, spread according to no rules that for many generations at least have been known in the refined world; an anomaly in the eyes of certainly one of the company. Yet the board had a character of its own, very far removed from vulgarity, and suiting remarkably well with the condition and demeanour of those who presided over it—a comfortable, well-to-do, substantial look, that could afford to dispense with minor graces; a self-respect that was not afraid of criticism. Aunt Miriam's successful efforts deserve to be celebrated.

In the middle of the table the polished amber of the pig's arched back elevated itself,—a striking object,—but worthy of the place he filled, as the honours paid him by everybody abundantly testified. Aunt Miriam had sent down a basket of her own bread, made out of the new flour, brown and white, both as sweet and fine as it is possible for bread to be; the piled-up slices were really beautiful. The superb butter had come from aunt Miriam's dairy too, for on such an occasion she would not trust to the very doubtful excellence of Miss Cynthia's doings. Every spare place on the table was filled with dishes of potatoes and pickles and sweetmeats, that left nothing to be desired in their respective kinds; the cake was a delicious presentment of the finest of material; and the pies, pumpkin pies, such as only aunt Miriam could make, rich compounds of everything *but* pumpkin with enough of that to give them a name—Fleda smiled to think how pleased aunt Miriam must secretly be to see the homage paid her through them. And most happily Mrs. Plumfield had discovered that the last tea Mr. Ringgan had brought from the little Queechy store was not very good, and there was no time to send up on "the hill" for more, so she made coffee. Verily it was not Mocha, but the thick yellow cream with which the cups were filled really made up the difference. The most curious palate found no want.

Everybody was in a high state of satisfaction, even to Miss Cynthia Gall; who having some lurking suspicion that Mrs. Plumfield might design to cut her out of her post of tea-making, had slipped herself into her usual chair behind the tea-tray before anybody else was ready to sit down. No one at table bestowed a thought upon Miss Cynthia, but as she thought of nothing else she may be said to have had her fair share of attention. The most unqualified satisfaction however was no doubt little Fleda's. Forgetting with a child's happy readiness the fears and doubts which had lately troubled her, she was full of the present, enjoying with a most unselfish enjoyment everything that pleased anybody else. *She* was glad that the supper was a fine one, and so approved, because it was her grandfather's hospitality and her aunt Miriam's housekeeping; little beside was her care for pies or coffee. She saw with secret glee the expression of both her aunt's and Mr. Ringgan's face; partly from pure sympathy, and partly because, as she knew, the cause of it was Mr. Carleton, whom privately Fleda liked very much. And after all perhaps he had directly more to do with her enjoyment than all other causes together.

Certainly that was true of him with respect to the rest of the dinner-table. None at that dinner-table had ever seen the like. With all the graceful charm of manner with which he would have delighted a courtly circle, he came out from his reserve and was brilliant, gay, sensible, entertaining, and witty, to a degree that assuredly has very rarely been thrown away upon an old farmer in the country and his un-polite sister. They appreciated him though, as well as any courtly circle could have done, and he knew it. In aunt Miriam's strong sensible face, when not full of some hospitable care, he could see the reflection of every play of his own; the grave practical eye twinkled and brightened, giving a ready answer to every turn of sense or humour in what he was saying. Mr. Ringgan, as much of a child for the moment as Fleda herself, had lost everything disagreeable and was in the full genial enjoyment of talk, rather listening than talking, with his cheeks in a perpetual dimple of gratification, and a low laugh of hearty amusement now and then rewarding the conversational and kind efforts of his guest with a complete triumph. Even the subtle charm which they could not quite recognise wrought fascination. Miss Cynthia declared afterwards, half admiring and half vexed, that he spoiled her supper, for she forgot to think how it tasted. Rossitur—his good humour was entirely restored; but whether even Mr. Carleton's power could have achieved that without the perfect seasoning of the pig and the smooth persuasion of the richly-creamed coffee, it may perhaps be doubted. He stared, mentally, for he had never known his friend condescend to bring himself out in the same manner before; and he wondered what he could see in the present occasion to make it worth while.

But Mr. Carleton did not think his efforts thrown away. He understood and admired his fine old host and hostess; and with all their ignorance of conventionalities and absence of what is called *polish* of manner, he could enjoy the sterling sense, the good feeling, the true hearty hospitality, and the dignified courtesy, which both of them shewed. No matter of the outside; this was in the grain. If mind had lacked much opportunity it had also made good use of a little; his host, Mr. Carleton found, had been a great reader, was well acquainted with history and a very intelligent reasoner upon it; and both he and his sister shewed a strong and quick aptitude for intellectual subjects of conversation. No doubt aunt Miriam's courtesy had not been taught by a dancing-master, and her brown satin gown had seen many a fashion come and go since it was made, but a *lady* was in both; and while Rossitur covertly smiled, Mr. Carleton paid his sincere respect where he felt it was due. Little Fleda's quick eye hardly saw, but more than half felt, the difference. Mr. Carleton had no more eager listener now than she, and perhaps none whose unaffected interest and sympathy gave him more pleasure.

When they rose from the table Mr. Ringgan would not be *insinuated* into the cold front room again.

"No, no," said he,—"what's the matter?—the table? Push the table back, and let it take care of itself,—come, gentlemen, sit down—draw up your chairs round the fire, and a fig for ceremony! Comfort, sister Miriam, against politeness, any day in the year;—don't you say so too, Fairy? Come here by me."

"Miss Fleda," said Mr. Carleton. "will you take a ride with me to Montepoole to-morrow? I should like to make you acquainted with my mother."

Fleda coloured and looked at her grandfather.

"What do you say, deary?" he inquired fondly; "will you go?—I believe, sir, your proposal will prove a very acceptable one. You will go, won't you, Fleda?"

Fleda would very much rather not! But she was always exceedingly afraid of hurting people's feelings; she could not bear that Mr. Carleton should think she disliked to go with him, so she answered yes, in her usual sober manner.

Just then the door opened and a man unceremoniously walked in, his entrance immediately following a little sullen knock that had made a mockery of asking permission. An ill-looking man, in the worst sense; his face being a mixture of cunning, meanness, and insolence. He shut the door and came with a slow leisurely step into the middle of the room without speaking a word. Mr. Carleton saw the blank change in Fleda's face. She knew him.

"Do you wish to see me, Mr. McGowan?" said Mr. Ringgan, not without something of the same change.

"I guess I ha'n't come here for nothing," was the gruff retort.

"Wouldn't another time answer as well?"

"I don't mean to find you here another time," said the man chuckling,—"I have given you notice to quit, and now I have come to tell you you'll clear out. I ain't a going to be kept out of my property for ever. If I can't get my money from you, Elzevir Ringgan, I'll see you don't get no more of it in your hands."

"Very well, sir," said the old gentleman;—"You have said all that is necessary."

"You have got to hear a little more, though," returned the other, "I've an idee that there's a satisfaction in speaking one's mind. I'll have that much out of you! Mr. Ringgan, a man hadn't ought to make an agreement to pay what he doesn't *mean* to pay, and what he has made an agreement to pay he ought to meet and be up to, if he sold his soul for it! You call yourself a Christian, do you, to stay in another man's house, month after month, when you know you ha'n't got the means to give him the rent for it! That's what *I* call stealing, and it's what I'd live in the County House before I'd demean myself to do! and so ought you."

"Well, well! neighbour," said Mr. Ringgan, with patient dignity,—"it's no use calling names. You know as well as I do how all this came about. I hoped to be able to pay you, but I haven't been able to make it out, without having more time."

"Time!" said the other. "Time to cheat me out of a little more houseroom. If I was agoing to live on charity,

Mr. Ringgan, I'd come out and say so, and not put my hand in a man's pocket this way. You'll quit the house by the day after to-morrow, or if you don't I'll let you hear a little more of me that you won't like!"

He stalked out, shutting the door after him with a bang. Mr. Carleton had quitted the room a moment before him.

Nobody moved or spoke at first, when the man was gone, except Miss Cynthia, who as she was taking something from the table to the pantry remarked, probably for Mr. Rossitur's benefit, that "Mr. Ringgan had to have that man punished for something he did a few years ago when he was justice of the peace, and she guessed likely that was the reason he had a grudge agin him ever since." Beyond this piece of dubious information nothing was said. Little Fleda stood beside her grandfather with a face of quiet distress; the tears silently running over her flushed cheeks, and her eyes fixed upon Mr. Ringgan with a tender touching look of sympathy, most pure from self-recollection.

Mr. Carleton presently came in to take leave of the disturbed family. The old gentleman rose and returned his shake of the hand with even a degree more than usual of his manly dignity, or Mr. Carleton thought so.

"Good day to you, sir!" he said heartily. "We have had a great deal of pleasure in your society, and I shall always be very happy to see you—wherever I am." And then following him to the door and wringing his hand with a force he was not at all aware of, the old gentleman added in a lower tone, "I shall let her go with you!"

Mr. Carleton read his whole story in the stern self-command of brow, and the slight convulsion of feature which all the self-command could not prevent. He returned warmly the grasp of the hand answering merely, "I will see you again."

Fleda wound her arms round her grandfather's neck when they were gone, and did her best to comfort him, assuring him that "they would be just as happy somewhere else." And aunt Miriam earnestly proffered her own home. But Fleda knew that her grandfather was not comforted. He stroked her head with the same look of stern gravity and troubled emotion which had grieved her so much the other day. She could not win him to a smile, and went to bed at last feeling desolate. She had no heart to look out at the night. The wind was sweeping by in wintry gusts; and Fleda cried herself to sleep thinking how it would whistle round the dear old house when their ears would not be there to hear it.

CHAPTER VII.

He from his old hereditary nook
Must part; the summons came,—our final leave we took.
WORDSWORTH.

MR. CARLETON came the next day, but not early, to take Fleda to Montepoole. She had told her grandfather that she did not think he would come, because after last night he must know that she would not want to go. About twelve o'clock however he was there, with a little wagon, and Fleda was fain to get her sun-bonnet and let him put her in. Happily it was her maxim never to trust to uncertainties, so she was quite ready when he came and they had not to wait a minute.

Though Fleda had a little dread of being introduced to a party of strangers and was a good deal disappointed at being obliged to keep her promise, she very soon began to be glad. She found her fear gradually falling away before Mr. Carleton's quiet kind reassuring manner; he took such nice care of her; and she presently made up her mind that he would manage the matter so that it would not be awkward. They had so much pleasant talk too. Fleda had found before that she could talk to Mr. Carleton, nay she could not help talking to him; and she forgot to think about it. And besides, it was a pleasant day, and they drove fast, and Fleda's particular delight was driving; and though the horse was a little gay she had a kind of intuitive perception that Mr. Carleton knew how to manage him. So she gave up every care and was very happy.

When Mr. Carleton asked after her grandfather, Fleda answered with great animation, "O he's very well! and such a happy thing—You heard what that man said last night, Mr. Carleton, didn't you?"

"Yes."

"Well it is all arranged;—this morning Mr Jolly—he's a friend of grandpa's that lives over at Queechy Run and knew about all this—he's a lawyer—he came this morning and told grandpa that he had found some one that could lend him the money he wanted and there was no trouble about it; and we are so happy, for we thought we should have to go away from where we live now, and I know grandpa would have felt it dreadfully. If it hadn't been for that,—I mean, for Mr. Jolly's coming,—I couldn't have gone to Montepoole to-day."

"Then I am very glad Mr. Jolly made his appearance," said Mr. Carleton.

"So am I," said Fleda;—"but I think it was a little strange that Mr. Jolly wouldn't tell us who it was that he had got the money from. Grandpa said he never saw Mr. Jolly so curious."

When they got to the Pool Fleda's nervousness returned a little; but she went through the dreaded introduction with great demureness and perfect propriety. And throughout the day Mr. Carleton had no reason to fear rebuke for the judgment which he had pronounced upon his little paragon. All the flattering attention which was shewn her, and it was a good deal, could not draw Fleda a line beyond the dignified simplicity which seemed natural to her; any more than the witty attempts at raillery and endeavours to amuse themselves at her expense, in which some of the gentlemen shewed their wisdom, could move her from her modest self-possession. *Very* quiet, *very* modest, as she invariably was, awkwardness could not fasten upon her; her colour might come and her timid eye fall; it often did; but Fleda's wits were always in their place and within call. She would shrink from a stranger's eye, and yet when spoken to her answers were as ready and acute as they were marked for simplicity and gentleness. She was kept to dinner; and though the arrangement and manner of the service must have been strange to little Fleda, it was impossible to guess from word or look that it was the first time within her recollection that she had ever seen the like. Her native instincts took it all as quietly as any old liberalized traveller looks upon the customs of a new country.

Mr. Carleton smiled as he now and then saw a glance of intelligence or admiration pass between one and another of the company; and a little knowing nod from Mrs. Evelyn and many a look from his mother confessed he had been quite right.

Those two, Mrs. Evelyn and Mrs. Carleton, were by far the most kind and eager in their attention to Fleda. Mrs. Thorn did little else but look at her. The gentlemen amused themselves with her. But Mr. Carleton, true to the hopes Fleda had founded upon his good-nature, had stood her friend all the day, coming to her help if she needed any, and placing himself easily and quietly between her and anything that threatened to try or annoy her too much. Fleda felt it with grateful admiration. Yet she noticed, too, that he was a very different person at this dinner-table from what he had been the other day at her grandfather's. Easy and graceful, always, he filled his own place, but did not seem to care to do more; there was even something bordering on haughtiness in his air of grave reserve. He was not the life of the company here; he contented himself with being all that the company could possibly require of him.

On the whole Fleda was exceedingly well pleased with her day, and thought all the people in general very kind. It was quite late before she set out to go home again; and then Mrs. Evelyn and Mrs. Carleton were extremely afraid lest she should take cold, and Mr. Carleton without saying one word about it wrapped her up so very nicely after she got into the wagon, in a warm cloak of his mother's. The drive home, through the gathering shades of twilight, was to little Fleda thoroughly charming. It was almost in perfect silence, but she liked that; and all the way home her mind was full of a shadowy beautiful world that seemed to lie before and around her.

It was a happy child that Mr. Carleton lifted from the wagon when they reached Queechy. He read it in the utter lightheartedness of brow and voice, and the spring to the ground which hardly needed the help of his hands.

"Thank you, Mr. Carleton," she said when she had reached her own door; (he would not go in) "I have had a very nice time!"

He smiled.

"Good night," said he. "Tell your grandfather I will come to-morrow to see him about some business."

Fleda ran gayly into the kitchen. Only Cynthia was there.

"Where is grandpa, Cynthy?"

"He went off into his room a half an hour ago. I believe he's layin' down. He ain't right well, I s'pect. What's made you so late?"

"O they kept me," said Fleda. Her gayety suddenly sobered, she took off her bonnet and coat and throwing them down in the kitchen stole softly along the passage to her grandfather's room. She stopped a minute at the door and held her breath to see if she could hear any movement which might tell her he was not asleep. It was all still, and pulling the iron latch with her gentlest hand Fleda went on tiptoe into the room. He was lying on the bed, but awake, for she had made no noise and the blue eyes opened and looked upon her as she came near.

"Are you not well, dear grandpa?" said the little girl.

Nothing made of flesh and blood ever spoke words of more spirit-like sweetness,—not the beauty of a fine organ, but such as the sweetness of angel-speech might be; a whisper of love and tenderness that was hushed by its own intensity. He did not answer, or did not notice her first question; she repeated it.

"Don't you feel well?"

"Not exactly, dear!" he replied.

There was the shadow of somewhat in his tone, that fell upon his little granddaughter's heart and brow at once. Her voice next time, though not suffered to be anything but clear and cheerful still, had in part the clearness of apprehension.

"What is the matter?"

"Oh—I don't know, dear!"

She felt the shadow again, and he seemed to say that time would shew her the meaning of it. She put her little hand in one of his which lay outside the coverlets, and stood looking at him; and presently said, but in a very different key from the same speech to Mr. Carleton,

"I have had a very nice time, dear grandpa."

Her grandfather made her no answer. He brought the dear little hand to his lips and kissed it twice, so earnestly that it was almost passionately; then laid it on the side of the bed again, with his own upon it, and patted it slowly and fondly and with an inexpressible kind of sadness in the manner. Fleda's lip trembled and her heart was fluttering, but she stood so that he could not see her face in the dusk, and kept still till the rebel features were calm again and she had schooled the heart to be silent.

Mr. Ringgan had closed his eyes, and perhaps was asleep, and his little granddaughter sat quietly down on a chair by the bedside to watch by him, in that gentle sorrowful patience which women often know but which hardly belongs to childhood. Her eye and thoughts, as she sat there in the dusky twilight, fell upon the hand of her grandfather which still fondly held one of her own; and fancy travelled fast and far, from what it was to what it had been. Rough, discoloured, stiff, as it lay there now, she thought how it had once had the hue and the freshness and the grace of youth, when it had been the instrument of uncommon strength and wielded an authority that none could stand against. Her fancy wandered over the scenes it had known; when it had felled trees in the wild forest, and those fingers, then supple and slight, had played the fife to the struggling men of the Revolution; how its activity had outdone the activity of all other hands in clearing and cultivating those very fields where her feet loved to run; how in its pride of strength it had handled the scythe and the sickle and the flail, with a grace and efficiency that no other could attain; and how in happy manhood that strong hand had fondled and sheltered and led the little children that now had grown up and were gone! —Strength and activity, ay, and the fruits of them, were passed away;—his children were dead;—his race was run; —the shock of corn was in full season, ready to be gathered. Poor little Fleda! her thought had travelled but a very little way before the sense of these things entirely overcame her; her head bowed on her knees, and she wept tears that all the fine springs of her nature were moving to feed—many, many,—but poured forth as quietly as bitterly; she smothered every sound. That beautiful shadowy world with which she had been so busy a little while ago,—alas! she had left the fair outlines and the dreamy light and had been tracking one solitary path through the wilderness, and she saw how the traveller foot-sore and weather-beaten comes to the end of his way. And after all, he comes to *the end.*—"Yes, and I must travel through life and come to the end, too," thought little Fleda;—"life is but a passing through the world; my hand must wither and grow old too, if I live long enough, and whether or no, I must come to *the end*—Oh, there is only one thing that ought to be very much minded in this world!"

That thought, sober though it was, brought sweet consolation. Fleda's tears, if they fell as fast, grew brighter, as she remembered with singular tender joy that her mother and her father had been ready to see the end of their journey, and were not afraid of it; that her grandfather and her aunt Miriam were happy in the same quiet confidence, and she believed she herself was a lamb of the Good Shepherd's flock. "And he will let none of his lambs be lost," she thought. "How happy I am! How happy we all are!"

Her grandfather still lay quiet as if asleep, and gently drawing her hand from under his, Fleda went and got a candle and sat down by him again to read, carefully shading the light so that it might not awake him.

He presently spoke to her, and more cheerfully.

"Are you reading, dear?"

"Yes, grandpa!" said the little girl looking up brightly. "Does the candle disturb you?"

"No dear!—What have you got there?"

"I just took up this volume of Newton that has the hymns in it."

"Read out."

Fleda read Mr. Newton's long beautiful hymn, "The Lord will provide;" but with her late thoughts fresh in her mind it was hard to get through the last verses;—

"No strength of our own,
  Or goodness we claim;
But since we have known
  The Saviour's great name,
In this, our strong tower,
  For safety we hide;
The Lord is our power,
  The Lord will provide.

"When life sinks apace,
And death is in view,
This word of his grace
Shall comfort us through.
No fearing nor doubting,—
With Christ on our side,
We hope to die shouting
The Lord will provide!"

The little reader's voice changed, almost broke, but she struggled through, and then was quietly crying behind her hand.

"Read it again," said the old gentleman after a pause.

There is no 'cannot' in the vocabulary of affection. Fleda waited a minute or two to rally her forces, and then went through it again, more steadily than the first time.

"Yes—" said Mr. Ringgan calmly, folding his hands,—"that will do! That trust won't fail, for it is founded upon a rock. 'He is a rock; and he knoweth them that put their trust in him!' I have been a fool to doubt ever that he would make all things work well—The Lord will provide!"

"Grandpa," said Fleda, but in an unsteady voice, and shading her face with her hand still,—"I can remember reading this hymn to my mother once when I was so little that 'suggestions' was a hard word to me."

"Ay, ay,—I dare say," said the old gentleman,—"your mother knew that Rock and rested her hope upon it,—where mine stands now. If ever there was a creature that might have trusted to her own doings, I believe she was one, for I never saw her do anything wrong,—as I know. But she knew Christ was all. Will you follow him as she did, dear?"

Fleda tried in vain to give an answer.

"Do you know what her last prayer for you was, Fleda?"

"No, grandpa."

"It was that you might be kept 'unspotted from the world.' I heard her make that prayer myself." And stretching out his hand the old gentleman laid it tenderly upon Fleda's bowed head, saying with strong earnestness and affection, even *his* voice somewhat shaken, "God grant that prayer!—whatever else he do with her, keep my child from the evil!—and bring her to join her father and mother in heaven!—and me!"

He said no more;—but Fleda's sobs said a great deal. And when the sobs were hushed, she still sat shedding quiet tears, sorrowed and disturbed by her grandfather's manner. She had never known it so grave, so solemn; but there was that shadow of something else in it besides, and she would have feared if she had known what to fear. He told her at last that she had better go to bed, and to say to Cynthy that he wanted to see her. She was going, and had near reached the door, when he said,

"Elfleda!"

She hastened back to the bedside.

"Kiss me."

He let her do so twice, without moving, and then holding her to his breast he pressed one long earnest passionate kiss upon her lips, and released her.

Fleda told Cynthy that her grandfather wished her to come to him, and then mounted the stairs to her little bedroom. She went to the window and opening it looked out at the soft moonlit sky; the weather was mild again and a little hazy, and the landscape was beautiful. But little Fleda was tasting realities, and she could not go off upon dream-journeys to seek the light food of fancy through the air. She did not think to-night about the people the moon was shining on; she only thought of one little sad anxious heart,—and of another down stairs, more sad and anxious still, she feared;—what could it be about? Now that Mr. Jolly had settled all that troublesome business with McGowan?—

As she stood there at the window, gazing out aimlessly into the still night,—it was very quiet,—she heard Cynthy at the back of the house calling out, but as if she were afraid of making too much noise, "Watkins!—Watkins!"

The sound had business, if not anxiety, in it. Fleda instinctively held her breath to listen. Presently she heard Watkins reply; but they were round the corner, she could not easily make out what they said. It was only by straining her ears that she caught the words,

"Watkins, Mr. Ringgan wants you to go right up on the hill to Mis' Plumfield's and tell her he wants her to come right down—he thinks"—the voice of the speaker fell, and Fleda could only make out the last words,—"Dr. James."

More was said, but so thick and low that she could understand nothing.

She had heard enough. She shut the window, trembling, and fastened again the parts of her dress she had loosened; and softly and hastily went down the stairs into the kitchen.

"Cynthy!—what is the matter with grandpa?"

"Why ain't you in bed, Flidda?" said Cynthy with some sharpness. "That's what you had ought to be. I am sure your grandpa wants you to be abed."

"But tell me," said Fleda anxiously.

"I don't know as there's anything the matter with him," said Cynthy. "Nothing much, I suppose. What makes you think anything is the matter?"

"Because I heard you telling Watkins to go for aunt Miriam." Fleda could not say,—"and the doctor."

"Well your grandpa thought he'd like to have her come down, and he don't feel right well,—so I sent Watkins up; but you'd better go to bed, Flidda; you'll catch cold if you sit up o' night."

Fleda was unsatisfied, the more because Cynthy would not meet the keen searching look with which the little girl tried to read her face. She was not to be sent to bed, and all Cynthy's endeavours to make her change her mind were of no avail. Fleda saw in them but fresh reason for staying, and saw besides, what Cynthy could not hide, a somewhat of wandering and uneasiness in her manner which strengthened her resolution. She sat down in the chimney corner, resolved to wait till her aunt Miriam came; there would be satisfaction in her, for aunt Miriam always told the truth, the whole truth, and nothing but the truth.

It was a miserable three quarters of an hour. The kitchen seemed to wear a strange desolate look, though seen in its wonted bright light of fire and candles, and in itself nice and cheerful as usual. Fleda looked at it also through that vague fear which casts its own lurid colour upon everything. The very flickering of the candle blaze seemed of ill omen, and her grandfather's empty chair stood a signal of pain to little Fleda whenever she looked at it. She sat still, in submissive patience, her cheek pale with the working of a heart too big for that little body. Cynthia was going in and out of her grandfather's room, but Fleda would not ask her any more questions, to be disappointed with word-answers; she waited, but the minutes seemed very long,—and very sad.

The characteristic outward calm which Fleda had kept, and which belonged to a nature uncommonly moulded to patience and fortitude, had yet perhaps heightened the pressure of excited fear within. When at last she saw the cloak and hood of aunt Miriam coming through the moonlight to the kitchen door, she rushed to open it, and quite overcome for the moment threw her arms around her and was speechless. Aunt Miriam's tender and quiet voice comforted her.

"You up yet, Fleda! Hadn't you better go to bed? 'Tisn't good for you."

"That's what I've been a telling her," said Cynthy, "but she wa'n't a mind to listen to me."

But the two little arms embraced aunt Miriam's cloak and wrappers and the little face was hid there still, and Fleda's answer was a half smothered ejaculation.

"I am *so* glad you are come, dear aunt Miriam!"

Aunt Miriam kissed her again, and again repeated her request.

"O no—I can't go to bed," said Fleda crying;—"I can't till I know—I am *sure* something is the matter, or Cynthy wouldn't look so. *Do* tell me, aunt Miriam!"

"I can't tell you anything, dear, except that grandpa is not well—that is all I know—I am going in to see him. I will tell you in the morning how he is."

"No," said Fleda, "I will wait here till you come out. I couldn't sleep."

Mrs. Plumfield made no more efforts to persuade her, but rid herself of cloak and hood and went into Mr. Ringgan's room. Fleda placed herself again in her chimney corner. Burying her face in her hands, she sat waiting more quietly; and Cynthy, having finished all her business, took a chair on the hearth opposite to her. Both were silent and motionless, except when Cynthy once in a while got up to readjust the sticks of wood on the fire. They sat there waiting so long that Fleda's anxiety began to quicken again.

"Don't you think the doctor is a long time coming, Cynthy?" said she raising her head at last. Her question, breaking that forced silence, sounded fearful.

"It seems kind o' long," said Cynthy. "I guess Watkins ha'n't found him to hum."

Watkins indeed presently came in and reported as much, and that the wind was changing and it was coming off cold; and then his heavy boots were heard going up the stairs to his room overhead; but Fleda listened in vain for the sound of the latch of her grandfather's door, or aunt Miriam's quiet foot-fall in the passage; listened and longed, till the minutes seemed like the links of a heavy chain which she was obliged to pass over from hand to hand, and the last link could not be found. The noise of Watkins' feet ceased overhead, and nothing stirred or moved but the crackling flames and Cynthia's elbows, which took turns each in resting upon the opposite arm, and now and then a tell-tale gust of wind in the trees. If Mr. Ringgan was asleep, why did not aunt Miriam come out and see them,—if he was better, why not come and tell them so. He had been asleep when she first went into his room, and she had come back for a minute then to try again to get Fleda to bed; why could she not come out for a minute once more. Two hours of watching and trouble had quite changed little Fleda; the dark ring of anxiety had come under each eye in her little pale face; she looked herself almost ill.

Aunt Miriam's grave step was heard coming out of the room at last,—it did not sound cheerfully in Fleda's ears. She came in, and stopping to give some direction to Cynthy, walked up to Fleda. Her face encouraged no questions. She took the child's head tenderly in both her hands, and told her gently, but it was in vain that she tried to make her voice quite as usual, that she had better go to bed—that she would be sick.

Fleda looked up anxiously in her face.

"How is he?"

But her next word was the wailing cry of sorrow,—"Oh grandpa!—"

The old lady took the little child in her arms and they both sat there by the fire until the morning dawned.

CHAPTER VIII.

> Patience and sorrow strove
> Who should express her goodliest.
>
> KING LEAR.

WHEN Mr. Carleton knocked at the front door the next day about two o'clock it was opened to him by Cynthy. He asked for his late host.

"Mr. Ringgan is dead."

"Dead!" exclaimed the young man much shocked;—"when? how?"

"Won't you come in, sir?" said Cynthy;—"maybe you'll see Mis' Plumfield."

"No, certainly," replied the visiter. "Only tell me about Mr. Ringgan."

"He died last night."

"What was the matter with him?"

"I don't know," said Cynthy in a business-like tone of voice,—"I s'pose the doctor knows, but he didn't say nothing about it. He died very sudden."

"Was he alone?"

"No—his sister was with him; he had been complaining all the evening that he didn't feel right, but I didn't think nothing of it and I didn't know as he did; and towards evening he went and laid down, and Flidda was with him a spell, talking to him; and at last he sent her to bed and called me in and said he felt mighty strange and he didn't know what it was going to be, and that he had as lieve I should send up and ask Mis' Plumfield to come down, and perhaps I might as well send for the doctor too. And I sent right off, but the doctor wa'n't to hum, and didn't get here till long after. Mis' Plumfield, she come; and Mr. Ringgan was asleep then, and I didn't know as it was going to be anything more after all than just a turn, such as anybody might take; and Mis' Plumfield went in and sot by him; and there wa'n't no one else in the room; and after a while he come to, and talked to her, she said, a spell; but he seemed to think it was something more than common ailed him; and all of a sudden he just riz up half way in bed and then fell back and died,—with no more warning than that."

"And how is the little girl?"

"Why," said Cynthy, looking off at right angles from her visiter, "she's middling now, I s'pose, but she won't be before long, or else she must be harder to make sick than other folks.—We can't get her out of the room," she added, bringing her eyes to bear, for an instant, upon the young gentleman,—"she stays in there the hull time since morning—I've tried, and Mis' Plumfield's tried, and everybody has tried, and there can't none of us manage it; she will stay in there, and it's an awful cold room when there ain't no fire."

Cynthy and her visiter were both taking the benefit of the chill blast which rushed in at the opon door.

"*The room?*" said Mr. Carleton. "The room where the body lies?"

"Yes—it's dreadful chill in there when the stove ain't heated, and she sits there the hull time. And she ha'n't got much to boast of now; she looks as if a feather would blow her away."

The door at the further end of the hall opened about two inches and a voice called out through the crack,

"Cynthy!—Mis' Plumfield wants to know if that is Mr. Carleton?"

"Yes."

"Well she'd like to see him. Ask him to walk into the front room, she says."

Cynthy upon this shewed the way, and Mr. Carleton walked into the same room where a very few days before he had been so kindly welcomed by his fine old host. Cold indeed it was now, as was the welcome he would have given. There was no fire in the chimney, and even all the signs of the fire of the other day had been carefully cleared away; the clean empty fireplace looked a mournful assurance that its cheerfulness would not soon come back again. It was a raw disagreeable day; the paper window-shades fluttered uncomfortably in the wind, which had its way now; and the very chairs and tables seemed as if they had taken leave of life and society for ever. Mr. Carleton walked slowly up and down, his thoughts running perhaps somewhat in the train where poor little Fleda's had been so busy last night; and wrapped up in broadcloth as he was to the chin, he shivered when he heard the chill wind moaning round the house and rustling the paper hangings and thought of little Fleda's delicate frame, exposed as Cynthia had described it. He made up his mind it must not be.

Mrs. Plumfield presently came in, and met him with the calm dignity of that sorrow which needs no parade and that truth and meekness of character which can make none. Yet there was nothing like stoicism, no affected or proud repression of feeling; her manner was simply the dictate of good sense borne out by a firm and quiet spirit. Mr. Carleton was struck with it; it was a display of character different from any he had ever before met with; it was something he could not quite understand. For he wanted the key. But all the high respect he had felt for this lady from the first was confirmed and strengthened.

After quietly receiving Mr. Carleton's silent grasp of the hand, aunt Miriam said,

"I troubled you to stop, sir, that I might ask you how much longer you expect to stop at Montepoole."

Not more than two or three days, he said.

"I understood," said aunt Miriam after a minute's pause, "that Mrs. Carleton was so kind as to say she would take care of Elfleda to France and put her in the hands of her aunt."

"She would have great pleasure in doing it," said Mr. Carleton. "I can promise for your little niece that she shall have a mother's care so long as my mother can render it."

Aunt Miriam was silent, and he saw her eyes fill.

"You should not have had the pain of seeing me to-day," said he gently, "if I could have known it would give you any; but since I am here, may I ask, whether it is your determination that Fleda shall go with us?"

"It was my brother's," said aunt Miriam, sighing;—"he

told me—last night—that he wished her to go with Mrs. Carleton—if she would still be so good as to take her."

"I have just heard about her, from the housekeeper," said Mr. Carleton, "what has disturbed me a good deal. Will you forgive me, if I venture to propose that she should come to us at once. Of course we will not leave the place for several days—till you are ready to part with her."

Aunt Miriam hesitated, and again the tears flushed to her eyes.

"I believe it would be best," she said,—"since it must be—I cannot get the child away from her grandfather—I am afraid I want firmness to do it—and she ought not to be there—she is a tender little creature—"

For once self-command failed her—she was obliged to cover her face.

"A stranger's hands cannot be more tender of her than ours will be," said Mr. Carleton, his warm pressure of aunt Miriam's hand repeating the promise. "My mother will bring a carriage for her this afternoon, if you will permit."

"If you please, sir,—since it must be, it does not matter a day sooner or later," repeated aunt Miriam,—"if she can be got away—I don't know whether it will be possible."

Mr. Carleton had his own private opinion on that point. He merely promised to be there again in a few hours and took his leave.

He came, with his mother, about five o'clock in the afternoon. They were shewn this time into the kitchen, where they found two or three neighbours and friends with aunt Miriam and Cynthy. The former received them with the same calm simplicity that Mr. Carleton had admired in the morning, but said she was afraid their coming would be in vain; she had talked with Fleda about the proposed plan and could not get her to listen to it. She doubted whether it would be possible to persuade her. And yet—

Aunt Miriam's self-possession seemed to be shaken when she thought of Fleda; she could not speak of her without watering eyes.

"She's fixing to be sick as fast as ever she can," remarked Cynthia dryly, in a kind of aside meant for the audience;—"there wa'n't a grain of colour in her face when I went in to try to get her out a little while ago; and Mis'

Plumfield ha'n't the heart to do anything with her, nor nobody else."

"Mother, will you see what you can do?" said Mr. Carleton.

Mrs. Carleton went, with an expression of face that her son, nobody else, knew meant that she thought it a particularly disagreeable piece of business. She came back after the lapse of a few minutes, in tears.

"I can do nothing with her," she said hurriedly;—"I don't know what to say to her; and she looks like death. Go yourself, Guy; you can manage her if any one can."

Mr. Carleton went immediately.

The room into which a short passage admitted him was cheerless indeed. On a fair afternoon the sun's rays came in there pleasantly, but this was a true November day; a grey sky and a chill raw wind that found its way in between the loose window-sashes and frames. One corner of the room was sadly tenanted by the bed which held the remains of its late master and owner. At a little table between the windows, with her back turned towards the bed, Fleda was sitting, her face bowed in her hands upon the old quarto bible that lay there open; a shawl round her shoulders.

Mr. Carleton went up to the side of the table and softly spoke her name. Fleda looked up at him for an instant, and then buried her face in her hands on the book as before. That look might have staggered him, but that Mr. Carleton rarely was staggered in any purpose when he had once made up his mind. It did move him,—so much that he was obliged to wait a minute or two before he could muster firmness to speak to her again. Such a look,—so pitiful in its sorrow, so appealing in its helplessness, so imposing in its purity,—he had never seen, and it absolutely awed him. Many a child's face is lovely to look upon for its innocent purity, but more commonly it is not like this; it is the purity of snow, unsullied, but not unsullyable; there is another kind more ethereal, like that of light, which you feel is from another sphere and will not know soil. But there were other signs in the face that would have nerved Mr. Carleton's resolution if he had needed it. Twenty-four hours had wrought a sad change. The child looked as if she had been ill for weeks. Her cheeks were colourless; the delicate brow would have seemed pencilled on marble but for the dark lines which weeping and watching, and still more sorrow, had drawn underneath; and the beautiful moulding of the features shewed under the transparent skin like the work of the sculptor. She was not crying then, but the open pages of the great bible had been wet with very many tears since her head had rested there.

"Fleda," said Mr. Carleton after a moment,—"you must come with me."

The words were gently and tenderly spoken, yet they had that tone which young and old instinctively know it is vain to dispute. Fleda glanced up again, a touching imploring look it was very difficult to bear, and her "Oh no—I cannot,"—went to his heart. It was not resistance but entreaty, and all the arguments she would have urged seemed to lie in the mere tone of her voice. She had no power of urging them in any other way, for even as she spoke her head went down again on the bible with a burst of sorrow. Mr. Carleton was moved, but not shaken in his purpose. He was silent a moment, drawing back the hair that fell over Fleda's forehead with a gentle caressing touch; and then he said, still lower and more tenderly than before, but without flinching, "You must come with me, Fleda."

"Mayn't I stay," said Fleda, sobbing, while he could see in the tension of the muscles a violent effort at self-control which he did not like to see,—"mayn't I stay till—till—the day after to-morrow?"

"No, dear Fleda," said he, still stroking her head kindly,—"I will bring you back, but you must go with me now. Your aunt wishes it and we all think it is best. I will bring you back."—

She sobbed bitterly for a few minutes. Then she begged in smothered words that he would leave her alone a little while. He went immediately.

She checked her sobs when she heard the door close upon him, or as soon as she could, and rising went and knelt down by the side of the bed. It was not to cry, though what she did could not be done without many tears,—it was to repeat with equal earnestness and solemnity her mother's prayer, that she might be kept pure from the world's contact. There beside the remains of her last dear earthly friend, as it were before going out of his sight forever, little Fleda knelt down to set the seal of faith and hope to his wishes, and to lay the constraining hand of Memory upon her conscience. It was soon done,—and then there was but one thing more to do. But oh, the tears that fell as she stood there! before she could go on; how the little hands were pressed to the bowed face, as if *they* would have borne up the load they could not reach; the convulsive struggle, before the last look could be taken, the last good-by said! But the sobs were forced back, the hands wiped off the tears, the quivering features were bidden into some degree of calmness; and she leaned forward, over the loved face that in death had kept all its wonted look of mildness and placid dignity. It was in vain to try to look through Fleda's blinded eyes; the hot tears dropped fast, while her trembling lips kissed—and kissed,—those cold and silent that could make no return; and then feeling that it was the last, that the parting was over, she stood again by the side of the bed as she had done a few minutes before, in a convulsion of grief, her face bowed down and her little frame racked with feeling too strong for it; shaken visibly, as if too frail to bear the trial to which it was put.

Mr. Carleton had waited and waited, as he thought long enough, and now at last came in again, guessing how it was with her. He put his arm round the child and gently drew her away, and sitting down took her on his knee; and endeavoured rather with actions than with words to soothe and comfort her; for he did not know what to say. But his gentle delicate way, the soft touch with which he again stroked back her hair or took her hand, speaking kindness and sympathy, the loving pressure of his lips once or twice to her brow, the low tones in which he told her that she was making herself sick,—that she must not do so,—that she must let him take care of her,—were powerful to soothe or quiet a sensitive mind, and Fleda felt them. It was a very difficult task, and if undertaken by any one else would have been more likely to disgust and distress her. But his spirit had taken the measure of hers, and he knew precisely how to temper every word and tone so as just to meet the nice sensibilities of her nature. He had said hardly any thing, but she had understood all he meant to say, and when he told her at last, softly, that it was getting late and she must let him take her away, she made no more difficulty; rose up and let him lead her out of the room without once turning her head to look back.

Mrs. Carleton looked relieved that there was a prospect of getting away, and rose up with a happy adjusting of her shawl round her shoulders. Aunt Miriam came forward to say good-by, but it was very quietly said. Fleda clasped her round the neck convulsively for an instant, kissed her as if a kiss could speak a whole heartful, and then turned submissively to Mr. Carleton and let him lead her to the carriage.

There was no fault to be found with Mrs. Carleton's kindness when they were on the way. She held the forlorn little child tenderly in her arm, and told her how glad she was to have her with them, how glad she should be if she were going to keep her always; but her saying so only made Fleda cry, and she soon thought it best to say nothing. All the rest of the way Fleda was a picture of resignation; transparently pale, meek and pure, and fragile seemingly, as the delicatest wood-flower that grows. Mr. Carleton looked grieved, and leaning forward he took one of her hands in his own and held it affectionately till they got to the end of their journey. It marked Fleda's feeling towards him that she let it lie there without making a motion to draw it away. She was so still for the last few miles that her friends thought she had fallen asleep; but when the carriage stopped and the light of the lantern was flung inside, they saw the grave hazel eyes broad open and gazing intently out of the window.

"You will order tea for us in your dressing-room, mother?" said Mr. Carleton.

"*Us*—who is *us?*"

"Fleda and me,—unless you will please to make one of the party."

"Certainly I will, but perhaps Fleda might like it better down stairs. Wouldn't you, dear?"

"If you please, ma'am," said Fleda. "Wherever you please."

"But which would you rather, Fleda?" said Mr. Carleton.

"I would *rather* have it up-stairs," said Fleda gently, "but it's no matter."

"We will have it up stairs," said Mrs. Carleton. "We will be a nice little party up there by ourselves. You shall not come down till you like."

"You are hardly able to walk up," said Mr. Carleton tenderly. "Shall I carry you?"

The tears rushed to Fleda's eyes, but she said no, and managed to mount the stairs, though it was evidently an exertion. Mrs. Carleton's dressing-room, as her son had called it, looked very pleasant when they got there. It was well lighted and warmed and something answering to curtains had been summoned from its obscurity in store-room or garret and hung up at the windows,—"them air fussy English folks had made such a pint of it," the landlord said. Truth was, that Mr. Carleton as well as his mother wanted this room as a retreat for the quiet and privacy which travelling in company as they did they could have nowhere else. Everything the hotel could furnish in the shape of comfort had been drawn together to give this room as little the look of a public house as possible. Easy chairs, as Mrs. Carleton remarked with a disgusted face, one could not expect to find in a country inn; there were instead as many as half a dozen of "those miserable substitutes" as she called rocking-chairs, and sundry fashions of couches and sofas, in various degrees of elegance and convenience. The best of these, a great chintz-covered thing, full of pillows, stood invitingly near the bright fire. There Mr. Carleton placed little Fleda, took off her bonnet and things, and piled the cushions about her just in the way that would make her most easy and comfortable. He said little, and she nothing, but her eyes watered again at the kind tenderness of his manner. And then he left her in peace till the tea came.

The tea was made in that room for those three alone. Fleda knew that Mr. and Mrs. Carleton staid up there only for her sake, and it troubled her, but she could not help it. Neither could she be very sorry so far as one of them was concerned. Mr. Carleton was too good to be wished away. All that evening his care of her never ceased. At tea, which the poor child would hardly have shared but for him, and after tea, when in the absence of bustle she had leisure to feel more fully her strange circumstances and position, he hardly permitted her to feel either, doing everything for her ease and pleasure and quietly managing at the same time to keep back his mother's more forward and less happily adapted tokens of kind feeling. Though she knew he was constantly occupied with her Fleda could not feel oppressed; his kindness was as pervading and as unobtrusive as the summer air itself; she felt as if she was in somebody's hands that knew her wants before she did, and quietly supplied or prevented them, in a way she could not tell how. It was very rarely that she even got a chance to utter the quiet and touching "thank you," which invariably answered every token of kindness or thoughtfulness that permitted an answer. How greatly that harsh and sad day was softened to little Fleda's heart by the good feeling and fine breeding of one person. She thought when she went to bed that night, thought seriously and gratefully, that since she must go over the ocean and take that long journey to her aunt, how glad she was, how thankful she ought to be, that she had so very kind and pleasant people to go with. Kind and pleasant she counted them both; but what more she thought of Mr. Carleton it would be hard to say. Her admiration of him was very high, appreciating as she did to the full all that charm of manner which she could neither analyze nor describe.

Her last words to him that night, spoken with a most wistful anxious glance into his face, were,

"You will take me back again, Mr. Carleton?"

He knew what she meant.

"Certainly I will. I promised you, Fleda."

"Whatever Guy promises you may be very sure he will do," said his mother with a smile.

Fleda believed it. But the next morning it was very plain that this promise he would not be called upon to perform; Fleda would not be well enough to go to the funeral. She was able indeed to get up, but she lay all day upon the sofa in the dressing-room. Mr. Carleton had bargained for no company last night; to-day female curiosity could stand it no longer; and Mrs. Thorn and Mrs. Evelyn came up to look and gossip openly and to admire and comment privately, when they had a chance. Fleda lay perfectly quiet and still, seeming not much to notice or care for their presence; they thought she was tolerably easy in body and mind, perhaps tired and sleepy, and like to do well enough after a few days. How little they knew! How little they could imagine the assembly of Thought which was holding in that child's mind; how little they deemed of the deep, sad, serious look into life which that little spirit was taking. How far they were from fancying while they were discussing all manner of trifles before her, sometimes when they thought her sleeping, that in the intervals between sadder and weighter things her nice instincts were taking the gauge of all their characters; unconsciously, but surely; how they might have been ashamed if they had known that while they were busy with all affairs in the universe but those which most nearly concerned them, the little child at their side whom they had almost forgotten was secretly looking up to her Father in heaven, and asking to be kept pure from the world! "Not unto the wise and prudent;"—how strange it may seem in one view of the subject,—in another, how natural, how beautiful, how reasonable!

Fleda did not ask again to be taken to Queechy. But as the afternoon drew on she turned her face away from the company and shielded it from view among the cushions, and lay in that utterly motionless state of body which betrays a concentrated movement of the spirits in some hidden direction. To her companions it betrayed nothing. They only lowered their tones a little lest they should disturb her.

It had grown dark, and she was sitting up again, leaning against the pillows and in her usual quietude, when Mr. Carleton came in. They had not seen him since before dinner. He came to her side and taking her hand made some gentle inquiry how she was.

"She has had a fine rest," said Mrs. Evelyn.

"She has been sleeping all the afternoon," said Mrs. Carleton,—"she lay as quiet as a mouse, without stirring;—you were sleeping, weren't you, dear?"

Fleda's lips hardly formed the word "no," and her features were quivering sadly. Mr. Carleton's were impenetrable.

"Dear Fleda," said he, stooping down and speaking with equal gravity and kindliness of manner,—"you were not able to go."

Fleda's shake of the head gave a meek acquiescence. But her face was covered, and the gay talkers around her were silenced and sobered by the heaving of her little frame with sobs that she could not keep back. Mr. Carleton secured the permanence of their silence for that evening. He dismissed them the room again and would have nobody there but himself and his mother.

Instead of being better the next day Fleda was not able to get up; she was somewhat feverish and exceedingly weak. She lay like a baby, Mrs. Carleton said, and gave as little trouble. Gentle and patient always, she made no complaint, and even uttered no wish, and whatever they did made no objection. Though many a tear that day and the following paid its faithful tribute to the memory of what she had lost, no one knew it; she was never seen to weep; and the very grave composure of her face and her passive unconcern as to what was done or doing around her alone gave her friends reason to suspect that the mind was not as quiet as the body. Mr. Carleton was the only one who saw deeper; the only one that guessed why the little hand often covered the eyes so carefully, and read the very, very grave lines of the mouth that it could not hide.

As soon as she could bear it he had her brought out to the dressing-room again, and laid on the sofa; and it was several days before she could be got any further. But there he could be more with her and devote himself more to her pleasure; and it was not long before he had made himself necessary to the poor child's comfort in a way beyond what he was aware of.

He was not the only one who shewed her kindness. Unwearied care and most affectionate attention were lavished upon her by his mother and both her friends; they all thought they could not do enough to mark their feeling and regard for her. Mrs. Carleton and Mrs. Evelyn nursed her by night and by day. Mrs. Evelyn read to her. Mrs. Thorn would come often to look and smile at her and say a few words of heart-felt pity and sympathy. Yet Fleda could not feel quite at home with any one of them. They did not see it. Her manner was affectionate and grateful, to the utmost of their wish; her simple natural politeness, her nice sense of propriety, were at every call; she seemed after a few days to be as cheerful and to enter as much into what was going on about her as they had any reason to expect she could; and they were satisfied. But while moving thus smoothly among her new companions, in secret her spirit stood aloof; there was not one of them that could touch her, that could understand her, that could meet the want of her nature. Mrs. Carleton was incapacitated for it by education; Mrs. Evelyn by character; Mrs. Thorn by natural constitution. Of them all, though by far the least winning and agreeable in personal qualifications, Fleda would soonest have relied on Mrs. Thorn, could soonest have loved her. Her homely sympathy and kindness made their way to the child's heart; Fleda felt them and trusted them. But there were too few points of contact. Fleda thanked her, and did not wish to see her again. With Mrs. Carleton Fleda had almost nothing at all in common. And that notwithstanding all this lady's politeness, intelligence, cultivation, and real kindness towards herself. Fleda would readily have given her credit for them all; and yet, the nautilus may as soon compare notes with the navigator, the canary might as well study Maelzel's Metronome, as a child of nature and a woman of the world comprehend and suit each other. The nature of the one must change or the two must remain the world wide apart. Fleda felt it, she did not know why. Mrs. Carleton was very kind, and perfectly polite; but Fleda had no pleasure in her kindness, no trust in her politeness; or if that be saying too much, at least she felt that for some inexplicable reason both were unsatisfactory. Even the tact which each possessed in an exquisite degree was not the same in each; in one it was the self-graduating power of a clever machine,—in the other, the delicateness of the sensitive-plant. Mrs. Carleton herself was not without some sense of this distinction; she confessed, secretly, that there was something in Fleda out of the reach of her discernment, and consequently beyond the walk of her skill; and felt, rather uneasily, that more delicate hands were needed to guide so delicate a nature. Mrs. Evelyn came nearer the point. She was very pleasant, and she knew how to do things in a charming way; and there were times, frequently, when Fleda thought she was everything lovely. But yet, now and then a mere word, or look, would contradict this fair promise, a something of *hardness* which Fleda could not reconcile with the soft gentleness of other times; and on the whole Mrs. Evelyn was unsure ground to her; she could not adventure her confidence there.

With Mr. Carleton alone Fleda felt at home. He only, she knew, completely understood and appreciated her. Yet she saw also that with others he was not the same as with her. Whether grave or gay there was about him an air of cool indifference, very often reserved and not seldom haughty; and the eye which could melt and glow when turned upon her, was sometimes as bright and cold as a winter sky. Fleda felt sure however that she might trust him entirely so far as she herself was concerned; of the rest she stood in doubt. She was quite right in both cases. Whatever else there might be in that blue eye, there was truth in it when it met hers; she gave that truth her full confidence and was willing to honour every draught made upon her charity for the other parts of his character.

He never seemed to lose sight of her. He was always doing something for which Fleda loved him, but so quietly and happily that she could neither help his taking the trouble nor thank him for it. It might have been matter of surprise that a gay young man of fashion should concern himself like a brother about the wants of a little child; the young gentlemen down stairs who were not of the society in the dressing-room did make themselves very merry upon the subject, and rallied Mr. Carleton with the common amount of wit and wisdom about his little sweetheart; a raillery which met the most flinty indifference. But none of those who saw Fleda ever thought strange of anything that was done for her; and Mrs. Carleton was rejoiced to have her son take up the task she was fain to lay down. So he really, more than any one else, had the management of her; and Fleda invariably greeted his entrance into the room with a faint smile, which even the ladies who saw agreed was well worth working for.

CHAPTER IX.

If large possessions, pompous titles, honourable charges, and profitable commissions, could have made this proud man happy, there would have been nothing wanting.—L'ESTRANGE.

SEVERAL days had passed. Fleda's cheeks had gained no colour, but she had grown a little stronger, and it was thought the party might proceed on their way without any more tarrying; trusting that change and the motion of travelling would do better things for Fleda than could be hoped from any further stay at Montepoole. The matter was talked over in an evening consultation in the dressing-room, and it was decided that they would set off on the second day thereafter.

Fleda was lying quietly on her sofa, with her eyes closed, having had nothing to say during the discussion. They thought she had perhaps not heard it. Mr. Carleton's sharper eyes, however, saw that one or two tears were glimmering just under the eyelash. He bent down over her and whispered,

"I know what you are thinking of Fleda, do I not?"

"I was thinking of aunt Miriam," Fleda said in an answering whisper, without opening her eyes.

"I will take care of that."

Fleda looked up and smiled most expressively her thanks, and in five minutes was asleep. Mr. Carleton stood watching her, querying how long those clear eyes would have nothing to hide,—how long that bright purity could resist the corrosion of the world's breath; and half thinking that it would be better for the spirit to pass away, with its lustre upon it, than stay till self-interest should sharpen the eye, and the lines of diplomacy write themselves on that fair brow. "Better so; better so."

"What are you thinking of so gloomily, Guy?" said his mother.

"That is a tender little creature to struggle with a rough world."

"She won't have to struggle with it," said Mrs. Carleton.

"She will do very well," said Mrs. Evelyn.

"I don't think she'd find it a rough world, where *you* were, Mr. Carleton," said Mrs. Thorn.

"Thank you ma'am," he said smiling. "But unhappily my power reaches very little way."

"Perhaps," said Mrs. Evelyn with a sly smile,—"that might be arranged differently—Mrs. Rossitur—I have no doubt—would desire nothing better than a smooth world for her little niece—and Mr. Carleton's power might be unlimited in its extent."

There was no answer, and the absolute repose of all the lines of the young gentleman's face bordered too nearly on contempt to encourage the lady to pursue her jest any further.

The next day Fleda was well enough to bear moving. Mr. Carleton had her carefully bundled up, and then carried her down stairs and placed her in the little light wagon which had once before brought her to the Pool. Luckily it was a mild day, for no close carriage was to be had for love or money. The stage-coach in which Fleda had been fetched from her grandfather's was in use, away somewhere. Mr. Carleton drove her down to aunt Miriam's, and leaving her there he went off again; and whatever he did with himself it was a good two hours before he came back. All too little yet they were for the tears and the sympathy which went to so many things both in the past and in the future. Aunt Miriam had not said half she wished to say, when the wagon was at the gate again, and Mr. Carleton came to take his little charge away.

He found her sitting happily in aunt Miriam's lap. Fleda was very grateful to him for leaving her such a nice long time, and welcomed him with even a brighter smile than usual. But her head rested wistfully on her aunt's bosom after that; and when he asked her if she was almost ready to go, she hid her face there and put her arms about her neck. The old lady held her close for a few minutes, in silence.

"Elfleda," said aunt Miriam gravely and tenderly,—"do you know what was your mother's prayer for you?"

"Yes,"—she whispered.

"What was it?"

"That I—might be kept—"

"Unspotted from the world!" repeated aunt Miriam, in a tone of tender and deep feeling;—"My sweet blossom!—how wilt thou keep so? Will you remember always your mother's prayer?"

"I will try."

"How will you try, Fleda?"

"I will pray."

Aunt Miriam kissed her again and again, fondly repeating, "The Lord hear thee!—The Lord bless thee!—The Lord keep thee!—as a lily among thorns, my precious little babe;—though in the world, not of it.—"

"Do you think that is possible?" said Mr. Carleton significantly, when a few moments after they had risen and were about to separate. Aunt Miriam looked at him in surprise and asked,

"What, sir?"

"To live in the world and not be like the world?"

She cast her eyes upon Fleda, fondly smoothing down her soft hair with both hands for a minute or two before she answered,

"By the help of one thing sir, yes!"

"And what is that?" said he quickly.

"The blessing of God, with whom all things are possible."

His eyes fell, and there was a kind of incredulous sadness in his half smile which aunt Miriam understood better than he did. She sighed as she folded Fleda again to her breast and whisperingly bade her "Remember!" But Fleda knew nothing of it; and when she had finally parted from aunt Miriam and was seated in the little wagon on her way home, to her fancy the best friend she had in the world was sitting beside her.

Neither was her judgment wrong, so far as it went. She

saw true where she saw at all. But there was a great deal she could not see.

Mr. Carleton was an unbeliever. Not maliciously,—not wilfully,—not stupidly;—rather the fool of circumstance. His skepticism might be traced to the joint workings of a very fine nature and a very bad education. That is, education in the broad sense of the term; of course none of the means and appliances of mental culture had been wanting to him.

He was an uncommonly fine example of what nature alone can do for a man. A character of nature's building is at best a very ragged affair, without religion's finishing hand;—at the utmost a fine ruin—no more. And if that be the *utmost*, of nature's handiwork, what is at the other end of the scale?—alas! the rubble stones of the ruin; what of good and fair nature had reared there was not strong enough to stand alone. But religion cannot work alike on every foundation; and the varieties are as many as the individuals. Sometimes she must build the whole, from the very ground; and there are cases where nature's work stands so strong and fair that religion's strength may be expended in perfecting and enriching and carrying it to an uncommon height of grace and beauty, and dedicating the fair temple to a new use.

Of religion Mr. Carleton had nothing at all, and a true Christian character had never crossed his path near enough for him to become acquainted with it. His mother was a woman of the world; his father had been a man of the world; and what is more, so deep-dyed a politician that to all intents and purposes, except as to bare natural affection, he was nothing to his son and his son was nothing to him. Both mother and father thought the son a piece of perfection, and mothers and fathers have very often indeed thought so on less grounds. Mr. Carleton saw, whenever he took time to look at him, that Guy had no lack either of quick wit or manly bearing; that he had pride enough to keep him from low company and make him abhor low pursuits; if anything more than pride and better than pride mingled with it, the father's discernment could not reach so far. He had a love for knowledge too, that from a child made him eager in seeking it, in ways both regular and desultory; and tastes which his mother laughingly said would give him all the elegance of a woman, joined to the strong manly character which no one ever doubted he possessed. *She* looked mostly at the outside, willing if that pleased her to take everything else upon trust; and the grace of manner which a warm heart and fine sensibilities and a mind entirely frank and above-board had given him, from his earliest years had more than met all her wishes. No one suspected the stubbornness and energy of will which was in fact the back-bone of his character. Nothing tried it. His father's death early left little Guy to his mother's guardianship. Contradicting him was the last thing she thought of, and of course it was attempted by no one else.

If she would ever have allowed that he had a fault, which she never would, it was one that grew out of his greatest virtue, an unmanageable truth of character; and if she ever unwillingly recognised its companion virtue, firmness of will, it was when she endeavoured to combat certain troublesome demonstrations of the other. In spite of all the grace and charm of manner in which he was allowed to be a model, and which was as natural to him as it was universal, if ever the interests of truth came in conflict with the dictates of society he flung minor considerations behind his back and came out with some startling piece of bluntness at which his mother was utterly confounded. These occasions were very rare; he never sought them. Always where it was possible he chose either to speak or be silent in an unexceptionable manner. But sometimes the barrier of conventionalities, or his mother's unwise policy, pressed too hard upon his integrity or his indignation; and he would then free the barrier and present the shut-out truth in its full size and proportions before his mother's shocked eyes. It was in vain to try to coax or blind him; a marble statue is not more unruffled by the soft airs of summer; and Mrs. Carleton was fain to console herself with the reflection that Guy's very next act after one of these breaks would be one of such happy fascination that the former would be forgotten; and that in this world of discordancies it was impossible on the whole for any one to come nearer perfection. And if there was inconvenience there were also great comforts about this character of truthfulness.

So nearly up to the time of his leaving the University the young heir lived a life of as free and uncontrolled enjoyment as the deer on his grounds, happily led by his own fine instincts to seek that enjoyment in pure and natural sources. His tutor was proud of his success; his dependants loved his frank and high bearing; his mother rejoiced in his personal accomplishments, and was secretly well pleased that his tastes led him another way from the more common and less safe indulgences of other young men. He had not escaped the temptations of opportunity and example. But gambling was not intellectual enough, jockeying was too undignified, and drinking too coarse a pleasure for him. Even hunting and coursing charmed him but for a few times; when he found he could out-ride and out-leap all his companions, he hunted no more; telling his mother when she attacked him on the subject, that he thought the hare the worthier animal of the two upon a chase; and that the fox deserved an easier death. His friends twitted him with his want of spirit and want of manliness; but such light shafts bounded back from the buff suit of cool indifference in which their object was cased; and his companions very soon gave over the attempt either to persuade or annoy him, with the conclusion that "nothing could be done with Carleton."

The same wants that had displeased him in the sports soon led him to decline the company of those who indulged in them. From the low-minded, from the uncultivated, from the unrefined in mind and manner, and such there are in the highest class of society as well as in the less-favoured, he shrank away in secret disgust or weariness. There was no affinity. To his books, to his grounds, which he took endless delight in overseeing, to the fine arts in general, for which he had a great love and for one or two of them a great talent,—he went with restless energy and no want of companionship; and at one or the other, always pushing eagerly forward after some point of excellence or some new attainment not yet reached, and which sprang up after one another as fast as ever "Alps on Alps," he was happily and constantly busy. Too solitary, his mother thought,—

caring less for society than she wished to see him; but that she trusted would mend itself. He would be through the University and come of age and go into the world, as a matter of necessity.

But years brought a change—not the change his mother looked for. That restless active energy which had made the years of his youth so happy, became, in connection with one or two other qualities, a troublesome companion when he had reached the age of manhood and obeying manhood's law had "put away childish things." On what should it spend itself? It had lost none of its strength; while his fastidious notions of excellence and a far-reaching clear-sightedness which belonged to his truth of nature, greatly narrowed the sphere of its possible action. He could not delude himself into the belief that the oversight of his plantations and the perfecting his park scenery could be a worthy end of existence; or that painting and music were meant to be the stamina of life; or even that books were their own final cause. These things had refined and enriched him;—they might go on doing so to the end of his days;—but *for what?* For what?

It is said that everybody has his niche, failing to find which nobody fills his place or acts his part in society. Mr. Carleton could not find his niche, and he consequently grew dissatisfied everywhere. His mother's hopes from the University and the World, were sadly disappointed.

At the University he had not lost his time. The pride of character which joined with less estimable pride of birth was a marked feature in his composition, made him look with scorn upon the ephemeral pursuits of one set of young men; while his strong intellectual tastes drew him in the other direction; and the energetic activity which drove him to do everything well that he once took in hand, carried him to high distinction. Being there he would have disdained to be anywhere but at the top of the tree. But out of the University and in possession of his estates, what should he do with himself and them?

A question easy to settle by most young men! very easy to settle by Guy, if he had had the clue of Christian truth to guide him through the labyrinth. But the clue was wanting, and the world seemed to him a world of confusion.

A certain clearness of judgment is apt to be the blessed handmaid of uncommon truth of character; the mind that knows not what it is to play tricks upon its neighbours is rewarded by a comparative freedom from self-deception. Guy could not sit down upon his estates and lead an insect life like that recommended by Rossitur. His energies wanted room to expend themselves. But the world offered no sphere that would satisfy him; even had his circumstances and position laid all equally open. It was a busy world, but to him people seemed to be busy upon trifles, or working in a circle, or working mischief; and his nice notions of what *ought to be* were shocked by what he saw *was*, in every direction around him. He was disgusted with what he called the drivelling of some unhappy specimens of the Church which had come in his way; he disbelieved the truth of what such men professed. If there had been truth in it, he thought, they would deserve to be drummed out of the profession. He detested the crooked involvments and double-dealing of the law. He despised the butterfly life of a soldier; and as to the other side of a soldier's life, again he thought, what is it for?—to humour the arrogance of the proud,—to pamper the appetite of the full,—to tighten the grip of the iron hand of power;—and though it be sometimes for better ends, yet the soldier cannot choose what letters of the alphabet of obedience he will learn. Politics was the very shaking of the government sieve, where if there were any solid result it was accompanied with a very great flying about of chaff indeed. Society was nothing but whip syllabub,—a mere conglomeration of bubbles,—as hollow and as unsatisfying. And in lower departments of human life, as far as he knew, he saw evils yet more deplorable. The Church played at shuttlecock with men's credulousness, the law with their purses, the medical profession with their lives, the military with their liberties and hopes. He acknowledged that in all these lines of action there was much talent, much good intention, much admirable diligence and acuteness brought out—but to what great general end? He saw in short that the machinery of the human mind, both at large and in particular, was out of order. He did not know what was the broken wheel the want of which set all the rest to running wrong.

This was a strange train of thought for a very young man; but Guy had lived much alone, and in solitude one is like a person who has climbed a high mountain; the air is purer about him, his vision is freer; the eye goes straight and clear to the distant view which below on the plain a thousand things would come between to intercept. But there was some morbidness about it too. Disappointment in two or three instances where he had given his full confidence and been obliged to take it back had quickened him to generalize unfavourably upon human character, both in the mass and in individuals. And a restless dissatisfaction with himself and the world did not tend to a healthy view of things. Yet truth was at the bottom; truth rarely arrived at without the help of revelation. He discerned a want he did not know how to supply. His fine perceptions felt the jar of the machinery which other men are too busy or too deaf to hear. It seemed to him hopelessly disordered.

This habit of thinking wrought a change very unlike what his mother had looked for. He mingled more in society, but Mrs. Carleton saw that the eye with which he looked upon it was yet colder than it wont to be. A cloud came over the light gay spirited manner he had used to wear. The charm of his address was as great as ever where he pleased to shew it, but much more generally now he contented himself with a cool reserve, as impossible to disturb as to find fault with. His temper suffered the same eclipse. It was naturally excellent. His passions were not hastily moved. He had never been easy to offend; his careless good-humour and an unbounded proud self-respect made him look rather with contempt than anger upon the things that fire most men; though when once moved to displeasure it was stern and abiding in proportion to the depth of his character. The same good-humour and cool self-respect forbade him even then to be eager in shewing resentment; the offender fell off from his esteem and apparently from the sphere of his notice as easily as a drop of water from a duck's wing, and could with as much ease regain his lost lodgment; but unless there were wrong to be righted or truth to be vindicated he was in general safe from any further tokens of displeasure. In those cases Mr. Carleton was an adversary to be dreaded. As cool, as unwavering, as persevering there as in other things, he there as in other things no more failed of his end. And at bottom these characteristics remained the same; it was rather his humour than his temper that suffered a change. That grew more gloomy and less gentle. He was more easily irritated and would shew it more freely than in the old happy times had ever been.

Mrs. Carleton would have been glad to have those times back again. It could not be. Guy could not be content any longer in the Happy Valley of Amhara. Life had something for him to do beyond his park palings. He had carried manly exercises and personal accomplishments to an uncommon point of perfection; he knew his library well and his grounds thoroughly, and had made excellent improvement of both; it was in vain to try to persuade him that seed-time and harvest were the same thing, and that he had nothing to do but to rest in what he had done; shew his bright colours and flutter like a moth in the sunshine, or sit down like a degenerate bee in the summer time and eat his own honey. The power of action which he knew in himself could not rest without something to act upon. It longed to be doing.

But what?

Conscience is often morbidly far-sighted. Mr. Carleton had a very large tenantry around him and depending upon him, in bettering whose condition, if he had but known it, all those energies might have found full play. It never entered into his head. He abhorred *business*,—the detail of business; and his fastidious tastes especially shrank from having anything to do among those whose business was literally their life. The eye sensitively fond of elegance, the extreme of elegance, in everything, and permitting no other around or about him, could not bear the tokens of mental and bodily wretchedness among the ignorant poor; he escaped from them as soon as possible; thought that poverty was one of the irregularities of this wrong-working machine of a world, and something utterly beyond his power to do away or alleviate; and left to his steward all the responsibility that of right rested on his own shoulders.

And at last unable to content himself in the old routine of things he quitted home and England, even before he was of age, and roved from place to place, trying, and trying in vain, to soothe the vague restlessness that called for a very different remedy.

"On change de ciel,—l'on ne change point de soi."

CHAPTER X.

> Faire Christabelle, that ladye bright,
> Was had forth of the towre:
> But ever she droopeth in her minde,
> As, nipt by an ungentle winde,
> Doth some faire lillye flowre.
>
> SYR CAULINE.

THAT evening, the last of their stay at Montepoole, Fleda was thought well enough to take her tea in company. So Mr. Carleton carried her down, though she could have walked, and placed her on the sofa in the parlour.

Whatever disposition the young officers might have felt to renew their pleasantry on the occasion, it was shamed into silence. There was a pure dignity about that little pale face which protected itself. They were quite struck, and Fleda had no reason to complain of want of attention from any of the party. Mr. Evelyn kissed her. Mr. Thorn brought a little table to the side of the sofa for her cup of tea to stand on, and handed her the toast most dutifully; and her cousin Rossitur went back and forth between her and the tea-urn. All of the ladies seemed to take immense satisfaction in looking at her, they did it so much; standing about the hearth-rug with their cups in their hands, sipping their tea. Fleda was quite touched with everybody's kindness, but somebody at the back of the sofa whom she did not see was the greatest comfort of all.

"You must let me carry you up stairs wnen you go, Fleda," said her cousin. "I shall grow quite jealous of your friend Mr. Carleton."

"No," said Fleda smiling a little,—"I shall not let any one but him carry me up,—if he will."

"We shall all grow jealous of Mr. Carleton," said Thorn.

"He means to monopolize you, keeping you shut up there, up stairs."

"He didn't keep me shut up," said Fleda.

Mr. Carleton was welcome to monopolize her, if it depended on her vote.

"Not fair play, Carleton," continued the young officer wisely shaking his head,—"all start alike, or there's no fun in the race. You've fairly distanced us—left us nowhere."

He might have talked Chinese and been as intelligible to Fleda,—and as interesting to Guy, for all that appeared.

"How are we going to proceed to-morrow, Mr. Evelyn?" said Mrs. Carleton. "Has the missing stage-coach returned yet? or will it be forthcoming in the morning?"

"Promised, Mrs. Carleton. The landlord's faith stands pledged for it."

"Then it won't disappoint us, of course. What a dismal way of travelling!"

"This young country has'n't grown up to post-coaches yet," said Mrs. Evelyn.

"How many will it hold?" inquired Mrs. Carleton.

"Hum!—Nine inside, I suppose."

"And we number ten, with the servants."

"Just take us," said Mr. Evelyn. "There's room on the box for one."

"It will not take me," said Mr. Carleton.

"How will you go? ride?" said his mother. "I should think you would, since you have found a horse you like so well."

"By George! I wish there was another that *I* liked," said Rossitur, "and I'd go on horseback too. Such weather! The landlord says it's the beginning of Indian summer."

"It's too early for that," said Thorn.

"Well, eight inside will do very well for one day," said Mrs. Carleton. "That will give little Fleda a little more space to lie at her ease."

"You may put Fleda out of your calculations too, mother," said Mr. Carleton. "I will take care of her."

"How in the world," exclaimed his mother,—"if you are on horseback?"

And Fleda twisted herself round so as to give a look of bright inquiry at his face. She got no answer beyond a smile, which however completely satisfied her. As to the rest he told his mother that he had arranged it and they should see in the morning. Mrs. Carleton was far from being at ease on the subject of his arrangements, but she let the matter drop.

Fleda was secretly very much pleased. She thought she would a great deal rather go with Mr. Carleton in the little wagon than in the stage-coach with the rest of the people. Privately she did not at all admire Mr. Thorn or her cousin Rossitur. They amused her though; and feeling very much better and stronger in body, and at least quiet in mind, she sat in tolerable comfort on her sofa, looking and listening to the people who were gayly talking around her.

In the gaps of talk she sometimes thought she heard a distressed sound in the hall. The buzz of tongues covered it up,—then again she heard it,—and she was sure at last that it was the voice of a dog. Never came an appeal in vain from any four-footed creature to Fleda's heart. All the rest being busy with their own affairs, she quietly got up and opened the door and looked out, and finding that she was right went softly into the hall. In one corner lay her cousin Rossitur's beautiful black pointer, which she well remembered and had greatly admired several times. The poor creature was every now and then uttering short cries, in a manner as if he would not but they were forced from him.

"What is the matter with him?" asked Fleda, stepping fearfully towards the dog, and speaking to Mr. Carleton who had come out to look after her. As she spoke the dog rose and came crouching and wagging his tail to meet them.

"O Mr. Carleton!" Fleda almost screamed,—"look at him! O what is the matter with him! he's all over bloody! Poor creature!"—

"You must ask your cousin, Fleda," said Mr. Carleton, with as much cold disgust in his countenance as it often expressed; and that is saying a good deal.

Fleda could speak in the cause of a dog, where she would have been silent in her own. She went back to the parlour and begged her cousin with a face of distress to come out into the hall,—she did not say for what. Both he and Thorn followed her. Rossitur's face darkened as Fleda repeated her enquiry, her heart so full by this time as hardly to allow her to make any.

"Why the dog didn't do his duty and has been punished," he said gloomily.

"Punished?" said Fleda.

"Shot," said Mr. Carleton coolly.

"Shot!" exclaimed Fleda, bursting into heartwrung tears,—"Shot!—O how *could* any one do it! Oh how could you, how could you, cousin Charlton?"

It was a picture. The child was crying bitterly, her fingers stroking the poor dog's head with a touch in which lay, O what tender healing, if the will had but had magnetic power. Carleton's eye glanced significantly from her to the young officers. Rossitur looked at Thorn.

"It was not Charlton—it was I, Miss Fleda," said the latter. "Charlton lent him to me to-day, and he disobeyed me, and so I was angry with him and punished him a little severely; but he'll soon get over it."

But all Fleda's answer was, "I am very sorry!—I am very sorry!—poor dog!!"—and to weep such tears as made the young gentlemen for once ashamed of themselves. It almost did the child a mischief. She did not get over it all the evening. And she never got over it as far as Mr. Thorn was concerned.

Mrs. Carleton hoped, faintly, that Guy would come to reason by the next morning and let Fleda go in the stage-coach with the rest of the people. But he was as unreasonable as ever, and stuck to his purpose. She had supposed however, with Fleda, that the difference would be only an open vehicle and his company instead of a covered one and her own. Both of them were sadly discomfited when on coming to the hall door to take their carriages it was found that Mr. Carleton's meaning was no less than to take Fleda before him on horseback. He was busy even then in arranging a cushion on the pommel of the saddle for her to sit upon. Mrs. Carleton burst into indignant remonstrances; Fleda silently trembled.

But Mr. Carleton had his own notions on the subject, and they were not moved by anything his mother could say. He quietly went on with his preparations; taking very slight notice of the raillery of the young officers, answering Mrs. Evelyn with polite words, and silencing his mother as he came up with one of those looks out of his dark eyes to which she always forgave the wilfulness for the sake of the beauty and the winning power. She was completely conquered, and stepped back with even a smile.

"But Carleton!" cried Rossitur impatiently,—"you can't ride so! you'll find it deucedly inconvenient."

"Possibly," said Mr. Carleton.

"Fleda would be a great deal better off in the stage-coach."

"Have you studied medicine, Mr. Rossitur?" said the young man. "Because I am persuaded of the contrary."

"I don't believe your horse will like it," said Thorn.

"My horse is always of my mind, sir; or if he be not I generally succeed in convincing him."

"But there is somebody else that deserves to be consulted," said Mrs. Thorn. "I wonder how little Fleda will like it."

"I will ask her when we get to our first stopping-place," said Mr. Carleton smiling. "Come, Fleda!"

Fleda would hardly have said a word if his purpose had been to put her under the horse's feet instead of on his back. But she came forward with great unwillingness and a very tremulous little heart. He must have understood the want of alacrity in her face and manner, though he took no notice of it otherwise than by the gentle kindness with which he led her to the horse-block and placed her upon it. Then mounting, and riding the horse up close to the block, he took Fleda in both hands and bidding her spring, in a moment she was safely seated before him.

At first it seemed dreadful to Fleda to have that great horse's head so near her, and she was afraid that her feet touching him would excite his most serious disapprobation. However a minute or so went by and she could not see that his tranquillity seemed to be at all ruffled, or even that he was sensible of her being upon his shoulders. They waited to see the stage-coach off, and then gently set forward. Fleda feared very much again when she felt the horse moving under her, easy as his gait was, and looking after the stage-coach in the distance, now beyond call, she felt a little as if she was a great way from help and dry land, cast away on a horse's back. But Mr. Carleton's arm was gently passed round her, and she knew it held her safely and would not let her fall; and he bent down his face to her and asked her so kindly and tenderly, and with such a look too, that seemed to laugh at her fears, whether she felt afraid?—and with such a kind little pressure of his arm that promised to take care of her,—that Fleda's courage mounted twenty degrees at once. And it rose higher every minute; the horse went very easily, and Mr. Carleton held her so that she could not be tired, and made her lean against him; and before they had gone a mile Fleda began to be delighted. Such a charming way of travelling! Such a free view of the country!—and in this pleasant weather too, neither hot nor cold, and when all nature's features were softened by the light veil of haze that hung over them and kept off the sun's glare. Mr. Carleton was right. In the stage-coach Fleda would have sat quiet in a corner and moped the time sadly away; now she was roused, excited, interested, even cheerful; forgetting herself, which was the very thing of all others to be desired for her. She lost her fears; she was willing to have the horse trot or canter as fast as his rider pleased; but the trotting was too rough for her, so they cantered or paced along most of the time, when the hills did not oblige them to walk quietly up and down, which happened pretty often. For several miles the country was not very familiar to Fleda. It was however extremely picturesque; and she sat silently and gravely looking at it, her head lying upon Mr. Carleton's breast, her little mind very full of thoughts and musings, curious, deep, sometimes sorrowful, but not unhappy.

"I am afraid I tire you, Mr. Carleton!" said she in a sudden fit of recollection, starting up.

His look answered her, and his arm drew her back to her place again.

"Are *you* not tired, Elfie?"

"Oh no!——You have got a new name for me, Mr. Carleton," said she a moment after, looking up and smiling.

"Do you like it?"

"Yes."

"You are my good genius," said he,—"so I must have

a peculiar title for you, different from what other people know you by."

"What is a genius, sir?" said Fleda.

"Well a sprite then," said he smiling.

"A sprite!" said Fleda.

"I have read a story of a lady, Elfie, who had a great many little unearthly creatures, a kind of sprites, to attend upon her. Some sat in the ringlets of her hair and took charge of them; some hid in the folds of her dress and made them lie gracefully; another lodged in a dimple in her cheek, and another perched on her eyebrows, and so on."

"To take care of her eyebrows?" said Fleda laughing.

"Yes—to smooth out all the ill-humoured wrinkles and frowns, I suppose."

"But am I such a sprite?" said Fleda.

"Something like it."

"Why what do I do?" said Fleda, rousing herself in a mixture of gratification and amusement that was pleasant to behold.

"What office would you choose, Elfie? what good would you like to do me?"

It was a curious wistful look with which Fleda answered this question, an innocent look, in which Mr. Carleton read perfectly that she felt something was wanting in him, and did not know exactly what. His smile almost made her think she had been mistaken.

"You are just the sprite you would wish to be, Elfie," he said.

Fleda's head took its former position, and she sat for some time musing over his question and answer, till a familiar waymark put all such thoughts to flight. They were passing Deepwater Lake, and would presently be at aunt Miriam's. Fleda looked now with a beating heart. Every foot of ground was known to her. She was seeing it perhaps for the last time. It was with even an intensity of eagerness that she watched every point and turn of the landscape, endeavouring to lose nothing in her farewell view, to give her farewell look at every favourite clump of trees and old rock, and at the very mill-wheels, which for years whether working or at rest had had such interest for her. If tears came to bid their good-by too, they were hastily thrown off, or suffered to roll quietly down; *they* might bide their time; but eyes must look now or never. How pleasant, how pleasant, the quiet old country seemed to Fleda as they went along!—in that most quiet light and colouring; the brightness of the autumn glory gone, and the sober warm hue which the hills still wore seen under that hazy veil. All the home-like peace of the place was spread out to make it hard going away. Would she ever see any other so pleasant again? Those dear old hills and fields, among which she had been so happy,—they were not to be her home any more; would she ever have the same sweet happiness anywhere else?—"The Lord will provide!" thought little Fleda with swimming eyes.

It was hard to go by aunt Miriam's. Fleda eagerly looked, as well as she could, but no one was to be seen about the house. It was just as well. A sad gush of tears must come then, but she got rid of them as soon as possible, that she might not lose the rest of the way, promising them another time. The little settlement on "the hill" was passed,—the factories and mills and mill-ponds, one after the other; they made Fleda feel very badly, for here she remembered going with her grandfather to see the work, and there she had stopped with him at the turner's shop to get a wooden bowl turned, and there she had been with Cynthy when she went to visit an acquaintance; and there never was a happier little girl than Fleda had been in those old times. All gone!—It was no use trying to help it; Fleda put her two hands to her face and cried at last a silent but not the less bitter leave-taking of the shadows of the past.

She forced herself into quiet again, resolved to look to the last. As they were going down the hill past the saw-mill Mr. Carleton noticed that her head was stretched out to look back at it, with an expression of face he could not withstand. He wheeled about immediately and went back and stood opposite to it. The mill was not working to-day. The saw was standing still, though there were plenty of huge trunks of trees lying about in all directions waiting to be cut up. There was a desolate look of the place. No one was there; the little brook, most of its waters cut off, did not go roaring and laughing down the hill, but trickled softly and plaintively over the stones. It seemed exceeding sad to Fleda.

"Thank you, Mr. Carleton," she said after a little earnest fond looking at her old haunt;—"you needn't stay any longer."

But as soon as they had crossed the little rude bridge at the foot of the hill they could see the poplar trees which skirted the courtyard fence before her grandfather's house. Poor Fleda's eyes could hardly serve her. She managed to keep them open till the horse had made a few steps more and she had caught the well-known face of the old house looking at her through the poplars. Her fortitude failed, and bowing her little head she wept so exceedingly that Mr. Carleton was fain to draw bridle and try to comfort her.

"My dear Elfie!—do not weep so," he said tenderly. "Is there anything you would like?—Can I do anything for you?"

He had to wait a little. He repeated his first query.

"O—it's no matter," said Fleda, striving to conquer her tears, which found their way again,—"if I only could have gone into the house once more!—but it's no matter—you needn't wait, Mr. Carleton—"

The horse however remained motionless.

"Do you think you would feel better, Elfie, if you had seen it again?"

"Oh yes!——But never mind, Mr. Carleton,—you may go on."

Mr. Carleton ordered his servant to open the gate, and rode up to the back of the house.

"I am afraid there is nobody here, Elfie," he said;—"the house seems all shut up."

"I know how I can get in," said Fleda,—"there's a window down stairs—I don't believe it is fastened,—if you wouldn't mind waiting, Mr. Carleton,—I won't keep you long?"

The child had dried her tears, and there was the eagerness of something like hope in her face. Mr. Carleton dismounted and took her off.

"I must find a way to get in too, Elfie,—I cannot let you go alone."

"O I can open the door when I get in," said Fleda.

"But you have not the key."

"There's no key—it's only bolted on the inside, that door. I can open it."

She found the window unfastened, as she had expected; Mr. Carleton held it open while she crawled in and then she undid the door for him. He more than half questioned the wisdom of his proceeding. The house had a dismal look; cold, empty, deserted,—it was a dreary reminder of Fleda's loss, and he feared the effect of it would be anything but good. He followed and watched her, as with an eager business step she went through the hall and up the stairs, putting her head into every room and giving an earnest wistful look all round it. Here and there she went in and stood a moment, where associations were more thick and strong; sometimes taking a look out of a particular window, and even opening a cupboard door, to give that same kind and sorrowful glance of recognition at the old often-resorted-to hiding-place of her own or her grandfather's treasures and trumpery. Those old corners seemed to touch Fleda more than all the rest; and she turned away from one of them with a face of such extreme sorrow that Mr. Carleton very much regretted he had brought her into the house. For her sake,—for his own, it was a curious show of character. Though tears were sometimes streaming, she made no delay and gave him no trouble; with the calm steadiness of a woman she went regularly through the house, leaving no place unvisited, but never obliging him to hasten her away. She said not a word during the whole time; her very crying was still; the light tread of her little feet was the only sound in the silent empty rooms; and the noise of their footsteps in the halls and of the opening and shutting doors echoed mournfully through the house.

She had left her grandfather's room for the last. Mr. Carleton did not follow her in there, guessing that she would rather be alone. But she did not come back, and he was forced to go to fetch her.

The chill desolateness of that room had been too much for poor little Fleda. The empty bedstead, the cold stove, the table bare of books, only one or two lay upon the old bible,—the forlorn order of the place that bespoke the master far away, the very sunbeams that stole in at the little windows and met now no answering look of gladness or gratitude,—it had struck the child's heart too heavily, and she was standing crying by the window. A second time in that room Mr. Carleton sat down and drew his little charge to his breast and spoke words of soothing and sympathy.

"I am very sorry I brought you here, dear Elfie," he said kindly. "It was too hard for you."

"O no!"—even through her tears Fleda said,—"she was very glad!"

"Hadn't we better try to overtake our friends?" he whispered after another pause.

She immediately, almost immediately, put away her tears, and with a quiet obedience that touched him went with him from the room; fastened the door and got out again at the little window.

"O Mr. Carleton!" she said with great earnestness when they had almost reached the horses, "won't you wait for me *one* minute more?—I just want a piece of the burning bush"—

Drawing her hand from him she rushed round to the front of the house. A little more slowly Mr. Carleton followed, and found her under the burning bush, tugging furiously at a branch beyond her strength to break off.

"That's too much for you, Elfie," said he, gently taking her hand from the tree,—"let my hand try."

She stood back and watched, tears running down her face, while he got a knife from his pocket and cut off the piece she had been trying for, nicely, and gave it to her. The first movement of Fleda's head was down, bent over the pretty spray of red berries; but by the time she stood at the horse's side she looked up at Mr. Carleton and thanked him with a face of more than thankfulness.

She was crying however, constantly, till they had gone several miles on their way again, and Mr. Carleton doubted he had done wrong. It passed away, and she had been sitting quite peacefully for some time, when he told her they were near the place where they were to stop and join their friends. She looked up most gratefully in his face.

"I am very much obliged to you, Mr. Carleton, for what you did!"

"I was afraid I had made a mistake, Elfie."

"Oh no you didn't."

"Do you think you feel any easier after it, Elfie?"

"Oh yes!—indeed I do," said she looking up again,—"thank you, Mr. Carleton."

A gentle kind pressure of his arm answered her thanks.

"I ought to be a good sprite to you, Mr. Carleton," Fleda said after musing a little while,—"you are so very good to me!"

Perhaps Mr. Carleton felt too much pleasure at this speech to make any answer, for he made none.

"It is only selfishness, Elfie," said he presently, looking down to the quiet sweet little face which seemed to him, and was, more pure than anything of earth's mould he had ever seen.—"You know I must take care of you for my own sake."

Fleda laughed a little.

"But what will you do when we get to Paris?"

"I don't know. I should like to have you always, Elfie."

"You'll have to get aunt Lucy to give me to you," said Fleda.

"Mr. Carleton," said she a few minutes after,—"is that story in a book?"

"What story?"

"About the lady and the little sprites that waited on her."

"Yes, it is in a book; you shall see it, Elfie.—Here we are!"

And here it was proposed to stay till the next day, lest Fleda might not be able to bear so much travelling at first. But the country inn was not found inviting; the dinner was bad and the rooms were worse; uninhabitable, the ladies said; and about the middle of the afternoon they began to cast about for the means of reaching Albany that night. None very comfortable could be had; however it was thought better to push on at any rate than wear out the night in such a place. The weather was very mild; the moon at the full.

"How is Fleda to go this afternoon?" said Mrs. Evelyn.

"She shall decide herself," said Mrs. Carleton. "How will you go, my sweet Fleda?"

Fleda was lying upon a sort of rude couch which had

been spread for her, where she had been sleeping incessantly ever since she arrived, the hour of dinner alone excepted. Mrs. Carleton repeated her question.

"I am afraid Mr. Carleton must be tired," said Fleda, without opening her eyes.

"That means that you are, don't it?" said Rossitur.

"No," said Fleda gently.

Mr. Carleton smiled and went out to press forward the arrangements. In spite of good words and good money there was some delay. It was rather late before the cavalcade left the inn; and a journey of several hours was before them. Mr. Carleton rode rather slowly too, for Fleda's sake, so the evening had fallen while they were yet a mile or two from the city.

His little charge had borne the fatigue well, thanks partly to his admirable care, and partly to her quiet pleasure in being with him. She had been so perfectly still for some distance that he thought she had dropped asleep. Looking down closer however to make sure about it he saw her thoughtful clear eyes most unsleepily fixed upon the sky.

"What are you gazing at, Elfie?"

The look of thought changed to a look of affection as the eyes were brought to bear upon him, and she answered with a smile,

"Nothing,—I was looking at the stars."

"What are you dreaming about?"

"I wasn't dreaming," said Fleda,—"I was thinking."

"Thinking of what?"

"O of pleasant things."

"Mayn't I know them?—I like to hear of pleasant things."

"I was thinking,—" said Fleda, looking up again at the stars, which shone with no purer ray than those grave eyes sent back to them,—"I was thinking—of being ready to die."

The words, and the calm thoughtful manner in which they were said, thrilled upon Mr. Carleton with a disagreeable shock.

"How came you to think of such a thing?" said he lightly.

"I don't know,"—said Fleda, still looking at the stars,—"I suppose—I was thinking—"

"What?" said Mr. Carleton, inexpressibly curious to get at the workings of the child's mind, which was not easy, for Fleda was never very forward to talk of herself;—"what were you thinking? I want to know how you could get such a thing into your head."

"It wasn't very strange," said Fleda. "The stars made me think of heaven, and grandpa's being there, and then I thought how he was ready to go there and that made him ready to die—"

"I wouldn't think of such things, Elfie," said Mr. Carleton after a few minutes.

"Why not, sir?" said Fleda quickly.

"I don't think they are good for you."

"But Mr. Carleton," said Fleda gently,—"if I don't think about it, how shall *I* ever be ready to die?"

"It is not fit for you," said he evading the question,—"it is not necessary now,—there's time enough. You are a little body and should have none but gay thoughts."

"But Mr. Carleton," said Fleda with timid earnestness,—"don't you think one could have gay thoughts better if one knew one was ready to die?"

"What makes a person ready to die, Elfie?" said her friend, disliking to ask the question, but yet more unable to answer hers, and curious to hear what she would say.

"O—to be a Christian," said Fleda.

"But I have seen Christians," said Mr. Carleton, "who were no more ready to die than other people."

"Then they were make-believe Christians," said Fleda decidedly.

"What makes you think so?" said her friend, carefully guarding his countenance from anything like a smile.

"Because," said Fleda, "grandpa was ready, and my father was ready, and my mother too; and I know it was because they were Christians."

"Perhaps your kind of Christians are different from my kind," said Mr. Carleton, carrying on the conversation half in spite of himself. "What do you mean by a Christian, Elfie?"

"Why, what the Bible means," said Fleda, looking at him with innocent earnestness.

Mr. Carleton was ashamed to tell her he did not know what that was, or he was unwilling to say what he felt would trouble the happy confidence she had in him. He was silent; but as they rode on, a bitter wish crossed his mind that he could have the simple purity of the little child in his arms; and he thought he would give his broad acres, supposing it possible that religion could be true,—in exchange for that free happy spirit that looks up to all its possessions in heaven.

CHAPTER XI.

Starres are poore books and oftentimes do misse;
This book of starres lights to eternall blisse.
GEORGE HERBERT.

THE voyage across the Atlantic was not, in itself, at all notable. The first half of the passage was extremely unquiet, and most of the passengers uncomfortable to match. Then the weather cleared; and the rest of the way, though lengthened out a good deal by the tricks of the wind, was very fair and pleasant.

Fifteen days of tossing and sea-sickness had brought little Fleda to look like the ghost of herself. So soon as the weather changed and sky and sea were looking gentle again, Mr. Carleton had a mattress and cushions laid in a sheltered corner of the deck for her, and carried her up. She had hardly any more strength than a baby.

"What are you looking at me so for, Mr. Carleton?" said she, a little while after he had carried her up, with a sweet serious smile that seemed to know the answer to her question.

He stooped down and clasped her little thin hand, as reverentially as if she really had not belonged to the earth.

"You are more like a sprite than I like to see you just now," said he, unconsciously fastening the child's heart to himself with the magnetism of those deep eyes.—"I must get some of the sailors' salt beef and sea-biscuit for you—they say that is the best thing to make people well."

"O I feel better already," said Fleda, and settling her little face upon the cushion and closing her eyes, she added,—"thank you, Mr. Carleton!"

The fresh air began to restore her immediately; she was

no more sick; her appetite came back; and from that time, without the help of beef and sea-biscuit, she mended rapidly. Mr. Carleton proved himself as good a nurse on the sea as on land. She seemed to be never far from his thoughts. He was constantly finding out something that would do her good or please her; and Fleda could not discover that he took any trouble about it; she could not feel that she was a burden to him; the things seemed to come as a matter of course. Mrs. Carleton was not wanting in any shew of kindness or care, and yet, when Fleda looked back upon the day, it somehow was Guy that had done everything for her; she thought little of thanking anybody but him.

There were other passengers that petted her a great deal, or would have done so, if Fleda's very timid retiring nature had not stood in the way. She was never bashful, nor awkward; but yet it was only a very peculiar, sympathetic, style of address that could get within the wall of reserve which in general hid her from other people. Hid, what it could; for through that reserve a singular modesty, sweetness, and gracefulness of spirit would shew themselves. But there was much more behind. There were no eyes however on board that did not look kindly on little Fleda, excepting only two pair. The Captain shewed her a great deal of flattering attention, and said she was a pattern of a passenger; even the sailors noticed and spoke of her and let slip no occasion of shewing the respect and interest she had raised. But there were two pair of eyes, and one of them Fleda thought most remarkably ugly, that were an exception to the rest; these belonged to her cousin Rossitur and Lieut. Thorn. Rossitur had never forgiven her remarks upon his character as a gentleman and declared preference of Mr. Carleton in that capacity; and Thorn was mortified at the invincible childish reserve which she opposed to all his advances; and both, absurd as it seems, were jealous of the young Englishman's advantage over them. Both not the less, because their sole reason for making her a person of consequence was that he had thought fit to do so. Fleda would permit neither of them to do anything for her that she could help.

They took their revenge in raillery, which was not always

good-natured. Mr. Carleton never answered it in any other way than by his look of cold disdain,—not always by that; little Fleda could not be quite so unmoved. Many a time her nice sense of delicacy confessed itself hurt, by the deep and abiding colour her cheeks would wear after one of their ill-mannered flings at her. She bore them with a grave dignity peculiar to herself, but the same nice delicacy forbade her to mention the subject to any one; and the young gentlemen contrived to give the little child in the course of the voyage a good deal of pain. She shunned them at last as she would the plague. As to the rest Fleda liked her life on board ship amazingly. In her quiet way she took all the good that offered and seemed not to recognise the ill.

Mr. Carleton had bought for her a copy of The Rape of the Lock, and Bryant's poems. With these, sitting or lying among her cushions, Fleda amused herself a great deal; and it was an especial pleasure when he would sit down by her and read and talk about them. Still a greater was to watch the sea, in its changes of colour and varieties of agitation, and to get from Mr. Carleton, bit by bit, all the pieces of knowledge concerning it that he had ever made his own. Even when Fleda feared it she was fascinated; and while the fear went off the fascination grew deeper. Daintily nestling among her cushions she watched with charmed eyes the long rollers that came up in detachments of three to attack the good ship, that like a slandered character rode patiently over them; or the crested green billows, or sometimes the little rippling waves that shewed old Ocean's placidest face; while with ears as charmed as if he had been delivering a fairy tale she listened to all Mr. Carleton could tell her of the green water where the whales feed, or the blue water where Neptune sits in his own solitude, the furthest from land, and the pavement under his feet outdoes the very canopy overhead in its deep colouring; of the transparent seas where the curious mysterious marine plants and animals may be clearly seen many feet down, and in the North where hundreds of feet of depth do not hide the bottom; of the icebergs; and whirling great fields of ice, between which if a ship get she had as good be an almond in a pair of strong nut-crackers. How the water grows colder and murkier as it is nearer the shore; how the mountain waves are piled together; and how old Ocean, like a wise man, however roughened and tumbled outwardly by the currents of Life, is always calm at heart. Of the signs of the weather; the out-riders of the winds, and the use the seaman makes of the tidings they bring; and before Mr. Carleton knew where he was he found himself deep in the science of navigation, and making a star-gazer of little Fleda. Sometimes kneeling beside him as he sat on her mattress, with her hand leaning on his shoulder, Fleda asked, listened, and looked; as engaged, as rapt, as interested, as another child would be in Robinson Crusoe, gravely drinking in knowledge with a fresh healthy taste for it that never had enough. Mr. Carleton was about as amused and as interested as she. There is a second taste of knowledge that some minds get in imparting it, almost as sweet as the first relish. At any rate Fleda never felt that she had any reason to fear tiring him; and his mother complaining of his want of sociableness said she believed Guy did not like to talk to anybody but that little pet of his and one or two of the old sailors. If left to her own resources Fleda was never at a loss; she amused herself with her books, or watching the sailors, or watching the sea, or with some fanciful manufacture she had learned from one of the ladies on board, or with what the company about her were saying and doing.

One evening she had been some time alone, looking out upon the restless little waves that were tossing and tumbling in every direction. She had been afraid of them at first and they were still rather fearful to her imagination. This evening as her musing eye watched them rise and fall her childish fancy likened them to the up-springing chances of life,—uncertain, unstable, alike too much for her skill and her strength to manage. She was not more helpless before the attacks of the one than of the other. But then —that calm blue Heaven that hung over the sea. It was like the heaven of power and love above her destinies; only this was far higher and more pure and abiding. "He knoweth them that trust in him." "There shall not a hair of your head perish."

Not these words perhaps, but something like the sense of them was in little Fleda's head. Mr. Carleton coming up saw her gazing out upon the water with an eye that seemed to see nothing.

"Elfie!—Are you looking into futurity!"

"No,—yes—not exactly," said Fleda smiling.

"No, yes, and not exactly!" said he throwing himself down beside her.—"What does all that mean?"

"I wasn't exactly looking into futurity," said Fleda.

"What then?—Don't tell me you were 'thinking;' I know that already. What?"

Fleda was always rather shy of opening her cabinet of thoughts. She glanced at him, and hesitated, and then yielded to a fascination of eye and smile that rarely failed of its end. Looking off to the sea again as if she had left her thoughts there, she said,

"I was only thinking of that beautiful hymn of Mr Newton's."

"What hymn?"

"That long one, 'The Lord will provide.'"

"Do you know it?—Tell it to me, Elfie—let us see whether I shall think it beautiful."

Fleda knew the whole and repeated it.

"Though troubles assail,
 And dangers affright,
Though friends should all fail,
 And foes all unite;
Yet one thing secures us
 Whatever betide,
The Scripture assures us
 'The Lord will provide.'

"The birds without barn
 Or storehouse are fed;
From them let us learn
 To trust for our bread.
His saints what is fitting
 Shall ne'er be denied,
So long as 'tis written,
 'The Lord will provide.'

"His call we obey,
 Like Abraham of old,
Not knowing our way,
 But faith makes us bold.
And though we are strangers
 We have a good guide,
And trust in all dangers
 'The Lord will provide.'

"We may like the ships
In tempests be tossed
On perilous deeps,
But cannot be lost.
Though Satan enrages
The wind and the tide,
The promise engages
'The Lord will provide.'

"When Satan appears
To stop up our path,
And fills us with fears,
We triumph by faith.
He cannot take from us,
Though oft he has tried,
This heart-cheering promise,
'The Lord will provide.'

"He tells us we're weak,
Our hope is in vain,
The good that we seek
We ne'er shall obtain;
But when such suggestions
Our spirits have tried,
This answers all questions,
'The Lord will provide.'

"No strength of our own,
Or goodness we claim;
But since we have known
The Saviour's great name,
In this, our strong tower,
For safety we hide;
The Lord is our power!
'The Lord will provide!'

"When life sinks apace,
And death is in view,
This word of his grace
Shall comfort us through.
No fearing nor doubting,
With Christ on our side,
We hope to die shouting
'The Lord will provide!'"

Guy listened very attentively to the whole. He was very far from understanding the meaning of several of the verses, but the bounding expression of confidence and hope he did understand, and did feel.

"Happy to be so deluded!" he thought.—"I almost wish I could share the delusion!"

He was gloomily silent when she had done, and little Fleda's eyes were so full that it was a little while before she could look towards him and ask in her gentle way, "Do you like it, Mr. Carleton?"

She was gratified by his grave, "yes!"

"But Elfie," said he smiling again, "you have not told me your thoughts yet. What had these verses to do with the sea you were looking at so hard?"

"Nothing—I was thinking,"said Fleda slowly,—"that the sea seemed something like the world,—I don't mean it was like, but it made me think of it;—and I thought how pleasant it is to know that God takes care of his people."

"Don't he take care of everybody?"

"Yes—in one sort of way," said Fleda; "but then it is only his children that he has promised to keep from everything that will hurt them."

"I don't see how that promise is kept, Elfie. I think those who call themselves so meet with as many troubles as the rest of the world, and perhaps more."

"Yes," said Fleda quickly, "they have troubles, but then God won't let the troubles do them any harm."

A subtle evasion, thought Mr. Carleton.—"Where did you learn that, Elfie?"

"The Bible says so," said Fleda.

"Well, how do you know it from that?" said Mr. Carleton, impelled, he hardly knew whether by his bad or his good angel, to carry on the conversation.

"Why," said Fleda, looking as if it were a very simple question and Mr. Carleton were catechising her,—"you know, Mr. Carleton, the Bible was written by men who were taught by God exactly what to say, so there could be nothing in it that is not true."

"How do you know those men were so taught?"

"The Bible says so."

A child's answer!—but with a child's wisdom in it, not learnt of the schools. "He that is of God heareth God's words." To little Fleda, as to every simple and humble intelligence, the Bible proved itself; she had no need to go further.

Mr. Carleton did not smile, for nothing would have tempted him to hurt her feelings; but he said, though conscience did not let him do it without a twinge,

"But don't you know, Elfie, there are some people who do not believe the Bible?"

"Ah but those are bad people," replied Fleda quickly; —"all good people believe it."

A child's reason again, but hitting the mark this time. Unconsciously, little Fleda had brought forward a strong argument for her cause. Mr. Carleton felt it, and rising up that he might not be obliged to say anything more, he began to pace slowly up and down the deck, turning the matter over.

Was it so? that there were hardly any good men (he thought there might be a few) who did not believe in the Bible and uphold its authority? and that all the worst portion of society was comprehended in the other class?—and if so how had he overlooked it? He had reasoned most unphilosophically from a few solitary instances that had come under his own eye; but applying the broad principle of induction it could not be doubted that the Bible was on the side of all that is sound, healthful, and hopeful, in this disordered world. And whatever might be the character of a few exceptions, it was not supposable that a wide system of hypocrisy should tell universally for the best interests of mankind. Summoning history to produce her witnesses, as he went on with his walk up and down, he saw with increasing interest, what he had never seen before, that the Bible had come like the breath of spring upon the moral waste of mind; that the ice-bound intellect and cold heart of the world had waked into life under its kindly influence and that all the rich growth of the one and the other had come forth at its bidding. And except in that sun-lightened tract, the world was and had been a waste indeed. Doubtless in that waste, intellect had at different times put forth sundry barren shoots, such as a vigorous plant can make in the absence of the sun, but also like them immature, unsound, and groping vainly after the light in which alone they could expand and perfect themselves; ripening no seed for a future and richer growth. And flowers the wilderness had none. The affections were stunted and overgrown.

All this was so,—how had he overlooked it? His unbelief had come from a thoughtless, ignorant, one-sided view of life and human things. The disorder and ruin which he saw, where he did not also see the adjusting hand at work, had led him to refuse his credit to the Supreme Fabricator. He thought the waste would never be reclaimed, and did not know how much it already owed to the sun of revelation; but what was the waste where that light had not been! —Mr. Carleton was staggered. He did not know what to think. He began to think he had been a fool.

Poor little Fleda was meditating less agreeably the while. With the sure tact of truth she had discerned that there was more than jest in the questions that had been put to her. She almost feared that Mr. Carleton shared himself the doubts he had so lightly spoken of, and the thought gave her great distress. However, when he came to take her down to tea, with all his usual manner, Fleda's earnest look at him ended in the conviction that there was nothing very wrong under that face.

For several days Mr. Carleton pondered the matter of this evening's conversation, characteristically restless till he had made up his mind. He wished very much to draw Fleda to speak further upon the subject, but it was not easy; she never led to it. He sought in vain an opportunity to bring it in easily, and at last resolved to make one.

"Elfie," said he one morning when all the rest of the passengers were happily engaged at a distance with the letter-bags,—"I wish you would let me hear that favourite hymn of yours again,—I like it very much."

Fleda was much gratified and immediately with great satisfaction repeated the hymn. Its peculiar beauty struck him yet more the second time than the first.

"Do you understand those two last verses?" said he when she had done.

Fleda said "yes!" rather surprised.

"I do not," he said gravely.

Fleda paused a minute or two, and then finding that it depended on her to enlighten him, said in her modest way,

"Why it means that we have no goodness of our own, and only expect to be forgiven and taken to heaven for the Saviour's sake."

Mr. Carleton asked, "How *for his sake?*"

"Why you know Mr. Carleton, we don't deserve to go there, and if we are forgiven at all it must be for what he has done."

"And what is that, Elfie?"

"He died for us," said Fleda, with a look of some anxiety into Mr. Carleton's face.

"Died for us!—And what end was that to serve, Elfie?" said he, partly willing to hear the full statement of the matter, and partly willing to see how far her intelligence could give it.

"Because we are sinners," said Fleda, "and God has said that sinners shall die."

"Then how can he keep his word and forgive at all?'

"Because Christ has died *for us*," said Fleda eagerly;—"instead of us."

"Do you understand the justice of letting one take the place of others?"

"He was willing, Mr. Carleton," said Fleda, with a singular wistful expression that touched him.

"Still Elfie," said he after a minute's silence,—"how could the ends of justice be answered by the death of one man in the place of millions?"

"No, Mr. Carleton, but he was God as well as man," Fleda said, with a sparkle in her eye which perhaps delayed her companion's rejoinder.

"What should induce him, Elfie," he said gently, "to do such a thing for people who had displeased him?"

"Because he loved us, Mr. Carleton."

She answered with so evident a strong and clear appreciation of what she was saying that it half made its way into Mr. Carleton's mind by the force of sheer sympathy. Her words came almost as something new.

Certainly Mr. Carleton had heard these things before, though perhaps never in a way that appealed so directly to his intelligence and his candour. He was again silent an instant, pondering, and so was Fleda.

"Do you know, Elfie," said Mr. Carleton, "there are some people who do not believe that the Saviour was anything more than a man?"

"Yes I know it," said Fleda;—"it is very strange!"

"Why is it strange?"

"Because the Bible says it so plainly."

"But those people hold I believe that the Bible does not say it."

"I don't see how they could have read the Bible," said Fleda. "Why he said so himself."

"Who said so?"

"Jesus Christ. Don't *you* believe it, Mr. Carleton?"

She saw he did not, and the shade that had come over her face was reflected in his before he said "no."

"But perhaps I shall believe it yet, Elfie," he said kindly. "Can you shew me the place in your bible where Jesus says this of himself?"

Fleda looked in despair. She hastily turned over the leaves of her bible to find the passages he had asked for, and Mr. Carleton was cut to the heart to see that she twice was obliged to turn her face from him and brush her hand over her eyes, before she could find them. She turned to Matt. xxvi. 63, 64, 65, and without speaking gave him the book, pointing to the passage. He read it with great care, and several times over.

"You are right, Elfie," he said. "I do not see how those who honour the authority of the Bible and the character of Jesus Christ can deny the truth of his own declaration. If that is false so must those be."

Fleda took the bible and hurriedly sought out another passage.

"Grandpa shewed me these places," she said, "once when we were talking about Mr. Didenhover—*he* didn't believe that. There are a great many other places, grandpa said; but one is enough;"—

She gave him the latter part of the twentieth chapter of John.—

"You see, Mr. Carleton, he let Thomas fall down and worship him and call him God; and if he had *not* been, you know——God is more displeased with that than with anything."

"With what, Elfie?"

"With men's worshipping any other than himself. He says he 'will not give his glory to another.'"

"Where is that?"

"I am afraid I can't find it," said Fleda,—"it is somewhere in Isaiah, I know"—

She tried in vain; and failing, then looked up in Mr. Carleton's face to see what impression had been made.

"You see Thomas believed when he *saw*," said he, answering her;—"I will believe too when I see."

"Ah if you wait for that—" said Fleda.

Her voice suddenly checked she bent her face down again to her little bible, and there was a moment's struggle with herself.

"Are you looking for something more to shew me?" said Mr. Carleton kindly, stooping his face down to hers.

"Not much," said Fleda hurriedly; and then making a great effort she raised her head and gave him the book again.

"Look here, Mr. Carleton,—Jesus said, 'Blessed are they that have *not* seen and yet have believed.'"

Mr. Carleton was profoundly struck, and the thought recurred to him afterwards and was dwelt upon. "Blessed are they that have *not* seen, and yet have believed." It was strange at first, and then he wondered that it should ever have been so. His was a mind peculiarly open to conviction, peculiarly accessible to truth; and his attention being called to it he saw faintly now what he had never seen before, the beauty of the principle of *faith;*—how natural, how reasonable, how *necessary*, how honourable to the Supreme Being, how happy even for man, that the grounds of his trust in God being established, his acceptance of many other things should rest on that trust alone.

Mr. Carleton now became more reserved and unsociable than ever. He wearied himself with thinking. If he could have got at the books, he would have spent his days and nights in studying the evidences of Christianity; but the ship was bare of any such books, and he never thought of turning to the most obvious of all, the Bible itself. His unbelief was shaken; it was within an ace of falling in pieces to the very foundation; or rather he began to suspect how foundationless it had been. It came at last to one point with him;—If there were a God, he would not have left the world without a revelation,—no more would he have suffered that revelation to defeat its own end by becoming corrupted or alloyed; if there was such a revelation it could be no other than the Bible;—and his acceptance of the whole scheme of Christianity now hung upon the turn of a hair. Yet he could not resolve himself. He balanced the counter doubts and arguments, on one side and on the other, and strained his mind to the task;—he could not weigh them nicely enough. He was in a maze; and seeking to clear and calm his judgment that he might see the way out, it was in vain that he tried to shake his dizzied head from the effect of the turns it had made. By dint of anxiety to find the right path reason had lost herself in the wilderness.

Fleda was not, as Mr. Carleton had feared she would be, at all alienated from him by the discovery that had given her so much pain. It wrought in another way, rather to add a touch of tender and anxious interest to the affection she had for him. It gave her however much more pain than he thought. If he had seen the secret tears that fell on his account he would have been grieved; and if he had known of the many petitions that little heart made for him—he could hardly have loved her more than he did.

One evening Mr. Carleton had been a long while pacing up and down the deck in front of little Fleda's nest, thinking and thinking, without coming to any end. It was a most fair evening, near sunset, the sky without a cloud except two or three little dainty strips which set off its blue. The ocean was very quiet, only broken into cheerful mites of waves that seemed to have nothing to do but sparkle. The sun's rays were almost level now, and a long path of glory across the sea led off towards his sinking disk. Fleda sat watching and enjoying it all in her happy fashion, which always made the most of everything good, and was especially quick in catching any form of natural beauty.

Mr. Carleton's thoughts were elsewhere; too busy to take note of things around him. Fleda looked now and then as he passed at his gloomy brow, wondering what he was thinking of, and wishing that he could have the same reason to be happy that she had. In one of his turns his eye met her gentle glance; and vexed and bewildered as he was with study there was something in that calm bright face that impelled him irresistibly to ask the little child to set the proud scholar right. Placing himself beside her, he said,

"Elfie, how do you know there is a God?—what reason have you for thinking so, out of the Bible?"

It was a strange look little Fleda gave him. He felt it at the time, and he never forgot it. Such a look of reproach, sorrow, and *pity*, he afterwards thought, as an angel's face might have worn. The *question* did not seem to occupy her a moment. After this answering look she suddenly pointed to the sinking sun and said,

"Who made that, Mr. Carleton?"

Mr. Carleton's eyes, following the direction of hers, met the long bright rays whose still witness-bearing was almost too powerful to be borne. The sun was just dipping majestically into the sea, and its calm self-assertion seemed to him at that instant hardly stronger than its vindication of its Author.

A slight arrow may find the joint in the armour before which many weightier shafts have fallen powerless. Mr. Carleton was an unbeliever no more from that time.

CHAPTER XII.

He borrowed a box of the ear of the Englishman, and swore he would pay him again when he was able.—MERCHANT OF VENICE.

ONE other incident alone in the course of the voyage deserves to be mentioned; both because it served to bring out the characters of several people, and because it was not,—what is?—without its lingering consequences.

Thorn and Rossitur had kept up indefatigably the game of teasing Fleda about her "English admirer," as they sometime styled him. Poor Fleda grew more and more sore on the subject. She thought it was very strange that two grown men could not find enough to do to amuse themselves without making sport of the comfort of a little child. She wondered they could take pleasure in what gave her so much pain; but so it was; and they had it up so often that at last others caught it from them; and though not in malevolence yet in thoughtless folly many a light remark was made and question asked of her that set little Fleda's sensitive nerves a quivering. She was only too happy that they were never said before Mr. Carleton; that would have been a thousand times worse. As it was, her gentle nature was constantly suffering from the pain or the fear of these attacks.

"Where's Mr. Carleton?" said her cousin coming up one day.

"I don't know," said Fleda,—"I don't know but he is gone up into one of the tops."

"Your humble servant leaves you to yourself a great while this morning, it seems to me. He is growing very inattentive."

"I wouldn't permit it, Miss Fleda, if I were you," said

Thorn maliciously. "You let him have his own way too much.'"

"I wish you wouldn't talk so, cousin Charlton!" said Fleda.

"But seriously," said Charlton, "I think you had better call him to account. He is very suspicious lately. I have observed him walking by himself and looking very glum indeed. I am afraid he has taken some fancy into his head that would not suit you. I advise you to enquire into it."

"I wouldn't give myself any concern about it!" said Thorn lightly, enjoying the child's confusion and his own fanciful style of backbiting,—"I'd let him go if he has a mind to, Miss Fleda. He's no such great catch. He's neither lord nor knight—nothing in the world but a private gentleman, with plenty of money I dare say, but you don't care for that;—and there's as good fish in the sea as ever came out of it. I don't think much of him!"

He is wonderfully better than *you*, thought Fleda as she looked in the young gentleman's face for a second, but she said nothing.

"Why Fleda," said Charlton laughing, "it wouldn't be a killing affair, would it? How has this English admirer of yours got so far in your fancy?—praising your pretty eyes, eh?—Eh?" he repeated, as Fleda kept a dignified silence.

"No," said Fleda in displeasure,—"he never says such things."

"No?" said Charlton. "What then? What does he say? I wouldn't let him make a fool of me if I were you. Fleda!—did he ever ask you for a kiss?"

"No!" exclaimed Fleda half beside herself and bursting into tears;—"I wish you wouldn't talk so! How can you!"

They had carried the game pretty far that time, and thought best to leave it. Fleda stopped crying as soon as she could, lest somebody should see her; and was sitting quietly again, alone as before, when one of the sailors whom she had never spoken to came by, and leaning over towards her with a leer as he passed, said,

"Is this the young English gentleman's little sweetheart?"

Poor Fleda! She had got more than she could bear. She jumped up and ran down into the cabin; and in her berth Mrs. Carleton found her some time afterwards, quietly crying, and most sorry to be discovered. She was exceeding unwilling to tell what had troubled her. Mrs. Carleton, really distressed, tried coaxing, soothing, reasoning, promising, in a way the most gentle and kind that she could use.

"Oh it's nothing—it's nothing," Fleda said at last eagerly,—"it's because I am foolish—it's only something they said to me."

"Who, love?"

Again was Fleda most unwilling to answer, and it was after repeated urging that she at last said,

"Cousin Charlton and Mr. Thorn."

"Charlton and Mr. Thorn!—What did they say? What did they say, darling Fleda?"

"O it's only that they tease me," said Fleda, trying hard to put an end to the tears which caused all this questioning, and to speak as if they were about a trifle. But Mrs. Carleton persisted.

"What do they say to tease you, love? what is it about? —Guy, come in here and help me to find out what is the matter with Fleda."

Fleda hid her face in Mrs. Carleton's neck, resolved to keep her lips sealed. Mr. Carleton came in, but to her great relief his question was directed not to her but his mother.

"Fleda has been annoyed by something those young men, her cousin and Mr. Thorn, have said to her;—they tease her, she says, and she will not tell me what it is."

Mr. Carleton did not ask, and he presently left the stateroom.

"O I am afraid he will speak to them!" exclaimed Fleda as soon as he was gone.—"O I oughtn't to have said that!"—

Mrs. Carleton tried to soothe her and asked what she was afraid of. But Fleda would not say any more. Her anxious fear that she had done mischief helped to dry her tears, and she sorrowfully resolved she would keep her griefs to herself next time.

Rossitur and Thorn were in company with a brother officer and friend of the latter when Mr. Carleton approached them.

"Mr. Rossitur and Mr. Thorn," said he, "you have indulged yourselves in a style of conversation extremely displeasing to the little girl under my mother's care. You will oblige me by abandoning it for the future."

There was certainly in Mr. Carleton's manner a sufficient degree of the cold haughtiness with which he usually expressed displeasure; though his words gave no other cause of offence. Thorn retorted rather insolently.

"I shall oblige myself in the matter, and do as I think proper."

"I have a right to speak as I please to my own cousin," said Rossitur sulkily,—"without asking anybody's leave. I don't see what you have to do with it."

"Simply that she is under my protection and that I will not permit her to be annoyed."

"I don't see how she is under your protection," said Rossitur.

"And I do not see how the potency of it will avail in this case," said his companion.

"Neither position is to be made out in words," said Mr. Carleton calmly. "You see that I desire there be no repetition of the offence. The rest I will endeavour to make clear if I am compelled to it."

"Stop sir!" said Thorn, as the young Englishman was turning away, adding with an oath,—"I won't bear this! You shall answer this to me, sir!"

"Easily," said the other.

"And me too," said Rossitur. "You have an account to settle with me, Carleton."

"I will answer what you please," said Carleton carelessly, —"and as soon as we get to land,—provided you do not in the mean time induce me to refuse you the honour."

However incensed, the young men endeavoured to carry it off with the same coolness that their adversary shewed. No more words passed. But Mrs. Carleton, possibly quickened by Fleda's fears, was not satisfied with the carriage of all parties, and resolved to sound her son, happy in knowing that nothing but truth was to be had from him.

She found an opportunity that very afternoon when he was sitting alone on the deck. The neighbourhood of little Fleda she hardly noticed. Fleda was curled up among her cushions, luxuriously bending over a little old black bible which was very often in her hand at times when she was quiet and had no observation to fear.

"Reading!—always reading?" said Mrs. Carleton, as she came up and took a place by her son.

"By no means!" he said, closing his book with a smile;—"not enough to tire any one's eyes on this voyage, mother."

"I wish you liked intercourse with living society," said Mrs. Carleton, leaning her arm on his shoulder and looking at him rather wistfully.

"You need not wish that,—when it suits me," he answered.

"But none suits you. Is there any on board?"

"A small proportion," he said, with the slight play of feature which always effected a diversion of his mother's thoughts, no matter in what channel they had been flowing.

"But those young men," she said, returning to the charge,—"you hold yourself very much aloof from them?"

He did not answer, even by a look, but to his mother the perfectly quiet composure of his face was sufficiently expressive.

"I know what you think; but Guy, you always had the same opinion of them?"

"I have never shewn any other."

"Guy," she said speaking low and rather anxiously,—"have you got into trouble with those young men?"

"*I* am in no trouble, mother," he answered somewhat haughtily;—"I cannot speak for them."

Mrs. Carleton waited a moment.

"You have done something to displease them, have you not?"

"They have displeased me, which is somewhat more to the purpose."

"But their folly is nothing to you?"

"No,—not their folly."

"Guy," said his mother, again pausing a minute, and pressing her hand more heavily upon his shoulder, "you will not suffer this to alter the friendly terms you have been on?—whatever it be,—let it pass."

"Certainly—if they choose to apologize and behave themselves."

"What, about Fleda?"

"Yes."

"I have no idea they meant to trouble her—I suppose they did not at all know what they were doing,—thoughtless nonsense,—and they could have had no design to offend you. Promise me that you will not take any further notice of this!"

He shook off her beseeching hand as he rose up, and answered haughtily, and not without something like an oath, that he *would*.

Mrs. Carleton knew him better than to press the matter any further; and her fondness easily forgave the offence against herself, especially as her son almost immediately resumed his ordinary manner.

It had well nigh passed from the minds of both parties, when in the middle of the next day Mr. Carleton asked what had become of Fleda?—he had not seen her except at the breakfast table. Mrs. Carleton said she was not well.

"What's the matter?"

"She complained of some headache—I think she made herself sick yesterday—she was crying all the afternoon, and I could not get her to tell me what for. I tried every means I could think of, but she would not give me the least clue—she said 'no' to everything I guessed—I can't bear to see her do so—it makes it all the worse she does it so quietly—it was only by a mere chance I found she was crying at all, but I think she cried herself ill before she stopped. She could not eat a mouthful of breakfast."

Mr. Carleton said nothing and with a changed countenance went directly down to the cabin. The stewardess, whom he sent in to see how she was, brought back word that Fleda was not asleep but was too ill to speak to her. Mr. Carleton went immediately into the little crib of a state-room. There he found his little charge, sitting bolt upright, her feet on the rung of a chair and her hands grasping the top to support herself. Her eyes were closed, her face without a particle of colour, except the dark shade round the eyes which bespoke illness and pain. She made no attempt to answer his shocked questions and words of tender concern, not even by the raising of an eyelid, and he saw that the intensity of pain at the moment was such as to render breathing itself difficult. He sent off the stewardess with all despatch after iced water and vinegar and brandy, and himself went on an earnest quest of restoratives among the lady passengers in the cabin, which resulted in sundry supplies of salts and cologne; and also offers of service, in greater plenty still, which he all refused. Most tenderly and judiciously he himself applied various remedies to the suffering child, who could not direct him otherwise than by gently putting away the things which she felt would not avail her. Several were in vain. But there was one bottle of strong aromatic vinegar which was destined to immortalize its owner in Fleda's remembrance. Before she had taken three whiffs of it her colour changed. Mr. Carleton watched the effect of a few whiffs more, and then bade the stewardess take away all the other things and bring him a cup of fresh strong coffee. By the time it came Fleda was ready for it, and by the time Mr. Carleton had administered the coffee he saw it would do to throw his mother's shawl round her and carry her up on deck, which he did without asking any questions. All this while Fleda had not spoken a word, except once when he asked her if she felt better. But she had given him, on finishing the coffee, a full look and half smile of such pure affectionate gratitude that the young gentleman's tongue was tied for some time after.

With happy skill, when he had safely bestowed Fleda among her cushions on deck, Mr. Carleton managed to keep off the crowd of busy inquirers after her well-doing and even presently to turn his mother's attention another way, leaving Fleda to enjoy all the comfort of quiet and fresh air at once. He himself, seeming occupied with other things, did no more but keep watch over her, till he saw that she was able to bear conversation again. Then he seated himself beside her and said softly,

"Elfie,—what were you crying about all yesterday afternoon?"

Fleda changed colour, for soft and gentle as the tone was she heard in it a determination to have the answer; and looking up beseechingly into his face she saw in the steady full blue eye that it was a determination she could not escape from. Her answer was an imploring request that he would not ask her. But taking one of her little hands and carrying it to his lips, he in the same tone repeated his question. Fleda snatched away her hand and burst into very frank tears; Mr. Carleton was silent, but she knew through his silence that he was only quietly waiting for her to answer him.

"I wish you wouldn't ask me sir," said poor Fleda, who still could not turn her face to meet his eye;—"It was only something that happened yesterday."

"What was it, Elfie?—You need not be afraid to tell me."

"It was only—what you said to Mrs. Carleton yesterday,—when she was talking—"

"About my difficulty with those gentlemen?"

"Yes," said Fleda, with a new gush of tears, as if her grief stirred afresh at the thought.

Mr. Carleton was silent a moment; and when he spoke there was no displeasure and more tenderness than usual in his voice.

"What troubled you in that, Elfie? tell me the whole."

"I was sorry, because,—it wasn't right," said Fleda, with a grave truthfulness which yet lacked none of her universal gentleness and modesty.

"What wasn't right?"

"To speak—I am afraid you won't like me to say it, Mr. Carleton."

"I will Elfie,—for I ask you."

"To speak to Mrs. Carleton so, and besides,—you know what you said, Mr. Carleton—"

"It was *not* right," said he after a minute,—"and I very seldom use such an expression, but you know one cannot always be on one's guard, Elfie?"

"But," said Fleda with gentle persistence, "one can always do what is right."

The deuce one can!—thought Mr. Carleton to himself.

"Elfie,—was this all that troubled you?—that I had said what was not right?"

"It wasn't quite that only," said Fleda hesitating,—

"What else?"

She stooped her face from his sight and he could but just understand her words.

"I was disappointed—"

"What, in me!"

Her tears gave the answer; she could add to them nothing but an assenting nod of her head.

They would have flowed in double measure if she had guessed the pain she had given. Her questioner heard her with a keen pang which did not leave him for days. There was some hurt pride in it, though other and more generous feelings had a far larger share. He, who had been admired, lauded, followed, cited, and envied, by all ranks of his countrymen, and countrywomen;—in whom nobody found a fault that could be dwelt upon amid the lustre of his perfections and advantages;—one of the first young men in England, thought so by himself as well as by others;—this little pure being had been *disappointed* in him. He could not get over it. He reckoned the one judgment worth all the others. Those whose direct or indirect flatteries had been poured at his feet were the proud, the worldly, the ambitious, the interested, the corrupted;—their praise was given to what they esteemed, and that, his candour said, was the least estimable part of him. Beneath all that, this truth-loving, truth-discerning little spirit had found enough to weep for. She was right and they were wrong. The sense of this was so keen upon him that it was ten or fifteen minutes befere he could recover himself to speak to his little reprover. He paced up and down the deck, while Fleda wept more and more from the fear of having offended or grieved him. But she was soon reassured on the former point. She was just wiping away her tears, with the quiet expression of patience her face often wore, when Mr. Carleton sat down beside her and took one of her hands.

"Elfie," said he,—"I promise you I will never say such a thing again."

He might well call her his good angel, for it was an angelic look the child gave him. So purely humble, grateful, glad,—so rosy with joyful hope,—the eyes were absolutely sparkling through tears. But when she saw that his were not dry, her own overflowed. She clasped her other hand to his hand and bending down her face affectionately upon it, she wept,—if ever angels weep,—such tears as they.

"Elfie," said Mr. Carleton, as soon as he could,—"I want you to go down stairs with me; so dry those eyes, or my mother will be asking all sorts of difficult questions."

Happiness is a quick restorative. Elfie was soon ready to go where he would.

They found Mrs. Carleton fortunately wrapped up in a new novel, some distance apart from the other persons in the cabin. The novel was immediately laid aside to take Fleda on her lap and praise Guy's nursing.

"But she looks more like a wax figure yet than anything else, don't she, Guy?"

"Not like any that ever I saw," said Mr. Carleton gravely. "Hardly substantial enough. Mother I have come to tell you I am ashamed of myself for having given you such cause of offence yesterday."

Mrs. Carleton's quick look, as she laid her hand on her son's arm, said sufficiently well that she would have excused him from making any apology rather than have him humble himself in the presence of a third person.

"Fleda heard me yesterday," said he;—"it was right she should hear me to-day."

"Then my dear Guy," said his mother, with a secret eagerness which she did not allow to appear,—"if I may make a condition for my forgiveness, which you had before you asked for it,—will you grant me one favour?"

"Certainly, mother,—if I can."

"You promise me?"

"As well in one word as in two."

"Promise me that you will never, by any circumstances, allow yourself to be drawn into—what is called *an affair of honour*."

Mr. Carleton's brow changed, and without making any reply, perhaps to avoid his mother's questioning gaze, he rose up and walked two or three times the length of the cabin. His mother and Fleda watched him doubtfully.

"Do you see how you have got me into trouble, Elfie?" said he, stopping before them.

Fleda looked wonderingly, and Mrs. Carleton exclaimed, "What trouble?"

"Elfie," said he, without immediately answering his mother, "what would your conscience do with two promises both of which cannot be kept?"

"What such promises have you made?" said Mrs. Carleton eagerly.

"Let me hear first what Fleda says to my question."

"Why," said Fleda, looking a little bewildered,—"I would keep the right one."

"Not the one first made?" said he smiling.

"No," said Fleda,—"not unless it was the right one."

"But don't you think one ought to keep one's word, in any event?"

"I don't think anything can make it right to do wrong," Fleda said gravely, and not without a secret trembling consciousness to what point she was speaking.

He left them and again took several turns up and down the cabin before he sat down.

"You have not given me your promise yet, Guy," said his mother, whose eye had not once quitted him. "You said you would."

"I said, if I could."

"Well?—you can?"

"I have two honourable meetings of the proscribed kind now on hand, to which I stand pledged."

Fleda hid her face in an agony. Mrs. Carleton's agony was in every line of hers as she grasped her son's wrist exclaiming, "Guy, promise me!" She had words for nothing else. He hesitated still a moment, and then meeting his mother's look he said gravely and steadily,

"I promise you, mother, I never will."

His mother threw herself upon his breast and hid her face there, too much excited to have any thought of her customary regard to appearances; sobbing out thanks and blessings even audibly. Fleda's gentle head was bowed in almost equal agitation; and Mr. Carleton at that moment had no doubt that he had chosen well which promise to keep.

There remained however a less agreeable part of the business to manage. After seeing his mother and Fleda quite happy again, though without satisfying in any degree the curiosity of the former, Guy went in search of the two young West Point officers. They were together, but without Thorn's friend, Capt. Beebee. Him Carleton next sought and brought to the forward deck where the others were enjoying their cigars; or rather Charlton Rossitur was enjoying his, with the happy self-satisfaction of a pair of epaulettes off duty. Thorn had too busy a brain to be much of a smoker. Now, however, when it was plain that Mr. Carleton had something to say to them, Charlton's cigar gave way to his attention; it was displaced from his mouth and held in abeyance; while Thorn puffed away more intently than ever.

"Gentlemen," Carleton began,—"I gave you yesterday reason to expect that so soon as circumstances permitted, you should have the opportunity which offended honour desires of trying sounder arguments than those of reason upon the offender. I have to tell you to-day that I will not give it you. I have thought further of it."

"Is it a new insult that you mean by this, sir?" exclaimed Rossitur in astonishment. Thorn's cigar did not stir.

"Neither new nor old. I mean simply that I have changed my mind."

"But this is very extraordinary!" said Rossitur. "What reason do you give?"

"I give none, sir."

"In that case," said Capt. Beebee, "perhaps Mr. Carleton will not object to explain or unsay the things which gave offence yesterday."

"I apprehend there is nothing to explain, sir,—I think I must have been understood; and I never take back my words for I am in the habit of speaking the truth."

"Then we are to consider this as a further, unprovoked, unmitigated insult for which you will give neither reason nor satisfaction!" cried Rossitur.

"I have already disclaimed that, Mr. Rossitur."

"Are we, on mature deliberation, considered unworthy of the *honour* you so condescendingly awarded to us yesterday?"

"My reasons have nothing to do with you, sir, nor with your friend; they are entirely personal to myself."

"Mr. Carleton must be aware," said Capt. Beebee, "that his conduct, if unexplained, will bear a very strange construction."

Mr. Carleton was coldly silent.

"It never was heard of," the Captain went on,—"that a gentleman declined both to explain and to give satisfaction for any part of his conduct which had called for it."

"It never was heard that a *gentleman* did," said Thorn, removing his cigar a moment for the purpose of supplying the emphasis which his friend had carefully omitted to make.

"Will you say, Mr. Carleton," said Rossitur, "that you did not mean to offend us yesterday in what you said?"

"No, Mr. Rossitur."

"You will not!" cried the Captain.

"No sir; for your friends had given me, as I conceived, just cause of displeasure; and I was, and am, careless of offending those who have done so."

"You consider yourself aggrieved, then, in the first place?" said Beebee.

"I have said so, sir."

"Then," said the Captain after a puzzled look out to sea, "supposing that my friends disclaim all intention to offend you, in that case—"

"In that case I should be glad, Capt. Beebee, that they had changed their line of tactics—there is nothing to change in my own."

"Then what are we to understand by this strange refusal of a meeting, Mr. Carleton? what does it mean?"

"It means one thing in my own mind, sir, and probably another in yours; but the outward expression I choose to give it is that I will not reward uncalled-for rudeness with an opportunity of self-vindication."

"You are," said Thorn sneeringly, "probably careless as to the figure your own name will cut in connection with this story?"

"Entirely so," said Mr. Carleton, eying him steadily.

"You are aware that your character is at our mercy?"

A slight bow seemed to leave at their disposal the very small portion of his character he conceived to lie in that predicament.

"You will expect to hear yourself spoken of in terms that befit a man who has cowed out of an engagement he dared not fulfil?"

"Of course," said Carleton haughtily, "by my present refusal I give you leave to say all that, and as much more as your ingenuity can furnish in the same style; but not in my hearing, sir."

"You can't help yourself," said Thorn, with the same sneer. "You have rid yourself of a gentleman's means of protection,—what others will you use?"

"I will leave that to the suggestion of the moment—I do not doubt it will be found fruitful."

Nobody doubted it who looked just then on his steady sparkling eye.

"I consider the championship of yesterday given up of course," Thorn went on in a kind of aside, not looking at anybody, and striking his cigar against the guards to clear it of ashes;—"the champion has quitted the field; and the little princess but lately so walled in with defences must now listen to whatever knight and squire may please to address to her. Nothing remains to be seen of her defender but his spurs."

"They may serve for the heels of whoever is disposed to annoy her," said Mr. Carleton. "He will need them."

He left the group with the same air of imperturbable self-possession which he had maintained during the conference. But presently Rossitur, who had his private reasons for wishing to keep friends with an acquaintance who might be of service in more ways than one, followed him and declared himself to have been, in all his nonsense to Fleda, most undesirous of giving displeasure to her temporary guardian, and sorry that it had fallen out so. He spoke frankly, and Mr. Carleton, with the same cool gracefulness with which he had carried on the quarrel, waived his displeasure, and admitted the young gentleman apparently to stand as before in his favour. Their reconciliation was not an hour old when Capt. Beebee joined them.

"I am sorry I must trouble you with a word more on this disagreeable subject, Mr. Carleton," he began, after a ceremonious salutation,—"My friend, Lieut. Thorn, considers himself greatly outraged by your determination not to meet him. He begs to ask, by me, whether it is your purpose to abide by it at all hazards?"

"Yes, sir."

"There is some misunderstanding here, which I greatly regret.—I hope you will see and excuse the disagreeable necessity I am under of delivering the rest of my friend's message."

"Say on, sir."

"Mr. Thorn declares that if you deny him the common courtesy which no gentleman refuses to another, he will proclaim your name with the most opprobrious adjuncts to all the world; and in place of his former regard he will hold you in the most unlimited contempt, which he will have no scruple about shewing on all occasions."

Mr. Carleton coloured a little, but replied coolly,

"I have not lived in Mr. Thorn's favour. As to the rest, I forgive him!—except indeed he provoke me to measures for which I never will forgive him."

"Measures!" said the Captain.

"I hope not! for my own self-respect would be more grievously hurt than his. But there is an unruly spring somewhere about my composition that when it gets wound up is once in a while too much for me."

"But," said Rossitur, "pardon me,—have you no regard to the effect of his misrepresentations?"

"You are mistaken, Mr. Rossitur," said Carleton slightly;—"this is but the blast of a bellows,—not the Simoom."

"Then what answer shall I have the honour of carrying back to my friend?" said Capt Beebee, after a sort of astounded pause of a few minutes.

"None, of my sending, sir."

Capt. Beebee touched his cap, and went back to Mr. Thorn, to whom he reported that the young Englishman was thoroughly impracticable, and that there was nothing to be gained by dealing with him; and the vexed conclusion of Thorn's own mind, in the end, was in favour of the wisdom of letting him alone.

In a very different mood, saddened and disgusted, Mr. Carleton shook himself free of Rossitur, and went and stood alone by the guards looking out upon the sea. He did not at all regret his promise to his mother, nor wish to take other ground than that he had taken. Both the theory and the practice of duelling he heartily despised, and he was not weak enough to fancy that he had brought any discredit upon either his sense or his honour by refusing to comply with an unwarrantable and barbarous custom. And he valued mankind too little to be at all concerned about their judgment in the matter. His own opinion was at all times enough for him. But the miserable folly and puerility of such an altercation as that in which he had just been engaged, the poor display of human character, the little low passions which had been called up, even in himself, alike destitute of worthy cause and aim, and which had perhaps but just missed ending in the death of some and the living death of others,—it all wrought to bring him back to his old wearying of human nature and despondent eying of the everywhere jarrings, confusions and discordances in the moral world. The fresh sea-breeze that swept by the ship, roughening the play of the waves, and brushing his own cheek with its health-bearing wing, brought with it a sad feeling of contrast. Free, and pure, and steadily directed, it sped on its way, to do its work. And like it all the rest of the natural world, faithful to the law of its Maker, was stamped with the same signet of perfection. Only man, in all the universe, seemed to be at cross purposes with the end of his being. Only man, of all animate or inanimate things, lived an aimless, fruitless, broken life,—or fruitful only in evil. How was this? and whence? and when would be the end? and would this confused mass of warring elements ever be at peace? would this disordered machinery ever work smoothly, without let or stop any more, and work out the beautiful something for which sure it was designed? And could any hand but its first Maker mend the broken wheel or supply the spring that was wanting?

Has not the Desire of all nations been often sought of eyes that were never taught where to look for him.

Mr. Carleton was standing still by the guards, looking thoughtfully out to windward to meet the fresh breeze, as if the Spirit of the Wilderness were in it and could teach him the truth that the Spirit of the World knew not and had not to give, when he became sensible of something close beside him; and looking down met little Fleda's upturned face, with such a look of purity, freshness, and peace, it said as plainly as ever the dial-plate of a clock that *that* little piece of machinery was working right. There was a sunlight upon it too, of happy confidence and affection. Mr. Carleton's mind experienced a sudden revulsion. Fleda might see the reflection of her own light in his face as he helped her up to a stand where she could be more on a level with him; putting his arm round her to guard against any sudden roll of the ship.

"What makes you wear such a happy face?" said he, with an expression half envious, half regretful.

"I don't know!" said Fleda innocently. "You, I suppose."

He looked as bright as she did, for a minute.

"Were you ever angry, Elfie?"

"I don't know—" said Fleda. "I don't know but I have."

He smiled to see that although evidently her memory could not bring the charge, her modesty would not deny it.

"Were you not angry yesterday with your cousin and that unmannerly friend of his?"

"No," said Fleda, a shade crossing her face,—"I was not *angry*"—

And as she spoke her hand was softly put upon Mr. Carleton's; as if partly in the fear of what might have grown out of *his* anger, and partly in thankfulness to him that he had rendered it unnecessary. There was a singular delicate timidity and tenderness in the action.

"I wish I had your secret, Elfie," said Mr. Carleton, looking wistfully into the clear eyes that met his.

"What secret?" said Fleda smiling.

"You say one can always do right—is that the reason you are happy?—because you follow that out?"

"No," said Fleda seriously. "But I think it is a great deal pleasanter."

"I have no doubt at all of that, neither, I dare say, have the rest of the world; only somehow when it comes to the point they find it is easier to do wrong. What's your secret, Elfie?"

"I haven't any secret," said Fleda. But presently seeming to bethink herself, she added gently and gravely,

"Aunt Miriam says—"

"What?"

"She says that when we love Jesus Christ it is easy to please him."

"And do you love him, Elfie?" Mr. Carleton asked after a minute.

Her answer was a very quiet and sober "yes."

He doubted still whether she were not unconsciously using a form of speech the spirit of which she did not quite realize. That one might "not see and yet believe," he could understand; but for *affection* to go forth towards an unseen object was another matter. His question was grave and acute.

"By what do you judge that you do, Elfie?"

"Why, Mr. Carleton," said Fleda, with an instant look of appeal, "who else *should* I love?"

"If not him"—her eye and her voice made sufficiently plain. Mr. Carleton was obliged to confess to himself that she spoke intelligently, with deeper intelligence than he could follow. He asked no more questions. Yet truth shines by its own light, like the sun. He had not perfectly comprehended her answers, but they struck him as something that deserved to be understood, and he resolved to make the truth of them his own.

The rest of the voyage was perfectly quiet. Following the earnest advice of his friend Capt. Beebee, Thorn had given up trying to push Mr. Carleton to extremity; who on his part did not seem conscious of Thorn's existence.

CHAPTER XIII.

There the most daintie paradise on ground
Itselfe doth offer to his sober eye,—
—— The painted flowres, the trees upshooting hye,
The dales for shade, the hills for breathing space,
The trembling groves, the christall running by;
And that, which all faire works doth most aggrace,
The art which all that wrought appeared in no place.

FAERY QUEENE.

THEY had taken ship for London, as Mr. and Mrs. Carleton wished to visit home for a day or two before going on to Paris. So leaving Charlton to carry news of them to the French capital, so soon as he could persuade himself to leave the English one, they with little Fleda in company posted down to Carleton, in ——shire.

It was a time of great delight to Fleda, that is, as soon as Mr. Carleton had made her feel at home in England; and somehow he had contrived to do that and to scatter some clouds of remembrance that seemed to gather about her, before they had reached the end of their first day's journey. To be out of the ship was itself a comfort, and to be alone with kind friends was much more. With great joy Fleda put her cousin Charlton and Mr. Thorn at once out of sight and out of mind; and gave herself with even more than her usual happy readiness to everything the way and the end of the way had for her. Those days were to be painted days in Fleda's memory.

She thought Carleton was a very odd place. That is, the house, not the village which went by the same name. If the manner of her two companions had not been such as to put her entirely at her ease she would have felt strange and shy. As it was she felt half afraid of losing herself in the house; to Fleda's unaccustomed eyes it was a labyrinth of halls and staircases, set with the most unaccountable number and variety of rooms; old and new, quaint and comfortable, gloomy and magnificent; some with stern old-fashioned massiveness of style and garniture; others absolutely bewitching (to Fleda's eyes and understanding) in the rich beauty and luxuriousness of their arrangements. Mr. Carleton's own particular haunts were of these; his private room, the little library as it was called, the library, and the music-room, which was indeed rather a gallery of the fine arts, so many treasures of art were gathered there. To an older and nice-judging person these rooms would have given no slight indications of their owner's mind—it had been at work on every corner of them. No particular fashion had been followed, in anything, nor any model consulted but that which fancy had built to the mind's order. The wealth of years had drawn together an enormous assemblage of matters, great and small, every one of which was fitted either to excite fancy, or suggest thought, or to satisfy the eye by its nice adaptation. And if pride had had the ordering of them, all these might have been but a costly museum, a literary alphabet that its possessor could not put together, an ungainly confession of ignorance on the part of the intellect that could do nothing with this rich heap of material. But pride was not the genius of the place. A most refined taste and curious fastidiousness had arranged and harmonized all the heterogeneous items; the mental hieroglyphics had been ordered by one to whom the reading of them was no mystery. Nothing struck a stranger at first entering, except the very rich effect and faultless air of the whole, and perhaps the delicious facilities for every kind of intellectual cultivation which appeared on every hand; facilities which it must be allowed do seem in general *not* to facilitate the work they are meant to speed. In this case however it was different. The mind that wanted them had brought them together to satisfy its own craving.

These rooms were Guy's peculiar domain. In other parts of the house, where his mother reigned conjointly with him, their joint tastes had struck out another style of adornment which might be called a style of superb elegance. Not superb alone, for taste had not permitted so heavy a characteristic to be predominant; not merely elegant, for the fineness of all the details would warrant an ampler word. A larger part of the house than both these together had been left as generations past had left it, in various stages of refinement, comfort and comeliness. It was a day or two before Fleda found out that it was all one; she thought at first that it was a collection of several houses that had somehow inexplicably sat down there with their backs to each other; it was so straggling and irregular a pile of building, covering so much ground, and looking so very unlike the different parts to each other. One portion was quite old; the other parts ranged variously between the present and the far past. After she once understood this it was a piece of delicious wonderment and musing and great admiration to Fleda; she never grew weary of wandering round it and thinking about it, for from a child fanciful meditation was one of her delights. Within doors she best liked Mr. Carleton's favourite rooms. Their rich colouring and moderated light and endless stores of beauty and curiosity made them a place of fascination.

Out of doors she found still more to delight her. Morning noon and night she might be seen near the house gazing, taking in pictures of natural beauty which were for ever after to hang in Fleda's memory as standards of excellence in that sort. Nature's hand had been very kind to the place, moulding the ground in beautiful style. Art had made happy use of the advantage thus given her; and now what appeared was neither art nor nature, but a perfection that can only spring from the hands of both. Fleda's eyes were bewitched. She stood watching the rolling slopes of green turf, *so* soft and lovely, and the magnificent trees, that had kept their ground for ages and seen generations rise and fall before their growing strength and grandeur. They were scattered here and there on the lawn, and further back stood on the heights and stretched along the ridges of the undulating ground, the outposts of a wood of the same growth still beyond them.

"How do you like it, Elfie?" Mr. Carleton asked her the evening of the first day, as he saw her for a length of time looking out gravely and intently from before the hall door.

"I think it is beautiful!" said Fleda. "The ground is a great deal smoother here than it was at home."

"I'll take you to ride to-morrow," said he smiling, "and shew you rough ground enough."

"As you did when we came from Montepoole?" said Fleda rather eagerly.

"Would you like that?"

"Yes, very much,—if *you* would like it, Mr. Carleton."

"Very well," said he. "So it shall be."

And not a day passed during their short stay that he did not give her one of those rides. He shewed her rough ground, according to his promise, but Fleda still thought it did not look much like the mountains "at home." And indeed unsightly roughnesses had been skilfully covered or removed; and though a large part of the park, which was a very extensive one, was wildly broken and had apparently been left as nature left it, the hand of taste had been there; and many an unsuspected touch instead of hindering had heightened both the wild and the beautiful character. Landscape gardening had long been a great hobby of its owner.

"How far does your ground come, Mr. Carleton?" inquired Fleda on one of these rides, when they had travelled a good distance from home.

"Further than you can see, Elfie."

"Further than I can see!—It must be a very large farm!"

"This is not a farm where we are now," said he;—"did you mean that?—this is the park; we are almost at the edge of it on this side."

"What is the difference between a farm and a park?" said Fleda.

"The grounds of a farm are tilled for profit; a park is an uncultivated enclosure kept merely for men and women and deer to take pleasure in."

"*I* have taken a good deal of pleasure in it," said Fleda. "And have you a farm besides, Mr. Carleton?"

"A good many, Elfie."

Fleda looked surprised; and then remarked that it must be very nice to have such a beautiful piece of ground just for pleasure.

She enjoyed it to the full during the few days she was there. And one thing more, the grand piano in the music-room. The first evening of their arrival she was drawn by the far-off sounds, and Mrs. Carleton seeing it went immediately to the music-room with her. The room had no light, except from the moonbeams that stole in through two glass doors which opened upon a particularly private and cherished part of the grounds, in summer-time full of flowers; for in the very refinement of luxury delights had been crowded about this favourite apartment. Mr. Carleton was at the instrument, playing. Fleda sat down quietly in one corner and listened,—in a rapture of pleasure she had hardly ever known from any like source. She did not think it could be greater; till after a time, in a pause of the music, Mrs. Carleton asked her son to sing a particular ballad; and that one was followed by two or three more. Fleda left her corner, she could not contain herself, and favoured by the darkness came forward and stood quite near; and if the performer had had light to see by, he would have been gratified with the tribute paid to his power by the unfeigned tears that ran down her cheeks. This pleasure was also repeated from evening to evening.

"Do you know we set off for Paris to-morrow?" said Mrs. Carleton the last evening of their stay, as Fleda came up to the door after a prolonged ramble in the park, leaving Mr. Carleton with one or two gardeners at a little distance.

"Yes!" said Fleda, with a sigh that was more than half audible.

"Are you sorry?" said Mrs. Carleton smiling.

"I cannot be glad," said Fleda, giving a sober look over the lawn.

"Then you like Carleton?"

"Very much!—It is a prettier place than Queechy."

"But we shall have you here again, dear Fleda," said Mrs. Carleton, restraining her smile at this, to her, very moderate compliment.

"Perhaps not," said Fleda quietly.—"Mr. Carleton said," she added a minute after with more animation, "that a park was a place for men and women and deer to take pleasure in. I am sure it is for children too!"

"Did you have a pleasant ride this morning?"

"O very!—I always do. There isn't anything I like so well."

"What, as to ride on horseback with Guy?" said Mrs. Carleton looking exceedingly benignant.

"Yes,—unless—"

"Unless what, my dear Fleda?"

"Unless, perhaps,—I don't know,—I was going to say, unless perhaps to hear him sing."

Mrs. Carleton's delight was unequivocally expressed; and she promised Fleda that she should have both rides and songs there in plenty another time; a promise upon which Fleda built no trust at all.

The short journey to Paris was soon made. The next morning Mrs. Carleton making an excuse of her fatigue left Guy to end the care he had rather taken upon himself by delivering his little charge into the hands of her friends. So they drove to the Hotel ——, Rue ——, where Mr. Rossitur had apartments in very handsome style. They found him alone in the saloon.

"Ha! Carleton—come back again. Just in time—very glad to see you. And who is this?—Ah, another little daughter for aunt Lucy."

Mr. Rossitur, who gave them this greeting very cordially, was rather a fine-looking man; decidedly agreeable both in person and manner. Fleda was pleasantly disappointed after what her grandfather had led her to expect. There might be something of sternness in his expression; people gave him credit for a peremptory, not to say imperious temper; but if truly, it could not often meet with opposition. The sense and gentlemanly character which marked his face and bearing had an air of smooth politeness which seemed habitual. There was no want of kindness nor even of tenderness in the way he drew Fleda within his arm and held her there, while he went on talking to Mr. Carleton; now and then stooping his face to look in at her bonnet and kiss her, which was his only welcome. He said nothing to her after his first question.

He was too busy talking to Guy. He seemed to have a great deal to tell him. There was this for him to see, and that for him to hear, and charming new things which had been done or doing since Mr. Carleton left Paris. The impression upon Fleda's mind after listening awhile was that the French capital was a great Gallery of the Fine Arts, with a magnified likeness of Mr. Carleton's music-room at one end of it. She thought her uncle must be most extraordinarily fond of pictures and works of art in general, and must have a great love for seeing company and hearing people sing. This latter taste Fleda was disposed to allow might be a very reasonable one. Mr. Carleton, she observed, seemed much more cool on the whole subject. But meanwhile where was aunt Lucy?—and had Mr. Rossitur forgotten the little armful that he held so fast and so perseveringly? No, for here was another kiss, and another look into her face, so kind that Fleda gave him a piece of her heart from that time.

"Hugh!" said Mr. Rossitur suddenly to somebody she had not seen before,—"Hugh!—here is your little cousin. Take her off to your mother."

A child came forward at this bidding hardly larger than herself. He was a slender graceful little figure, with nothing of the boy in his face or manner; delicate as a girl, and with something almost melancholy in the gentle sweetness of his countenance. Fleda's confidence was given to it on the instant, which had not been the case with anything in her uncle, and she yielded without reluctance the hand he took to obey his father's command. Before two steps had been taken however, she suddenly broke away from him and springing to Mr. Carleton's side silently laid her hand in his. She made no answer whatever to a light word or two of kindness that he spoke just for her ear. She listened with downcast eyes and a lip that he saw was too unsteady to be trusted, and then after a moment more, without looking, pulled away her hand and followed her cousin. Hugh did not once get a sight of her face on the way to his mother's room, but owing to her exceeding efforts and quiet generalship he never guessed the cause. There was nothing in her face to raise suspicion when he reached the door and opening it announced her with,

"Mother, here's cousin Fleda come."

Fleda had seen her aunt before, though several years back, and not long enough to get acquainted with her. But no matter;—it was her mother's sister sitting there, whose face gave her so lovely a welcome at that speech of Hugh's, whose arms were stretched out so eagerly towards her; and springing to them as to a very haven of rest Fleda wept on her bosom those delicious tears that are only shed where the heart is at home. And even before they were dried the ties were knit that bound her to her new sphere.

"Who came with you, dear Fleda?" said Mrs. Rossitur then. "Is Mrs. Carleton here? I must go and thank her for bringing you to me."

"*Mr.* Carleton is here." said Hugh.

"I must go and thank him then. Jump down, dear Fleda—I'll be back in a minute."

Fleda got off her lap, and stood looking in a kind of enchanted maze, while her aunt hastily arranged her hair at the glass. Looking, while fancy and memory were making strong the net in which her heart was caught. She was trying to see something of her mother in one who had shared her blood and her affection so nearly. A miniature of that mother was left to Fleda, and she had studied it till she could hardly persuade herself that she had not some recollection of the original; and now she thought she caught a precious shadow of something like it in her aunt Lucy. Not in those pretty bright eyes which had looked through kind tears so lovingly upon her; but in the graceful ringlets about the temples, the delicate contour of the face, and a something, Fleda could only have said it was "a something," about the mouth *when at rest*, the shadow of her mother's image rejoiced her heart. Rather that faint shadow of the loved lost one for little Fleda, than any other form or combination of beauty on earth. As she stood fascinated, watching the movements of her aunt's light figure, Fleda drew a long breath with which went off the whole burden of doubt and anxiety that had lain upon her mind ever since the journey began. She had not known it was there, but she felt it go. Yet even when that sigh of relief was breathed, and while fancy and feeling were weaving their rich embroidery into the very tissue of Fleda's happiness, most persons would have seen merely that the child looked very sober, and have thought probably that she felt very tired and strange. Perhaps Mrs. Rossitur thought so, for again tenderly kissing her before she left the room she told Hugh to take off her things and make her feel at home.

Hugh upon this made Fleda sit down and proceeded to untie her tippet strings and take off her coat with an air of delicate tenderness which shewed he had great pleasure in his task, and which made Fleda take a good deal of pleasure in it too.

"Are you tired, cousin Fleda?" said he gently.

"No," said Fleda. "O no!"

"Charlton said you were tired on board ship."

"I wasn't tired," said Fleda, in not a little surprise; "I liked it very much."

"Then maybe I mistook. I know Charlton said *he* was tired, and I thought he said you were too. You know my brother Charlton, don't you?"

"Yes."

"Are you glad to come to Paris?"

"I am glad now," said Fleda. "I wasn't glad before."

"I am very glad," said Hugh. "I think you will like it. We didn't know you were coming till two or three days ago when Charlton got here. Do you like to take walks?"

"Yes, very much."

"Father and mother will take us delightful walks in the Tuileries, the gardens you know, and the Champs Elysées, and Versailles, and the Boulevards, and ever so many places; and it will be a great deal pleasanter now you are here. Do you know French?"

"No."

"Then you'll have to learn. I'll help you if you will let me. It is very easy. Did you get my last letter?"

"I don't know," said Fleda,—"the last one I had came with one of aunt Lucy's, telling me about Mrs. Carleton—I got it just before"—

Alas! before what? Fleda suddenly remembered, and was stopped short. From all the strange scenes and interests which lately had whirled her along, her spirit leapt back with strong yearning recollection to her old home and her old ties; and such a rain of tears witnessed the dearness of what she had lost and the tenderness of the memory that had let them slip for a moment, that Hugh was as much distressed as startled. With great tenderness and touching delicacy he tried to soothe her and at the same time, though guessing, to find out what was the matter, lest he should make a mistake.

"Just before what?" said he, laying his hand caressingly on his little cousin's shoulder;—"Don't grieve so, dear Fleda!"

"It was only just before grandpa died," said Fleda.

Hugh had known of that before, though like her he had forgotten it for a moment. A little while his feeling was too strong to permit any further attempt at condolence; but as he saw Fleda grow quiet he took courage to speak again.

"Was he a good man?" he asked softly.

"Oh yes!"

"Then," said Hugh," you know he is happy now, Fleda. If he loved Jesus Christ he is gone to be with him. That ought to make you glad as well as sorry."

Fleda looked up, though tears were streaming yet, to give that full happy answer of the eye that no words could do. This was consolation, and sympathy. The two children had a perfect understanding of each other from that time forward; a fellowship that never knew a break nor a weakening.

Mrs. Rossitur found on her return that Hugh had obeyed her charge to the letter. He had made Fleda feel at home. They were sitting close together, Hugh's hand affectionately clasping hers, and he was holding forth on some subject with a gracious politeness that many of his elders might have copied; while Fleda listened and assented with entire satisfaction. The rest of the morning she passed in her aunt's arms; drinking draughts of pleasure from those dear bright eyes; taking in the balm of gentlest words of love, and soft kisses, every one of which was felt at the bottom of Fleda's heart, and the pleasure of talking over her young sorrows with one who could feel them all and answer with tears as well as words of sympathy. And Hugh stood by the while looking at his little orphan cousin as if she might have dropped from the clouds into his mother's lap, a rare jewel or delicate flower, but much more delicate and precious than they or any other possible gift

Hugh and Fleda dined alone. For as he informed her his father never would have children at the dinner-table when he had company; and Mr. and Mrs. Carleton and other people were to be there to-day. Fleda made no remark on the subject, by word or look, but she thought none the less. She thought it was a very mean fashion. *She* not come to the table when strangers were there! And who would enjoy them more? When Mr. Rossitur and Mr. Carleton had dined with her grandfather, had she not taken as much pleasure in their society, and in the whole thing, as any other one of the party? And at Carleton, had she not several times dined with a tableful, and been unspeakably amused to watch the different manners and characteristics of people who were strange to her? However, Mr. Rossitur had other notions. So she and Hugh had their dinner in aunt Lucy's dressing-room, by themselves; and a very nice dinner it was, Fleda thought; and Rosaline, Mrs. Rossitur's French maid, was well affected and took admirable care of them. Indeed before the close of the day Rosaline privately informed her mistress, "qu'elle serait entêtée sûrement de cet enfant dans trois jours;" and "que son regard vraiment lui serrait le cœur." And Hugh was excellent company, failing all other, and did the honours of the table with the utmost thoughtfulness, and amused Fleda the whole time with accounts of Paris and what they would do and what she should see; and how his sister Marion was at school at a convent, and what kind of a place a convent was; and how he himself always staid at home and learned of his mother and his father; "or by himself," he said, "just as it happened;" and he hoped they would keep Fleda at home too. So Fleda hoped exceedingly, but this stern rule about the dining had made her feel a little shy of her uncle; she thought perhaps he was not kind and indulgent to children like her aunt Lucy; and if he said she must go to a convent she would not dare to ask him to let her stay. The next time she saw him however, she was obliged to change her opinion again, in part; for he was very kind and indulgent, both to her and Hugh; and more than that he was very amusing. He shewed her pictures, and told her new and interesting things; and finding that she listened eagerly he seemed pleased to prolong her pleasure, even at the expense of a good deal of his own time.

Mr. Rossitur was a man of cultivated mind and very refined and fastidious taste. He lived for the pleasures of Art and Literature and the society where these are valued. For this, and not without some secret love of display, he lived in Paris; not extravagant in his pleasures, nor silly in his ostentation, but leading, like a gentleman, as worthy and rational a life as a man can lead who lives only to himself, with no further thought than to enjoy the passing hours. Mr. Rossitur enjoyed them elegantly, and for a man of the world, moderately, bestowing however few of those precious hours upon his children. It was his maxim that they should be kept out of the way whenever their presence might by any chance interfere with the amusements of their elders; and this maxim, a good one certainly in some hands, was in his reading of it a very broad one. Still when he did take time to give his family he was a delightful companion to those of them who could understand him. If they shewed no taste for sensible pleasure he had no patience with them nor desire of their company. Report had done him no wrong in giving him a stern temper; but this almost never came out in actual exercise; Fleda knew it only from an occasional hint now and then, and by her childish intuitive reading of the lines it had drawn round the mouth and brow. It had no disagreeable bearing on his everyday life and manner; and the quiet fact probably served but to heighten the love and reverence in which his family held him very high.

Mr. Rossitur did once moot the question whether Fleda should not join Marion at her convent. But his wife looked very grave and said that she was too tender and delicate a little thing to be trusted to the hands of strangers; Hugh pleaded, and argued that she might share all his lessons; and Fleda's own face pleaded more powerfully. There was something appealing in its extreme delicacy and purity which seemed to call for shelter and protection from every rough breath of the world; and Mr. Rossitur was easily persuaded to let her remain in the stronghold of home. Hugh had never quitted it. Neither father nor mother ever thought of such a thing. He was the cherished idol of the whole family. Always a delicate child, always blameless in life and behaviour, his loveliness of mind and person, his affectionateness, the winning sweetness that was about him like a halo, and the slight tenure by which they seemed to hold him, had wrought to bind the hearts of father and mother to this child, as it were, with the very life-strings of both. Not his mother was more gentle with Hugh than his much sterner father. And now little Fleda, sharing somewhat of Hugh's peculiar claims upon their tenderness and adding another of her own, was admitted, not to the same place in their hearts,—that could not be,—but to their honour be it spoken, to the same place in all outward shew of thought and feeling. Hugh had nothing that Fleda did not have, even to the time, care and caresses of his parents. And not Hugh rendered them a more faithful return of devoted affection.

Once made easy on the question of school, which was never seriously stirred again, Fleda's life became very happy. It was easy to make her happy; affection and sympathy would have done it almost anywhere; but in Paris she had much more; and after time had softened the sorrow she brought with her, no bird ever found existence less of a burden, nor sang more light-heartedly along its life. In her aunt she had all but the name of a mother; in her uncle, with kindness and affection, she had amusement, interest, and improvement; in Hugh everything;—love, confidence, sympathy, society, help; their tastes, opinions, pursuits, went hand in hand. The two children were always together. Fleda's spirits were brighter than Hugh's, and her intellectual tastes stronger and more universal. That might be as much from difference of physical as of mental constitution. Hugh's temperament led him somewhat to melancholy, and to those studies and pleasures which best side with subdued feeling and delicate nerves. Fleda's nervous system was of the finest too, but—in short, she was as like a bird as possible. Perfect health, which yet a slight thing was enough to shake to the foundation;—joyous spirits, which a look could quell;—happy energies, which a harsh hand might easily crush for ever. Well for little Fleda that so tender a plant was permitted to unfold in so nicely tempered an atmosphere. A cold wind would soon have killed it. Besides all this there were charming studies to be gone through every day with Hugh; some for aunt Lucy to hear, some for masters and and mistresses. There were amusing walks in the Boulevards, and delicious pleasure-taking in the gardens of Paris, and a new world of people and manners and things and histories for the little American. And despite her early rustic experience Fleda had from nature an indefeasible taste for the elegancies of life; it suited her well to see all about her, in dress, in furniture, in various appliances, as commodious and tasteful as wealth and refinement could contrive it; and she very soon knew what was right in each kind. There were now and then most gleeful excursions in the environs of Paris, when she and Hugh found in earth and air a world of delights more than they could tell anybody but each other. And at home, what peaceful times they two had,—what endless conversations, discussions, schemes, air-journeys of memory and fancy, backward and forward; what sociable dinners alone, and delightful evenings with Mr. and Mrs. Rossitur in the saloon when nobody or only a very few people were there; how pleasantly in those evenings the foundations were laid of a strong and enduring love for the works of art, painted, sculptured, or engraven; what a multitude of curious and excellent bits of knowledge Fleda's ears picked up from the talk of different people. They were capital ears; what they caught they never let fall. In the course of the year her gleanings amounted to more than many another person's harvest.

CHAPTER XIV.

Heav'n bless thee;
Thou hast the sweetest face I ever look'd on.
SHAKSPEARE.

ONE of the greatest of Fleda's pleasures was when Mr. Carleton came to take her out with him. He did that often. Fleda only wished he would have taken Hugh too, but somehow he never did. Nothing but that was wanting to make the pleasure of those times perfect. Knowing that she saw the *common things* in other company, Guy was at the pains to vary the amusement when she went with him. Instead of going to Versailles or St. Cloud, he would take her long delightful drives into the country and shew her some old or interesting place that nobody else went to see. Often there was a history belonging to the spot, which Fleda listened to with the delight of eye and fancy at once. In the city, where they more frequently walked, still he shewed her what she would perhaps have seen under no other other guidance. He made it his business to give her pleasure; and understanding the inquisitive active little spirit he had to do with he went where his own tastes would hardly have led him. The Quai aux Fleurs was often visited, but also the Halle aux Blés, the great Halle aux Vins, the Jardin des Plantes, and the Marché des Innocens. Guy even took the trouble, more for her sake than his own, to go to the latter place once very early in the morning, when the market bell had not two hours sounded, while the interest and prettiness of the scene were yet in their full life. Hugh was in company this time, and the delight of both children was beyond words, as it would have been beyond anybody's patience that had not a strong motive to back it. They never discovered that Mr. Carleton was in a hurry, as indeed he was not. They bargained for fruit with any number of people, upon all sorts of inducements, and to an extent of which they had no competent notion, but Hugh had his mother's purse, and Fleda was skilfully commissioned to purchase what she pleased for Mrs. Carleton. Verily the two children that morning bought pleasure, not peaches. Fancy and Benevolence held the purse strings, and Economy did not even look on. They revelled too, Fleda especially, amidst the bright pictures of the odd, the new, and the picturesque, and the varieties of character and incident, that were displayed around them; even till the country people began to go away and the scene to lose its charm. It never lost it in memory; and many a time in after life Hugh and Fleda recurred to something that was seen or done "that morning when we bought fruit at the Innocens."

Besides these scenes of everyday life, which interested and amused Fleda to the last degree, Mr. Carleton shewed her many an obscure part of Paris where deeds of daring and of blood had been, and thrilled the little listener's ear with histories of the Past. He judged her rightly. She would rather at any time have gone to walk with him, than with anybody else to see any show that could be devised. His object in all this was in the first place to give her pleasure, and in the second place to draw out her mind into free communion with his own, which he knew could only be done by talking sense to her. He succeeded as he wished. Lost in the interest of the scenes he presented to her eye and mind, she forgot everything else and shewed him herself; precisely what he wanted to see.

It was strange that a young man, an admired man of fashion, a flattered favourite of the gay and great world, and furthermore a reserved and proud repeller of almost all who sought his intimacy, should seek and delight in the society of a little child. His mother would have wondered if she had known it. Mrs. Rossitur did marvel that even Fleda should have so won upon the cold and haughty young Englishman; and her husband said he probably chose to have Fleda with him because he could make up his mind to like nobody else. A remark which perhaps arose from the utter failure of every attempt to draw him and Charlton nearer together. But Mr. Rossitur was only half right. The reason lay deeper.

Mr. Carleton had admitted the truth of Christianity, upon what he considered sufficient grounds, and would now have steadily fought for it, as he would for anything else that he believed to be truth. But there he stopped. He had not discovered nor tried to discover whether the truth of Christianity imposed any obligation upon him. He had cast off his unbelief, and looked upon it now as a singular folly. But his belief was almost as vague and as fruitless as his infidelity had been. Perhaps, a little, his bitter dissatisfaction with the world and human things, or rather his despondent view of them, was mitigated. If there was, as he now held, a Supreme Orderer of events, it might be, and it was rational to suppose there would be, in the issues of time, an entire change wrought in the disordered and dishonoured state of his handiwork. There might be a remedial system somewhere,—nay, it might be in the Bible; he meant to look some day. But that *he* had anything to do with that change—that the working of the remedial system called for hands—that *his* had any charge in the matter—had never entered into his imagination or stirred his conscience. He was living his old life at Paris, with his old dissatisfaction, perhaps a trifle less bitter. He was seeking pleasure in whatever art, learning, literature, refinement and luxury can do for a man who has them all at command; but there was something within him that spurned this ignoble existence and called for higher aims and worthier exertion. He was not vicious, he never had been vicious, or, as somebody else said, his vices were all refined vices; but a life of mere self-indulgence although pursued without self-satisfaction, is constantly lowering the standard and weakening the forces of virtue,—lessening the whole man. He felt it so; and to leave his ordinary scenes and occupations and lose a morning with little Fleda was a freshening of his better nature; it was like breathing pure air after the fever-heat of a sick room; it was like hearing the birds sing after the meaningless jabber of Bedlam. Mr. Carleton indeed did not put the matter quite so strongly to himself. He called Fleda his good angel. He did not exactly know that the office this good angel performed was simply to hold a candle to his conscience. For conscience was not by any means dead in him; it only wanted light to see by. When he turned from the gay and corrupt world in which he lived, where the changes were rung incessantly upon self-interest, falsehood, pride, and the various more or less refined forms of sensuality, and when he looked upon that pure bright little face, so free from selfishness, those clear eyes so innocent of evil, the peaceful brow under which a thought of double-dealing had never hid, Mr. Carleton felt himself in a healthier region. Here as elsewhere, he honoured and loved the image of truth; in the broad sense of truth;—that which suits the perfect standard of right. But his pleasure in this case was invariably mixed with a slight feeling of self-reproach; and it was this hardly recognised stir of his better nature, this clearing of his mental eyesight under the light of a bright example, that made him call the little torch-bearer his good angel. If this were truth, this purity, uprightness and singleness of mind, as conscience said it was, where was he? how far wandering from his beloved Idol!

One other feeling saddened the pleasure he had in her society—a belief that the ground of it could not last. "If she could grow up so!"—he said to himself. "But it is impossible. A very few years, and all that clear sunshine of the mind will be overcast;—there is not a cloud now!"—

Under the working of these thoughts Mr. Carleton sometimes forgot to talk to his little charge, and would walk for a length of way by her side wrapped up in sombre musings. Fleda never disturbed him then, but waited contentedly and patiently for him to come out of them, with her old feeling wondering what he could be thinking of and wishing he were as happy as she. But he never left her very long; he was sure to waive his own humour and give her all the graceful kind attention which nobody else could bestow so well. Nobody understood and appreciated it better than Fleda.

One day, some months after they had been in Paris, they were sitting in the Place de la Concorde, Mr. Carleton was in one of these thinking fits. He had been giving Fleda a long detail of the scenes that had taken place in that spot—

a history of it from the time when it had lain an unsightly waste;—such a graphic lively account as he knew well how to give. The absorbed interest with which she had lost everything else in what he was saying had given him at once reward and motive enough as he went on. Standing by his side, with one little hand confidingly resting on his knee, she gazed alternately into his face and towards the broad highly-adorned square by the side of which they had placed themselves, and where it was hard to realize that the ground had once been soaked in blood while madness and death filled the air; and her changing face like a mirror gave him back the reflection of the times he held up to her view. And still standing there in the same attitude after he had done she had been looking out towards the square in a fit of deep meditation. Mr. Carleton had forgotten her for awhile in his own thoughts, and then the sight of the little gloved hand upon his knee brought him back again.

"What are you musing about, Elfie, dear?" he said cheerfully, taking the hand in one of his.

Fleda gave a swift glance into his face, as if to see whether it would be safe for her to answer his question; a kind of exploring look, in which her eyes often acted as scouts for her tongue. Those she met pledged their faith for her security; yet Fleda's look went back to the square and then again to his face in silence.

"How do you like living in Paris?" said he. "You should know by this time."

"I like it very much indeed," said Fleda.

"I thought you would."

"I like Queechy better though," she went on gravely, her eyes turning again to the square.

"Like Queechy better! Were you thinking of Queechy just now when I spoke to you?"

"Oh no!"—with a smile.

"Were you going over all those horrors I have been distressing you with?"

"No," said Fleda;—"I *was* thinking of them, awhile ago."

"What then?" said he pleasantly. "You were looking so sober I should like to know how near your thoughts were to mine."

"I was thinking," said Fleda gravely, and a little unwillingly, but Guy's manner was not to be withstood,—"I was wishing I could be like the disciple whom Jesus loved."

Mr. Carleton let her see none of the surprise he felt at this answer.

"Was there one more loved than the rest?"

"Yes—the Bible calls him 'the disciple whom Jesus loved.' That was John."

"Why was he preferred above the others?"

"I don't know. I suppose he was more gentle and good than the others, and loved Jesus more. I think Aunt Miriam said so when I asked her once."

Mr. Carleton thought Fleda had not far to seek for the fulfilment of her wish.

"But how in the world, Elfie, did you work round to this gentle and good disciple from those scenes of blood you set out with?"

"Why," said Elfie,—"I was thinking how unhappy and bad people are, especially people here, I think; and how much must be done before they will all be brought right;—and then I was thinking of the work Jesus gave his disciples to do; and so I wished I could be like *that* disciple.—Hugh and I were talking about it this morning."

"What is the work he gave them to do?" said Mr. Carleton, more and more interested.

"Why," said Fleda, lifting her gentle wistful eyes to his and then looking away,—"to bring everybody to be good and happy."

"And how in the world are they to do that?" said Mr. Carleton, astonished to see his own problem quietly handled by this child.

"By telling them about Jesus Christ, and getting them to believe and love him," said Fleda, glancing at him again,—"and living so beautifully that people cannot help believing them."

"That last is an important clause," said Mr. Carleton thoughtfully. "But suppose people will not hear when they are spoken to, Elfie?"

"Some will at any rate," said Fleda,—"and by and by everybody will."

"How do you know?"

"Because the Bible says so."

"Are you sure of that, Elfie?"

"Why yes, Mr. Carleton—God has promised that the world shall be full of good people, and then they will be all happy. I wish it was now."

"But if that be so, Elfie, God can make them all good without our help?"

"Yes, but I suppose he chooses to do it with our help, Mr. Carleton," said Fleda with equal naiveté and gravity.

"But is not this you speak of," said he half smiling,—"rather the business of clergymen? you have nothing to do with it?"

"No," said Fleda,—"everybody has something to do with it; the Bible says so; ministers must do it in their way and other people in other ways; everybody has his own work. Don't you remember the parable of the ten talents, Mr. Carleton?"

Mr. Carleton was silent for a minute.

"I do not know the Bible quite as well as you do, Elfie," he said then,—"nor as I ought to do."

Elfie's only answer was by a look somewhat like that he well remembered on shipboard he had thought was angel-like,—a look of gentle sorrowful wistfulness which she did not venture to put into words. It had not for that the less power. But he did not choose to prolong the conversation. They rose up and began to walk homeward, Elfie thinking with all the warmth of her little heart that she wished very much Mr. Carleton knew the Bible better; divided between him and "that disciple" whom she and Hugh had been talking about.

"I suppose you are very busy now, Elfie," observed her companion, when they had walked the length of several squares in silence.

"O yes!" said Fleda. "Hugh and I are as busy as we can be. We are busy every minute."

"Except when you are on some chase after pleasure?"

"Well," said Fleda laughing,—"that is a kind of business; and all the business is pleasure too. I didn't mean that we were always busy about *work*. O Mr. Carleton we had such a nice time the day before yesterday!"—And she went on to give him the history of a very successful chase after pleasure which they had made to St. Cloud.

"And yet you like Queechy better?"

"Yes," said Fleda, with a gentle steadiness peculiar to herself,—"if I had aunt Lucy and Hugh and uncle Rolf there and everybody that I care for, I should like it a great deal better."

"Unspotted" yet, he thought.

"Mr. Carleton," said Fleda presently,—"do you play and sing every day here in Paris?"

"Yes," said he smiling,—"about every day. Why?"

"I was thinking how pleasant it was at your house, in England."

"Has Carleton the honour of rivalling Queechy in your liking?"

"I haven't lived there so long, you know," said Fleda. "I dare say it would if I had. I think it is quite as pretty a place."

Mr. Carleton smiled with a very pleased expression. Truth and politeness had joined hands in her answer with a child's grace.

He brought Fleda to her own door and there was leaving her.

"Stop!—O Mr. Carleton," cried Fleda, "come in just for one minute—I want to shew you something."

He made no resistance to that. She led him to the saloon, where it happened that nobody was, and repeating "One minute!"—rushed out of the room. In less than that time she came running back with a beautiful half-blown bud of a monthly rose in her hand, and in her face such a bloom of pleasure and eagerness as more than rivalled it. The rose was fairly eclipsed. She put the bud quietly but with a most satisfied air of affection into Mr. Carleton's hand. It had come from a little tree which he had given her on one of their first visits to the Quai aux Fleurs. She had had the choice of what she liked best, and had characteristically taken a flourishing little rose-bush that as yet shewed nothing but leaves and green buds; partly because she would have the pleasure of seeing its beauties come forward, and partly because she thought having no flowers it would not cost much. The former reason however was all that she had given to Mr. Carleton's remonstrances.

"What is all this, Elfie?" said he. "Have you been robbing your rose-tree?"

"No," said Elfie;—"there are plenty more buds! Isn't it lovely? This is the first one. They've been a great while coming out."

His eye went from the rose to her; he thought the one was a mere emblem of the other. Fleda was usually very quiet in her demonstrations; it was as if a little green bud had suddenly burst into a flush of loveliness; and he saw, it was as plain as possible, that good-will to him had been the moving power. He was so much struck and moved that his thanks, though as usual perfect in their kind, were far shorter and graver than he would have given if he had felt less. He turned away from the house, his mind full of the bright unsullied purity and single-hearted good-will that had looked out of that beaming little face; he seemed to see them again in the flower he held in his hand, and he saw nothing else as he went.

Mr. Carleton preached to himself all the way home, and his text was a rose.

Laugh who will. To many it may seem ridiculous; and to most minds it would have been impossible; but to a nature very finely wrought and highly trained, many a voice that grosser senses cannot hear comes with an utterance as clear as it is sweet-spoken; many a touch that coarser nerves cannot heed reaches the springs of the deeper life; many a truth that duller eyes have no skill to see shews its fair features, hid away among the petals of a rose, or peering out between the wings of a butterfly, or reflected in a bright drop of dew. The material is but a veil for the spiritual; but then eyes must be quickened, or the veil becomes an impassable cloud.

That particular rose was to Mr. Carleton's eye a most perfect emblem and representative of its little giver. He traced out the points of resemblance as he went along. The delicacy and character of refinement for which that kind of rose is remarkable above many of its more superb kindred; a refinement essential and unalterable by decay or otherwise, as true a characteristic of the child as of the flower; a delicacy that called for gentle handling and tender cherishing;—the sweetness, rare indeed, but asserting itself as it were timidly, at least with equally rare modesty; —the very style of the beauty, that with all its loveliness would not startle nor even catch the eye among its more showy neighbours;—and the breath of purity that seemed to own no kindred with earth, nor liability to infection.

As he went on with his musing, and drawing out this fair character from the type before him, the feeling of *contrast*, that he had known before, pressed upon Mr. Carleton's mind; the feeling of self-reproach, and the bitter wish that he could be again what he once had been, something like this. How changed now he seemed to himself—not a point of likeness left. How much less honourable, how much less worth, how much less dignified, than that fair innocent child. How much better a part she was acting in life—what an influence she was exerting,—as pure, as sweet-breathed, and as unobtrusive, as the very rose in his hand. And he—doing no good to an earthly creature and losing himself by inches.

He reached his room, put the flower in a glass on the table, and walked up and down before it. It had come to a struggle between the sense of what was and the passionate wish for what might have been.

"It is late, sir," said his servant opening the door,—"and you were—"

"I am not going out."

"This evening, sir?"

"No—not at all to-day. Spenser!—I don't wish to see anybody—let no one come near me."

The servant retired and Guy went on with his walk and his meditations; looking back over his life and reviewing, with a wiser ken now, the steps by which he had come. He compared the selfish disgust with which he had cast off the world with the very different spirit of little Fleda's look upon it that morning; the useless, self-pleasing, vain life he was leading, with her wish to be like the beloved disciple and do something to heal the troubles of those less happy than herself. He did not very well comprehend the grounds of her feeling or reasoning, but he began to see, mistily, that his own had been mistaken and wild.

His step grew slower, his eye more intent, his brow quiet.

"She is right and I am wrong," he thought. "She is by far the nobler creature—worth many such as I. *Like her* I cannot be—I cannot regain what I have lost,—I cannot undo what years have done. But I can be something other than I am! If there be a system of remedy, as there well may, it may as well take effect on myself first. She says everybody has his work; I believe her. It must in the nature of things be so. I will make it my business to find out what mine is; and when I have made that sure I will give myself to the doing of it. An Allwise Governor must look for service of me. He shall have it. Whatever my life be it shall be to some end. If not what I would, what I can. If not the purity of the rose, that of tempered steel!"

Mr. Carleton walked his room for three hours; then rung for his servant and ordered him to prepare everything for leaving Paris the second day thereafter.

The next morning over their coffee he told his mother of his purpose.

"Leave Paris!—To-morrow!—My dear Guy, that is rather a sudden notice."

"No mother—for I am going alone."

His mother immediately bent an anxious and somewhat terrified look upon him. The frank smile she met put half her suspicions out of her head at once.

"What is the matter?"

"Nothing at all—if by 'matter' you mean mischief."

"You are not in difficulty with those young men again?"

"No mother," said he coolly. "I am in difficulty with no one but myself."

"With yourself! But why will you not let me go with you?"

"My business will go on better if I am quite alone."

"What business?"

"Only to settle this question with myself," said he smiling.

"But Guy! you are enigmatical this morning. Is it the question that of all others I wish to see settled?"

"No mother," said he laughing and colouring a little,—"I don't want another half to take care of till I have this one under management."

"I don't understand you," said Mrs. Carleton. "There is no hidden reason under all this that you are keeping from me?"

"I won't say that. But there is none that need give you the least uneasiness. There are one or two matters I want to study out—I cannot do it here, so I am going where I shall be free."

"Where?"

"I think I shall pass the summer between Switzerland and Germany."

"And when and where shall I meet you again?"

"I think at home;—I cannot say when."

"At home!" said his mother with a brightening face. "Then you are beginning to be tired of wandering at last?"

"Not precisely, mother,—rather out of humour."

"I shall be glad of anything," said his mother, gazing at him admiringly, "that brings you home again, Guy."

"Bring me home a better man, I hope, mother," said he kissing her as he left the room. "I will see you again by and by."

"'A better man!'" thought Mrs. Carleton, as she sat with full eyes, the image of her son filling the place where his presence had been;—"I would be willing never to see him better and be sure of his never being worse!"

Mr. Carleton's farewell visit found Mr. and Mrs. Rossitur not at home. They had driven out early into the country to fetch Marion from her convent for some holiday. Fleda came alone into the saloon to receive him.

"I have your rose in safe keeping, Elfie," he said. "It has done me more good than ever a rose did before."

Fleda smiled an innocently pleased smile. But her look changed when he added,

"I have come to tell you so and to bid you good-bye."

"Are you going away, Mr. Carleton!"

"Yes."

"But you will be back soon?"

"No, Elfie,—I do not know that I shall ever come back."

He spoke gravely, more gravely than he was used; and Fleda's acuteness saw that there was some solid reason for this sudden determination. Her face changed sadly, but she was silent, her eyes never wavering from those that read hers with such gentle intelligence.

"You will be satisfied to have me go, Elfie, when I tell you that I am going on business which I believe to be duty. Nothing else takes me away. I am going to try to do right," said he smiling.

Elfie could not answer the smile. She wanted to ask whether she should never see him again, and there was another thought upon her tongue too; but her lip trembled and she said nothing.

"I shall miss my good fairy," Mr. Carleton went on lightly;—"I don't know how I shall do without her. If your wand was long enough to reach so far I would ask you to touch me now and then, Elfie."

Poor Elfie could not stand it. Her head sank. She knew she had a wand that could touch him, and well and gratefully she resolved that its light blessing should "now and then" rest on his head; but he did not understand that; he was talking, whether lightly or seriously, and Elfie knew it was a little of both,—he was talking of wanting her help, and was ignorant of the help that alone could avail him. "Oh that he knew but that!"—What with this feeling and sorrow together the child's distress was exceeding great; and the tokens of grief in one so accustomed to hide them were the more painful to see. Mr. Carleton drew the sorrowing little creature within his arm and endeavoured with a mixture of kindness and lightness in his tone to cheer her.

"I shall often remember you, dear Elfie," he said;—"I shall keep your rose always and take it with me wherever I go.—You must not make it too hard for me to quit Paris—you are glad to have me go on such an errand, are you not?"

She presently commanded herself, bade her tears wait till another time as usual, and trying to get rid of those that covered her face, asked him, "What errand?"

He hesitated.

"I have been thinking of what we were talking of yesterday, Elfie," he said at length. "I am going to try to discover my duty, and then to do it."

But Fleda at that clasped his hand, and squeezing it in

both hers bent down her little head over it to hide her face and the tears that streamed again. He hardly knew how to understand or what to say to her. He half suspected that there were depths in that childish mind beyond his fathoming. He was not however left to wait long. Fleda, though she might now and then be surprised into shewing it, never allowed her sorrow of any kind to press upon the notice or the time of others. She again checked herself and dried her face.

"There is nobody else in Paris that will be so sorry for my leaving it," said Mr. Carleton, half tenderly and half pleasantly.

"There is nobody else that has so much cause," said Elfie, near bursting out again, but she restrained herself.

"And you will not come here again, Mr. Carleton?" she said after a few minutes.

"I do not say that—it is possible—if I do, it will be to see you, Elfie."

A shadow of a smile passed over her face at that. It was gone instantly.

"My mother will not leave Paris yet," he went on,—"you will see her often."

But he saw that Fleda was thinking of something else; she scarce seemed to hear him. She was thinking of something that troubled her.

"Mr. Carleton—" she began, and her colour changed.

"Speak, Elfie."

Her colour changed again. "Mr. Carleton—will you be displeased if I say something?"

"Don't you know me better than to ask me that, Elfie?" he said gently.

"I want to ask you something,—if you won't mind my saying it."

"What is it?" said he, reading in her face that a request was behind. "I will do it."

Her eyes sparkled, but she seemed to have some difficulty in going on.

"I will do it, whatever it is," he said watching her.

"Will you wait for me one moment, Mr. Carleton?"

"Half an hour."

She sprang away, her face absolutely flashing pleasure

through her tears. It was much soberer, and again doubtful and changing colour, when a few minutes afterwards she came back with a book in her hand. With a striking mixture of timidity, modesty, and eagerness in her countenance she came forward, and putting the little volume, which was her own bible, into Mr. Carleton's hands said under her breath, "Please read it." She did not venture to look up.

He saw what the book was; and then taking the gentle hand which had given it, he kissed it two or three times. If it had been a princess's he could not with more respect.

"You have my promise, Elfie," he said. "I need not repeat it?"

She raised her eyes and gave him a look so grateful, so loving, so happy, that it dwelt for ever in his remembrance. A moment after it had faded, and she stood still where he had left her, listening to his footsteps as they went down the stairs. She heard the last of them, and then sank upon her knees by a chair and burst into a passion of tears. Their time was now and she let them come. It was not only the losing a loved and pleasant friend, it was not only the stirring of sudden and disagreeable excitement;—poor Elfie was crying for her bible. It had been her father's own—it was filled with his marks—it was precious to her above price—and Elfie cried with all her heart for the loss of it. She had done what she had on the spur of the emergency—she was satisfied she had done right; she would not take it back if she could; but not the less her bible was gone, and the pages that loved eyes had looked upon were for hers to look upon no more. Her very heart was wrung that she should have parted with it,—and yet,—what could she do?—It was as bad as the parting with Mr. Carleton.

That agony was over, and even that was shortened for "Hugh would find out that she had been crying." Hours had passed, and the tears were dried, and the little face was bending over the wonted tasks with a shadow upon its wonted cheerfulness,—when Rosaline came to tell her that Victor said there was somebody in the passage who wanted to see her and would not come in.

It was Mr. Carleton himself. He gave her a parcel, smiled at her without saying a word, kissed her hand earnestly, and was gone again. Fleda ran to her own room, and took the wrappers off such a beauty of a bible as she had never seen; bound in blue velvet, with clasps of gold, and her initials in letters of gold upon the cover. Fleda hardly knew whether to be most pleased or sorry; for to have its place so supplied seemed to put her lost treasure further away than ever. The result was another flood of very tender tears; in the very shedding of which however the new little bible was bound to her heart with cords of association as bright and as incorruptible as its gold mountings.

CHAPTER XV.

Her sports were such as carried riches of knowledge upon the stream of delight.—SIDNEY.

FLEDA had not been a year in Paris when her uncle suddenly made up his mind to quit it and go home. Some trouble in money affairs, felt or feared, brought him to this step, which a month before he had no definite purpose of ever taking. There was cloudy weather in the financial world of New York and he wisely judged it best that his own eyes should be on the spot to see to his own interests. Nobody was sorry for this determination. Mrs. Rossitur always liked what her husband liked, but she had at the same time a decided predilection for home. Marion was glad to leave her convent for the gay world, which her parents promised she should immediately enter. And Hugh and Fleda had too lively a spring of happiness within themselves to care where its outgoings should be.

So home they came, in good mood, bringing with them all manner of Parisian delights that Paris could part with. Furniture, that at home at least they might forget where they were; dresses, that at home or abroad nobody might forget where they had been; pictures and statuary and engravings and books, to satisfy a taste really strong and well cultivated. And indeed the other items were quite as much for this purpose as for any other. A French cook for Mr. Rossitur, and even Rosaline for his wife, who declared she was worth all the rest of Paris. Hugh cared little for any of these things; he brought home a treasure of books and a flute, to which he was devoted. Fleda cared for them all, even Monsieur Emile and Rosaline, for her uncle's and aunt's sake; but her special joy was a beautiful little King Charles which had been sent her by Mr. Carleton a few weeks before. It came with the kindest of letters, saying that some matters had made it inexpedient for him to pass through Paris on his way home but that he hoped nevertheless to see her soon. That intimation was the only thing that made Fleda sorry to leave Paris. The little dog was a beauty, allowed to be so not only by his mistress but by every one else; of the true black and tan colours; and Fleda's dearly loved and constant companion.

The life she and Hugh led was little changed by the change of place. They went out and came in as they had done in Paris, and took the same quiet but intense happiness in the same quiet occupations and pleasures; only the Tuileries and Champs Elysées had a miserable substitute in the Battery, and no substitute at all anywhere else. And the pleasant drives in the environs of Paris were missed too and had nothing in New York to supply their place. Mrs. Rossitur always said it was impossible to get out of New York by land, and not worth the trouble to do it by water. But then in the house Fleda thought there was a great gain. The dirty Parisian Hotel was well exchanged for the bright clean well-appointed house in State street. And if Broadway was disagreeable, and the Park a weariness to the eyes, after the dressed gardens of the French capital, Hugh and Fleda made it up in the delights of the luxuriously furnished library and the dear at-home feeling of having the whole house their own.

They were left, those two children, quite as much to themselves as ever. Marion was going into company, and she and her mother were swallowed up in the consequent necessary calls upon their time. Marion never had been anything to Fleda. She was a fine handsome girl, outwardly, but seemed to have more of her father than her mother in her composition, though colder-natured and more wrapped up in self than Mr. Rossitur would be called by anybody that knew him. She had never done anything to draw Fleda towards her, and even Hugh had very little of her attention. They did not miss it. They were everything to each other.

Everything,—for now morning and night there was a sort of whirlwind in the house which carried the mother and daughter round and round and permitted no rest; and Mr.

Rossitur himself was drawn in. It was worse than it had been in Paris. There, with Marion in her convent, there were often evenings when they did not go abroad nor receive company and spent the time quietly and happily in each other's society. No such evenings now; if by chance there were an unoccupied one Mrs. Rossitur and her daughter were sure to be tired and Mr. Rossitur busy.

Hugh and Fleda in those bustling times retreated to the library; Mr. Rossitur would rarely have that invaded; and while the net was so eagerly cast for pleasure among the gay company below, pleasure had often slipped away and hid herself among the things on the library table, and was dancing on every page of Hugh's book and minding each stroke of Fleda's pencil and cocking the spaniel's ears whenever his mistress looked at him. King, the spaniel, lay on a silk cushion on the library table, his nose just touching Fleda's fingers. Fleda's drawing was mere amusement; she and Hugh were not so burthened with studies that they had not always their evenings free, and to tell truth, much more than their evenings. Masters indeed they had; but the heads of the house were busy with the interests of their grown-up child, and perhaps with other interests; and took it for granted that all was going right with the young ones.

"Haven't we a great deal better time than they have down stairs, Fleda?" said Hugh one of these evenings.

"Hum—yes—" answered Fleda abstractedly, stroking into order some old man in her drawing with great intentness.—"King!—you rascal—keep back and be quiet, sir!—"

Nothing could be conceived more gentle and loving than Fleda's tone of fault-finding, and her repulse only fell short of a caress.

"What's he doing?"

"Wants to get into my lap."

"Why don't you let him!"

"Because I don't choose to—a silk cushion is good enough for his majesty. King!—" (laying her soft cheek against the little dog's soft head and forsaking her drawing for the purpose.)

"How you do love that dog!" said Hugh.

"Very well—why shouldn't I?—provided he steals no love from anybody else," said Fleda, still caressing him.

"What a noise somebody is making down stairs!" said Hugh. "I don't think I should ever want to go to large parties, Fleda, do you?"

"I don't know," said Fleda, whose natural taste for society was strongly developed;—"it would depend upon what kind of parties they were."

"I shouldn't like them, I know, of whatever kind," said Hugh. "What are you smiling at?"

"Only Mr. Pickwick's face, that I am drawing here."

Hugh came round to look and laugh, and then began again.

"I can't think of anything pleasanter than this room as we are now."

"You should have seen Mr. Carleton's library," said Fleda in a musing tone, going on with her drawing.

"Was it so much better than this?"

Fleda's eyes gave a slight glance at the room and then looked down again with a little shake of her head sufficiently expressive.

"Well," said Hugh, "you and I do not want any better than this, do we, Fleda?"

Fleda's smile, a most satisfactory one, was divided between him and King.

"I don't believe," said Hugh, "you would have loved that dog near so well if anybody else had given him to you."

"I don't believe I should!—not a quarter," said Fleda with sufficient distinctness.

"I never liked that Mr. Carleton as well as you did."

"That is because you did not know him," said Fleda quietly.

"Do you think he was a good man, Fleda?"

"He was very good to me," said Fleda, "always. What rides I did have on that great black horse of his!"—

"A black horse?"

"Yes, a great black horse, strong, but so gentle, and he went so delightfully. His name was Harold. Oh I should like to see that horse!—When I wasn't with him, Mr. Carleton used to ride another, the greatest beauty of a horse, Hugh; a brown Arabian—so slender and delicate—her name was Zephyr, and she used to go like the wind to be sure. Mr. Carleton said he wouldn't trust me on such a fly-away thing."

"But you didn't use to ride alone?" said Hugh.

"Oh no!—and *I* wouldn't have been afraid if he had chosen to take me on any one."

"But do you think, Fleda, he was a *good* man? as I mean?"

"I am sure he was better than a great many others," answered Fleda evasively;—"the worst of him was infinitely better than the best of half the people down stairs,—Mr. Sweden included."

"Sweden!—you don't call his name right."

"The worse it is called the better, in my opinion," said Fleda.

"Well, I don't like him; but what makes you dislike him so much?"

"I don't know—partly because Uncle Rolf and Marion like him so much, I believe—I don't think there is any moral expression in his face."

"I wonder why they like him," said Hugh.

It was a somewhat irregular and desultory education that the two children gathered under this system of things. The masters they had were rather for accomplishments and languages than for anything solid; the rest they worked out for themselves. Fortunately they both loved books, and rational books; and hours and hours, when Mrs. Rossitur and her daughter were paying or receiving visits, they, always together, were stowed away behind the book-cases or in the library window poring patiently over pages of various complexion; the soft turning of the leaves or Fleda's frequent attentions to King the only sound in the room. They walked together, talking of what they had read, though indeed they ranged beyond that into nameless and numberless fields of speculation, where if they sometimes found fruit they as often lost their way. However the habit of ranging was something. Then when they joined the rest of the family at the dinner-table, especially if others were present, and most especially if a certain German gentleman happened to be there who the second winter after their return Fleda thought came very often, she and Hugh would be sure to find the strange talk of the world that was going on unsuited and wearisome to them, and they would make their escape up stairs again to handle the pencil and to play the flute and to read, and to draw plans for the future, while King crept upon the skirts of his mistress's gown and laid his little head on her feet. Nobody ever thought of sending them to school. Hugh was a child of frail health, and though not often very ill was often near it; and as for Fleda, she and Hugh were inseparable; and besides by this time her uncle and aunt would almost as soon have thought of taking the mats off their delicate shrubs in winter as of exposing her to any atmosphere less genial than that of home.

For Fleda this doubtful course of mental training wrought singularly well. An uncommonly quick eye and strong memory and clear head, which she had even in childhood, passed over no field of truth or fancy without making their quiet gleanings; and the stores thus gathered, though somewhat miscellaneous and unarranged, were both rich and uncommon, and more than any one or she herself knew. Perhaps such a mind thus left to itself knew a more free and luxuriant growth than could ever have flourished within the confinement of rules. Perhaps a plant at once so strong and so delicate was safest without the hand of the dresser. At all events it was permitted to spring and to put forth all its native gracefulness alike unhindered and unknown. Cherished as little Fleda dearly was, her mind kept company with no one but herself,—and Hugh. As to externals,—music was uncommonly loved by both the children, and by both cultivated with great success. So much came under Mrs. Rossitur's knowledge. Also every foreign Signor and Madame that came into the house to teach them spoke with enthusiasm of the apt minds and flexile tongues that honoured their instructions. In private and in public the gentle, docile, and affectionate children answered every wish both of taste and judgment. And perhaps, in a world where education is *not* understood, their guardians might be pardoned for taking it for granted that all was right where nothing appeared that was wrong; certainly they took no pains to make sure of the fact. In this case, one of a thousand, their neglect was not punished with disappointment. They never found out that Hugh's mind wanted the strengthening that early skilful training might have given it. His intellectual tastes were not so strong as Fleda's; his reading was more superficial; his gleanings not so sound and in far fewer fields, and they went rather to nourish sentiment and fancy than to stimulate thought or lay up food for it. But his parents saw nothing of this.

The third winter had not passed, when Fleda's discernment saw that Mr. Sweden, as she called him, the German gentleman, would not cease coming to the house till he had carried off Marion with him. Her opinion on the subject was delivered to no one but Hugh.

That winter introduced them to a better acquaintance. One evening Dr. Gregory, an uncle of Mrs. Rossitur's, had been dining with her and was in the drawing-room. Mr. Schwiden had been there too, and he and Marion and one or two other young people had gone out to some popular entertainment. The children knew little of Dr. Gregory but that he was a very respectable-looking elderly gentleman, a little rough in his manners; the doctor had not long been returned from a stay of some years in Europe where he had been collecting rare books for a fine public library, the charge of which was now entrusted to him. After talking some time with Mr. and Mrs. Rossitur the doctor pushed round his chair to take a look at the children.

"So that's Amy's child," said he. "Come here Amy."

"That is not my name," said the little girl coming forward.

"Isn't it? It ought to be. What *is* then?"

"Elfleda."

"Elfleda!—Where in the name of all that is auricular did you get such an outlandish name?"

"My father gave it to me, sir," said Fleda, with a dignified sobriety which amused the old gentleman.

"Your father!—Hum—I understand. And couldn't your father find a cap that fitted you without going back to the old-fashioned days of King Alfred?"

"Yes sir; it was my grandmother's cap."

"I am afraid your grandmother's cap isn't all of her that's come down to you," said he, tapping his snuff-box and looking at her with a curious twinkle in his eyes. "What do you call yourself? Haven't you some variations of this tongue-twisting appellative to serve for every day and save trouble?"

"They call me Fleda," said the little girl, who could not help laughing.

"Nothing better than that?"

Fleda remembered two prettier nick-names which had been hers; but one had been given by dear lips long ago, and she was not going to have it profaned by common use; and "Elfie" belonged to Mr. Carleton. She would own to nothing but Fleda.

"Well Miss Fleda," said the doctor, "are you going to school?"

"No sir."

"You intend to live without such a vulgar thing as learning?"

"No sir—Hugh and I have our lessons at home?"

"Teaching each other, I suppose?"

"O no, sir," said Fleda laughing;—"Mme. Lascelles and Mr. Schweppenhesser and Signor Barytone come to teach us, besides our music masters."

"Do you ever talk German with this Mr. What's-his-name who has just gone out with your cousin Marion?"

"I never talk to him at all, sir."

"Don't you? why not? Don't you like him?"

Fleda said "not particularly," and seemed to wish to let the subject pass, but the doctor was amused and pressed it.

"Why why don't you like him?" said he; "I am sure he's a fine-looking dashing gentleman,—dresses as well as anybody, and talks as much as most people,—why don't you like him? Isn't he a handsome fellow, eh?"

"I dare say he is, to many people," said Fleda.

"She said she didn't think there was any moral expression in his face," said Hugh, by way of settling the matter.

"Moral expression!" cried the doctor,—"moral expression!—and what if there isn't, you Elf!—what if there isn't?"

"I shouldn't care what other kind of expression it had," said Fleda, colouring a little.

Mr. Rossitur 'pished' rather impatiently. The doctor glanced at his niece, and changed the subject.

"Well who teaches you English, Miss Fleda? you haven't told me that yet."

"O that we teach ourselves," said Fleda, smiling as if it was a very innocent question.

"Hum!—you do! Pray how do you teach yourselves?"

"By reading, sir."

"Reading! And what do you read? what have you read in the last twelve months, now?"

"I don't think I could remember all exactly," said Fleda.

"But you have got a list of them all," said Hugh, who chanced to have been looking over said list a day or two before and felt quite proud of it.

"Let's have it—let's have it," said the doctor. And Mrs. Rossitur laughing said "Let's have it;" and even her husband commanded Hugh to go and fetch it; so poor Fleda, though not a little unwilling, was obliged to let the list be forthcoming. Hugh brought it, in a neat little book covered with pink blotting paper.

"Now for it," said the doctor;—"let us see what this English amounts to. Can you stand fire, Elfleda?"

* 'Jan. 1. Robinson Crusoe.'

"Hum—that sounds reasonable, at all events."

"I had it for a New Year present," remarked Fleda, who stood by with down-cast eyes, like a person undergoing an examination.

'Jan. 2. Histoire de France.'

"What history of France is this?"

Fleda hesitated and then said it was by Lacretelle.

"Lacretelle?—what, of the Revolution?"

"No sir, it is before that; it is in five or six large volumes."

"What, Louis XV's time!" said the doctor muttering to himself.

'Jan. 27. 2. ditto, ditto.'

"'Two' means the second volume I suppose?"

"Yes sir."

"Hum—if you were a mouse you would gnaw through the wall in time at that rate. This is in the original?"

"Yes sir."

'Feb. 3. Paris. L. E. K.'

"What do these hieroglyphics mean?"

* A true list made by a child of that age.

"That stands for the 'Library of Entertaining Knowledge,'" said Fleda.

"But how is this?—do you go hop skip and jump through these books, or read a little and then throw them away? Here it is only seven days since you began the second volume of Lacretelle—not time enough to get through it."

"O no, sir," said Fleda smiling,—"I like to have several books that I am reading in at once,—I mean—at the same time, you know; and then if I am not in the mood of one I take up another."

"She reads them all through," said Hugh,—"always, though she reads them very quick."

"Hum—I understand," said the old doctor with a humorous expression, going on with the list.

'March 3. 3 Hist. de France.'

"But you finish one of these volumes, I suppose, before you begin another; or do you dip into different parts of the same work at once?"

"O no, sir;—of course not!"

'Mar. 5. Modern Egyptians. L. E. K. Ap. 13.'

"What are these dates on the right as well as on the left?"

"Those on the right shew when I finished the volume."

"Well I wonder what you were cut out for!" said the doctor. "A Quaker!—you aren't a Quaker, are you?"

"No sir," said Fleda laughing.

"You look like it," said he.

'Feb. 24. Five Penny Magazines, finished Mar. 4.'

"They are in paper numbers, you know, sir."

'April 4. 4 Hist. de. F.'

"Let us see—the third volume was finished March 29—I declare you keep it up pretty well."

'Ap. 19. Incidents of Travel.'

"Whose is that?"

"It is by Mr. Stephens."

"How did you like it?"

"O very much indeed."

"Ay, I see you did; you finished it by the first of May. 'Tour to the Hebrides'—what? Johnson's?"

"Yes sir."

"Read it all fairly through?"

"Yes sir, certainly."

He smiled and went on.

'May 12. Peter Simple!'

There was quite a shout at the heterogeneous character of Fleda's reading, which she, not knowing exactly what to make of it, heard rather abashed.

"'Peter Simple'!" said the doctor, settling himself to go on with his list;—"well, let us see.—'World without Souls.' Why you Elf! read in two days."

"It is very short, you know, sir."

"What did you think of it?"

"I liked parts of it very much."

He went on, still smiling.

'June 15. Goldsmith's Animated Nature.'

' " 18. 1 Life of Washington.'

"What Life of Washington?"

"Marshall's."

"Hum.—'July 9. 2 Goldsmith's An. Na.' As I live, begun the very day the first volume was finished. Did you read the whole of that?"

"O yes, sir. I liked that book very much."

'July 12. 5 Hist. de France.'

"Two histories on hand at once! Out of all rule, Miss Fleda! We must look after you."

"Yes sir; sometimes I wanted to read one, and sometimes I wanted to read the other."

"And you always do what you want to do, I suppose?"

"I think the reading does me more good in that way."

'July 15. Paley's Natural Theology!'

There was another shout. Poor Fleda's eyes filled with tears.

"What in the world put that book into your head, or before your eyes?" said the doctor.

"I don't know, sir,—I thought I should like to read it," said Fleda, drooping her eyelids that the bright drops under them might not be seen.

"And finished in eleven days, as I live!" said the doctor wagging his head. 'July 19. 3 Goldsmith's A. N.'

'Aug. 6. 4 Do. Do.

"That is one of Fleda's favourite books," put in Hugh.

"So it seems. '6 Hist. de France.'—What does this little cross mean?"

"That shews when the book is finished," said Fleda, looking on the page,—"the last volume, I mean."

"'Retrospect of Western Travel'—'Goldsmith's A. N., last vol.'—'Memoirs de Sully'—in the French?"

"Yes sir."

"'Life of Newton'—What's this?—'Sep. 8. 1 Fairy Queen!'—not Spenser's?"

"Yes sir, I believe so—the Fairy Queen, in five volumes."

The doctor looked up comically at his niece and her husband, who were both sitting or standing close by.

"'Sep. 10. Paolo e Virginia.'—In what language?"

"Italian, sir; I was just beginning, and I haven't finished it yet."

"'Sep. 16. Milner's Church History'!—What the deuce!—'Vol. 2. Fairy Queen.'—Why this must have been a favourite book too."

"That's one of the books Fleda loves best," said Hugh; —"she went through that very fast."

"*Over* it, you mean, I reckon; how much did you skip, Fleda?"

"I didn't skip at all," said Fleda; "I read every word of it."

"'Sep. 20. 2 Mem. de Sully.'—Well, you're an industrious mouse, I'll say that for you.—What's this—'Don Quixotte!'—'Life of Howard'—'Nov. 17. 3 Fairy Queen.' —'Nov. 29. 4 Fairy Queen.'—'Dec. 8. 1 Goldsmith's England.'—Well if this list of books is a fair exhibit of your taste and capacity, you have a most happily proportioned set of intellectuals. Let us see—History, fun, facts, nature, theology, poetry and divinity!—upon my soul!—and poetry and history the leading features!—a little fun, —as much as you could lay your hand on, I'll warrant, by that pinch in the corner of your eye. And here, the eleventh of December, you finished the Fairy Queen;—and ever since, I suppose, you have been imagining yourself the 'faire Una,' with Hugh standing for Prince Arthur or the Red-cross knight,—haven't you?"

"No sir. I didn't imagine anything about it."

"Don't tell me! What did you read it for?"

"Only because I liked it, sir. I liked it better than any other book I read last year."

"You did! Well, the year ends, I see, with another volume of Sully. I won't enter upon this year's list. Pray how much of all these volumes do you suppose you remember? I'll try and find out, next time I come to see you. I can give a guess, if you study with that little pug in your lap."

"He is not a pug!" said Fleda, in whose arms King was lying luxuriously,—"and he never gets into my lap besides."

"Don't he! Why not?"

"Because I don't like it, sir. I don't like to see dogs in laps."

"But all the ladies in the land do it, you little Saxon! it is universally considered a mark of distinction."

"I can't help what all the ladies in the land do," said Fleda. "That won't alter my liking, and I don't think a lady's lap is a place for a dog."

"I wish you were *my* daughter!" said the old doctor, shaking his head at her with a comic fierce expression of countenance, which Fleda perfectly understood and laughed at accordingly. Then as the two children with the dog went off into the other room, he said, turning to his niece and Mr. Rossitur,

"If that girl ever takes a wrong turn with the bit in her teeth, you'll be puzzled to hold her. What stuff will you make the reins of?"

"I don't think she ever will take a wrong turn," said Mr. Rossitur.

"A look is enough to manage her, if she did," said his wife. "Hugh is not more gentle."

"I should be inclined rather to fear her not having stability of character enough," said Mr. Rossitur. "She is so very meek and yielding, I almost doubt whether anything would give her courage to take ground of her own and keep it."

"Hum——well, well!" said the old doctor, walking off after the children. "Prince Arthur, will you bring this damsel up to my den some of these days?—the 'faire

Una' is safe from the wild beasts, you know;—and I'll shew her books enough to build herself a house with, if she likes."

The acceptance of this invitation led to some of the pleasantest hours of Fleda's city life. The visits to the great library became very frequent. Dr. Gregory and the children were little while in growing fond of each other; he loved to see them and taught them to come at such times as the library was free of visiters and his hands of engagements. Then he delighted himself with giving them pleasure, especially Fleda, whose quick curiosity and intelligence were a constant amusement to him. He would establish the children in some corner of the large apartments, out of the way behind a screen of books and tables; and there shut out from the world they would enjoy a kind of fairyland pleasure over some volume or set of engravings that they could not see at home. Hours and hours were spent so. Fleda would stand clasping her hands before Audubon, or rapt over a finely illustrated book of travels, or going through and through with Hugh the works of the best masters of the pencil and the graver. The doctor found he could trust them, and then all the treasures of the library were at their disposal. Very often he put chosen pieces of reading into their hands; and it was pleasantest of all when he was not busy and came and sat down with them; for with all his odd manner he was extremely kind, and could and did put them in the way to profit greatly by their opportunities. The doctor and the children had nice times there together.

They lasted for many months, and grew more and more worth. Mr. Schwiden carried off Marion, as Fleda had foreseen he would, before the end of spring; and after she was gone something like the old pleasant Paris life was taken up again. They had no more company now than was agreeable, and it was picked not to suit Marion's taste but her father's,—a very different matter. Fleda and Hugh were not forbidden the dinner-table, and so had the good of hearing much useful conversation from which the former, according to custom, made her steady precious gleanings. The pleasant evenings in the family were still better enjoyed than they used to be; Fleda was older; and the snug handsome American house had a home-feeling to her that the wide Parisian saloons never knew. She had become bound to her uncle and aunt by all but the ties of blood; nobody in the house ever remembered that she was not born their daughter; except indeed Fleda herself, who remembered everything, and with whom the forming of any new affections or relations somehow never blotted out or even faded the register of the old. It lived in all its brightness; the writing of past loves and friendships was as plain as ever in her heart; and often, often the eye and the kiss of memory fell upon it. In the secret of her heart's core; for still, as at the first, no one had a suspicion of the movings of thought that were beneath that childish brow. No one guessed how clear a judgment weighed and decided upon many things. No one dreamed, amid their busy, bustling, thoughtless life, how often, in the street, in her bed, in company and alone, her mother's last prayer was in Fleda's heart; well cherished; never forgotten.

Her education and Hugh's meanwhile went on after the old fashion. If Mr. Rossitur had more time he seemed to have no more thought for the matter; and Mrs. Rossitur, fine-natured as she was, had never been trained to self-exertion and of course was entirely out of the way of training others. Her children were pieces of perfection, and needed no oversight; her house was a piece of perfection too. If either had not been, Mrs. Rossitur would have been utterly at a loss how to mend matters,—except in the latter instance by getting a new housekeeper; and as Mrs. Renney, the good woman who held that station, was in everybody's opinion another treasure, Mrs. Rossitur's mind was uncrossed by the shadow of such a dilemma. With Mrs. Renny as with every one else Fleda was held in highest regard; always welcome to her premises and to those mysteries of her trade which were sacred from other intrusion. Fleda's natural inquisitiveness carried her often to the housekeeper's room, and made her there the same curious and careful observer that she had been in the library or at the Louvre.

"Come," said Hugh one day when he had sought and found her in Mrs. Renney's precincts,—"come away, Fleda! What do you want to stand here and see Mrs. Renney roll butter and sugar for?"

"My dear Mr. Rossitur!" said Fleda,—"you don't understand quelquechoses. How do you know but I may have to get my living by making them, some day."

"By making what?" said Hugh.

"Quelquechoses,—anglicé, kickshaws,—alias, sweet trifles denominated merrings."

"Pshaw, Fleda!"

"Miss Fleda is more likely to get her living by eating them, Mr. Hugh, isn't she?" said the housekeeper.

"I hope to decline both lines of life," said Fleda laughingly as she followed Hugh out of the room. But her chance remark had grazed the truth sufficiently near.

Those years in New York were a happy time for little Fleda, a time when mind and body flourished under the sun of prosperity. Luxury did not spoil her; and any one that saw her in the soft furs of her winter wrappings would have said that delicate cheek and frame were never made to know the unkindliness of harsher things.

CHAPTER XVI.

Whereunto is money good?
Who has it not wants hardihood,
Who has it has much trouble and care,
Who once has had it has despair.
LONGFELLOW. *From the German.*

IT was the middle of winter. One day Hugh and Fleda had come home from their walk. They dashed into the parlour, complaining that it was bitterly cold, and began unrobing before the glowing grate, which was a mass of living fire from end to end. Mrs. Rossitur was there in an easy chair, alone and doing nothing. That was not a thing absolutely unheard of, but Fleda had not pulled off her second glove before she bent down towards her and in a changed tone tenderly asked if she did not feel well?

Mrs. Rossitur looked up in her face a minute, and then drawing her down kissed the blooming cheeks one and the other several times. But as she looked off to the fire again Fleda saw that it was through watering eyes. She dropped on her knees by the side of the easy chair that she might have a better sight of that face, and tried to read it as she asked again what was the matter; and Hugh coming to the other side repeated her question. His mother passed an arm round each, looking wistfully from one to the other and kissing them earnestly, but she said only, with a very heart-felt emphasis, "Poor children!"

Fleda was now afraid to speak, but Hugh pressed his inquiry.

"Why 'poor' mamma? what makes you say so?"

"Because you are poor really, dear Hugh. We have lost everything we have in the world."

"Mamma! What do you mean?"

"Your father has failed."

"Failed!—But mamma I thought he wasn't in business?"

"So I thought," said Mrs. Rossitur;—"I didn't know people could fail that were not in business; but it seems they can. He was a partner in some concern or other, and it's all broken to pieces, and your father with it, he says."

Mrs. Rossitur's face was distressful. They were all silent for a little; Hugh kissing his mother's wet cheeks. Fleda had softly nestled her head in her bosom. But Mrs. Rossitur soon recovered herself.

"How bad is it, mother?" said Hugh.

"As bad as can possibly be."

"Is *everything* gone?"

"Everything!"—

"You don't mean the house, mamma?"

"The house, and all that is in it."

The children's hearts were struck, and they were silent again, only a trembling touch of Fleda's lips spoke sympathy and patience if ever a kiss did.

"But mamma," said Hugh, after he had gathered breath for it,—"do you mean to say that *everything*, literally *everything*, is gone? is there nothing left?"

"Nothing in the world—not a sou."

"Then what are we going to do!"

Mrs. Rossitur shook her head, and had no words.

Fleda *looked* across to Hugh to ask no more, and putting her arms round her aunt's neck and laying cheek to cheek, she spoke what comfort she could.

"Don't, dear aunt Lucy!—there will be some way—things always turn out better than at first—I dare say we shall find out it isn't so bad by and by. Don't you mind it, and then we won't. We can be happy anywhere together."

If there was not much in the reasoning there was something in the tone of the words to bid Mrs. Rossitur bear herself well. Its tremulous sweetness, its anxious love, was without a taint of self-recollection; its sorrow was for *her*. Mrs. Rossitur felt that she must not shew herself overcome. She again kissed and blessed and pressed closer in her arms her little comforter, while her other hand was given to Hugh.

"I have only heard about it this morning. Your uncle was here telling me just now,—a little while before you came in. Don't say anything about it before him."

Why not? The words struck Fleda disagreeably.

"What will be done with the house, mamma?" said Hugh.

"Sold—sold, and everything in it."

"Papa's books, mamma! and all the things in the library!" exclaimed Hugh, looking terrified.

Mrs. Rossitur's face gave the answer; do it in words she could not.

The children were a long time silent, trying hard to swallow this bitter pill; and still Hugh's hand was in his mother's and Fleda's head lay on her bosom. Thought was busy, going up and down, and breaking the companionship they had so long held with the pleasant drawing-room and the tasteful arrangements among which Fleda was so much at home;—the easy chairs in whose comfortable arms she had had so many an hour of nice reading; the soft rug where in the very wantonness of frolic she had stretched herself to play with King; that very luxurious bright grateful of fire, which had given her so often the same warm welcome home, an apt introduction to the other stores of comfort which awaited her above and below stairs; the rich-coloured curtains and carpet, the beauty of which had been such a constant gratification to Fleda's eye; and the exquisite French table and lamps they had brought out with them, in which her uncle and aunt had so much pride and which could nowhere be matched for elegance;—they must all be said 'good-bye' to; and as yet fancy had nothing to furnish the future with; it looked very bare.

King had come in and wagged himself up close to his mistress, but even he could obtain nothing but the touch of most abstracted finger-ends. Yet, though keenly recognised, these thoughts were only passing compared with the anxious and sorrowful ones that went to her aunt and uncle; for Hugh and her, she judged, it was less matter. And Mrs. Rossitur's care was most for her husband; and Hugh's was for them all. His associations were less quick and his tastes less keen than Fleda's and less a part of himself. Hugh lived in his affections· with a salvo to them, he could bear to lose anything and go any where.

"Mamma," said he after a long time,—"will anything be done with Fleda's books?"

A question that had been in Fleda's mind before, but which she had patiently forborne just then to ask.

"No indeed!" said Mrs. Rossitur, pressing Fleda more closely and kissing in a kind of rapture the sweet thoughtful face;—"not yours, my darling; they can't touch anything that belongs to you—I wish it was more—and I don't suppose they will take anything of mine either."

"Ah, well!" said Fleda raising her head, "you have got quite a parcel of books, aunt Lucy, and I have a good many —how well it is I have had so many given me since I have been here!—That will make quite a nice little library, both together, and Hugh has some; I thought perhaps we shouldn't have one at all left, and that would have been rather bad."

'Rather bad'! Mrs. Rossitur looked at her, and was dumb.

"Only don't you wear a sad face for anything!" Fleda went on earnestly;—"we shall be perfectly happy if you and uncle Rolf only will be."

"My dear children!" said Mrs. Rossitur wiping her eyes, —"it is for you I am unhappy—you and your uncle;—I do not think of myself."

"And we do not think of ourselves, mamma," said Hugh.

"I know it—but having good children don't make one care less about them," said Mrs. Rossitur, the tears fairly raining over her fingers.

Hugh pulled the fingers down and again tried the efficacy of his lips.

"And you know papa thinks most of you, mamma."

"Ah, your father!"—said Mrs. Rossitur shaking her head,—"I am afraid it will go hard with him!—But I will be happy as long as I have you two, or else I should be a very wicked woman. It only grieves me to think of your education and prospects—"

"Fleda's piano, mamma!" said Hugh with sudden dismay.

Mrs. Rossitur shook her head again and covered her eyes, while Fleda stretching across to Hugh gave him by look and touch an earnest admonition to let that subject alone. And then with a sweetness and gentleness like nothing but the breath of the south wind, she wooed her aunt to hope and resignation. Hugh held back, feeling, or thinking, that Fleda could do it better than he, and watching her progress, as Mrs. Rossitur took her hand from her face, and smiled, at first mournfully and then really mirthfully in Fleda's face, at some sally that nobody but a nice observer would have seen was got up for the occasion. And it was hardly that, so completely had the child forgotten her own sorrow in ministering to that of another. "Blessed are the peacemakers"! It is always so.

"You are a witch or a fairy," said Mrs. Rossitur, catching her again in her arms,—"nothing else! You must try your powers of charming upon your uncle."

Fleda laughed, without any effort; but as to trying her slight wand upon Mr. Rossitur she had serious doubts. And the doubts became certainty when they met at dinner; he looked so grave that she dared not attack him. It was a gloomy meal, for the face that should have lighted the whole table cast a shadow there.

Without at all comprehending the whole of her husband's character the sure magnetism of affection had enabled Mrs. Rossitur to divine his thoughts. Pride was his ruling passion; not such pride as Mr. Carleton's, which was rather like exaggerated self-respect, but wider and more indiscriminate in its choice of objects. It was pride in his family name; pride in his own talents, which were considerable; pride in his family, wife and children and all of which he thought did him honour,—if they had not his love for them assuredly would have known some diminishing;—pride in his wealth and in the attractions with which it surrounded him; and lastly, pride in the skill, taste and connoisseurship which enabled him to bring those attractions together. Furthermore, his love for both literature and art was true and strong; and for many years he had accustomed himself to lead a life of great luxuriousness; catering for body and mind in every taste that could be elegantly enjoyed; and again proud of the elegance of every enjoyment. The change of circumstances which touched his pride wounded him at every point where he was vulnerable at all.

Fleda had never felt so afraid of him. She was glad to see Dr. Gregory come in to tea. Mr. Rossitur was not there. The Doctor did not touch upon affairs, if he had heard of their misfortune; he went on as usual in a rambling cheerful way all tea-time, talking mostly to Fleda and Hugh. But after tea he talked no more but sat still and waited till the master of the house came in.

Fleda thought Mr. Rossitur did not look glad to see him. But how could he look glad about anything? He did not sit down, and for a few minutes there was a kind of meaning silence. Fleda sat in the corner with the heartache, to see her uncle's gloomy tramp up and down the rich apartment, and her aunt Lucy's gaze at him.

"Humph!—well—So!" said the Doctor at last,—"You've all gone overboard with a smash, I understand?"

The walker gave him no regard.

"True, is it?" said the doctor.

Mr. Rossitur made no answer, unless a smothered grunt might be taken for one.

"How came it about?"

"Folly and Devilry."

"Humph!—bad capital to work upon. I hope the principal is gone with the interest. What's the amount of your loss?"

"Ruin."

"Humph.—French ruin, or American ruin? because there's a difference. What do you mean?"

"I am not so happy as to understand you sir, but we shall not pay seventy cents on the dollar."

The old gentleman got up and stood before the fire with his back to Mr. Rossitur, saying "that was rather bad."

"What are you going to do?"

Mr. Rossitur hesitated a few moments for an answer and then said,

"Pay the seventy cents and begin the world anew with nothing."

"Of course!" said the doctor. "I understand that; but where and how? What end of the world will you take up first?"

Mr. Rossitur writhed in impatience or disgust, and after

again hesitating answered dryly that he had not determined.

"Have you thought of anything in particular?"

"Zounds! no sir, except my misfortune. That's enough for one day."

"And too much," said the old doctor, "unless you can mix some other thought with it. That's what I came for. Will you go into business?"

Fleda was startled by the vehemence with which her uncle said "No, never!"—and he presently added, "I'll do nothing here."

"Well,—well," said the doctor to himself;—"Will you go into the country?"

"Yes!—anywhere!—the further the better."

Mrs. Rossitur startled, but her husband's face did not encourage her to open her lips.

"Ay but on a farm, I mean?"

"On anything, that will give me a standing."

"I thought that too," said Dr. Gregory, now whirling about. "I have a fine piece of land that wants a tenant. You may take it at an easy rate, and pay me when the crops come in. I shouldn't expect so young a farmer, you know, to keep any closer terms."

"How far is it?"

"Far enough—up in Wyandot County."

"How large?"

"A matter of two or three hundred acres or so. It is very fine, they say. It came into a fellow's hands that owed me what I thought was a bad debt, so for fear he would never pay me I thought best to take it and pay him; whether the place will ever fill my pockets again remains to be seen; doubtful, I think."

"I'll take it, Dr. Gregory, and see if I cannot bring that about."

"Pooh, pooh! fill your own. I am not careful about it; the less money one has the more it jingles, unless it gets *too* low indeed."

"I will take it, Dr. Gregory, and feel myself under obligation to you."

"No, I told you, not till the crops come in. No obligation

is binding till the term is up. Well, I'll see you further about it."

"But Rolf!" said Mrs. Rossitur,—"stop a minute, uncle, don't go yet,—Rolf don't know anything in the world about the management of a farm, neither do I."

"The 'faire Una' can enlighten you," said the doctor, waving his hand towards his little favourite in the corner,—"but I forgot!—Well, if you don't know, the crops won't come in—that's all the difference."

But Mrs. Rossitur looked anxiously at her husband. "Do you know exactly what you are undertaking, Rolf?" she said.

"If I do not, I presume I shall discover in time."

"But it may be too late," said Mrs. Rossitur, in the tone of sad remonstrance that had gone all the length it dared.

"It *can not* be too late!" said her husband impatiently. "If I do not know what I am taking up, I know very well what I am laying down; and it does not signify a straw what comes after—if it was a snail-shell, that would cover my head!"

"Hum—" said the old doctor,—"the snail is very well in his way, but I have no idea that he was ever cut out for a farmer."

"Do you think you will find it a business you would like, Mr. Rossitur?" said his wife timidly.

"I tell you," said he facing about, "it is not a question of liking. I will like anything that will bury me out of the world!"

Poor Mrs. Rossitur. She had not yet come to wishing herself buried alive, and she had small faith in the permanence of her husband's taste for it. She looked desponding.

"You don't suppose," said Mr. Rossitur stopping again in the middle of the floor after another turn and a half,—"you do not suppose that I am going to take the labouring of the farm upon myself? I shall employ some one of course, who understands the matter, to take all that off my hands."

The doctor thought of the old proverb and the alternative the plough presents to those who would thrive by it; Fleda thought of Mr. Didenhover; Mrs. Rossitur would fain have suggested that such an important person must be well paid; but neither of them spoke.

"Of course," said Mr. Rossitur haughtily as he went on with his walk, "I do not expect any more than you to live in the backwoods the life we have been leading here. That is at an end."

"Is it a very wild country?" asked Mrs. Rossitur of the doctor.

"No wild beasts, my dear, if that is your meaning,—and I do not suppose there are even many snakes left by this time."

"No, but dear uncle, I mean, is it in an unsettled state?"

"No my dear, not at all,—perfectly quiet."

"Ah but, do not play with me," exclaimed poor Mrs. Rossitur between laughing and crying;—"I mean is it far from any town and not among neighbours?"

"Far enough to be out of the way of morning calls," said the doctor;—"and when your neighbours come to see you they will expect tea by four o'clock. There are not a great many near by, but they don't mind coming from five or six miles off."

Mrs. Rossitur looked chilled and horrified. To her he had described a very wild country indeed. Fleda would have laughed if it had not been for her aunt's face; but that settled down into a doubtful anxious look that pained her. It pained the old doctor too.

"Come," said he touching her pretty chin with his fore finger,—"what are you thinking of? folks may be good folks and yet have tea at four o'clock, mayn't they?"

"When do they have dinner!" said Mrs. Rossitur.

"I really don't know. When you get settled up there I'll come and see."

"Hardly," said Mrs. Rossitur. "I don't believe it would be possible for Emile to get dinner before the tea-time; and I am sure I shouldn't like to propose such a thing to Mrs. Renney."

The doctor fidgeted about a little on the hearth-rug and looked comical, perfectly understood by one acute observer in the corner.

"Are you wise enough to imagine, Lucy," said Mr. Rossitur sternly, "that you can carry your whole establishment with you? What do you suppose Emile and Mrs. Renney would do in a farm-house?"

"I can do without whatever you can," said Mrs. Rossitur meekly. "I did not know that you would be willing to part with Emile, and I do not think Mrs. Renney would like to leave us."

"I told you before, it is no more a question of liking," answered he.

"And if it were," said the doctor, "I have no idea that Monsieur Emile and Madame Renney would be satisfied with the style of a country kitchen, or think the interior of Yankee land a hopeful sphere for their energies."

"What sort of a house is it?" said Mrs. Rossitur.

"A wooden frame house, I believe."

"No but, dear uncle, do tell me."

"What sort of a house?—Humph—Large enough, I am told. It will accommodate you, in one way."

"Comfortable?"

"I don't know," said the doctor shaking his head;—"depends on who's in it. No house is that per se. But I reckon there isn't much plate glass. I suppose you'll find the doors all painted blue, and every fireplace with a crane in it."

"A crane!" said Mrs. Rossitur, to whose imagination the word suggested nothing but a large water-bird with a long neck.

"Ay!" said the doctor. "But it's just as well. You won't want hanging lamps there,—and candelabra would hardly be in place either, to hold tallow candles."

"Tallow candles!" exclaimed Mrs. Rossitur. Her husband winced, but said nothing.

"Ay," said the doctor again,—"and make them yourself if you are a good housewife. Come Lucy," said he taking her hand, "do you know how the wild fowl do on the Chesapeake?—duck and swim under water till they can shew their heads with safety? 'Twon't spoil your eyes to see by a tallow candle."

Mrs. Rossitur half smiled, but looked anxiously towards her husband.

"Pooh, pooh! Rolf won't care what the light burns that lights him to independence,—and when you get there you may illuminate with a whole whale if you like. By the way, Rolf, there is a fine water power up yonder, and a saw-mill in good order, they tell me, but a short way from the house. Hugh might learn to manage it, and it would be fine employment for him."

"Hugh!" said his mother disconsolately. Mr. Rossitur neither spoke nor looked an answer. Fleda sprang forward.

"A saw-mill!—Uncle Orrin!—where is it?"

"Just a little way from the house, they say. *You* can't manage it, fair Saxon!—though you look as if you would undertake all the mills in creation, for a trifle."

"No but the place, uncle Orrin;—where is the place?"

"The place? Hum—why it's up in Wyandot County—some five or six miles from the Montepoole Spring—what's this they call it?—Queechy!—By the way!" said he, reading Fleda's countenance, "it is the very place where your father was born!—it is! I didn't think of that before."

Fleda's hands were clasped.

"O I am very glad!" she said. "It's my old home. It is the most lovely place, aunt Lucy!—most lovely—and we shall have some good neighbours there too. O I am very glad!—The dear old saw-mill!—"

"Dear old saw-mill!" said the doctor looking at her. "Rolf, I'll tell you what, you shall give me this girl. I want her. I can take better care of her, perhaps, now than you can. Let her come to me when you leave the city—it will be better for her than to help work the saw-mill; and I have as good a right to her as anybody, for Amy before her was like my own child."

The doctor spoke not with his usual light jesting manner but very seriously. Hugh's lips parted,—Mrs. Rossitur looked with a sad thoughtful look at Fleda,—Mr. Rossitur walked up and down looking at nobody. Fleda watched him.

"What does Fleda herself say?" said he stopping short suddenly. His face softened and his eye changed as it fell upon her, for the first time that day. Fleda saw her opening; she came to him, within his arms, and laid her head upon his breast.

"What does Fleda say?" said he, softly kissing her.

Fleda's tears said a good deal, that needed no interpreter.

She felt her uncle's hand passed more and more tenderly over her head, so tenderly that it made it all the more difficult for her to govern herself and stop her tears. But she did stop them, and looked up at him then with such a face—so glowing through smiles and tears—it was like a very rainbow of hope upon the cloud of their prospects. Mr. Rossitur felt the power of the sunbeam wand, it reached his heart; it was even with a smile that he said as he looked at her,

"Will you go to your uncle Orrin, Fleda?"

"Not if uncle Rolf will keep me."

"Keep you!" said Mr. Rossitur;—"I should like to see who wouldn't keep you!—There, Dr. Gregory, you have your answer."

"Hum!—I might have known," said the doctor, "that the 'faire Una' would abjure cities.—Come here, you Elf!"—and he wrapped her in his arms so tight she could not stir,—"I have a spite against you for this. What amends will you make me for such an affront?"

"Let me take breath," said Fleda laughing, "and I'll tell you. You don't want any amends, uncle Orrin."

"Well," said he, gazing with more feeling than he cared to shew into that sweet face, so innocent of apology-making,—"you shall promise me that you will not forget uncle Orrin and the old house in Bleecker street."

Fleda's eyes grew more wistful.

"And will you promise me that if ever you want anything you will come or send straight there?"

"If ever I want anything I can't get nor do without," said Fleda.

"Pshaw!" said the doctor letting her go, but laughing at the same time. "Mind my words, Mr. and Mrs. Rossitur;—if ever that girl takes the wrong bit in her mouth—Well, well! I'll go home."

Home he went. The rest drew together particularly near, round the fire; Hugh at his father's shoulder, and Fleda kneeling on the rug between her uncle and aunt with a hand on each; and there was not one of them whose gloom was not lightened by her bright face and cheerful words of hope that in the new scenes they were going to "they would all be so happy."

The days that followed were gloomy; but Fleda's ministry was unceasing. Hugh seconded her well, though more passively. Feeling less pain himself, he perhaps for that very reason was less acutely alive to it in others; not so quick to foresee and ward off, not so skilful to allay it. Fleda seemed to have intuition for the one and a charm for the other. To her there was pain in every parting; her sympathies clung to whatever wore the livery of habit. There was hardly any piece of furniture, there was no book or marble or picture, that she could take leave of without a pang. But it was kept to herself; her sorrowful good-byes were said in secret; before others, in all those weeks, she was a very Euphrosyne; light, bright, cheerful, of eye and foot and hand; a shield between her aunt and every annoyance that *she* could take instead; a good little fairy, that sent her sunbeam wand, quick as a flash, where any eye rested gloomily. People did not always find out where the light came from, but it was her witchery.

The creditors would touch none of Mrs. Rossitur's things, her husband's honourable behaviour had been so thorough. They even presented him with one or two pictures which he sold for a considerable sum; and to Mrs. Rossitur they gave up all the plate in daily use; a matter of great rejoicing to Fleda who knew well how sorely it would have been missed. She and her aunt had quite a little library too, of their own private store; a little one it was indeed, but the worth of every volume was now trebled in her eyes. Their furniture was all left behind; and in its stead went some of neat light painted wood which looked to Fleda deliciously countryfied. A promising cook and housemaid were engaged to go with them to the wilds; and about the first of April they turned their backs upon the city.

CHAPTER XVII.

> The thresher's weary flingin-tree
> The lee-lang day had tired me:
> And whan the day had closed his e'e,
> Far i' the west,
> Ben i' the spence, right pensivelie,
> I 'gaed to rest.
>
> BURNS.

QUEECHY was reached at night. Fleda had promised herself to be off almost with the dawn of light the next morning to see aunt Miriam, but a heavy rain kept her fast at home the whole day. It was very well; she was wanted there.

Despite the rain and her disappointment it was impossible for Fleda to lie abed from the time the first grey light began to break in at her windows,—those old windows that had rattled their welcome to her all night. She was up and dressed and had had a long consultation with herself over matters and prospects, before anybody else had thought of leaving the indubitable comfort of a feather bed for the doubtful contingency of happiness that awaited them down stairs. Fleda took in the whole length and breadth of it, half wittingly and half through some finer sense than that of the understanding.

The first view of things could not strike them pleasantly; it was not to be looked for. The doors did not happen to be painted blue; they were a deep chocolate colour; doors and wainscot. The fireplaces were not all furnished with cranes, but they were all uncouthly wide and deep. Nobody would have thought them so indeed in the winter, when piled up with blazing hickory logs, but in summer they yawned uncomfortably upon the eye. The ceilings were low; the walls rough papered or rougher white-washed; the sashes not hung; the rooms, otherwise well enough proportioned, stuck with little cupboards, in recesses and corners and out of the way places, in a style impertinently suggestive of housekeeping, and fitted to shock any symmetrical set of nerves. The old house had undergone a thorough putting in order, it is true; the chocolate paint was just dry, and the paper hangings freshly put up; and the bulk of the new furniture had been sent on before and unpacked, though not a single article of it was in its right place. The house was clean and tight, that is, as tight as it ever was. But the colour had been unfortunately chosen —perhaps there was no help for that;—the paper was *very* coarse and countryfied; the big windows were startling they looked so bare, without any manner of drapery; and the long reaches of wall were unbroken by mirror or picture-frame. And this to eyes trained to eschew ungracefulness and that abhorred a vacuum as much as nature is said to do! Even Fleda felt there was something disagreeable in the change, though it reached her more through the channel of other people's sensitiveness than her own. To her it was the dear old house still, though her eyes had seen better things since they loved it. No corner or recess could have a pleasanter filling, to her fancy, than the old brown cupboard or shelves which had always been there. But what *would* her uncle say to them! and to that dismal paper! and what would aunt Lucy think of those rattling window-sashes! this cool raw day too, for the first!—

Think as she might Fleda did not stand still to think. She had gone softly all over the house, taking a strange look at the old places and the images with which memory filled them, thinking of the last time, and many a time before that;—and she had at last come back to the sitting-room, long before anybody else was down stairs; the two tired servants were just rubbing their eyes open in the kitchen and speculating themselves awake. Leaving them, at their peril, to get ready a decent breakfast, (by the way she grudged them the old kitchen) Fleda set about trying what her wand could do towards brightening the face of affairs in the other part of the house. It was quite cold enough for a fire, luckily. She ordered one made, and meanwhile busied herself with the various stray packages and articles of wearing apparel that lay scattered about giving the whole place a look of discomfort. Fleda gathered them up and bestowed them in one or two of the impertinent cupboards, and then undertook the labour of carrying out all the wrong furniture that had got into the breakfast-room and bringing in that which really belonged there from the hall and the parlour beyond; moving like a mouse that she might not disturb the people up stairs. A quarter of an hour was spent in arranging to the best advantage these various pieces of furniture in the room; it was the very same in which Mr. Carleton and Charlton Rossitur had been received the memorable day of the roast pig dinner, but that was not the uppermost association in Fleda's mind. Satisfied at last that a happier effect could not be produced with the given materials, and well pleased too with her success, Fleda turned to the fire. It was made, but not by any means doing its part to encourage the other portions of the room to look their best. Fleda knew something of wood fires from old times; she laid hold of the tongs, and touched and loosened and coaxed a stick here and there, with a delicate hand, till, seeing the very opening it had wanted,—without which neither fire nor hope can keep its activity,—the blaze sprang up energetically, crackling through all the piled oak and hickory and driving the smoke clean out of sight. Fleda had done her work. It would have been a misanthropical person indeed that could have come into the room then and not felt his face brighten. One other thing remained,—setting the breakfast table; and Fleda would let no hands but hers do it this morning; she was curious about the setting of tables. How she remembered or divined where everything had been stowed; how quietly and efficiently her little fingers unfastened hampers and pried into baskets, without making any noise; till all the breakfast paraphernalia of silver, china, and table-linen was found, gathered from various receptacles, and laid in most exquisite order on the table. State street never saw better. Fleda stood and looked at it then, in immense satisfaction, seeing that her uncle's eye would miss nothing of its accustomed gratification. To her the old room, shining with firelight and new furniture, was perfectly charming. If those great windows were staringly bright, health and cheerfulness seemed to look in at them. And what other images of association, with "nods and becks and wreathed smiles," looked at her out of the curling flames in the old wide fireplace! And one other angel stood there unseen,—the one whose errand it is to see fulfilled the promise, "Give and it shall be given to you; full measure, and pressed down, and heaped up, and running over."

A little while Fleda sat contentedly eying her work; then a new idea struck her and she sprang up. In the next meadow, only one fence between, a little spring of purest water ran through from the woodland; water cresses used to grow there. Uncle Rolf was very fond of them. It was pouring with rain, but no matter. Her heart beating between haste and delight, Fleda slipped her feet into galoches and put an old cloak of Hugh's over her head, and ran out through the kitchen, the old accustomed way. The servants exclaimed and entreated, but Fleda only flashed a bright look at them from under her cloak as she opened the door, and ran off, over the wet grass, under the fence, and over half the meadow, till she came to the stream. She was getting a delicious taste of old times, and though the spring water was very cold and with it and the rain one half of each sleeve was soon thoroughly wetted, she gathered her cresses and scampered back with a pair of eyes and cheeks that might have struck any city belle chill with envy.

"Then but that's a sweet girl!" said Mary the cook to Jane the housemaid.

"A lovely countenance she has," answered Jane, who was refined in her speech.

"Take her away and you've taken the best of the house, I'm a thinking."

"Mrs. Rossitur is a lady," said Jane in a low voice.

"Ay, and a very proper-behaved one she is, and him the same, that is, for a gentleman I maan; but Jane! I say, I'm thinking he'll have eat too much sour bread lately! I wish I knowed how they'd have their eggs boiled, till I'd have 'em ready."

"Sure it's on the table itself they'll do 'em," said Jane. "They've an elegant little fixture in there for the purpose."

"Is that it!"

Nobody found out how busy Fleda's wand had been in

the old breakfast room. But she was not disappointed; she had not worked for praise. Her cresses were appreciated; that was enough. She enjoyed her breakfast, the only one of the party that did. Mr. Rossitur looked moody; his wife looked anxious; and Hugh's face was the reflection of theirs. If Fleda's face reflected anything it was the sunlight of heaven.

"How sweet the air is after New York!" said she.

They looked at her. There was a fresh sweetness of another kind about that breakfast-table. They all felt it, and breathed more freely.

"Delicious cresses!" said Mrs. Rossitur.

"Yes, I wonder where they came from," said her husband. "Who got them?"

"I guess Fleda knows," said Hugh.

"They grow in a little stream of spring water over here in the meadow," said Fleda demurely.

"Yes, but you don't answer my question," said her uncle, putting his hand under her chin and smiling at the blushing face he brought round to view;—"Who got them?"

"I did."

"You have been out in the rain?"

"O Queechy rain don't hurt me, uncle Rolf."

"And don't it wet you either?"

"Yes sir—a little."

"How much?"

"My sleeves,—O I dried them long ago."

"Don't you repeat that experiment, Fleda," said he seriously, but with a look that was a good reward to her nevertheless.

"It is a raw day!" said Mrs. Rossitur, drawing her shoulders together as an ill-disposed window sash gave one of its admonitory shakes.

"What little panes of glass for such big windows!" said Hugh.

"But what a pleasant prospect through them," said Fleda,—"look, Hugh!—worth all the Batteries and Parks in the world."

"In the world!—in New York you mean," said her uncle. "Not better than the Champs Elysées?"

"Better to me," said Fleda.

"For to-day I must attend to the prospect in-doors," said Mrs. Rossitur.

"Now aunt Lucy," said Fleda, "you are just going to put yourself down in the corner, in the rocking-chair there, with your book, and make yourself comfortable; and Hugh and I will see to all these things. Hugh and I and Mary and Jane,—that makes quite an army of us, and we can do everything without you, and you must just keep quiet. I'll build you up a fine fire, and then when I don't know what to do I will come to you for orders. Uncle Rolf, would you be so good as just to open that box of books in the hall? because I am afraid Hugh isn't strong enough. I'll take care of you, aunt Lucy."

Fleda's plans were not entirely carried out, but she contrived pretty well to take the brunt of the business on her own shoulders. She was as busy as a bee the whole day. To her all the ins and outs of the house, its advantages and disadvantages, were much better known than to anybody else; nothing could be done but by her advice; and more than that, she contrived by some sweet management to baffle Mrs. Rossitur's desire to spare her, and to bear the larger half of every burden that should have come upon her aunt. What she had done in the breakfast room she did or helped to do in the other parts of the house; she unpacked boxes and put away clothes and linen, in which Hugh was her excellent helper; she arranged her uncle's dressing-table with a scrupulosity that left nothing uncared-for;—and the last thing before tea she and Hugh dived into the book-box to get out some favourite volumes to lay upon the table in the evening, that the room might not look to her uncle quite so dismally bare. He had been abroad notwithstanding the rain near the whole day.

It was a weary party that gathered round the supper-table that night, weary it seemed as much in mind as in body; and the meal exerted its cheering influence over only two of them; Mr. and Mrs. Rossitur sipped their cups of tea abstractedly.

"I don't believe that fellow Donohan knows much about his business," remarked the former at length.

"Why don't you get somebody else, then?" said his wife.

"I happen to have engaged him, unfortunately."

A pause.——

"What doesn't he know?"

Mr. Rossitur laughed, not a pleasant laugh.

"It would take too long to enumerate. If you had asked me what part of his business he *does* understand, I could have told you shortly that I don't know."

"But you do not understand it very well yourself. Are you sure?"

"Am I sure of what?"

"That this man does not know his business?"

"No further sure than I can have confidence in my own common sense."

"What will you do?" said Mrs. Rossitur after a moment.

A question men are not fond of answering, especially when they have not made up their minds. Mr. Rossitur was silent, and his wife too, after that.

"If I could get some long-headed Yankee to go along with him"—he remarked again, balancing his spoon on the edge of his cup in curious illustration of his own mental position at the moment; Donohan being the only fixed point and all the rest wavering in uncertainty. There were a few silent minutes before anybody answered.

"If you want one and don't know of one, uncle Rolf," said Fleda, "I dare say cousin Seth might."

That gentle modest speech brought his attention round upon her. His face softened.

"Cousin Seth? who is cousin Seth?"

"He is aunt Miriam's son," said Fleda. "Seth Plumfield. He's a very good farmer, I know; grandpa used to say he was; and he knows everybody."

"Mrs. Plumfield," said Mrs. Rossitur, as her husband's eyes went inquiringly to her,—"Mrs. Plumfield was Mr. Ringgan's sister, you remember. This is her son."

"Cousin Seth, eh?" said Mr. Rossitur dubiously. "Well—Why Fleda, your sweet air don't seem to agree with you, as far as I see; I have not known you look so—so *triste*—since we left Paris. What have you been doing, my child?"

"She has been doing everything, father," said Hugh.

"O! it's nothing," said Fleda, answering Mr. Rossitur's

look and tone of affection with a bright smile. "I'm a little tired, that's all."

'A little tired!' She went to sleep on the sofa directly after supper and slept like a baby all the evening; but her power did not sleep with her; for that quiet, sweet, tired face, tired in their service, seemed to bear witness against the indulgence of anything harsh or unlovely in the same atmosphere. A gentle witness-bearing, but strong in its gentleness. They sat close together round the fire, talked softly, and from time to time cast loving glances at the quiet little sleeper by their side. They did not know that she was a fairy, and that though her wand had fallen out of her hand it was still resting upon them.

CHAPTER XVIII.

Gon. Here is everything advantageous to life.
Ant. True; save means to live.
TEMPEST.

FLEDA'S fatigue did not prevent her being up before sunrise the next day. Fatigue was forgotten, for the light of a fair spring morning was shining in at her windows and she meant to see aunt Miriam before breakfast. She ran out to find Hugh, and her merry shout reached him before she did, and brought him to meet her.

"Come, Hugh!—I'm going off up to aunt Miriam's, and I want you. Come! Isn't this delicious?"

"Hush!—" said Hugh. "Father's just here in the barn. I can't go, Fleda."

Fleda's countenance clouded.

"Can't go! what's the matter?—can't you go, Hugh?"

He shook his head and went off into the barn.

A chill came upon Fleda. She turned away with a very sober step. What if her uncle was in the barn, why should she hush? He never had been a check upon her merriment, never; what was coming now? Hugh too looked disturbed. It was a spring morning no longer. Fleda forgot the glittering wet grass that had set her own eyes a sparkling but a minute ago; she walked along, cogitating, swinging her bonnet by the strings in thoughtful vibration,—till by the help of sunlight and sweet air, and the loved scenes, her spirits again made head and swept over the sudden hindrance they had met. There were the blessed old sugar maples, seven in number, that fringed the side of the road,—how well Fleda knew them. Only skeletons now, but she remembered how beautiful they looked after the October frosts; and presently they would be putting out their new green leaves and be beautiful in another way. How different in their free-born luxuriance from the dusty and city-prisoned elms and willows she had left. She came to the bridge then, and stopped with a thrill of pleasure and pain to look and listen. Unchanged! —all but herself. The mill was not going; the little brook went by quietly chattering to itself, just as it had done the last time she saw it, when she rode past on Mr. Carleton's horse. Four and a half years ago!—And now how strange that she had come to live there again.

Drawing a long breath, and swinging her bonnet again, Fleda softly went on up the hill; past the saw-mill, the ponds, the factories, the houses of the settlement. The same, and not the same!—Bright with the morning sun, and yet somehow a little browner and homelier than of old they used to be. Fleda did not care for that; she would hardly acknowledge it to herself; her affection never made any discount for infirmity. Leaving the little settlement behind her thoughts as behind her back, she ran on now towards aunt Miriam's, breathlessly, till field after field was past and her eye caught a bit of the smooth lake and the old farmhouse in its old place. Very brown it looked, but Fleda dashed on, through the garden and in at the front door.

Nobody at all was in the entrance-room, the common sitting-room of the family. With trembling delight Fleda opened the well-known door and stole noiselessly through the little passage-way to the kitchen. The door of that was only on the latch and a gentle movement of it gave to Fleda's eye the tall figure of aunt Miriam, just before her, stooping down to look in at the open mouth of the oven which she was at that moment engaged in supplying with more work to do. It was a huge one, and beyond her aunt's head Fleda could see in the far end the great loaves of bread, half baked, and more near a perfect squad of pies and pans of gingerbread just going in to take the benefit of the oven's milder mood. Fleda saw all this as it were without seeing it; she stood still as a mouse and breathless till her aunt turned; and then, a spring and a half shout of joy, and she had clasped her in her arms and was crying with her whole heart. Aunt Miriam was taken all aback; she could do nothing but sit down and cry too and forgot her oven door.

"Ain't breakfast ready yet, mother?" said a manly voice coming in. "I must be off to see after them ploughs. Hollo!—why mother!—"

The first exclamation was uttered as the speaker put the door to the oven's mouth; the second as he turned in quest of the hand that should have done it. He stood wondering, while his mother and Fleda between laughing and crying tried to rouse themselves and look up.

"What is all this?"

"Don't you see, Seth?"

"I see somebody that had like to have spoiled your whole baking—I don't know who it is, yet."

"Don't you now, cousin Seth?" said Fleda shaking away her tears and getting up.

"I ha'n't quite lost my recollection. Cousin, you must give me a kiss.—How do you do? You ha'n't forgot how to colour, I see, for all you've been so long among the pale city-folks."

"I haven't forgotten any thing, cousin Seth," said Fleda, blushing indeed but laughing and shaking his hand with as hearty good-will.

"I don't believe you have,—anything that is good," said he. "Where have you been all this while?"

"O part of the time in New York, and part of the time in Paris, and some other places."

"Well you ha'n't seen anything better than Queechy, or Queechy bread and butter, have you?"

"No indeed!"

"Come, you shall give me another kiss for that," said he, suiting the action to the word;—"and now sit down and eat as much bread and butter as you can. It's just as good as it used to be. Come mother!—I guess breakfast is ready by the looks of that coffee-pot."

"Breakfast ready!" said Fleda.

"Ay indeed; it's a good half hour since it ought to ha' been ready. If it ain't I can't stop for it. Them boys will be running their furrows like sarpents if I ain't there to start them."

"Which like serpents," said Fleda,—"the furrows or the men?"

"Well, I was thinking of the furrows," said he glancing at her;—"I guess there ain't cunning enough in the others to trouble them. Come sit down, and let me see whether you have forgot a Queechy appetite."

"I don't know," said Fleda doubtfully,—"they will expect me at home."

"I don't care who expects you—sit down! you ain't going to eat any bread and butter this morning but my mother's—you haven't got any like it at your house. Mother, give her a cup of coffee, will you, and set her to work."

Fleda was too willing to comply with the invitation, were it only for the charm of old times. She had not seen such a table for years, and little as the conventionalities of delicate taste were known there, it was not without a comeliness of its own in its air of wholesome abundance and the extreme purity of all its arrangements. If but a piece of cold pork were on aunt Miriam's table, it was served with a nicety that would not have offended the most fastidious; and amid irregularities that the fastidious would scorn, there was a sound excellence of material and preparation that they very often fail to know. Fleda made up her mind she would be wanted at home; all the rather perhaps for Hugh's mysterious "hush"; and there was something in the hearty kindness and truth of these friends that she felt particularly genial. And if there was a lack of silver at the board its place was more than filled with the pure gold of association. They sat down to table, but aunt Miriam's eyes devoured Fleda. Mr. Plumfield set about his more material breakfast with all despatch.

"So Mr. Rossitur has left the city for good," said aunt Miriam. "How does he like it?"

"He hasn't been here but a day, you know, aunt Miriam," said Fleda evasively.

"Is he anything of a farmer?" asked her cousin.

"Not much," said Fleda.

"Is he going to work the farm himself?"

"How do you mean?"

22

"I mean, is he going to work the farm himself, or hire it out, or let somebody else work it on shares?"

"I don't know," said Fleda;—"I think he is going to have a farmer and oversee things himself."

"He'll get sick o' that," said Seth; "unless he's the luck to get hold of just the right hand."

"Has he hired anybody yet?" said aunt Miriam, after a little interval of supplying Fleda with 'bread and butter.'

"Yes ma'am, I believe so."

"What's his name?"

"Donohan,—an Irishman, I believe; uncle Rolf hired him in New York."

"For his head man?" said Seth, with a sufficiently intelligible look.

"Yes," said Fleda. "Why?"

But he did not immediately answer her.

"The land's in poor heart now," said he, "a good deal of it; it has been wasted; it wants first-rate management to bring it in order and make much of it for two or three years to come. I never see an Irishman's head yet that was worth more than a joke. Their hands are all of 'em that's good for anything."

"I believe uncle Rolf wants to have an American to go with this man," said Fleda.

Seth said nothing, but Fleda understood the shake of his head as he reached over after a pickle.

"Are you going to keep a dairy, Fleda?" said her aunt.

"I don't know, ma'am;—I haven't heard anything about it."

"Does Mrs. Rossitur know anything about country affairs?"

"No—nothing," Fleda said, her heart sinking perceptibly with every new question.

"She hasn't any cows yet?"

She!—any cows!—But Fleda only said they had not come; she believed they were coming.

"What help has she got?"

"Two women—Irishwomen," said Fleda.

"Mother you'll have to take hold and learn her," said Mr. Plumfield.

"Teach *her?*" cried Fleda, repelling the idea;—"aunt Lucy? she cannot do anything—she isn't strong enough;—not anything of that kind."

"What did she come here for?" said Seth.

"You know," said his mother, "that Mr. Rossitur's circumstances obliged him to quit New York."

"Ay, but that ain't my question. A man had better keep his fingers off anything he can't live by. A farm's one thing or t'other, just as it's worked. The land won't grow specie—it must be fetched out of it. Is Mr. Rossitur a smart man?"

"Very," Fleda said, "about everything but farming."

"Well if he'll put himself to school maybe he'll learn," Seth concluded as he finished his breakfast and went off. Fleda rose too, and was standing thoughtfully by the fire, when aunt Miriam came up and put her arms round her. Fleda's eyes sparkled again.

"You're not changed—you're the same little Fleda," she said.

"Not quite so little," said Fleda smiling.

"Not quite so little, but my own darling. The world hasn't spoiled thee yet."

"I hope not, aunt Miriam."

"You have remembered your mother's prayer, Fleda?"

"Always!"———

How tenderly aunt Miriam's hand was passed over the bowed head,—how fondly she pressed her. And Fleda's answer was as fond.

"I wanted to bring Hugh up to see you, aunt Miriam, with me, but he couldn't come. You will like Hugh. He is so good!"

"I will come down and see him," said aunt Miriam; and then she went to look after her oven's doings. Fleda stood by, amused to see the quantities of nice things that were rummaged out of it. They did not look like Mrs. Renney's work, but she knew from old experience that they were good.

"How early you must have have been up, to put these things in," said Fleda.

"Put them in! yes, and make them. These were all made this morning, Fleda."

"This morning!—before breakfast! Why the sun was only just rising when I set out to come up the hill; and I wasn't long coming, aunt Miriam."

"To be sure; that's the way to get things done. Before breakfast!—What time do you breakfast, Fleda?"

"Not till eight or nine o'clock."

"Eight or nine!—*Here?*"

"There hasn't been any change made yet, and I don't suppose there will be. Uncle Rolf is always up early, but he can't bear to have breakfast early."

Aunt Miriam's face shewed what she thought; and Fleda went away with all its gravity and doubt settled like lead upon her heart. Though she had one of the identical apple pies in her hands, which aunt Miriam had quietly said was "for her and Hugh," and though a pleasant savour of old times was about it, Fleda could not get up again the bright feeling with which she had come up the hill. There was a miserable misgiving at heart. It would work off in time.

It had begun to work off, when at the foot of the hill she met her uncle. He was coming after her to ask Mr. Plumfield about the desideratum of a Yankee. Fleda put her pie in safety behind a rock, and turned back with him, and aunt Miriam told them the way to Seth's ploughing ground.

A pleasant word or two had set Fleda's spirits a bounding again, and the walk was delightful. Truly the leaves were not on the trees, but it was April, and they soon would be; there was promise in the light, and hope in the air, and everything smelt of the country and spring-time. The soft tread of the sod, that her foot had not felt for so long,—the fresh look of the newly-turned earth,—here and there the brilliance of a field of winter grain,—and that nameless beauty of the budding trees, that the full luxuriance of summer can never equal,—Fleda's heart was springing for sympathy. And to her, with whom association was everywhere so strong, there was in it all a shadowy presence of her grandfather, with whom she had so often seen the spring-time bless those same hills and fields long ago. She walked on in silence, as her manner commonly was when deeply pleased; there were hardly two persons to whom she would speak her mind freely then. Mr. Rossitur had his own thoughts.

"Can anything equal the spring-time!" she burst forth at length.

Her uncle looked at her and smiled. "Perhaps not; but it is one thing," said he sighing, "for taste to enjoy and another thing for calculation to improve."

"But one can do both, can't one?" said Fleda brightly.

"I don't know," said he sighing again. "Hardly."

Fleda knew he was mistaken and thought the sighs out of place. But they reached her; and she had hardly condemned them before they set her off upon a long train of excuses for him, and she had wrought herself into quite a fit of tenderness by the time they reached her cousin.

They found him on a gentle side-hill, with two other men and teams, both of whom were stepping away in different parts of the field. Mr. Plumfield was just about setting off to work his way to the other side of the lot when they came up with him.

Fleda was not ashamed of her aunt Miriam's son, even before such critical eyes as those of her uncle. Farmer-like as were his dress and air, they shewed him nevertheless a well-built, fine-looking man, with the independent bearing of one who has never recognised any but mental or moral superiority. His face might have been called handsome; there was at least manliness in every line of it; and his excellent dark eye shewed an equal mingling of kindness and acute common sense. Let Mr. Plumfield wear what clothes he would one felt obliged to follow Burns' notable example and pay respect to the *man* that was in them.

"A fine day, sir," he remarked to Mr. Rossitur after they had shaken hands.

"Yes, and I will not interrupt you but a minute. Mr. Plumfield, I am in want of hands,—hands for this very business you are about, ploughing,—and Fleda says you know everybody; so I have come to ask if you can direct me."

"Heads or hands, do you want?" said Seth, clearing his boot-sole from some superfluous soil upon the share of his plough.

"Why both, to tell you the truth. I want hands, and teams, for that matter, for I have only two, and I suppose there is no time to be lost. And I want very much to get a person thoroughly acquainted with the business to go along with my man. He is an Irishman, and I am afraid not very well accustomed to the ways of doing things here."

"Like enough," said Seth;—"and the worst of 'em is you can't learn 'em."

"Well!—can you help me?"

"Mr. Douglass!"—said Seth, raising his voice to speak to one of his assistants who was approaching them,—"Mr. Douglass!—you're holding that 'ere plough a little too obleekly for my grounds."

"Very good, Mr. Plumfield!" said the person called upon, with a quick accent that intimated, "If you don't know what is best it is not my affair!"—the voice very peculiar, seeming to come from no lower than the top of his throat, with a guttural roll of the words.

"Is that Earl Douglass?" said Fleda.

"You remember him?" said her cousin smiling. "He's just where he was, and his wife too.—Well Mr. Rossitur, 'tain't very easy to find what you want just at this season, when most folks have their hands full and help is all taken up. I'll see if I can't come down and give you a lift myself with the ploughing, for a day or two, as I'm pretty beforehand with the spring, but you'll want more than that. I ain't sure—I haven't more hands than I'll want myself, but I think it is possible Squire Springer may spare you one of hisn. He ain't taking in any new land this year, and he's got things pretty snug; I guess he don't care to do any more than common—anyhow you might try. You know where uncle Joshua lives, Fleda? Well Philetus—what now?"

They had been slowly walking along the fence towards the furthest of Mr. Plumfield's coadjutors, upon whom his eye had been curiously fixed as he was speaking; a young man who was an excellent sample of what is called "the raw material." He had just come to a sudden stop in the midst of the furrow when his employer called to him; and he answered somewhat lack-a-daisically,

"Why I've broke this here clevis—I ha'n't touched anything nor nothing, and it broke right in teu!"

"What do you 'spose 'll be done now?" said Mr. Plumfield gravely going up to examine the fracture.

"Well 'twa'n't none of my doings," said the young man.

"I ha'n't touched anything nor nothing—and the mean thing broke right in teu. 'Tain't so handy as the old kind o' plough, by a long jump."

"You go 'long down to the house and ask my mother for a new clevis; and talk about ploughs when you know how to hold 'em," said Mr. Plumfield.

"It don't look so difficult a matter," said Mr. Rossitur,—"but I am a novice myself. What is the principal thing to be attended to in ploughing, Mr. Plumfield?"

There was a twinkle in Seth's eye, as he looked down upon a piece of straw he was breaking to bits, which Fleda, who could see, interpreted thoroughly.

"Well," said he, looking up,—"the breadth of the stitches and the width and depth of the furrow must be regulated according to the nature of the soil and the lay of the ground, and what you're ploughing for;—there's stubble ploughing, and breaking up old lays, and ploughing for fallow crops, and ribbing, where the land has been some years in grass, —and so on; and the plough must be geared accordingly, and so as not to take too much land nor go out of the land; and after that the best part of the work is to guide the plough right and run the furrows straight and even."

He spoke with the most impenetrable gravity, while Mr. Rossitur looked blank and puzzled. Fleda could hardly keep her countenance.

"That row of poles," said Mr. Rossitur presently,—"are they to guide you in running the furrow straight?"

"Yes sir—they are to mark out the crown of the stitch. I keep 'em right between the horses and plough 'em down one after another. It's a kind of way country folks play at ninepins," said Seth, with a glance half inquisitive, half sly, at his questioner.

Mr. Rossitur asked no more. Fleda felt a little uneasy again. It was rather a longish walk to uncle Joshua's, and hardly a word spoken on either side.

The old gentleman was "to hum;" and while Fleda went back into some remote part of the house to see "aunt Syra," Mr. Rossitur set forth his errand.

"Well,—and so you're looking for help, eh?" said uncle Joshua when he had heard him through.

"Yes sir,—I want help."

"And a team too?"

"So I have said, sir," Mr. Rossitur answered rather shortly. "Can you supply me?"

"Well,—I don't know as I can," said the old man, rubbing his hands slowly over his knees.—"You ha'n't got much done yet, I s'pose?"

"Nothing. I came the day before yesterday."

"Land's in rather poor condition in some parts, ain't it?"

"I really am not able to say, sir,—till I have seen it."

"It ought to be," said the old gentleman shaking his head, —"the fellow that was there last didn't do right by it—he worked the land too hard, and didn't put on it anywhere near what he had ought to—I guess you'll find it pretty poor in some places. He was trying to get all he could out of it, I s'pose. There's a good deal of fencing to be done too, ain't there?"

"All that there was, sir,—I have done none since I came."

"Seth Plumfield got through ploughing yet?"

"We found him at it."

"Ay, he's a smart man. What are you going to do, Mr. Rossitur, with that piece of marsh land that lies off to the south-east of the barn, beyond the meadow, between the hills? I had just sich another, and I"——

"Before I do anything with the wet land, Mr. —— I am so unhappy as to have forgotten your name?—"

"Springer, sir," said the old gentleman,—"Springer—Joshua Springer. That is my name, sir."

"Mr. Springer, before I do anything with the wet land I should like to have something growing on the dry; and as that is the present matter in hand will you be so good as to let me know whether I can have your assistance."

"Well I don't know,—" said the old gentleman; "there ain't anybody to send but my boy Lucas, and I don't know whether he would make up his mind to go or not."

"Well sir!"—said Mr. Rossitur rising,—"in that case I will bid you good morning. I am sorry to have given you the trouble."

"Stop," said the old man,—"stop a bit. Just sit down —I'll go in and see about it."

Mr. Rossitur sat down, and uncle Joshua left him to go into the kitchen and consult his wife, without whose counsel, of late years especially, he rarely did anything. They never varied in opinion, but aunt Syra's wits supplied the steel edge to his heavy metal.

"I don't know but Lucas would as leave go as not," the old gentleman remarked on coming back from this sharpening process,—"and I can make out to spare him, I guess. You calculate to keep him, I s'pose?"

"Until this press is over; and perhaps longer, if I find he can do what I want."

"You'll find him pretty handy at a' most anything; but I mean,—I s'pose he'll get his victuals with you."

"I have made no arrangement of the kind," said Mr. Rossitur controlling with some effort his rebelling muscles. "Donohan is boarded somewhere else, and for the present it will be best for all in my employ to follow the same plan."

"Very good," said uncle Joshua, "it makes no difference,—only of course in that case it is worth more, when a man has to find himself and his team."

"Whatever it is worth I am quite ready to pay, sir."

"Very good! You and Lucas can agree about that. He'll be along in the morning."

So they parted; and Fleda understood the impatient quick step with which her uncle got over the ground.

"Is that man a brother of your grandfather?"

"No sir—Oh no! only his brother-in-law. My grandmother was his sister, but they weren't in the least like each other."

"I should think they could not," said Mr. Rossitur.

"Oh they were not!" Fleda repeated. "I have always heard that."

After paying her respects to aunt Syra in the kitchen she had come back time enough to hear the end of the discourse in the parlour, and had felt its full teaching. Doubts returned, and her spirits were sobered again. Not another word was spoken till they reached home; when Fleda seized upon Hugh and went off to the rock after her forsaken pie.

"Have you succeeded?" asked Mrs. Rossitur while they were gone.

"Yes—that is, a cousin has kindly consented to come and help me."

"A cousin!" said Mrs. Rossitur.

"Ay,—we're in a nest of cousins."

"In a *what*, Mr. Rossitur?"

"In a nest of cousins; and I had rather be in a nest of rooks. I wonder if I shall be expected to ask my ploughmen to dinner! Every second man is a cousin, and the rest are uncles."

CHAPTER XIX.

Whilst skies are blue and bright,
Whilst flowers are gay,
Whilst eyes that change ere night
Make glad the day;
Whilst yet the calm hours creep,
Dream thou—and from thy sleep
Then wake to weep.

SHELLEY.

THE days of summer flew by, for the most part lightly over the heads of Hugh and Fleda. The farm was little to them but a place of pretty and picturesque doings and the scene of nameless delights by wood and stream, in all which, all that summer, Fleda rejoiced; pulling Hugh along with her even when sometimes he would rather have been poring over his books at home. She laughingly said it was good for him; and one half at least of every fine day their feet were abroad. They knew nothing practically of the dairy but that it was an inexhaustible source of the sweetest milk and butter, and indirectly of the richest custards and syllabubs. The flock of sheep that now and then came in sight running over the hill-side, were to them only an image of pastoral beauty and a soft link with the beauty of the past. The two children took the very cream of country life. The books they had left were read with greater eagerness than ever. When the weather was "too lovely to stay in the house," Shakspeare or Massillon or Sully or the "Curiosities of Literature" or "Corinne" or Milner's Church History, for Fleda's reading was as miscellaneous as ever, was enjoyed under the flutter of leaves and along with the rippling of the mountain spring; whilst King curled himself up on the skirt of his mistress's gown and slept for company; hardly more thoughtless and fearless of harm than his two companions. Now and then Fleda opened her eyes to see that her uncle was moody and not like himself, and that her aunt's gentle face was clouded in consequence; and she could not sometimes help the suspicion that he was not making a farmer of himself; but the next summer wind would blow these thoughts away, or the next look of her flowers would put them out of her head. The whole courtyard in front of the house had been given up to her peculiar use as a flower-garden, and there she and Hugh made themselves very busy.

But the summer-time came to an end.

It was a November morning, and Fleda had been doing some of the last jobs in her flower-beds. She was coming in with spirits as bright as her cheeks, when her aunt's attitude and look, more than usually spiritless, suddenly checked them. Fleda gave her a hopeful kiss and asked for the explanation.

"How bright you look, darling!" said her aunt, stroking her cheek.

"Yes, but you don't, aunt Lucy. What has happened?"

"Mary and Jane are going away."

"Going away!—What for?"

"They are tired of the place—don't like it, I suppose."

"Very foolish of them! Well, aunt Lucy, what matter? we can get plenty more in their room."

"Not from the city—not possible; they would not come at this time of year."

"Sure?—Well, then here we can at any rate."

"Here! But what sort of persons shall we get here? And your uncle—just think!"—

"O but I think we can manage," said Fleda. "When do Mary and Jane want to go?"

"Immediately!—to-morrow—they are not willing to wait till we can get somebody. Think of it!"

"Well let them go," said Fleda,—"the sooner the better."

"Yes, and I am sure I don't want to keep them; but—" and Mrs. Rossitur wrung her hands,—"I haven't money enough to pay them quite,—and they won't go without it."

Fleda felt shocked—so much that she could not help looking it.

"But can't uncle Rolf give it you?"

Mrs. Rossitur shook her head. "I have asked him."

"How much is wanting?"

"Twenty-five. Think of his not being able to give me that!"—

Mrs. Rossitur burst into tears.

"Now don't, aunt Lucy!"—said Fleda, guarding well her own composure;—"you know he has had a great deal to spend upon the farm and paying men, and all, and it is no wonder that he should be a little short just now,—now cheer up!—we can get along with this anyhow."

"I asked him," said Mrs. Rossitur through her tears, "when he would be able to give it to me; and he told me he didn't know!—"

Fleda ventured no reply but some of the tenderest caresses that lips and arms could give; and then sprang away and in three minutes was at her aunt's side again.

"Look here, aunt Lucy," said she gently,—"here is twenty dollars, if you can manage the five."

"Where did you get this?" Mrs. Rossitur exclaimed.

"I got it honestly. It is mine, aunt Lucy," said Fleda smiling. "Uncle Orrin gave me some money just before we came away, to do what I liked with; and I haven't wanted to do anything with it till now."

But this seemed to hurt Mrs. Rossitur more than all the rest. Leaning her head forward upon Fleda's breast and clasping her arms about her she cried worse tears than Fleda had seen her shed. If it had not been for the emergency Fleda would have broken down utterly too.

"That it should have come to this!—I can't take it, dear Fleda!"—

"Yes you must, aunt Lucy," said Fleda soothingly. "I couldn't do anything else with it that would give me so much pleasure. I don't want it—it would lie in my drawer till I don't know when. We'll let these people be off as soon as they please. Don't take it so—uncle Rolf will have money again—only just now he is out, I suppose—and we'll get somebody else in the kitchen that will do nicely—you see if we don't."

Mrs. Rossitur's embrace said what words were powerless to say.

"But I don't know how we're to find any one here in the country—I don't know who'll go to look—I am sure your uncle won't want to,—and Hugh wouldn't know—"

"I'll go," said Fleda cheerfully;—"Hugh and I. We can do famously—if you'll trust me. I won't promise to bring home a French cook."

"No indeed—we must take what we can get. But you can get no one to-day, and they will be off by the morning's coach—what shall we do to-morrow,—for dinner? Your uncle——"

"I'll get dinner," said Fleda caressing her;—"I'll take all that on myself. It sha'n't be a bad dinner either. Uncle Rolf will like what I do for him I dare say. Now cheer up, aunt Lucy!—do—that's all I ask of you. Won't you?—for me?"

She longed to speak a word of that quiet hope with which in every trouble she secretly comforted herself—she wanted to whisper the words that were that moment in her own mind, "Truly I know that it shall be well with them that fear God;"—but her natural reserve and timidity kept her lips shut; to her grief.

The women were paid off and dismissed and departed in the next day's coach from Montepoole. Fleda stood at the front door to see them go, with a curious sense that there was an empty house at her back, and indeed upon her back. And in spite of all the cheeriness of her tone to her aunt, she was not without some shadowy feeling that soberer times might be coming upon them.

"What is to be done now?" said Hugh close beside her.

"O we are going to get somebody else," said Fleda.

"Where?"

"I don't know!—You and I are going to find out."

"You and I!—"

"Yes. We are going out after dinner, Hugh dear," said she turning her bright merry face towards him,—"to pick up somebody."

Linking her arm within his she went back to the deserted kitchen premises to see how her promise about taking Mary's place was to be fulfilled.

"Do you know where to look?" said Hugh.

"I've a notion;—but the first thing is dinner, that uncle

Rolf mayn't think the world is turning topsy turvy. There is nothing at all here, Hugh!—nothing in the world but bread—it's a blessing there is that. Uncle Rolf will have to be satisfied with a coffee dinner to-day, and I'll make him the most superb omelette—that my skill is equal to! Hugh dear, you shall set the table.—You don't know how? —then you shall make the toast, and I will set it the first thing of all. You perceive it is well to know how to do everything, Mr. Hugh Rossitur."

"Where did you learn to make omelettes?" said Hugh with laughing admiration, as Fleda bared two pretty arms and ran about the very impersonation of good-humoured activity. The table was set; the coffee was making; and she had him established at the fire with two great plates, a pile of slices of bread, and the toasting-iron.

"Where? Oh don't you remember the days of Mrs. Renney? I have seen Emile make them. And by dint of trying to teach Mary this summer I have taught myself. There is no knowing, you see, what a person may come to."

"I wonder what father would say if he knew you had made all the coffee this summer!"

"That is an unnecessary speculation, my dear Hugh, as I have no intention of telling him. But see!—that is the way with speculators! 'While they go on refining'—the toast burns!"

The coffee and the omelette and the toast and Mr. Rossitur's favourite French salad, were served with beautiful accuracy; and he was quite satisfied. But aunt Lucy looked sadly at Fleda's flushed face and saw that her appetite seemed to have gone off in the steam of her preparations. Fleda had a kind of heart-feast however which answered as well.

Hugh harnessed the little wagon, for no one was at hand to do it, and he and Fleda set off as early as possible after dinner. Fleda's thoughts had turned to her old acquaintance Cynthia Gall, who she knew was out of employment and staying at home somewhere near Montepoole. They got the exact direction from aunt Miriam who approved of her plan.

It was a pleasant peaceful drive they had. They never

were alone together, they two, but vexations seemed to lose their power or be forgotten; and an atmosphere of quietness gather about them, the natural element of both hearts. It might refuse its presence to one, but the attraction of both together was too strong to be resisted.

Miss Cynthia's present abode was in an out of the way place, and a good distance off; they were some time in reaching it. The barest-looking and dingiest of houses, set plump in a green field, without one softening or home-like touch from any home-feeling within; not a flower, not a shrub, not an out-house, not a tree near. One would have thought it a deserted house, but that a thin wreath of smoke lazily stole up from one of the brown chimneys; and graceful as that was it took nothing from the hard stern barrenness below which told of a worse poverty than that of paint and glazing.

"Can this be the place?" said Hugh.

"It must be. You stay here with the horse, and I'll go in and seek my fortune.—Don't promise much," said Fleda shaking her head.

The house stood back from the road. Fleda picked her way to it along a little footpath which seemed to be the equal property of the geese. Her knock brought an invitation to "come in."

An elderly woman was sitting there whose appearance did not mend the general impression. She had the same dull and unhopeful look that her house had.

"Does Mrs. Gall live here?"

"I do," said this person.

"Is Cynthia at home?"

The woman upon this raised her voice and directed it at an inner door.

"Lucindy?" said she in a diversity of tones,—"Lucindy!—tell Cynthy here's somebody wants to see her."—But no one answered, and throwing the work from her lap the woman muttered she would go and see, and left Fleda with a cold invitation to sit down.

Dismal work! Fleda wished herself out of it. The house did not look poverty-stricken within, but poverty must have struck to the very heart, Fleda thought, where there was no apparent cherishing of anything. There was no absolute distress visible, neither was there a sign of real comfort or of a happy home. She could not fancy it was one.

She waited so long that she was sure Cynthia did not hold herself in readiness to see company. And when the lady at last came in it was with very evident marks of "smarting up" about her.

"Why it's Flidda Ringgan!" said Miss Gall after a dubious look or two at her visiter. "How *do* you do? I didn't 'spect to see *you*. How much you have growed!"

She looked really pleased and gave Fleda's hand a very strong grasp as she shook it.

"There ain't no fire here to-day," pursued Cynthy, paying her attentions to the fireplace,—"we let it go down on account of our being all busy out at the back of the house. I guess you're cold, ain't you?"

Fleda said no, and remembered that the woman she had first seen was certainly not busy at the back of the house, nor anywhere else but in that very room, where she had found her deep in a pile of patchwork.

"I heerd you had come to the old place. Were you glad to be back again?" Cynthy asked with a smile that might be taken to express some doubt upon the subject.

"I was very glad to see it again."

"I hain't seen it in a great while. I've been staying to hum this year or two. I got tired o' going out," Cynthy remarked, with again a smile very peculiar and Fleda thought a little sardonical. She did not know how to answer.

"Well, how do you come along down yonder?" Cynthy went on, making a great fuss with the shovel and tongs to very little purpose. "Ha' you come all the way from Queechy?"

"Yes. I came on purpose to see you, Cynthy."

Without staying to ask what for, Miss Gall now went out to "the back of the house" and came running in again with a live brand pinched in the tongs, and a long tail of smoke running after it. Fleda would have compounded for no fire and no choking. The choking was only useful to give her time to think. She was uncertain how to bring in her errand.

"And how is Mis' Plumfield?" said Cynthy, in an interval of blowing the brand.

"She is quite well; but Cynthy, you need not have taken all that trouble for me. I cannot stay but a few minutes."

"There is wood enough!" Cynthia remarked with one of her grim smiles; an assertion Fleda could not help doubting. Indeed she thought Miss Gall had grown altogether more disagreeable than she used to be in old times. Why, she could not divine, unless the souring effect had gone on with the years.

"And what's become of Earl Douglass and Mis' Douglass? I hain't heerd nothin' of 'em this great while. I always told your grandpa he'd ha' saved himself a great deal o' trouble if he'd ha' let Earl Douglass take hold of things. You ha'n't got Mr. Didenhover into the works again I guess, have you? He was there a good spell after your grandpa died."

"I haven't seen Mrs. Douglass," said Fleda. "But Cynthy, what do you think I have come here for?"

"I don't know," said Cynthy, with another of her peculiar looks directed at the fire. "I s'pose you want someh'n nother of me."

"I have come to see if you wouldn't come and live with my aunt, Mrs. Rossitur. We are left alone and want somebody very much; and I thought I would find you out and see if we couldn't have you, first of all,—before I looked for anybody else."

Cynthy was absolutely silent. She sat before the fire, her feet stretched out towards it as far as they would go, and her arms crossed, and not moving her steady gaze at the smoking wood, or the chimney-back, whichever it might be; but there was in the corners of her mouth the threatening of a smile that Fleda did not at all like.

"What do you say to it, Cynthy?"

"I reckon you'd best get somebody else," said Miss Gall with a kind of condescending dryness, and the smile shewing a little more.

"Why?" said Fleda. "I would a great deal rather have an old friend than a stranger."

"Be you the housekeeper?" said Cynthy a little abruptly.

"O I am a little of everything," said Fleda;—"cook and housekeeper and whatever comes first. I want you to come and be housekeeper, Cynthy."

"I reckon Mis' Rossitur don't have much to do with her help, does she?" said Cynthy after a pause, during which the corners of her mouth never changed. The tone of piqued independence let some light into Fleda's mind.

"She is not strong enough to do much herself, and she wants some one that will take all the trouble from her. You'd have the field all to yourself, Cynthy."

"Your aunt sets two tables I calculate, don't she?"

"Yes—my uncle doesn't like to have any but his own family around him."

"I guess I shouldn't suit!" said Miss Gall, after another little pause, and stooping very diligently to pick up some scattered shreds from the floor. But Fleda could see the flushed face and the smile which pride and a touch of spiteful pleasure in the revenge she was taking made particularly hateful. She needed no more convincing that Miss Gall "wouldn't suit;" but she was sorry at the same time for the perverseness that had so needlessly disappointed her; and went rather pensively back again down the little footpath to the waiting wagon.

"This is hardly the romance of life, dear Hugh," she said as she seated herself.

"Haven't you succeeded?"

Fleda shook her head.

"What's the matter?"

"O—pride,—injured pride of station! The wrong of not coming to our table and putting her knife into our butter."

"And living in such a place!"—said Hugh.

"You don't know what a place. They are miserably poor, I am sure; and yet—I suppose that the less people have to be proud of the more they make of what is left. Poor people!—"

"Poor Fleda!" said Hugh looking at her. "What will you do now?"

"O we'll do somehow," said she cheerfully. "Perhaps it is just as well after all, for Cynthy isn't the smartest woman in the world. I remember grandpa used to say he didn't believe she could get a bean into the middle of her bread."

"A bean into the middle of her bread!" said Hugh.

But Fleda's sobriety was quite banished by his mystified look, and her laugh rang along over the fields before she answered him.

That laugh had blown away all the vapours, for the present at least, and they jogged on again very sociably.

"Do you know," said Fleda, after a while of silent enjoyment in the changes of scene and the mild autumn weather,—"I am not sure that it wasn't very well for me that we came away from New York."

"I dare say it was," said Hugh,—"since we came; but what makes you say so?"

"I don't mean that it was for anybody else, but for me. I think I was a little proud of our nice things there."

"*You*, Fleda!" said Hugh with a look of appreciating affection.

"Yes I was, a little. It didn't make the greatest part of my love for them, I am sure; but I think I had a little, undefined, sort of pleasure in the feeling that they were better and prettier than other people had."

"You are sure you are not proud of your little King Charles now?" said Hugh.

"I don't know but I am," said Fleda laughing. "But how much pleasanter it is here on almost every account. Look at the beautiful sweep of the ground off among those hills —isn't it? What an exquisite horizon line, Hugh?"

"And what a sky over it!"

"Yes—I love these fall skies. Oh I would a great deal rather be here than in any city that ever was built!"

"So would I," said Hugh. "But the thing is——"

Fleda knew quite well what the thing was, and did not answer.

"But my dear Hugh," she said presently,—"I don't remember that sweep of hills when we were coming?"

"You were going the other way," said Hugh.

"Yes but, Hugh,—I am sure we did not pass these grain fields. We must have got into the wrong road."

Hugh drew the reins, and looked, and doubted.

"There is a house yonder," said Fleda,—"we had better drive on and ask."

"There is no house—"

"Yes there is—behind that piece of wood. Look over it—don't you see a light curl of blue smoke against the sky?—We never passed that house and wood, I am certain. We ought to make haste, for the afternoons are short now, and you will please to recollect there is nobody at home to get tea."

"I hope Lucas will get upon one of his everlasting talks with father," said Hugh.

"And that it will hold till we get home," said Fleda. "It will be the happiest use Lucas has made of his tongue in a good while."

Just as they stopped before a substantial-looking farm-house a man came from the other way and stopped there too, with his hand upon the gate.

"How far are we from Queechy, sir?" said Hugh.

"You're not from it at all, sir," said the man politely. "You're in Queechy, sir, at present."

"Is this the right road from Montepoole to Queechy village?"

"It is not, sir. It is a very tortuous direction indeed. Have I not the pleasure of speaking to Mr. Rossitur's young gentleman?"

Mr. Rossitur's young gentleman acknowledged his relationship and begged the favour of being set in the right way home.

"With much pleasure! You have been shewing Miss Rossitur the picturesque country about Montepoole?"

"My cousin and I have been there on business, and lost our way coming back."

"Ah I dare say. Very easy. First time you have been there?"

"Yes sir, and we are in a hurry to get home."

"Well sir,—you know the road by Deacon Patterson's?—comes out just above the lake?"

Hugh did not remember.

"Well—you keep this road straight on,—I'm sorry you are in a hurry,—you keep on till—do you know when you strike Mr. Harris's ground?"

No, Hugh knew nothing about it, nor Fleda.

"Well I'll tell you now how it is," said the stranger, "if you'll permit me. You and your—a—cousin—come in and do us the pleasure of taking some refreshment—I know my sister 'll have her table set out by this time—and I'll do myself the honour of introducing you to—a—these strange roads, afterwards."

"Thank you, sir, but that trouble is unnecessary—cannot you direct us?"

"No trouble—indeed sir, I assure you, I should esteem it a favour—very highly. I—I am Dr. Quackenboss, sir; you may have heard—"

"Thank you Dr. Quackenboss, but we have no time this afternoon—we are very anxious to reach home as soon as possible; if you would be so good as to put us in the way."

"I—really sir, I am afraid—to a person ignorant of the various localities—You will lose no time—I will just hitch your horse here, and I'll have mine ready by the time this young lady has rested. Miss—a—won't you join with me? I assure you I will not put you to the expense of a minute —Thank you!—Mr. Harden!—Just clap the saddle on to Lollypop and have him up here in three seconds.—Thank you!—My dear Miss—a—won't you take my arm? I am gratified, I assure you."

Yielding to the apparent impossibility of getting anything out of Dr. Quackenboss, except civility, and to the real difficulty of disappointing such very earnest good will, Fleda and Hugh did what older persons would not have done,—alighted and walked up to the house.

"This is quite a fortuitous occurrence," the doctor went on;—"I have often had the pleasure of seeing Mr. Rossitur's family in church—in the little church at Queechy Run—and that enabled me to recognise your cousin as soon as I saw him in the wagon. Perhaps Miss—a—you may have possibly heard of my name?—Quackenboss—I don't know that you understood——"

"I have heard it, sir."

"My Irishmen, Miss—a—my Irish labourers, can't get hold of but one end of it; they call me Boss—ha, ha, ha!"

Fleda hoped his patients did not get hold of the other end of it, and trembled, visibly.

"Hard to pull a man's name to pieces before his face,—ha, ha! but I am—a—not one thing myself,—a kind of heterogynous—I am a piece of a physician and a little in the agricultural line also; so it's all fair."

"The Irish treat my name as hardly, Dr. Quackenboss—they call me nothing but Miss Ring-again."

And then Fleda could laugh, and laugh she did, so heartily that the doctor was delighted.

"Ring-again! ha ha!—Very good!—Well, Miss—a—I shouldn't think that anybody in your service would ever—a—ever let you put your name in practice."

But Fleda's delight at the excessive gallantry and awkwardness of this speech was almost too much; or, as the doctor pleasantly remarked, her nerves were too many for her; and every one of them was dancing by the time they reached the hall-door. The doctor's flourishes lost not a bit of their angularity from his tall ungainly figure and a lantern-jawed face, the lower member of which had now and then a somewhat lateral play when he was speaking, which curiously aided the quaint effect of his words. He ushered his guests into the house, seeming in a flow of self-gratulation.

The supper-table was spread, sure enough, and hovering about it was the doctor's sister; a lady in whom Fleda only saw a Dutch face, with eyes that made no impression, disagreeable fair hair, and a string of gilt beads round her neck. A painted yellow floor under foot, a room that looked excessively *wooden* and smelt of cheese, bare walls and a well-filled table, was all that she took in besides.

"I have the honour of presenting you to my sister," said the doctor with suavity. "Flora, the Irish domestics of this young lady call her name Miss Ring-again—if she will let us know how it ought to be called we shall be happy to be informed."

Dr. Quackenboss was made happy.

"Miss *Ringgan*—and this young gentleman is young Mr. Rossitur—the gentleman that has taken Squire Ringgan's old place. We were so fortunate as to have them lose their way this afternoon, coming from the Pool, and they have just stepped in to see if you can't find 'em a mouthful of something they can eat, while Lollypop is a getting ready to see them home."

Poor Miss Flora immediately disappeared into the kitchen, to order a bit of superior cheese and to have some slices of ham put on the gridiron, and then coming back to the common room went rummaging about from cupboard to cupboard, in search of cake and sweetmeats. Fleda protested and begged in vain.

"She was so sorry she hadn't knowed," Miss Flora said,—"she'd ha' had some cakes made that maybe they could have eaten, but the bread was dry; and the cheese wa'n't as good somehow as the last one they cut; maybe Miss Ringgan would prefer a piece of newer-made, if she liked it; and she hadn't had good luck with her preserves last summer—the most of 'em had fomented—she thought it was the damp weather; but there was some stewed pears that maybe she would be so good as to approve—and there was some ham! whatever else it was it was hot!—"

It was impossible, it was impossible, to do dishonour to all this hospitality and kindness and pride that was brought out for them. Early or late, they must eat, in mere gratitude. The difficulty was to avoid eating everything. Hugh and Fleda managed to compound the matter with each other, one taking the cake and pears, and the other the ham and cheese. In the midst of all this overflow of good-will Fleda bethought her to ask if Miss Flora knew of any girl or woman that would go out to service. Miss Flora took the matter into grave consideration as soon as her anxiety on the subject of their cups of tea had subsided. She did not commit herself, but thought it possible that one of the Finns might be willing to go out.

"Where do they live?"

"It's—a—not far from Queechy Run," said the doctor, whose now and then hesitation in the midst of his speech was never for want of a thought but simply and merely for the best words to clothe it in.

"Is it in our way to-night?"

He could make it so, the doctor said, with pleasure, for it would give him permission to gallant them a little further.

They had several miles yet to go, and the sun went down

as they were passing through Queechy Run. Under that still cool clear autumn sky Fleda would have enjoyed the ride very much, but that her unfulfilled errand was weighing upon her, and she feared her aunt and uncle might want her services before she could be at home. Still, late as it was, she determined to stop for a minute at Mrs. Finn's and go home with a clear conscience. At her door, and not till there, the doctor was prevailed upon to part company, the rest of the way being perfectly plain.

Mrs. Finn's house was a great unprepossessing building, washed and dried by the rain and sun into a dark dingy colour, the only one that had ever supplanted the original hue of the fresh-sawn boards. This indeed was not an uncommon thing in the country; near all the houses of the Deepwater settlement were in the same case. Fleda went up a flight of steps to what seemed the front door, but the girl that answered her knock led her down them again and round to a lower entrance on the other side. This introduced Fleda to a large ground-floor apartment, probably the common room of the family, with the large kitchen fireplace and flagged hearth and wall cupboards, and the only furniture the usual red-backed splinter chairs and wooden table. A woman standing before the fire with a broom in her hand answered Fleda's inclination with a saturnine nod of the head, and fetching one of the red-backs from the wall bade her "sit down."

Poor Fleda's nerves bade her "go away." The people looked like their house. The principal woman, who remained standing broom in hand to hear Fleda's business, was in good truth a dark personage; her head covered with black hair, her person with a dingy black calico, and a sullen cloud lowering over her eye. At the corner of the fireplace was an old woman, laid by in an easy chair; disabled, it was plain, not from mental but bodily infirmity; for her face had a cast of mischief which could not stand with the innocence of second childhood. At the other corner sat an elderly woman sewing, with tokens of her trade for yards on the floor around her. Back at the far side of the room a young man was eating his supper at the table alone; and *under* the table, on the floor, the enormous family bread trough was unwontedly filled with the sewing-woman's child, which had with superhuman efforts crawled into it and lay kicking and crowing in delight at its new cradle. Fleda did not know how to enter upon her business.

"I have been looking," she began, "for a person who is willing to go out to work—Miss Flora Quackenboss told me perhaps I might find somebody here."

"Somebody to help?" said the woman beginning to use her broom upon the hearth.—"Who wants 'em?"

"Mrs. Rossitur—my aunt."

"Mrs. Rossitur?—what, down to old Squire Ringgan's place?"

"Yes. We are left alone and want somebody very much."

"Do you want her only a few days, or do you calculate to have her stop longer? because you know it wouldn't be worth the while to put oneself out for a week."

"O we want her to stay,—if we suit each other."

"Well I don't know," said the woman going on with her sweeping,—"I could let you have Hannah, but I 'spect I'll want her to hum—What does Mis' Rossitur calculate to give?"

"I don't know—anything that's reasonable."

"Hannah kin go—just as good as not," said the old woman in the corner rubbing her hands up and down her lap;—"Hannah kin go, just as good as not!"

"Hannah ain't a going," said the first speaker, answering without looking at her. "Hannah 'll be wanted to hum; and she ain't a well girl neither; she's kind o' weak in her muscles; and I calculate you want somebody that can take hold lively. There's Lucy—if she took a notion *she* could go—but she'd please herself about it. She won't do nothing without she has a notion."

This was inconclusive, and desiring to bring matters to a point Fleda after a pause asked if this lady thought Lucy would have a notion to go.

"Well I can't say—she ain't to hum or you could ask her. She's down to Mis' Douglass's, working for her today. Do you know Mis' Douglass?—Earl Douglass's wife?"

"O yes, I knew her long ago," said Fleda, thinking it

might be as well to throw in a spice of ingratiation;—"I am Fleda Ringgan. I used to live here with my grandfather."

"Don't say! Well I thought you had a kind o' look—the old Squire's granddarter, ain't you?"

"She looks like her father," said the sewing-woman laying down her needle, which indeed had been little hindrance to her admiration since Fleda came in.

"She's a real pretty gal," said the old woman in the corner.

"He was as smart a lookin' man as there was in Queechy township, or Montepoole either," the sewing-woman went on, "Do you mind him, Flidda?"

"Anastasy," said the old woman aside, "let Hannah go!"

"Hannah's a going to keep to hum!—Well about Lucy," she said, as Fleda rose to go,—"I can't just say—suppos'n you come here to-morrow afternoon—there's a few coming to quilt, and Lucy 'll be to hum then. I should admire to have you,—and then you and Lucy can agree what you'll fix upon. You can get somebody to bring you, can't you?"

Fleda inwardly shrank, but managed to get off with thanks and without making a positive promise, which Miss Anastasia would fain have had. She was glad to be out of the house and driving off with Hugh.

"How delicious the open air feels!"

"What has this visit produced?" said Hugh.

"An invitation to a party, and a slight possibility that at the party I may find what I want."

"A party!" said Hugh. Fleda laughed and explained.

"And do you intend to go?"

"Not I!—at least I think not. But Hugh, don't say anything about all this to aunt Lucy. She would be troubled."

Fleda had certainly when she came away no notion of improving her acquaintance with Miss Anastasia; but the supper, and the breakfast and the dinner of the next day, with all the nameless and almost numberless duties of housework that filled up the time between, wrought her to a very strong sense of the necessity of having some kind of "help" soon. Mrs. Rossitur wearied herself excessively with doing very little, and then looked so sad to see Fleda working on, that it was more disheartening and harder to bear than the fatigue. Hugh was a most faithful and invaluable coadjutor, and his lack of strength was like her own made up by energy of will; but neither of them could bear the strain long; and when the final clearing away of the dinner-dishes gave her a breathing-time she resolved to dress herself and put her thimble in her pocket and go over to Miss Finn's quilting. Miss Lucy might not be like Miss Anastasia; and if she were, anything that had hands and feet to move instead of her own would be welcome.

Hugh went with her to the door and was to come for her at sunset.

CHAPTER XX.

> With superfluity of breeding
> First makes you sick, and then with feeding.
>
> JENYNS.

MISS ANASTASIA was a little surprised and a good deal gratified, Fleda saw, by her coming, and played the hostess with great benignity. The quilting-frame was stretched in an upper room, not in the long kitchen, to Fleda's joy; most of the company were already seated at it, and she had to go through a long string of introductions before she was permitted to take her place. First of all Earl Douglass's wife, who rose up and taking both Fleda's hands squeezed and shook them heartily, giving her with eye and lip a most genial welcome. This lady had every look of being a very *clever* woman; "a manager" she was said to be; and indeed her very nose had a little pinch which prepared one for nothing superfluous about her. Even her dress could not have wanted another breadth from the skirt and had no fulness to spare about the body. Neat as a pin though; and a well-to-do look through it all. Miss Quackenboss Fleda recognised as an old friend, gilt beads and all. Catherine Douglass had grown up to a pretty girl during the five years since Fleda had left Queechy, and gave her a greeting half smiling half shy. There was a little more affluence about the flow of her drapery, and the pink ribbon round her neck was confined by a little dainty Jew's harp of a brooch; she had her mother's pinch of the nose too. Then there were two other young ladies;—Miss Letitia Ann Thornton, a tall grown girl in pantalettes, evidently a would-be aristocrat from the air of her head and lip, with a well-looking face and looking well knowing of the same, and sporting neat little white cuffs at her wrists, the only one who bore such a distinction. The third of these damsels, Jessie Healy, impressed Fleda with having been brought up upon coarse meat and having grown heavy in consequence; the other two were extremely fair and delicate, both in complexion and feature. Her aunt Syra Fleda recognised without particular pleasure and managed to seat herself at the quilt with the sewing-woman and Miss Hannah between them. Miss Lucy Finn she found seated at her right hand, but after all the civilities she had just gone through Fleda had not courage just then to dash into business with her, and Miss Lucy herself stitched away and was dumb.

So were the rest of the party—rather. The presence of the new-comer seemed to have the effect of a spell. Fleda could not think they had been as silent before her joining them as they were for some time afterwards. The young ladies were absolutely mute, and conversation seemed to flag even among the elder ones; and if Fleda ever raised her eyes from the quilt to look at somebody she was sure to see somebody's eyes looking at her, with a curiosity well enough defined and mixed with a more *or less* amount of benevolence and pleasure. Fleda was growing very industrious and feeling her cheeks grow warm, when the checked stream of conversation began to take revenge by turning its tide upon her.

"Are you glad to be back to Queechy, Fleda?" said Mrs. Douglass from the opposite far end of the quilt.

"Yes ma'am," said Fleda, smiling back her answer,—"on some accounts."

"Ain't she growed like her father, Mis' Douglass?" said the sewing-woman. "Do you recollect Walter Ringgan—what a handsome feller he was?"

The two opposite girls immediately found something to say to each other.

"She ain't a bit more like him than she is like her mother," said Mrs. Douglass, biting off the end of her thread energetically. "Amy Ringgan was a sweet good woman as ever was in this town."

Again her daughter's glance and smile went over to the speaker.

"You stay in Queechy and live like Queechy folks do,"

Mrs. Douglass added, nodding encouragingly, "and you'll beat both on 'em."

But this speech jarred, and Fleda wished it had not been spoken.

"How does your uncle like farming?" said aunt Syra.

A home-thrust, which Fleda parried by saying he had hardly got accustomed to it yet.

"What's been his business? what has he been doing all his life till now?" said the sewing-woman.

Fleda replied that he had had no business; and after the minds of the company had had time to entertain this statement she was startled by Miss Lucy's voice at her elbow.

"It seems kind o' curious, don't it, that a man should live to be forty or fifty years old and not know anything of the earth he gets his bread from?"

"What makes you think he don't?" said Miss Thornton rather tartly.

"She wa'n't speaking o' nobody," said aunt Syra.

"I was—I was speaking of *man*—I was speaking abstractly," said Fleda's right-hand neighbour.

"What's abstractly?" said Miss Anastasia scornfully.

"Where do you get hold of such hard words, Lucy?" said Mrs. Douglass.

"I don't know, Mis' Douglass;—they come to me;—it's practice, I suppose. I had no intention of being obscure."

"One kind o' word's as easy as another I suppose, when you're used to it, ain't it?" said the sewing-woman.

"What's abstractly?" said the mistress of the house again.

"Look in the dictionary, if you want to know," said her sister.

"I don't want to know—I only want you to tell."

"When do you get time for it, Lucy? ha'n't you nothing else to practise?" pursued Mrs. Douglass.

"Yes, Mis' Douglass; but then there are times for exertion, and other times less disposable; and when I feel thoughtful, or low, I commonly retire to my room and contemplate the stars or write a composition."

The sewing-woman greeted this speech with an unqualified ha! ha! and Fleda involuntarily raised her head to look at the last speaker; but there was nothing to be noticed about her, except that she was in rather nicer order than the rest of the Finn family.

"Did you get home safe last night?" inquired Miss Quackenboss, bending forward over the quilt to look down to Fleda.

Fleda thanked her, and replied that they had been overturned and had several ribs broken.

"And where have you been, Fleda, all this while?" said Mrs. Douglass.

Fleda told, upon which all the quilting-party raised their heads simultaneously to take another review of her.

"Your uncle's wife ain't a Frenchwoman, be she?" asked the sewing-woman.

Fleda said "oh no!"—and Miss Quackenboss remarked that "she thought she wa'n't;" whereby Fleda perceived it had been a subject of discussion.

"She lives like one, don't she?" said aunt Syra.

Which imputation Fleda also refuted to the best of her power.

"Well don't she have dinner in the middle of the afternoon?" pursued aunt Syra.

Fleda was obliged to admit that.

"And she can't eat without she has a fresh piece of roast meat on table every day, can she?"

"It is not always roast," said Fleda, half vexed and half laughing.

"I'd rather have a good dish o' bread and 'lasses than the hull on't;" observed old Mrs. Finn; from the corner where she sat manifestly turning up her nose at the far-off joints on Mrs. Rossitur's dinner-table.

The girls on the other side of the quilt again held counsel together, deep and low.

"Well didn't she pick up all them notions in that place yonder?—where you say she has been?" aunt Syra went on.

"No," said Fleda; "everybody does so in New York."

"I want to know what kind of a place New York is, now," said old Mrs. Finn drawlingly. "I s'pose it's pretty big, ain't it?"

Fleda replied that it was.

"I shouldn't wonder if it was a'most as far as from here to Queechy Run, now, ain't it?"

The distance mentioned being somewhere about one-eighth of New York's longest diameter, Fleda answered that it was quite as far.

"I s'pose there's plenty o' mighty rich folks there, ain't there?"

"Plenty, I believe," said Fleda.

"I should hate to live in it awfully!" was the old woman's conclusion.

"I should admire to travel in many countries," said Miss Lucy, for the first time seeming to intend her words particularly for Fleda's ear. "I think nothing makes people more genteel. I have observed it frequently."

Fleda said it was very pleasant; but though encouraged by this opening could not muster enough courage to ask if Miss Lucy had a "notion" to come and prove their gentility. Her next question was startling,—if Fleda had ever studied mathematics?

"No," said Fleda. "Have you?"

"O my, yes! There was a lot of us concluded we would learn it; and we commenced to study it a long time ago. I think it's a most elevating"———

The discussion was suddenly broken off, for the sewing-woman exclaimed, as the other sister came in and took her seat,

"Why Hannah! you ha'n't been makin' bread with that crock on your hands!"

"Well Mis' Barnes!" said the girl,—"I've washed 'em, and I've made bread with 'em, and even *that* didn't take it off!"

"Do you look at the stars, too, Hannah?" said Mrs. Douglass.

Amidst a small hubbub of laugh and talk which now became general, poor Fleda fell back upon one single thought—one wish; that Hugh would come to fetch her home before tea-time. But it was a vain hope. Hugh was not to be there till sundown, and supper was announced long before that. They all filed down, and Fleda with them, to the great kitchen below stairs; and she found herself placed in the seat of honour indeed, but an honour she would gladly have escaped, at Miss Anastasia's right hand.

A temporary locked-jaw would have been felt a blessing.

Fleda dared hardly even look about her; but under the eye of her hostess the instinct of good-breeding was found sufficient to swallow everything; literally and figuratively. There was a good deal to swallow. The usual variety of cakes, sweetmeats, beef, cheese, biscuits, and pies, was set out with some peculiarity of arrangement which Fleda had never seen before, and which left that of Miss Quackenboss elegant by comparison. Down each side of the table ran an advanced guard of little sauces, in Indian file, but in companies of three, the file leader of each being a saucer of custard, its follower a ditto of preserves, and the third keeping a sharp look-out in the shape of pickles; and to Fleda's unspeakable horror she discovered that the guests were expected to help themselves at will from these several stores with their own spoons, transferring what they took either to their own plates or at once to its final destination, which last mode several of the company preferred. The advantage of this plan was the necessary great display of the new silver tea-spoons which Mrs. Douglass slyly hinted to aunt Syra were the moving cause of the tea-party. But aunt Syra swallowed sweetmeats and would not give heed.

There was no relief for poor Fleda. Aunt Syra was her next neighbour, and opposite to her, at Miss Anastasia's left hand, was the disagreeable countenance and peering eyes of the old crone her mother. Fleda kept her own eyes fixed upon her plate and endeavoured to see nothing but that.

"Why here's Fleda ain't eating anything," said Mrs. Douglass. "Won't you have some preserves? take some custard, do!—Anastasy, she ha'n't a spoon—no wonder!"

Fleda had secretly conveyed hers under cover.

"There *was* one," said Miss Anastasia, looking about where one should have been,—"I'll get another as soon as I give Mis' Springer her tea."

"Ha'n't you got enough to go round?" said the old woman plucking at her daughter's sleeve,—"Anastasy!—ha'n't you got enough to go round?"

This speech which was spoken with a most spiteful simplicity Miss Anastasia answered with superb silence, and presently produced spoons enough to satisfy herself and the company. But Fleda! No earthly persuasion could prevail upon her to touch pickles, sweetmeats, or custard, that evening; and even in the bread and cakes she had a vision of hands before her that took away her appetite. She endeavoured to make a shew with hung beef and cups of tea, which indeed was not Pouchong; but her supper came suddenly to an end upon a remark of her hostess, addressed to the whole table, that they needn't be surprised if they found any bits of pudding in the gingerbread, for it was made from the molasses the children left the other day. Who "the children" were Fleda did not know, neither was it material.

It was sundown, but Hugh had not come when they went to the upper rooms again. Two were open now, for they were small and the company promised not to be such. Fathers and brothers and husbands began to come, and loud talking and laughing and joking took place of the quilting chit-chat. Fleda would fain have absorbed herself in the work again, but though the frame still stood there the minds of the company were plainly turned aside from their duty, or perhaps they thought that Miss Anastasia had had admiration enough to dispense with service. Nobody shewed a thimble but one or two old ladies; and as numbers and spirits gathered strength, a kind of romping game was set on foot in which a vast deal of kissing seemed to be the grand wit of the matter. Fleda shrank away out of sight behind the open door of communication between the two rooms, pleading with great truth that she was tired and would like to keep perfectly quiet; and she had soon the satisfaction of being apparently forgotten.

In the other room some of the older people were enjoying themselves more soberly. Fleda's ear was too near the crack of the door not to have the benefit of more of their conversation than she cared for. It soon put quiet of mind out of the question.

"He'll twist himself up pretty short; that's my sense of it; and he won't take long to do it, nother," said Earl Douglass's voice.

Fleda would have known it anywhere from its extreme peculiarity. It never either rose or fell much from a certain pitch; and at that level the words gurgled forth, seemingly from an ever-brimming fountain; he never wanted one; and the stream had neither let nor stay till his modicum of sense had fairly run out. People thought he had not a greater stock of that than some of his neighbours; but he issued an amount of word-currency sufficient for the use of the county.

"He'll run himself agin a post pretty quick," said uncle Joshua in a confirmatory tone of voice.

Fleda had a confused idea that somebody was going to hang himself.

"He ain't a workin' things right," said Douglass,—"he ain't a workin' things right; he's takin' hold o' everything by the tail end. He ain't studied the business; he doesn't know when things is right, and he doesn't know when things is wrong;—and if they're wrong he don't know how to set 'em right. He's got a feller there that ain't no more fit to be there than I am to be Vice President of the United States; and I ain't a going to say what I think I *am* fit for, but I ha'n't studied for *that* place and I shouldn't like to stand an examination for't; and a man hadn't ought to be a farmer no more if he ha'n't qualified himself. That's my idee. I like to see a thing done well if it's to be done at all; and there ain't a stitch o' land been laid right on the hull farm, nor a furrow driv' as it had ought to be, since he come on to it; and I say, Squire Springer, a man ain't going to get along in that way, and he hadn't ought to. I work hard myself, and I calculate to work hard; and I make a livin' by't; and I'm content to work hard. When I see a man with his hands in his pockets, I think he'll have nothin' else in 'em soon. I don't believe he's done a hand's turn himself on the land the hull season!"

And upon this Mr. Douglass brought up.

"My son Lucas has been workin' with him, off and on, pretty much the hull time since he come; and *he* says he ha'n't begun to know how to spell farmer yet."

"Ay, ay! My wife—she's a little harder on folks than I be—I think it ain't worth while to say nothin' of a man without I can say some good of him—that's my idee—and it don't do no harm, nother,—but my wife, she says he's got to let down his notions a peg or two afore they'll hitch just in the right place; and I won't say but what I think she ain't maybe fur from right. If a man's above his business he stands a pretty fair chance to be below it some day. I won't say myself, for I haven't any acquaintance with him, and a man oughtn't to speak but of what he is knowing to,—but I have heerd say, that he wa'n't as conversationable as it would ha' been handsome in him to be, all things considerin.' There seems to be a good many things said of him, somehow, and I always think men don't talk of a man if he don't give 'em occasion; but anyhow I've been past the farm pretty often myself this summer, workin' with Seth Plumfield; and I've took notice of things myself; and I know he's been makin' beds o' sparrowgrass when he had ought to ha' been makin' fences, and he's been helpin' that little girl o' his'n set her flowers, when he would ha' been better sot to work lookin' after his Irishman; but I don't know as it made much matter nother, for if he went wrong Mr. Rossitur wouldn't know how to set him right, and if he was a going right Mr. Rossitur would ha' been just as likely to ha' set him wrong. Well I'm sorry for him!"

"Mr. Rossitur is a most gentlemanlike man," said the voice of Dr. Quackenboss.

"Ay,—I dare say he is," Earl responded in precisely the same tone. "I was down to his house one day last summer to see him.—He wa'n't to hum, though."

"It would be strange if harm come to a man with such a guardian angel in the house as that man has in his'n," said Dr. Quackenboss.

"Well she's a pretty creetur'!" said Douglass, looking up with some animation. "I wouldn't blame any man that sot a good deal by her. I will say I think she's as handsome as my own darter; and a man can't go no furder than that I suppose."

"She won't help his farming much, I guess," said uncle Joshua,—"nor his wife nother."

Fleda heard Dr. Quackenboss coming through the doorway and started from her corner for fear he might find her out there and know what she had heard.

He very soon found her out in the new place she had chosen and came up to pay his compliments. Fleda was in a mood for anything but laughing, yet the mixture of the ludicrous which the doctor administered set her nerves a twitching. Bringing his chair down sideways at one angle and his person at another, so as to meet at the moment of the chair's touching the floor, and with a look and smile slanting to match, the doctor said,

"Well Miss Ringgan, has—a—Mrs. Rossitur,—does she feel herself reconciled yet?"

"Reconciled, sir?" said Fleda.

"Yes—a—to Queechy?"

"She never quarrelled with it, sir," said Fleda, quite unable to keep from laughing.

"Yes,—I mean—a—she feels that she can sustain her spirits in different situations?"

"She is very well, sir, thank you."

"It must have been a great change to her—and to you all—coming to this place."

"Yes sir; the country is very different from the city."

"In what part of New York was Mr. Rossitur's former residence?"

"In State street, sir."

"State street,—that is somewhere in the direction of the Park?"

"No sir, not exactly."

"Was Mrs. Rossitur a native of the city?"

"Not of New York. O Hugh, my dear Hugh," exclaimed Fleda in another tone,—"what have you been thinking of?"

"Father wanted me," said Hugh. "I could not help it, Fleda."

"You are not going to have the cruelty to take your—a—cousin away, Mr. Rossitur?" said the doctor.

But Fleda was for once happy to be cruel; she would hear no remonstrances. Though her desire for Miss Lucy's "help" had considerably lessened she thought she could not in politeness avoid speaking on the subject, after being invited there on purpose. But Miss Lucy said she "calculated to stay at home this winter," unless she went to live with somebody at Kenton for the purpose of attending a course of philosophy lectures that she heard were to be given there. So that matter was settled; and clasping Hugh's arm Fleda turned away from the house with a step and heart both lightened by the joy of being out of it.

"I couldn't come sooner, Fleda," said Hugh,

"No matter—O I'm so glad to be away! Walk a little faster, dear Hugh.—Have you missed me at home?"

"Do you want me to say no or yes?" said Hugh smiling. "We did very well—mother and I—and I have left everything ready to have tea the minute you get home. What sort of a time have you had?"

In answer to which Fleda gave him a long history; and then they walked on awhile in silence. The evening was still and would have been dark but for the extreme brilliancy of the stars through the keen clear atmosphere. Fleda looked up at them and drew large draughts of bodily and mental refreshment with the bracing air.

"Do you know to-morrow will be Thanksgiving day?"

"Yes—what made you think of it?"

"They were talking about it—they make a great fuss here Thanksgiving day."

"I don't think we shall make much of a fuss," said Hugh.

"I don't think we shall. I wonder what I shall do—I am afraid uncle Rolf will get tired of coffee and omelettes in the course of time; and my list of receipts is very limited."

"It is a pity you didn't beg one of Mrs. Renney's books," said Hugh laughing. "If you had only known—"

"'Tisn't too late!" said Fleda quickly,—"I'll send to New York for one. I will! I'll ask uncle Orrin to get it for me. That's the best thought!—"

"But Fleda! you're not going to turn cook in that fashion!"

"It would be no harm to have the book," said Fleda. "I can tell you we mustn't expect to get anybody here that can make an omelette, or even coffee, that uncle Rolf will drink. Oh Hugh!—"

"What?"

"I don't know where we are going to get anybody!—But don't say anything to aunt Lucy about it."

"Well, we can keep Thanksgiving day, Fleda, without a dinner," said Hugh cheerfully.

"Yes indeed;—I am sure I can—after being among these people to-night. How much I have that they want! Look at the Great Bear over there!—isn't that better than New York?"

"The Great Bear hangs over New York too," Hugh said with a smile.

"Ah but it isn't the same thing. Heaven hasn't the same eyes for the city and the country."

As Hugh and Fleda went quick up to the kitchen door they overtook a dark figure, at whom looking narrowly as she passed, Fleda recognised Seth Plumfield. He was joyfully let into the kitchen, and there proved to be the bearer of a huge dish carefully covered with a napkin.

"Mother guessed you hadn't any Thanksgiving ready," he said,—"and she wanted to send this down to you; so I thought I would come and fetch it myself."

"O thank her! and thank you, cousin Seth;—how good you are!"

"Mother ha'n't lost her old trick at 'em," said he, "so I hope *that's* good."

"O I know it is," said Fleda. "I remember aunt Miri am's Thanksgiving chicken-pies. Now cousin Seth, you must come in and see aunt Lucy."

"No," said he quietly,—"I've got my farm boots on—I guess I won't see anybody but you."

But Fleda would not suffer that, and finding she could not move him she brought her aunt out into the kitchen. Mrs. Rossitur's manner of speaking and thanking him quite charmed Seth, and he went away with a kindly feeling towards those gentle bright eyes which he never forgot.

"Now we've something for to-morrow, Hugh!" said Fleda;—"and such a chicken-pie I can tell you as *you* never saw. Hugh, isn't it odd how different a thing is in different circumstances? You don't know how glad I was when I put my hands upon that warm pie-dish and knew what it was; and when did I ever care in New York about Emile's doings?"

"Except the almond gauffres," said Hugh smiling.

"I never thought to be so glad of a chicken-pie," said Fleda, shaking her head.

Aunt Miriam's dish bore out Fleda's praise, in the opinion of all that tasted it; for such fowls, such butter, and such cream, as went to its composition could hardly be known but in an unsophisticated state of society. But one pie could not last for ever; and as soon as the signs of dinner were got rid of, Thanksgiving day though it was, poor Fleda was fain to go up the hill to consult aunt Miriam about the possibility of getting "help."

"I don't know, dear Fleda," said she;—"if you cannot get Lucy Finn—I don't know who else there is you can get. Mrs. Toles wants both her daughters at home I know this winter, because she is sick; and Marietta Winchel is working at aunt Syra's;—I don't know—Do you remember Barby Elster, that used to live with me?"

"O yes!"

"She *might* go—she has been staying at home these two years, to take care of her old mother, that's the reason she left me; but she has another sister come home now,—Hetty, that married and went to Montepoole,—she's lost her husband and come home to live; so perhaps Barby would go out again. But I don't know,—how do you think your aunt Lucy would get along with her?"

"Dear aunt Miriam! you know we must do as we can. We *must* have somebody."

"Barby is a little quick," said Mrs. Plumfield, "but I think she is good-hearted, and she is thorough, and faithful as the day is long. If your aunt and uncle can put up with her ways."

"I am sure we can, aunt Miriam. Aunt Lucy's the easiest person in the world to please, and I'll try and keep her away from uncle Rolf. I think we can get along. I know Barby used to like me."

"But then Barby knows nothing about French cooking, my child; she can do nothing but the common country things. What will your uncle and aunt say to that!"

"I don't know," said Fleda, "but anything is better than nothing. I must try and do what she can't do. I'll come up and get you to teach me, aunt Miriam."

Aunt Miriam hugged and kissed her before speaking.

"I'll teach you what I know, my darling;—and now we'll go right off and see Barby—we shall catch her just in a good time."

It was a poor little unpainted house, standing back from the road, and with a double row of boards laid down to serve as a path to it. But this board-walk was scrubbed perfectly clean. They went in without knocking. There was nobody there but an old woman seated before the fire, shaking all over with the St. Vitus's Dance. She gave them no salutation, calling instead on "Barby!"—who presently made her appearance from the inner door.

"Barby!—who's this?"

"That's Mis' Plumfield, mother," said the daughter, speaking loud as to a deaf person.

The old lady immediately got up and dropped a very quick and what was meant to be a very respect-shewing curtsey, saying at the same time with much deference and with one of her involuntary twitches,—"I ''maun' to know!"—The sense of the ludicrous and the feeling of pity together were painfully oppressive. Fleda turned away to the daughter who came forward and shook hands with a frank look of pleasure at the sight of her elder visiter.

"Barby," said Mrs. Plumfield, "this is little Fleda Ringgan—do you remember her?"

"I' mind to know!" said Barby, transferring her hand to Fleda's and giving it a good squeeze.—"She's growed a fine gal, Mis' Plumfield. You ha'n't lost none of your good looks—ha' you kept all your old goodness along with 'em?"

Fleda laughed at this abrupt question, and said she didn't know.

"If you ha'n't, I wouldn't give much for your eyes," said Barby letting go her hand.

Mrs. Plumfield laughed too at Barby's equivocal mode of complimenting.

"Who's that young gal, Barby?" inquired Mrs. Elster.

"That's Mis' Plumfield's niece, mother!"

"She's a handsome little creetur, ain't she?"

They all laughed at that, and Fleda's cheeks growing crimson, Mrs. Plumfield stepped forward to ask after the old lady's health; and while she talked and listened Fleda's eyes noted the spotless condition of the room—the white table, the nice rag-carpet, the bright many-coloured patchwork counterpane on the bed, the brilliant cleanliness of the floor where the small carpet left the boards bare, the tidy look of the two women; and she made up her mind that *she* could get along with Miss Barbara very well. Barby was rather tall, and in face decidedly a fine-looking woman, though her figure had the usual scantling proportions which nature or fashion assigns to the hard-working dwellers in the country. A handsome quick grey eye and the mouth were sufficiently expressive of character, and perhaps of temper, but there were no lines of anything sinister or surly; you could imagine a flash, but not a cloud.

"Barby, you are not tied at home any longer, are you?" said Mrs. Plumfield, coming back from the old lady and speaking rather low;—"now that Hetty is here can't your mother spare you?"

"Well I reckon she could, Mis' Plumfield,—if I could work it so that she'd be more comfortable by my being away."

"Then you'd have no objection to go out again?"

"Where to?"

"Fleda's uncle, you know, has taken my brother's old place, and they have no help. They want somebody to take the whole management—just you, Barby. Mrs. Rossitur isn't strong."

"Nor don't want to be, does she? I've heerd tell of her. Mis' Plumfield, I should despise to have as many legs and arms as other folks and not be able to help myself!"

"But you wouldn't despise to help other folks, I hope," said Mrs. Plumfield smiling.

"People that want you very much too," said Fleda; for she quite longed to have that strong hand and healthy eye to rely upon at home. Barby looked at her with a relaxed face, and after a little consideration said "she guessed she'd try."

"Mis' Plumfield," cried the old lady as they were moving,—"Mis' Plumfield, you said you'd send me a piece of pork."

"I haven't forgotten it, Mrs. Elster—you shall have it."

"Well you get it out for me yourself," said the old woman speaking very energetically,—"don't you send no one else to the barrel for't; because I know you'll give me the biggest piece."

Mrs. Plumfield laughed and promised.

"I'll come up and work it out some odd day," said the daughter nodding intelligently as she followed them to the door.

"We'll talk about that," said Mrs. Plumfield.

"She was wonderful pleased with the pie," said Barby, "and so was Hetty; she ha'n't seen anything so good, she says, since she quit Queechy."

"Well Barby," said Mrs. Plumfield, as she turned and grasped her hand, "did you remember your Thanksgiving over it?"

"Yes, Mis' Plumfield," and the fine grey eyes fell to the floor,—"but I minded it only because it had come from you. I seemed to hear you saying just that out of every bone I picked."

"You minded *my* message," said the other gently.

"Well I don't mind the things I had ought to most," said Barby in a subdued voice,—"never!—'cept mother—I ain't very apt to forget her."

Mrs. Plumfield saw a tell-tale glittering beneath the drooping eye-lid. She added no more but a sympathetic strong squeeze of the hand she held, and turned to follow Fleda who had gone on ahead.

"Mis' Plumfield!" said Barby, before they had reached the stile that led into the road, where Fleda was standing,—"Will I be sure of having the money regular down yonder? You know I hadn't ought to go otherways, on account of mother."

"Yes, it will be sure," said Mrs. Plumfield,—"and regular;" adding quietly, "I'll make it so."

There was a bond for the whole amount in aunt Miriam's eyes; and quite satisfied, Barby went back to the house.

"Will she expect to come to our table, aunt Miriam?" said Fleda when they had walked a little way.

"No—she will not expect that—but Barby will want a different kind of managing from those Irish women of yours. She won't bear to be spoken to in a way that don't suit her notions of what she thinks she deserves; and perhaps your aunt and uncle will think her notions rather high—I don't know."

"There is no difficulty with aunt Lucy," said Fleda;—"and I guess I can manage uncle Rolf—I'll try. *I* like her very much."

"Barby is very poor," said Mrs. Plumfield; "she has nothing but her own earnings to support herself and her old mother, and now I suppose her sister and her child; for Hetty is a poor thing—never did much and now I suppose does nothing."

"Are those Finns poor, aunt Miriam?"

"O no—not at all—they are very well off."

"So I thought—they seemed to have plenty of everything, and silver spoons and all—But why then do they go out to work?"

"They are a little too fond of getting money I expect," said aunt Miriam. "And they are a queer sort of people rather—the mother is queer and the children are queer—they ain't like other folks exactly—never were."

"I am very glad we are to have Barby instead of that Lucy Finn," said Fleda. "O aunt Miriam! you can't think how much easier my heart feels."

"Poor child!" said aunt Miriam looking at her. "But it isn't best, Fleda, to have things work too smooth in this world."

"No, I suppose not," said Fleda sighing. "Isn't it very strange, aunt Miriam, that it should make people worse instead of better to have everything go pleasantly with them?"

"It is because they are apt then to be so full of the present that they forget the care of the future."

"Yes and forget there is anything better than the present, I suppose," said Fleda.

"So we mustn't fret at the ways our Father takes to keep us from hurting ourselves?" said aunt Miriam cheerfully.

"O no!" said Fleda, looking up brightly in answer to the tender manner in which these words were spoken;—"and I didn't mean that *this* is much of a trouble—only I am very glad to think that somebody is coming to-morrow."

Aunt Miriam thought that gentle unfretful face could not stand in need of much discipline.

CHAPTER XXI.

Wise men alway
Affyrme and say,
That best is for a man,
Diligently,
For to apply,
The business that he can.
MORE.

FLEDA waited for Barby's coming the next day with a little anxiety. The introduction and installation however were happily got over. Mrs. Rossitur, as Fleda knew, was most easily pleased; and Barby Elster's quick eye was satisfied with the unaffected and universal gentleness and politeness of her new employer. She made herself at home in half an hour; and Mrs. Rossitur and Fleda were comforted to perceive, by unmistakeable signs, that their presence was not needed in the kitchen and they might retire to their own premises and forget there was another part of the house. Fleda had forgotten it utterly, and deliciously enjoying the rest of mind and body she was stretched upon the sofa, luxuriating over some volume from her remnant of a library; when the inner door was suddenly pushed open far enough to admit of the entrance of Miss Elster's head.

"Where's the soft soap?"

Fleda's book went down and her heart jumped to her mouth, for her uncle was sitting over by the window. Mrs. Rossitur looked up in a maze and waited for the question to be repeated.

"I say, where's the soft soap?"

"Soft soap!" said Mrs. Rossitur,—"I don't know whether there is any.—Fleda, do you know?"

"I was trying to think, aunt Lucy—I don't believe there is any."

"*Where* is it?" said Barby.

"There is none, I believe," said Mrs. Rossitur.

"Where *was* it, then?"

"Nowhere—there has not been any in the house," said Fleda, raising herself up to see over the back of her sofa.

"There ha'n't been none!" said Miss Elster, in a tone more significant than her words, and shutting the door as abruptly as she had opened it.

"What upon earth does the woman mean?" exclaimed Mr. Rossitur, springing up and advancing towards the kitchen door. Fleda threw herself before him.

"Nothing at all, uncle Rolf—she doesn't mean anything at all—she doesn't know any better."

"I will improve her knowledge—get out of the way, Fleda."

"But uncle Rolf, just hear me one moment—please don't!—she didn't mean any harm—these people don't know any manners—just let me speak to her, please uncle Rolf!—" said Fleda laying both hands upon her uncle's arms,—"I'll manage her."

Mr. Rossitur's wrath was high, and he would have run over or knocked down anything less gentle that had stood in his way; but even the harshness of strength shuns to set itself in array against the meekness that does not *oppose;* if the touch of those hands had been a whit less light, or the glance of her eye less submissively appealing, it would have availed nothing. As it was, he stopped and looked at her, at first scowling, but then with a smile.

"*You* manage her!" said he.

"Yes," said Fleda laughing, and now exerting her force she gently pushed him back towards the seat he had quitted,—"yes, uncle Rolf—you've enough else to manage—don't undertake our 'help.' Deliver over all your displeasure upon me when anything goes wrong—I will be the conductor to carry it off safely into the kitchen and discharge it just at that point where I think it will do most execution. Now will you uncle Rolf?—Because we have got a new-fashioned piece of firearms in the other room that I am afraid will go off unexpectedly if it is meddled with by an unskilful hand;—and that would leave us without arms, you see, or with only aunt Lucy's and mine, which are not reliable."

"You saucy girl!"—said her uncle, who was laughing partly at and partly with her,—"I don't know what you deserve exactly.—Well—keep this precious new operative of yours out of my way and I'll take care to keep out of hers. But mind, you must manage not to have your piece snapping in my face in this fashion, for I won't stand it."

And so, quieted, Mr. Rossitur sat down to his book again; and Fleda leaving hers open went to attend upon Barby.

"There ain't much yallow soap neither," said this personage,—"if this is all. There's one thing—if we ha'n't got it we can make it. I must get Mis' Rossitur to have a leach tub sot up right away. I'm a dreadful hand for havin' plenty o' soap."

"What is a leach-tub?" said Fleda.

"Why, a leach-tub, for to leach ashes in. That's easy enough. I'll fix it, afore we're any on us much older. If Mr. Rossitur 'll keep me in good hard wood I sha'n't cost him hardly anything for potash."

"I'll see about it," said Fleda, "and I will see about having the leach-tub, or whatever it is, put up for you. And Barby, whenever you want anything, will you just speak to me about it?—and if I am in the other room ask me to come out here. Because my aunt is not strong, and does not know where things are as well as I do; and when my uncle is in there he sometimes does not like to be disturbed with hearing any such talk. If you'll tell me I'll see and have everything done for you."

"Well—you get me a leach sot up—that's all I'll ask of you just now," said Barby good-humouredly;—"and help me to find the soap-grease, if there is any. As to the rest, I don't want to see nothin' o' him in the kitchen so I'll relieve him if he don't want to see much o' me in the parlour.—I shouldn't wonder if there wa'n't a speck of it in the house."

Not a speck was there to be found.

"Your uncle's pockets must ha' had a good hole in 'em by this time," remarked Barby as they came back from the cellar. "However, there never was a crock so empty it couldn't be filled. You get me a leach-tub sot up, and I'll find work for it."

From that time Fleda had no more trouble with her uncle and Barby. Each seemed to have a wholesome appreciation of the other's combative qualities and to shun them. With Mrs. Rossitur Barby was soon all-powerful. It was enough that she wanted a thing, if Mrs. Rossitur's own resources could compass it. For Fleda, to say that Barby had presently a perfect understanding with her and joined to that a most affectionate careful regard, is not perhaps saying much; for it was true of every one without exception with whom Fleda had much to do. Barby was to all of them a very great comfort and stand-by.

It was well for them that they had her within doors to keep things, as she called it, "right and tight;" for abroad the only system in vogue was one of fluctuation and uncertainty. Mr. Rossitur's Irishman, Donohan, staid his year out, doing as little good and as much at least negative harm as he well could; and then went, leaving them a good deal poorer than he found them. Dr. Gregory's generosity had added to Mr. Rossitur's own small stock of ready money, giving him the means to make some needed outlays on the farm. But the outlay, ill-applied, had been greater than the income; a scarcity of money began to be more and more felt; and the comfort of the family accordingly drew within more and more narrow bounds. The temper of the head of the family suffered in at least equal degree.

From the first of Barby's coming poor Fleda had done her utmost to prevent the want of Mons. Emile from being felt. Mr. Rossitur's table was always set by her careful hand, and all the delicacies that came upon it were, unknown to him, of her providing. Even the bread. One day at breakfast Mr. Rossitur had expressed his impatient displeasure at that of Miss Elster's manufacture. Fleda saw the distressed shade that came over her aunt's face, and took her resolution. It was the last time. She had followed her plan of sending for the receipts, and she studied them diligently, both at home and under aunt Miriam. Natural quickness of eye and hand came in aid of her affectionate zeal, and it was not long before she could trust herself to undertake any operation in the whole range of her cookery book. But meanwhile materials were growing scarce and hard to come by. The delicate French rolls which were now always ready for her uncle's plate in the morning had sometimes nothing to back them, unless the unfailing water-cress from the good little spring in the meadow. Fleda could not spare her eggs, for perhaps they might have nothing else to depend upon for dinner. It was no burden to her to do these things; she had a sufficient reward in seeing that her aunt and Hugh eat the better and that her uncle's brow was clear; but it *was* a burden when her hands were tied by the lack of means; for she knew the failure of the usual supply was bitterly felt, not for the actual want, but for that other want which it implied and prefigured.

On the first dismissal of Donohan Fleda hoped for a good turn of affairs. But Mr. Rossitur, disgusted with his first experiment resolved this season to be his own head man; and appointed Lucas Springer the second in command, with a posse of labourers to execute his decrees. It did not work well. Mr. Rossitur found he had a very tough prime minister, who would have every one of his plans to go through a kind of winnowing process by being tossed about in an argument. The arguments were interminable, until Mr. Rossitur not unfrequently quit the field with, "Well, do what you like about it!"—not conquered, but wearied. The labourers, either from want of ready money or of what they called "manners" in their employer, fell off at the wrong times, just when they were most wanted. Hugh threw himself then into the breach and wrought beyond his strength; and that tried Fleda worst of all. She was glad to see haying and harvest pass over; but the change of seasons seemed to bring only a change of disagreeableness, and she could not find that hope had any better breathing-time in the short days of winter than in the long days of summer. Her gentle face grew more gentle than ever, for under the shade of sorrowful patience which was always there now its meekness had no eclipse.

Mrs. Rossitur was struck with it one morning. She was coming down from her room and saw Fleda standing on the landing-place gazing out of the window. It was before breakfast one cold morning in winter. Mrs. Rossitur put her arms round her softly and kissed her.

"What are you thinking about, dear Fleda?—you ought not to be standing here."

"I was looking at Hugh," said Fleda, and her eye went back to the window. Mrs. Rossitur's followed it. The window gave them a view of the ground behind the house; and there was Hugh, just coming in with a large armful of heavy wood which he had been sawing.

"He isn't strong enough to do that, aunt Lucy," said Fleda softly.

"I know it," said his mother in a subdued tone, and not moving her eye, though Hugh had disappeared.

"It is too cold for him—he is too thinly clad to bear this exposure," said Fleda anxiously.

"I know it," said his mother again.

"Can't you tell uncle Rolf?—can't you get him to do it? I am afraid Hugh will hurt himself, aunt Lucy."

"I did tell him the other day—I did speak to him about it," said Mrs. Rossitur; "but he said there was no reason why Hugh should do it,—there were plenty of other people—"

"But how can he say so when he knows we never can ask Lucas to do anything of the kind, and that other man always contrives to be out of the way when he is wanted? —Oh what is he thinking of?"—said Fleda bitterly, as she saw Hugh again at his work.

It was so rarely that Fleda was seen to shed tears that they always were a signal of dismay to any of the household. There was even agony in Mrs. Rossitur's voice as she implored her not to give way to them. But notwithstanding that, Fleda's tears came this time from too deep a spring to be stopped at once.

"It makes me feel as if all was lost, Fleda, when I see you do so,"—

Fleda put her arms about her neck and whispered that "she would not"—that "she should not"—

Yet it was a little while before she could say any more.

"But aunt Lucy, he doesn't know what he is doing!"

"No—and I can't make him know. I cannot say anything more, Fleda—it would do no good. I don't know what is the matter—he is entirely changed from what he used to be—"

"I know what is the matter," said Fleda, now turning comforter in her turn as her aunt's tears fell more quietly, because more despairingly, than her own,—"I know what it is—he is not happy;—that is all. He has not succeeded well in these farm doings, and he wants money, and he is worried—it is no wonder if he don't seem exactly as he used to."

"And oh, that troubles me most of all!" said Mrs. Rossitur. "The farm is bringing in nothing, I know,—he don't know how to get along with it,—I was afraid it would be so;—and we are paying nothing to uncle Orrin—and it is just a dead weight on his hands;—and I can't bear to think of it!—And what will it come to!—"

Mrs. Rossitur was now in her turn surprised into shewing the strength of her sorrows and apprehensions. Fleda was fain to put her own out of sight and bend her utmost powers to soothe and compose her aunt, till they could both go down to the breakfast table. She had got ready a nice little dish that her uncle was very fond of; but her pleasure in it was all gone; and indeed it seemed to be thrown away upon the whole table. Half the meal was over before anybody said a word.

"I am going to wash my hands of these miserable farm affairs," said Mr. Rossitur.

"Are you!" said his wife.

"Yes,—of all personal concern in them, that is. I am wearied to death with the perpetual annoyances and vexations, and petty calls upon my time—life is not worth having at such a rate! I'll have done with it."

"You will give up the entire charge to Lucas?" said Mrs. Rossitur.

"Lucas!—No!—I wouldn't undergo that man's tongue for another year if he would take out his wages in talking. I could not have more of it in that case than I have had the last six months. After money, the thing that man loves best is certainly the sound of his own voice; and a most insufferable egotist! No,—I have been talking with a man who wants to take the whole farm for two years upon shares—that will clear me of all trouble."

There was sober silence for a few minutes, and then Mrs. Rossitur asked who it was.

"His name is Didenhover."

"O uncle Rolf, don't have anything to do with him!" exclaimed Fleda.

"Why not?"

"Because he lived with grandpa a great while ago, and behaved very ill. Grandpa had a great deal of trouble with him."

"How old were you then?"

"I was young, to be sure," said Fleda hanging her head, "but I remember very well how it was."

"You may have occasion to remember it a second time," said Mr. Rossitur dryly, "for the thing is done. I have engaged him."

Not another word was spoken.

Mr. Rossitur went out after breakfast, and Mrs. Rossitur busied herself with the breakfast cups and a tub of hot water, a work she never would let Fleda share with her and which lasted in consequence long enough, Barby said, to cook and eat three breakfasts. Fleda and Hugh sat looking at the floor and the fire respectively.

"I am going up the hill to get a sight of aunt Miriam," said Fleda, bringing her eyes from the fire upon her aunt.

"Well dear, do. You have been shut up long enough by the snow. Wrap yourself up well, and put on my snow-boots."

"No indeed!" said Fleda. "I shall just draw on another pair of stockings over my shoes, within my India-rubbers—I will take a pair of Hugh's woollen ones."

"What has become of your own?" said Hugh.

"My own what? Stockings?"

"Snow-boots."

"Worn out, Mr. Rossitur! I have run them to death, poor things. Is that a slight intimation that you are afraid of the same fate for your socks?"

"No," said Hugh, smiling in spite of himself at her manner,—"I will lend you anything I have got, Fleda."

His tone put Fleda in mind of the very doubtful pretensions of the socks in question to be comprehended under the term; she was silent a minute.

"Will you go with me, Hugh?"

"No dear, I can't;—I must get a little ahead with the wood while I can; it looks as if it would snow again; and Barby isn't provided for more than a day or two."

"And how for this fire?"

Hugh shook his head, and rose up to go forth into the kitchen. Fleda went too, linking her arm in his and bearing affectionately upon it, a sort of tacit saying that they would sink or swim together. Hugh understood it perfectly.

"I am very sorry you have to do it, dear Hugh—Oh that wood-shed!—if it had only been made!—"

"Never mind—can't help it now—we shall get through the winter by and by."

"Can't you get uncle Rolf to help you a little?" whispered Fleda;—"It would do him good."

But Hugh only shook his head.

"What are we going to do for dinner, Barby?" said Fleda, still holding Hugh there before the fire.

"Ain't much choice," said Barby. "It would puzzle anybody to spell much more out of it than pork and ham. There's plenty o' them. *I* shan't starve this some time."

"But we had ham yesterday and pork the day before yesterday and ham Monday," said Fleda. "There is plenty of vegetables, thanks to you and me, Hugh," she said with a little reminding squeeze of his arm. "I could make soups nicely, if I had anything to make them of!"

"There's enough to be had for the catching," said Barby. "If I hadn't a man-mountain of work upon me, I'd start out and shoot or steal something."

"*You* shoot, Barby!" said Fleda laughing.

"I guess I can do 'most anything I set my hand to. If I couldn't I'd shoot myself. It won't do to kill no more o' them chickens."

"O no,—now they are laying so finely. Well, I am going up the hill, and when I come home I'll try and make up something, Barby."

"Earl Douglass 'll go out in the woods now and then, of a day when he ha'n't no work particular to do, and fetch hum as many pigeons and woodchucks as you could shake a stick at."

"Hugh, my dear," said Fleda laughing, "it's a pity you aren't a hunter—I would shake a stick at you with great pleasure. Well Barby, we will see when I come home."

"I was just a thinkin," said Barby;—"Mis' Douglass sent round to know if Mis' Rossitur would like a piece of fresh meat—Earl's been killing a sheep—there's a nice quarter, she says, if she'd like to have it."

"A quarter of mutton!"—said Fleda,—"I don't know—no, I think not, Barby; I don't know when we should be able to pay it back again.—And yet—Hugh, do you think uncle Rolf will kill another sheep this winter?"

"I am sure he will not," said Hugh;—"there have so many died."

"If he only knowed it, that is a reason for killing more," said Barby,—"and have the good of them while he can."

"Tell Mrs. Douglass we are obliged to her but we do not want the mutton, Barby."

Hugh went to his chopping and Fleda set out upon her walk; the lines of her face settling into a most fixed gravity so soon as she turned away from the house. It was what might be called a fine winter's day; cold and still, and the sky covered with one uniform grey cloud. The snow lay in uncompromising whiteness thick over all the world; a kindly shelter for the young grain and covering for the soil; but Fleda's spirits just then in another mood saw in it only the cold refusal to hope and the barren check to exertion. The wind had cleared the snow from the trees and fences, and they stood in all their unsoftened blackness and nakedness, bleak and stern. The high grey sky threatened a fresh fall of snow in a few hours; it was just now a lull between two storms; and Fleda's spirits, that sometimes would have laughed in the face of nature's soberness, to-day sank to its own quiet. Her pace neither slackened nor quickened till she reached aunt Miriam's house and entered the kitchen.

Aunt Miriam was in high tide of business over a pot of boiling lard, and the enormous bread-tray by the side of the fire was half full of very tempting light-brown cruller, which however were little more than a kind of sweet bread for the workmen. In the bustle of putting in and taking out aunt Miriam could give her visiter but a word and a look. Fleda pulled off her hood and sitting down watched in unusual silence the old lady's operations.

"And how are they all at your house to-day?" aunt Miriam asked as she was carefully draining her cruller out of the kettle.

Fleda answered that they were as well as usual, but a slight hesitation and the tell-tale tone of her voice made the old lady look at her more narrowly. She came near and kissed that gentle brow and looking in her eyes asked her what the matter was?

"I don't know,—" said Fleda, eyes and voice wavering alike,—"I am foolish, I believe,—"

Aunt Miriam tenderly put aside the hair from her forehead and kissed it again, but the cruller was burning and she went back to the kettle.

"I got down-hearted somehow this morning," Fleda went on, trying to steady her voice and school herself.

"*You* down-hearted, dear? About what?"

There was a world of sympathy in these words, in the warmth of which Fleda's shut-up heart unfolded itself at once.

"It's nothing new, aunt Miriam,—only somehow I felt it particularly this morning,—I have been kept in the house so long by this snow I have got dumpish I suppose,—"

Aunt Miriam looked anxiously at the tears which seemed to come involuntarily, but she said nothing.

"We are not getting along well at home."

"I supposed that," said Mrs. Plumfield quietly. "But anything new?"

"Yes—uncle Rolf has let the farm—only think of it!—he has let the farm to that Didenhover."

"Didenhover!"

"For two years."

"Did you tell him what you knew about him?"

"Yes, but it was too late—the mischief was done."

Aunt Miriam went on skimming out her cruller with a very grave face.

"How came your uncle to do so without learning about him first?"

"O I don't know!—he was in a hurry to do anything

that would take the trouble of the farm off his hands;—he don't like it."

"On what terms has he let him have it?"

"On shares—and I know, I know, under that Didenhover it will bring us in nothing, and it has brought us in nothing all the time we have been here; and I don't know what we are going to live upon."—

"Has your uncle nor your aunt no property at all left?"

"Not a bit—except some waste lands in Michigan I believe, that were left to aunt Lucy a year or two ago; but they are as good as nothing."

"Has he let Didenhover have the saw-mill too?"

"I don't know—he didn't say—if he has there will be nothing at all left for us to live upon. I expect nothing from Didenhover,—his face is enough. I should have thought it might have been for uncle Rolf. O if it wasn't for aunt Lucy and Hugh I shouldn't care!—"

"What has your uncle been doing all this year past?"

"I don't know, aunt Miriam,—he can't bear the business and he has left the most of it to Lucas; and I think Lucas is more of a talker than a doer. Almost nothing has gone right. The crops have been ill managed—I do not know a great deal about it but I know enough for that; and uncle Rolf did not know anything about it but what he got from books. And the sheep are dying off—Barby says it is because they were in such poor condition at the beginning of winter, and I dare say she is right."

"He ought to have had a thorough good man at the beginning, to get along well."

"O yes!—but he hadn't, you see; and so we have just been growing poorer every month. And now, aunt Miriam, I really don't know from day to day what to do to get dinner. You know for a good while after we came we used to have our marketing brought every few days from Albany; but we have run up such a bill there already at the butcher's as I don't know when in the world will get paid; and aunt Lucy and I will do anything before we will send for any more; and if it wasn't for her and Hugh I wouldn't care, but they haven't much appetite, and I know that all this takes what little they have away—this, and seeing the effect it has upon uncle Rolf——"

"Does he think so much more of eating than of anything else?" said aunt Miriam.

"Oh no, it is not that!" said Fleda earnestly,—"it is not that at all—he is not a great eater—but he can't bear to have things different from what they used to be and from what they ought to be—O no, don't think that! I don't know whether I ought to have said what I have said, but I couldn't help it—"

Fleda's voice was lost for a little while.

"He is changed from what he used to be—a little thing vexes him now, and I know it is because he is not happy;—he used to be so kind and pleasant, and he is still, sometimes; but aunt Lucy's face—Oh aunt Miriam!—"

"Why, dear?" said aunt Miriam tenderly.

"It is so changed from what it used to be!"

Poor Fleda covered her own, and aunt Miriam came to her side to give softer and gentler expression to sympathy than words could do; till the bowed face was raised again and hid in her neck.

"I can't see thee do so my child—my dear child!—Hope for brighter days, dear Fleda."

"I could bear it," said Fleda after a little interval, "if it wasn't for aunt Lucy and Hugh—oh that is the worst!—"

"What about Hugh?" said aunt Miriam soothingly.

"Oh he does what he ought not to do, aunt Miriam, and there is no help for it,—and he did last summer—when we wanted men, and in the hot haying-time, he used to work, I know, beyond his strength,—and aunt Lucy and I did not know what to do with ourselves!—"

Fleda's head which had been raised sunk again and more heavily.

"Where was his father?" said Mrs. Plumfield.

"Oh he was in the house—he didn't know it—he didn't think about it."

"Didn't think about it!"

"No—O he didn't think Hugh was hurting himself, but he was—he shewed it for weeks afterward.—I have said what I ought not now," said Fleda looking up and seeming to check her tears and the spring of them at once.

"So much security any woman has in a man without religion!" said aunt Miriam, going back to her work. Fleda would have said something if she could; she was silent; she stood looking into the fire while the tears seemed to come as it were by stealth and ran down her face unregarded.

"Is Hugh not well?"

"I don't know,—" said Fleda faintly,—"he is not ill—but he never was very strong, and he exposes himself now I know in a way he ought not.—I am sorry I have just come and troubled you with all this now, aunt Miriam," she said after a little pause,—"I shall feel better by and by—I don't very often get such a fit."

"My dear little Fleda!"—and there was unspeakable tenderness in the old lady's voice, as she came up and drew Fleda's head again to rest upon her;—"I would not let a rough wind touch thee if I had the holding of it.—But we may be glad the arranging of things is not in my hand—I I should be a poor friend after all, for I do not know what is best. Canst thou trust him who does know, my child?"

"I do, aunt Miriam,—O I do," said Fleda, burying her face in her bosom;—"I don't often feel so as I did to-day."

"There comes not a cloud that its shadow is not wanted," said aunt Miriam. "I cannot see why,—but it is that thou mayest bloom the brighter, my dear one."

"I know it,—" Fleda's words were hardly audible,—"I will try—"

"Remember his own message to every one under a cloud —'cast all thy care upon him, for he careth for thee;'—thou mayest keep none of it;—and then the peace that passeth understanding shall keep thee.—'So he giveth his beloved sleep.'"

Fleda wept for a minute on the old lady's neck, and then she looked up, dried her tears, and sat down with a face greatly quieted and lightened of its burden; while aunt Miriam once more went back to her work. The one wrought and the other looked on in silence.

The cruller were all done at last; the great bread-trough was filled and set away; the remnant of the fat was carefully disposed of, and aunt Miriam's handmaid was called in to "take the watch." She herself and her visiter adjourned to the sitting-room.

"Well," said Fleda, in a tone again steady and clear,—

"I must go home to see about getting up a dinner. I am the greatest hand at making something out of nothing, aunt Miriam, that ever you saw. There is nothing like practice. I only wish the man uncle Orrin talks about would come along once in a while."

"Who was that?" said aunt Miriam.

"A man that used to go about from house to house," said Fleda laughing, "when the cottagers were making soup, with a ham-bone to give it a relish, and he used to charge them so much for a dip, and so much for a wallop."

"Come, come, I can do as much for you as that," said aunt Miriam, proceeding to her store-pantry,—"see here—wouldn't this be as good as a ham-bone?" said she, bringing out of it a fat fowl;—"how would a wallop of this do?"

"Admirably!—only—the ham-bone used to come out again,—and I am confident this never would."

"Well I guess I'll stand that," said aunt Miriam smiling,—"you wouldn't mind carrying this under your cloak, would you?"

"I have no doubt I shall go home lighter with it than without it, ma'am,—thank you dear aunty!—dear aunt Miriam!"

There was a change of tone, and of eye, as Fleda sealed each thank with a kiss.

"But how is it?—does all the charge of the house come upon you, dear?"

"O, this kind of thing, because aunt Lucy doesn't understand it and can't get along with it so well. She likes better to sew, and I had quite as lief do this."

"And don't you sew too?"

"O—a little. She does as much as she can," said Fleda gravely.

"Where is your other cousin?" said Mrs. Plumfield abruptly.

"Marion?—she is in England I believe;—we don't hear from her very often."

"No, no, I mean the one who is in the army?"

"Charlton!—O he is just ordered off to Mexico," said Fleda sadly, "and that is another great trouble to aunt Lucy. This miserable war!—"

"Does he never come home?"

"Only once since we came from Paris—while we were in New York. He has been stationed away off at the West."

"He has a captain's pay now, hasn't he?"

"Yes, but he doesn't know at all how things are at home—he hasn't an idea of it,—and he will not have. Well good-bye, dear aunt Miriam—I must run home to take care of my chicken."

She ran away; and if her eyes many a time on the way down the hill filled and overflowed, they were not bitter nor dark tears; they were the gushings of high and pure and generous affections, weeping for fulness, not for want.

That chicken was not wasted in soup; it was converted into the nicest possible little fricassee, because the toast would make so much more of it; and to Fleda's own dinner little went beside the toast, that a greater portion of the rest might be for her aunt and Hugh.

That same evening Seth Plumfield came into the kitchen while Fleda was there.

"Here is something belongs to you, I believe," said he with a covert smile, bringing out from under his cloak the mate to Fleda's fowl;—"mother said somethin' had run away with t'other one and she didn't know what to do with this one alone. Your uncle at home?"

The next news that Fleda heard was that Seth had taken a lease of the saw-mill for two years.

Mr. Didenhover did not disappoint Fleda's expectations. Very little could be got from him or the farm under him beyond the immediate supply wanted for the use of the family; and that in kind, not in cash. Mrs. Rossitur was comforted by knowing that some portion of rent had also gone to Dr. Gregory—how large or how small a portion she could not find out. But this left the family in increasing straits, which narrowed and narrowed during the whole first summer and winter of Didenhover's administration. Very straitened they would have been but for the means of relief adopted by the two *children*, as they were always called. Hugh, as soon as the spring opened, had a quiet hint, through Fleda, that if he had a mind to take the working of the saw-mill he might, for a consideration merely nominal. This offer was immediately and gratefully closed with; and Hugh's earnings were thenceforward very important at home. Fleda had her own ways and means. Mr. Rossitur, more low-spirited and gloomy than ever, seemed to have no heart to anything. He would have worked perhaps if he could have done it alone; but to join Didenhover and his men, or any other gang of workmen, was too much for his magnanimity. He helped nobody but Fleda. For her he would do anything, at any time; and in the garden and among her flowers in the flowery courtyard he might often be seen at work with her. But nowhere else.

CHAPTER XXII.

Some bring a capon, some a rurall cake,
Some nuts, some apples; some that thinke they make
The better cheeses, bring 'hem; or else send
By their ripe daughters, whom they would commend
This way to husbands; and whose baskets beare
An embleme of themselves, in plum or peare.

BEN JONSON.

SO the time walked away, for this family was not now of those "whom time runneth withal,"—to the second summer of Mr. Didenhover's term.

One morning Mrs. Rossitur was seated in the breakfast-room at her usual employment, mending and patching; no sinecure now. Fleda opened the kitchen door and came in folding up a calico apron she had just taken off.

"You are tired, dear," said Mrs. Rossitur sorrowfully;—"you look pale."

"Do I?"—said Fleda sitting down. "I am a little tired!"

"Why do you do so?"

"O it's nothing" said Fleda cheerfully;—"I haven't hurt myself. I shall be rested again in a few minutes."

"What have you been doing?"

"O I tired myself a little before breakfast in the garden, I suppose. Aunt Lucy, don't you think I had almost a bushel of peas?—and there was a little over a half bushel last time, so I shall call it a bushel. Isn't that fine?"

"You didn't pick them all yourself?"

"Hugh helped me a little while; but he had the horse to get ready, and I was out before him this morning—poor fellow, he was tired from yesterday, I dare say."

Mrs. Rossitur looked at her, a look between remonstrance and reproach, and cast her eyes down without saying a word, swallowing a whole heartful of thoughts and feelings. Fleda stooped forward till her own forehead softly touched Mrs. Rossitur's, as gentle a chiding of despondency as a very sunbeam could have given.

"Now aunt Lucy!—what do you mean? Don't you know it's good for me?—And do you know, Mr. Sweet will give me four shillings a bushel; and aunt Lucy, I sent three dozen heads of lettuce this morning besides. Isn't that doing well? and I sent two dozen day before yesterday. It is time they were gone for they are running up to seed, this set; I have got another fine set almost ready."

Mrs. Rossitur looked at her again, as if she had been a sort of terrestrial angel.

"And how much will you get for them?"

"I don't know exactly—threepence, or sixpence perhaps,—I guess not so much—they are so easily raised; though I don't believe there are so fine as mine to be seen in this region.—If I only had somebody to water the strawberries!—we should have a great many. Aunt Lucy, I am going to send as many as I can without robbing uncle Rolf—he sha'n't miss them; but the rest of us don't mind eating rather fewer than usual? I shall make a good deal by them. And I think these morning rides do Hugh good; don't you think so?"

"And what have you been busy about ever since breakfast, Fleda?"

"O—two or three things," said Fleda lightly.

"What?"

"I had bread to make—and than I thought while my hands were in I would make a custard for uncle Rolf."

"You needn't have done that, dear! it was not necessary."

"Yes it was, because you know we have only fried pork for dinner to-day, and while we have the milk and eggs it doesn't cost much—the sugar is almost nothing. He will like it better, and so will Hugh. As for you," said Fleda, gently touching her forehead again, "you know it is of no consequence!"

"I wish you would think yourself of some consequence," said Mrs. Rossitur.

"Don't I think myself of consequence!" said Fleda affectionately. "I don't know how you'd all get on without me. What do you think I have a mind to do now, by way of resting myself?"

"Well?" said Mrs. Rossitur, thinking of something else.

"It is the day for making presents to the minister you know?"

"The minister?"—

"Yes, the new minister—they expect him to-day;—you have heard of it;—the things are all to be carried to his house to-day. I have a great notion to go and see the fun—if I only had anything in the world I could possibly take with me—"

"Aren't you too tired, dear?"

"No—it would rest me—it is early yet—if I only had something to take!—I couldn't go without taking something——"

"A basket of eggs?" said Mrs. Rossitur.

"Can't, aunt Lucy—I can't spare them; so many of the hens are setting now.—A basket of strawberries!—that's the thing! I've got enough picked for that and to-night too. That will do!"

Fleda's preparations were soon made, and with her basket on her arm she was ready to set forth.

"If pride had not been a little put down in me," she said smiling, "I suppose I should rather stay at home than go with such a petty offering. And no doubt every one that sees it or hears of it will lay it to anything but the right reason. So much the world knows about the people it judges!—It is too bad to leave you all alone, aunt Lucy."

Mrs. Rossitur pulled her down for a kiss, a kiss in which how much was said on both sides!—and Fleda set forth, choosing as she very commonly did the old-time way through the kitchen.

"Off again?" said Barby who was on her knees scrubbing the great flag-stones of the hearth.

"Yes, I am going up to see the donation party."

"Has the minister come?"

"No, but he is coming to day, I understand."

"He ha'n't preached for 'em yet, has he?"

"Not yet; I suppose he will next Sunday."

"They are in a mighty hurry to give him a donation party!" said Barby. "I'd ha' waited till he was here first. I don't believe they'd be quite so spry with their donations if they had paid the last man up as they ought. I'd rather give a man what belongs to him, and make him presents afterwards."

"Why so I hope they will, Barby," said Fleda laughing. But Barby said no more.

The parsonage-house was about a quarter of a mile, a little more, from the saw-mill, in a line at right angles with the main road. Fleda took Hugh from his work to see her safe there. The road ran north, keeping near the level of the mid-hill where it branched off a little below the saw-mill; and as the ground continued rising towards the east and was well clothed with woods, the way at this hour was still pleasantly shady. To the left, the same slope of ground carried down to the foot of the hill gave them an uninterrupted view over a wide plain or bottom, edged in the distance with a circle of gently swelling hills. Close against the hills, in the far corner of the plain, lay the little village of Queechy Run, hid from sight by a slight intervening rise of ground; not a chimney shewed itself in the whole spread of country. A sunny landscape just now; but rich in picturesque associations of hay-cocks and winrows, spotting it near and far; and close by below them was a field of mowers at work; they could distinctly hear the measured rush of the scythes through the grass, and then the soft clink of the rifles would seem to play some old delicious tune of childish days. Fleda made Hugh stand still to listen. It was a warm day, but "the sweet south that breathes upon a bank of violets," could hardly be more sweet than the air which coming to them over the whole breadth of the valley had been charged by the new-made hay.

"How good it is, Hugh," said Fleda, "that one can get out of doors and forget everything that ever happened or ever will happen within four walls!"

"Do you?" said Hugh, rather soberly.

"Yes I do,—even in my flower-patch, right before the house-door; but *here*—" said Fleda, turning away and swinging her basket of strawberries as she went, "I have no idea I ever did such a thing as make bread!—and how clothes get mended I do not comprehend in the least!"

"And have you forgotten the peas and the asparagus too?"

"I am afraid you haven't, dear Hugh," said Fleda, linking her arm within his. "Hugh,—I must find some way to make money."

"More money?" said Hugh smiling.

"Yes—this garden business is all very well, but it doesn't come to any very great things after all, if you are aware of it; and Hugh, I want to get aunt Lucy a new dress. I can't bear to see her in that old merino and it isn't good for her. Why Hugh she couldn't possibly see anybody, if anybody should come to the house."

"Who is there to come?" said Hugh.

"Why nobody; but still, she ought not to be so."

"What more can you do, dear Fleda? You work a great deal too hard already," said Hugh sighing. "You should have seen the way father and mother looked at you last night when you were asleep on the sofa."

Fleda stifled her sigh, and went on.

"I am sure there are things that might be done—things for the booksellers—translating, or copying, or something,—I don't know exactly—I have heard of people's doing such things. I mean to write to uncle Orrin and ask him. I am sure he can manage it for me."

"What were you writing the other night?" said Hugh suddenly.

"When?"

"The other night—when you were writing by the firelight? I saw your pencil scribbling away at a furious rate over the paper, and you kept your hand up carefully between me and your face, but I could see it was something very interesting. Ha?—" said Hugh, laughingly trying to get another view of Fleda's face which was again kept from him. "Send *that* to uncle Orrin, Fleda;—or shew it to me first and then I will tell you."

Fleda made no answer; and at the parsonage door Hugh left her.

Two or three wagons were standing there but nobody to be seen. Fleda went up the steps and crossed the broad piazza, brown and unpainted, but picturesque still, and guided by the sound of tongues turned to the right where she found a large low room, the very centre of the stir. But the stir had not by any means reached the height yet. Not more than a dozen people were gathered. Here were aunt Syra and Mrs. Douglass, appointed a committee to receive and dispose the offerings as they were brought in.

"Why there is not much to be seen yet," said Fleda. "I did not know I was so early."

"Time enough," said Mrs. Douglass. "They'll come the thicker when they do come. Good morning, Dr. Quackenboss!—I hope you're a going to give us something else besides a bow? and I won't take none of your physic neither."

"I humbly submit," said the doctor graciously, "that nothing ought to be expected of gentlemen that—a—are so unhappy as to be alone; for they really—a—have nothing to give,—but themselves."

There was a shout of merriment.

"And suppos'n that's a gift that nobody wants?" said Mrs. Douglass's sharp eye and voice at once.

"In that case," said the doctor, "I really—Miss Ringgan, may I—a—may I relieve your hand of this fair burden?"

"It is not a very fair burden, sir," said Fleda, laughing and relinquishing her strawberries.

"Ah but, fair, you know, I mean,—we speak—in that sense——Mrs. Douglass, here is by far the most elegant offering that your hands will have the honour of receiving this day."

"I hope so," said Mrs. Douglass, "or there won't be much to eat for the minister. Did you never take notice how elegant things somehow made folks grow poor?"

"I guess he'd as leave see something a little substantial," said aunt Syra.

"Well now," said the doctor, "here is Miss Ringgan, who is unquestionably—a—elegant!—and I am sure nobody will say that she—looks poor!"

In one sense, surely not! There could not be two opinions. But with all the fairness of health, and the flush which two or three feelings had brought to her cheeks, there was a look as if the workings of the mind had refined away a little of the strength of the physical frame, and as if growing poor in Mrs. Douglass's sense, that is, thin, might easily be the next step.

"What's your uncle going to give us, Fleda?" said aunt Syra.

But Fleda was saved replying; for Mrs. Douglass, who if she was sharp could be good-natured too, and had watched to see how Fleda took the double fire upon elegance and poverty, could bear no more trial of that sweet gentle face. Without giving her time to answer she carried her off to see the things already stored in the closet, bidding the doctor over her shoulder "be off after his goods, whether he had got 'em or no."

There was certainly a promising beginning made for the future minister's comfort. One shelf was already completely stocked with pies, and another shewed a quantity of cake, and biscuits enough to last a good-sized family for several meals.

"That is always the way," said Mrs. Douglass;—"it's the strangest thing that folks has no sense! Now one half o' them pies 'll be dried up afore they can eat the rest;—'tain't much loss, for Mis' Prin sent 'em down, and if they are worth anything it's the first time anything ever come out of her house that was. Now look at them biscuit!"—

"How many are coming to eat them?" said Fleda.

"How?"

"How large a family has the minister?"

"He ha'n't a bit of a family! He ain't married."

"Not!"

At the grave way in which Mrs. Douglass faced round upon her and answered, and at the idea of a single mouth devoted to all that closetful, Fleda's gravity gave place to most uncontrollable merriment.

"No," said Mrs. Douglass, with a curious twist of her mouth but commanding herself,—"he ain't to be sure—not yet. He ha'n't any family but himself and some sort of a housekeeper, I suppose, they'll divide the house between 'em."

"And the biscuits, I hope," said Fleda. "But what will he do with all the other things, Mrs. Douglass?"

"Sell 'em if he don't want 'em," said Mrs. Douglass quizzically. "Shut up, Fleda, I forget who sent them biscuit—somebody that calculated to make a shew for a little, I reckon.—My sakes! I believe it was Mis' Springer herself!—she didn't hear me though," said Mrs. Douglass peeping out of the half open door. "It's a good thing the world ain't all alike;—there's Mis' Plumfield—stop now, and I'll tell you all she sent;—that big jar of lard, there's as good as eighteen or twenty pound,—and that basket of eggs, I don't know how many there is,—and that cheese, a real fine one I'll be bound, she wouldn't pick out the worst in her dairy,—and Seth fetched down a hundred weight of corn meal and another of rye flour; now that's what I call doing things something like; if everybody else would keep up their end as well as they keep up their'n the world wouldn't be quite so one-sided as it is. I never see the time yet when I couldn't tell where to find Mis' Plumfield."

"No, nor anybody else," said Fleda looking happy.

"There's Mis' Silbert couldn't find nothing better to send than a kag of soap," Mrs. Douglass went on, seeming very much amused;—"I *was* beat when I saw that walk in! I should think she'd feel streaked to come here by and by and see it a standing between Mis' Plumfield's lard and Mis' Clavering's pork—that's a handsome kag of pork, ain't it? What's that man done with your strawberries?—I'll put 'em up here afore somebody takes a notion to 'em.—I'll let the minister know who he's got to thank for 'em," said she, winking at Fleda. "Where's Dr. Quackenboss?"

"Coming, ma'am!" sounded from the hall, and forthwith at the open door entered the doctor's head, simultaneously with a large cheese which he was rolling before him, the rest of the doctor's person being thrown into the background in consequence. A curious natural representation of a wheelbarrow, the wheel being the only artificial part.

"Oh!—that's you, doctor, is it?" said Mrs. Douglass.

"This is me, ma'am," said the doctor, rolling up to the closet door,—"this has the honour to be—a—myself,—bringing my service to the feet of Miss Ringgan."

"'Tain't very elegant," said the sharp lady.

Fleda thought if his service was at her feet, her feet

should be somewhere else, and accordingly stepped quietly out of the way and went to one of the windows, from whence she could have a view both of the comers and the come; and by this time thoroughly in the spirit of the thing she used her eyes upon both with great amusement. People were constantly arriving now, in wagons and on foot; and stores of all kinds were most literally pouring in. Bags and even barrels of meal, flour, pork, and potatoes; strings of dried apples, *salt*, hams and beef; hops, pickles, vinegar, maple sugar and molasses; rolls of fresh butter, cheese, and eggs; cake, bread, and pies, without end. Mr. Penny, the storekeeper, sent a box of tea. Mr. Winegar, the carpenter, a new ox-sled. Earl Douglass brought a handsome axe-helve of his own fashioning; his wife a quantity of rolls of wool. Zan Finn carted a load of wood into the wood-shed, and Squire Thornton another. Home-made candles, custards, preserves, and smoked liver, came in a batch from two or three miles off up on the mountain. Half a dozen chairs from the factory man. Half a dozen brooms from the other store-keeper at the Deepwater settlement. A carpet for the best room from the ladies of the township, who had clubbed forces to furnish it; and a home-made concern it was, from the shears to the loom.

The room was full now, for every one after depositing his gift turned aside to see what others had brought and were bringing; and men and women, the young and old, had their several circles of gossip in various parts of the crowd. Apart from them all Fleda sat in her window, probably voted "elegant" by others than the doctor, for they vouchsafed her no more than a transitory attention and sheered off to find something more congenial. She sat watching the people; smiling very often as some odd figure, or look, or some peculiar turn of expression or tone of voice, caught her ear or her eye.

Both ear and eye were fastened by a young countryman with a particularly fresh face whom she saw approaching the house. He came up on foot, carrying a single fowl slung at his back by a stick thrown across his shoulder; and without stirring hat or stick he came into the room and made his way through the crowd of people, looking to the one hand and the other evidently in a maze of doubt to whom he should deliver himself and his chicken, till brought up by Mrs. Douglass's sharp voice.

"Well Philetus! what are you looking for?"

"Do, Mis' Douglass!"—it is impossible to express the abortive attempt at a bow which accompanied this salutation,—"I want to know if the minister 'll be in town today?"

"What do you want of him?"

"I don't want nothin' of him. I want to know if he'll be in town to-day?"

"Yes—I expect he'll be along directly—why, what then?"

"Cause I've got teu chickens for him here, and mother said they hadn't ought to be kept no longer, and if he wa'n't to hum I were to fetch 'em back, straight."

"Well he'll be here, so let's have 'em," said Mrs. Douglass biting her lips.

"What's become o' t'other one?" said Earl, as the young man's stick was brought round to the table;—"I guess you've lost it, ha'n't you?"

"My gracious!" was all Philetus's powers were equal to. Mrs. Douglass went off into fits which rendered her incapable of speaking and left the unlucky chicken-bearer to tell his story his own way, but all he brought forth was "Du tell!—I *am* beat!—"

"Where's t'other one?" said Mrs. Douglass between paroxysms.

"Why I ha'n't done nothin' to it," said Philetus dismally,—"there was teu on 'em afore I started, and I took and tied 'em together and hitched 'em onto the stick, and that one must ha' loosened itself off some way—I believe the darned thing did it o' purpose."

"I guess your mother knowed that one wouldn't keep till it got here," said Mrs. Douglass.

The room was now all one shout, in the midst of which poor Philetus took himself off as speedily as possible. Before Fleda had dried her eyes her attention was taken by a lady and gentleman who had just got out of a vehicle of more than the ordinary pretension and were coming up to the door. The gentleman was young, the lady was not, both had a particularly amiable and pleasant appearance;

but about the lady there was something that moved Fleda singularly and somehow touched the spring of old memories, which she felt stirring at the sight of her. As they neared the house she lost them—then they entered the room and came through it slowly, looking about them with an air of good-humoured amusement. Fleda's eye was fixed, but her mind puzzled itself in vain to recover what in her experience had been connected with that fair and lady-like physiognomy and the bland smile that was overlooked by those acute eyes. The eyes met hers, and then seemed to reflect her doubt, for they remained as fixed as her own while the lady quickening her steps came up to her.

"I am sure," she said, holding out her hand, and with a gentle graciousness that was very agreeable,—"I am sure you are somebody I know. What is your name?"

"Fleda Ringgan."

"I thought so!" said the lady, now shaking her hand warmly and kissing her,—"I knew nobody could have been your mother but Amy Charlton! How like her you look!—Don't you know me? don't you remember Mrs. Evelyn?"

"Mrs. Evelyn!" said Fleda, the whole coming back to her at once.

"You remember me now?—How well I recollect you! and all that old time at Montepoole. Poor little creature that you were! and dear little creature, as I am sure you have been ever since. And how is your dear aunt Lucy?"

Fleda answered that she was well.

"I used to love her very much—that was before I knew you—before she went abroad. *We* have just got home—this spring; and now we are staying at Montepoole for a few days. I shall come and see her to-morrow—I knew you were somewhere in this region, but I did not know exactly where to find you; that was one reason why I came here to-day—I thought I might hear something of you. And where are your aunt Lucy's children? and how are they?"

"Hugh is at home," said Fleda, "and rather delicate—Charlton is in the army."

"In the army. In Mexico!"—

"In Mexico he has been"—

"Your poor aunt Lucy!"

—"In Mexico he has been, but he is just coming home now—he has been wounded, and he is coming home to spend a long furlough."

"Coming home. That will make you all very happy. And Hugh is delicate—and how are you, love? you hardly look like a country-girl. Mr. Olmney!—" said Mrs. Evelyn looking round for her companion, who was standing quietly a few steps off surveying the scene,—"Mr. Olmney! —I am going to do you a favour, sir, in introducing you to Miss Ringgan—a very old friend of mine. Mr. Olmney, —these are not exactly the apple-cheeks and *robustious* demonstrations we are taught to look for in country-land?"

This was said with a kind of sly funny enjoyment which took away everything disagreeable from the appeal; but Fleda conceived a favourable opinion of the person to whom it was made from the fact that he paid her no compliment and made no answer beyond a very pleasant smile.

"What is Mrs. Evelyn's definition of a *very old* friend?" said he with another smile, as that lady moved off to take a more particular view of what she had come to see. "To judge by the specimen before me I should consider it very equivocal."

"Perhaps Mrs. Evelyn counts friendships by inheritance," said Fleda. "I think they ought to be counted so."

"'Thine own friend and thy father's friend forsake not'?" said the young man.

Fleda looked up and smiled a pleased answer.

"There is something very lovely in the faithfulness of tried friendship—and very uncommon."

"I know that it is uncommon only by hearsay," said Fleda. "I have so many good friends."

He was silent for an instant, possibly thinking there might be a reason for that unknown only to Fleda herself.

"Perhaps one must be in peculiar circumstances to realize it," he said sighing;—"circumstances that leave one of no importance to any one in the world.—But it is a kind lesson!—one learns to depend more on the one friendship that can never disappoint."

Fleda's eyes again gave an answer of sympathy, for she

thought from the shade that had come upon his face that these circumstances had probably been known to himself.

"This is rather an amusing scene," he remarked presently in a low tone.

"Very," said Fleda. "I have never seen such a one before."

"Nor I," said he. "It is a pleasant scene too; it is pleasant to see so many evidences of kindness and good feeling on the part of all these people."

"There is all the more shew of it, I suppose, to-day," said Fleda, "because we have a new minister coming;—they want to make a favourable impression."

"Does the old proverb of the 'new broom' hold good here too?" said he smiling. "What's the name of your new minister?"

"I am not certain," said Fleda,—"there were two talked of—the last I heard was that it was an old Mr. Carey; but from what I hear this morning I suppose it must be the other—a Mr. Ollum, or some such queer name, I believe."

Fleda thought her hearer looked very much amused, and followed his eye into the room, where Mrs. Evelyn was going about in all quarters looking at everything, and finding occasion to enter into conversation with at least a quarter of the people who were present. Whatever she was saying it seemed at that moment to have something to do with them, for sundry eyes turned in their direction; and presently Dr. Quackenboss came up, with even more than common suavity of manner.

"I trust Miss Ringgan will do me the favour of making me acquainted with—a—with our future pastor!" said the doctor, looking however not at all at Miss Ringgan but straight at the pastor in question. "I have great pleasure in giving you the first welcome, sir,—or, I should say, rather the second; since no doubt Miss Ringgan has been in advance of me. It is not un—a—appropriate, sir, for I may say we—a—divide the town between us. You are, I am sure, a worthy representative of Peter and Paul; and I am—a—a pupil of Esculapus, sir! You are the intellectual physician, and I am the external."

"I hope we shall both prove ourselves good workmen,

sir," said the young minister, shaking the doctor's hand heartily.

"This is Dr. Quackenboss, Mr. Olmney," said Fleda, making a tremendous effort. But though she could see corresponding indications about her companion's eyes and mouth, she admired the kindness and self-command with which he listened to the doctor's civilities and answered them; expressing his grateful sense of the favours received not only from him but from others.

"O—a little to begin with," said the doctor, looking round upon the room, which would certainly have furnished *that* for fifty people;—"I hope we ain't done yet by considerable—But here is Miss Ringgan, Mr.—a—Ummin, that has brought you some of the fruits of her own garden, with her own fair hands—a basket of fine strawberries—which I am sure—a—will make you forget everything else!"

Mr. Olmney had the good-breeding not to look at Fleda, as he answered, "I am sure the spirit of kindness was the same in all, Dr. Quackenboss, and I trust not to forget that readily."

Others now came up; and Mr. Olmney was walked off to be "made acquainted" with all or with all the chief of his parishioners then and there assembled. Fleda watched him going about, shaking hands, talking and smiling, in all directions, with about as much freedom of locomotion as a fly in a spider's web; till at Mrs. Evelyn's approach the others fell off a little, and taking him by the arm she rescued him.

"My dear Mr. Olmney!" she whispered, with an intensely amused face,—"I shall have a vision of you every day for a month to come, sitting down to dinner with a rueful face to a whortleberry pie; for there are so many of them your conscience will not let you have anything else cooked—you cannot manage more than one a day."

"Pies!" said the young gentleman, as Mrs. Evelyn left talking to indulge her feelings in ecstatic quiet laughing,—"I have a horror of pies!"

"Yes, yes," said Mrs. Evelyn nodding her head delightedly as she drew him towards the pantry,—"I know!—Come and see what is in store for you. You are to do penance for a month to come with tin pans of blackberry jam fringed with pie-crust—no, they can't be blackberries, they must be raspberries—the blackberries are not ripe yet. And you may sup upon cake and custards—unless you give the custards for the little pig out there—he will want something."

"A pig!—" said Mr. Olmney in a maze; Mrs. Evelyn again giving out in distress. "A pig?" said Mr. Olmney.

"Yes—a pig—a very little one," said Mrs. Evelyn convulsively, "I am sure he is hungry now!—"

They had reached the pantry, and Mr. Olmney's face was all that was wanting to Mrs. Evelyn's delight. How she smothered it, so that it should go no further than to distress his self-command, is a mystery known only to the initiated. Mrs. Douglass was forthwith called into council.

"Mrs. Douglass," said Mr. Olmney, "I feel very much inclined to play the host, and beg my friends to share with me some of these good things they have been so bountifully providing."

"He would enjoy them much more than he would alone, Mrs. Douglass," said Mrs. Evelyn, who still had hold of Mr. Olmney's arm, looking round to the lady with a most benign face.

"I reckon some of 'em would be past enjoying by the time he got to 'em wouldn't they?" said the lady. "Well, they'll have to take 'em in their fingers, for our crockery ha'n't come yet—I shall have to jog Mr. Flatt's elbow—but hungry folks ain't curious."

"In their fingers, or any way, provided you have only a knife to cut them with," said Mr. Olmney, while Mrs. Evelyn squeezed his arm in secret mischief;—"and pray if we can muster two knives let us cut one of these cheeses, Mrs. Douglass."

And presently Fleda saw pieces of pie walking about in all directions supported by pieces of cheese. And then Mrs. Evelyn and Mr. Olmney came out from the pantry and came towards her, the latter bringing her with his own hands a portion in a tin pan. The two ladies sat down in the window together to eat and be amused.

"My dear Fleda, I hope you are hungry!" said Mrs. Evelyn, biting her pie Fleda could not help thinking with an air of good-humoured condescension.

"I am, ma'am," she said laughing.

"You look just as you used to do," Mrs. Evelyn went on earnestly.

"Do I?" said Fleda, privately thinking that the lady must have good eyes for features of resemblance.

"Except that you have more colour in your cheeks and more sparkles in your eyes. Dear little creature that you were! I want to make you know my children. Do you remember that Mr. and Mrs. Carleton that took such care of you at Montepoole?"

"Certainly I do!—very well."

"We saw them last winter—we were down at their country-place in ——shire. They have a magnificent place there—everything you can think of to make life pleasant. We spent a week with them. My dear Fleda!—I wish I could shew you that place! you never saw anything like it."

Fleda eat her pie.

"We have nothing like it in this country—of course—cannot have. One of those superb English country-seats is beyond even the imagination of an American."

"Nature has been as kind to us, hasn't she?" said Fleda.

"O yes, but such fortunes you know. Mr. Olmney, what do you think of those overgrown fortunes? I was speaking to Miss Ringgan just now of a gentleman who has forty thousand pounds a year income—sterling, sir;—forty thousand pounds a year sterling. Somebody says, you know, that 'he who has more than enough is a thief of the rights of his brother,'—what do you think?"

But Mr. Olmney's attention was at the moment forcibly called off by the "income" of a parishioner.

"I suppose," said Fleda, "his thievish character must depend entirely on the use he makes of what he has."

"I don't know," said Mrs. Evelyn shaking her head,—"I think the possession of great wealth is very hardening."

"To a fine nature?" said Fleda.

Mrs. Evelyn shook her head again, but did not seem to think it worth while to reply; and Fleda was trying the question in her own mind whether wealth or poverty might be the most hardening in its effects; when Mr. Olmney having succeeded in getting free again came and took his station beside them; and they had a particularly pleasant talk, which Fleda who had seen nobody in a great while enjoyed very much. They had several such talks in the course of the day; for though the distractions caused by Mr. Olmney's other friends were many and engrossing, he generally contrived in time to find his way back to their window. Meanwhile Mrs. Evelyn had a great deal to say to Fleda and to hear from her; and left her at last under an engagement to spend the next day at the Pool.

Upon Mr. Olmney's departure with Mrs. Evelyn the attraction which had held the company together was broken, and they scattered fast. Fleda presently finding herself in the minority was glad to set out with Miss Anastasia Finn and her sister Lucy, who would leave her but very little way from her own door. But she had more company than she bargained for. Dr. Quackenboss was pleased to attach himself to their party, though his own shortest road certainly lay in another direction; and Fleda wondered what he had done with his wagon, which beyond a question must have brought the cheese in the morning. She edged herself out of the conversation as much as possible, and hoped it would prove so agreeable that he would not think of attending her home. In vain. When they made a stand at the cross roads the doctor stood on her side.

"I hope now you've made a commencement, you will come to see us again, Fleda," said Miss Lucy.

"What's the use of asking?" said her sister abruptly. "If she has a mind to she will, and if she ha'n't I am sure we don't want her."

They turned off.

"Those are excellent people," said the doctor when they were beyond hearing;—"really respectable!"

"Are they?" said Fleda.

"But your goodness does not look, I am sure, to find—a —Parisian graces, in so remote a circle?"

"Certainly not!" said Fleda.

"We have had a genial day!" said the doctor, quitting the Finns.

"I don't know," said Fleda, permitting a little of her inward merriment to work off,—"I think it has been rather too hot."

"Yes," said the doctor, "the sun has been ardent; but I

referred rather to the—a—to the warming of affections, and the pleasant exchange of intercourse on all sides which has taken place. How do you like our—a—the stranger?"

"Who, sir?"

"The new-comer,—this young Mr. Ummin?"

Fleda answered, but she hardly knew what, for she was musing whether the doctor would go away or come in. They reached the door, and Fleda invited him, with terrible effort after her voice; the doctor having just blandly offered an opinion upon the decided polish of Mr. Olmney's manners!

CHAPTER XXIII.

Labour is light, where love (quoth I) doth pay;
(Saith he) light burthens heavy, if far borne.
DRAYTON.

FLEDA pushed open the parlour door and preceded her convoy, in a kind of tip-toe state of spirits. The first thing that met her eyes was her aunt in one of the few handsome silks which were almost her sole relic of past wardrobe prosperity, and with a face uncommonly happy and pretty; and the next instant she saw the explanation of this appearance in her cousin Charlton, a little palish, but looking better than she had ever seen him, and another gentleman of whom her eye took in only the general outlines of fashion and comfortable circumstances; now too strange to it to go unnoted. In Fleda's usual mood her next movement would have been made with a demureness that would have looked like bashfulness. But the amusement and pleasure of the day just passed had for the moment set her spirits free from the burden that generally bound them down; and they were as elastic as her step as she came forward and presented to her aunt "Dr. Quackenboss,"—and then turned to shake her cousin's hand.

"Charlton!—Where did you come from? We didn't expect you so soon."

"You are not sorry to see me, I hope?"

"Not at all—very glad;"—and then as her eye glanced towards the other new-comer Charlton presented to her "Mr. Thorn;" and Fleda's fancy made a sudden quick leap on the instant to the old hall at Montepoole and the shot dog. And then Dr. Quackenboss was presented, an introduction which Capt. Rossitur received coldly, and Mr. Thorn with something more than frigidity.

The doctor's elasticity however defied depression, especially in the presence of a silk dress and a military coat. Fleda presently saw that he was agonizing her uncle. Mrs. Rossitur had drawn close to her son. Fleda was left to take care of the other visiter. The young men had both seemed more struck at the vision presented to them than she had been on her part. She thought neither of them was very ready to speak to her.

"I did not know," said Mr. Thorn softly, "what reason I had to thank Rossitur for bringing me home with him to-night—he promised me a supper and a welcome,—but I find he did not tell me the half of my entertainment."

"That was wise in him," said Fleda;—"the half that is not expected is always worth a great deal more than the other."

"In this case, most assuredly," said Thorn bowing, and Fleda was sure not knowing what to make of her.

"Have you been in Mexico too, Mr. Thorn?"

"Not I!—that's an entertainment I beg to decline. I never felt inclined to barter an arm for a shoulder-knot, or to abridge my usual means of locomotion for the privilege of riding on parade—or selling oneself for a name—Peter Schlemil's selling his shadow I can understand; but this is really lessening oneself that one's shadow may grow the larger."

"But you were in the army?" said Fleda.

"Yes—It wasn't my doing. There is a time, you know, when one must please the old folks—I grew old enough and wise enough to cut loose from the army before I had gained or lost much by it."

He did not understand the displeased gravity of Fleda's face, and went on insinuatingly;—

"Unless I have lost what Charlton has gained—something I did not know hung upon the decision—Perhaps you think a man is taller for having iron heels to his boots?"

"I do not measure a man by his inches," said Fleda.

"Then you have no particular predilection for shooting-men?"

"I have no predilection for shooting anything, sir."

"Then I am safe!" said he, with an arrogant little air of satisfaction. "I was born under an indolent star, but I confess to you, privately, of the two I would rather gather my harvests with the sickle than the sword. How does your uncle find it?"

"Find what, sir?"

"The worship of Ceres?—I remember he used to be devoted to Apollo and the Muses."

"Are they rival deities?"

"Why—I have been rather of the opinion that they were too many for one house to hold," said Thorn glancing at Mr. Rossitur. "But perhaps the Graces manage to reconcile them!"

"Did you ever hear of the Graces getting supper?" said Fleda. "Because Ceres sometimes sets them at that work. Uncle Rolf," she added as she passed him,—"Mr. Thorn is inquiring after Apollo—will you set him right, while I do the same for the table-cloth?"

Her uncle looked from her sparkling eyes to the rather puzzled expression of his guest's face.

"I was only asking your lovely niece," said Mr. Thorn coming down from his stilts,—"how you liked this country life?"

Dr. Quackenboss bowed, probably in approbation of the epithet.

"Well sir—what information did she give you on the subject?"

"Left me in the dark, sir, with a vague hope that you would enlighten me."

"I trust Mr. Rossitur can give a favourable report?" said the doctor benignly.

But Mr. Rossitur's frowning brow looked very little like it.

"What do you say to our country life, sir?"

"It's a confounded life, sir," said Mr. Rossitur, taking a pamphlet from the table to fold and twist as he spoke,—"it is a confounded life; for the head and the hands must either live separate, or the head must do no other work but wait upon the hands. It is an alternative of loss and waste, sir."

"The alternative seems to be of—a—limited application," said the doctor, as Fleda, having found that Hugh and Barby had been beforehand with her, now came back to the company. "I am sure this lady would not give such a testimony."

"About what?" said Fleda, colouring under the fire of so many eyes.

"The blighting influence of Ceres' sceptre," said Mr. Thorn.

"This country life," said her uncle;—"do you like it, Fleda?"

"You know uncle," said she cheerfully, "I was always of the old Douglasses' mind—I like better to hear the lark sing than the mouse squeak."

"Is that one of Earl Douglass's sayings?" said the doctor.

"Yes sir," said Fleda with quivering lips,—"but not the one you know—an older man."

"Ah!" said the doctor intelligently. "Mr. Rossitur,—speaking of hands,—I have employed the Irish very much of late years—they are as good as one can have, if you do not want a head."

"That is to say,—if you have a head," said Thorn.

"Exactly!" said the doctor, all abroad,—"and when there are not too many of them together. I had enough of that, sir, some years ago when a multitude of them were employed on the public works. The Irish were in a state of mutilation sir, all through the country."

"Ah!" said Thorn,—"had the military been at work upon them?"

"No sir, but I wish they had, I am sure; it would have been for the peace of the town. There were hundreds of them. We were in want of an army."

"Of surgeons,—I should think," said Thorn.

Fleda saw the doctor's dubious air and her uncle's compressed lips; and commanding herself, with even a look of something like displeasure she quitted her seat by Mr. Thorn and called the doctor to the window to look at a cluster of rose acacias just then in their glory. He admired, and she expatiated, till she hoped everybody but herself had forgotten what they had been talking about. But they had no sooner returned to their seats than Thorn began again.

"The Irish in your town are not in the same mutilated state now, I suppose, sir?"

"No sir, no," said the doctor;—"there are much fewer of them to break each other's bones. It was all among themselves, sir."

"The country is full of foreigners," said Mr. Rossitur with praiseworthy gravity.

"Yes sir," said Dr. Quackenboss thoughtfully;—"we shall have none of our ancestors left in a short time, if they go on as they are doing."

Fleda was beaten from the field, and rushing into the breakfast-room astonished Hugh by seizing hold of him and indulging in a most prolonged and unbounded laugh. She did not shew herself again till the company came in to supper; but then she was found as grave as Minerva. She devoted herself particularly to the care and entertainment of Dr. Quackenboss till he took leave; nor could Thorn get another chance to talk to her through all the evening.

When he and Rossitur were at last in their rooms Fleda told her story.

"You don't know how pleasant it was, aunt Lucy—how much I enjoyed it—seeing and talking to somebody again. Mrs. Evelyn was so very kind."

"I am very glad, my darling," said Mrs. Rossitur, stroking away the hair from the forehead that was bent down towards her;—"I am glad you had it to-day, and I am glad you will have it again to-morrow."

"You will have it too, aunt Lucy. Mrs. Evelyn will be here in the morning—she said so."

"I shall not see her."

"Why? Now aunt Lucy!—you will."

"I have nothing in the world to see her in—I cannot."

"You have this?"

"For the morning? A rich French silk?—It would be absurd. No, no,—it would be better to wear my old merino than that."

"But you will have to dress in the morning for Mr. Thorn?—he will be here to breakfast."

"I shall not come down to breakfast.—Don't look so, love!—I can't help it."

"Why was that calico got for me and not for you!" said Fleda bitterly.

"A sixpenny calico," said Mrs. Rossitur smiling,—"it would be hard if you could not have so much as that, love."

"And you will not see Mrs. Evelyn and her daughters at all!—and I was thinking that it would do you so much good!—"

Mrs. Rossitur drew her face a little nearer and kissed it, over and over.

"It will do you good, my darling—that is what I care for much more."

"It will not do me half as much," said Fleda sighing.

Her spirits were in their old place again; no more a tip-toe to-night. The short light of pleasure was overcast. She went to bed feeling very quiet indeed; and received Mrs. Evelyn and excused her aunt the next day, almost wishing the lady had not been as good as her word. But though in the same mood she set off with her to drive to Montepoole, it could not stand the bright influences with which she found herself surrounded. She came home again at night with dancing spirits.

It was some days before Capt. Rossitur began at all to comprehend the change which had come upon his family. One morning Fleda and Hugh having finished their morning's work were in the breakfast-room waiting for the rest of the family, when Charlton made his appearance, with the cloud on his brow which had been lately gathering.

"Where is the paper?" said he. "I haven't seen a paper since I have been here."

"You mustn't expect to find Mexican luxuries in Queechy, Capt. Rossitur," said Fleda pleasantly.—"Look at these roses, and don't ask me for papers!"

He did look a minute at the dish of flowers she was arranging for the breakfast table, and at the rival freshness and sweetness of the face that hung over them.

"You don't mean to say you live without a paper?"

"Well it's astonishing how many things people can live without," said Fleda rather dreamily, intent upon settling an uneasy rose that would topple over.

"I wish you'd answer me really," said Charlton. "Don't you take a paper here?"

"We would take one thankfully if it would be so good as to come; but seriously Charlton we haven't any," she said changing her tone.

"And have you done without one all through the war?"

"No—we used to borrow one from a kind neighbour once in a while, to make sure, as Mr. Thorn says, that you had not bartered an arm for a shoulder-knot."

"You never looked to see whether I was killed in the meanwhile, I suppose?"

"No—never," said Fleda gravely, as she took her place on a low seat in the corner,—"I always knew you were safe before I touched the paper."

"What do you mean?"

"I am not an enemy, Charlton," said Fleda laughing. "I mean that I used to make aunt Miriam look over the accounts before I did."

Charlton walked up and down the room for a little while in sullen silence; and then brought up before Fleda.

"What are you doing?"

Fleda looked up,—a glance that as sweetly and brightly as possible half asked half bade him be silent and ask no questions.

"What *are* you doing?" he repeated.

"I am putting a patch on my shoe."

His look expressed more indignation than anything else.

"What do you mean?"

"Just what I say," said Fleda, going on with her work.

"What in the name of all the cobblers in the land do you do it for?"

"Because I prefer it to having a hole in my shoe; which would give me the additional trouble of mending my stockings."

Charlton muttered an impatient sentence, of which Fleda only understood that "the devil" was in it, and then desired to know if whole shoes would not answer the purpose as well as either holes or patches?

"Quite—if I had them," said Fleda, giving him another glance which with all its gravity and sweetness carried also a little gentle reproach.

"But do you know," said he after standing still a minute

looking at her, "that any cobbler in the country would do what you are doing much better for sixpence?"

"I am quite aware of that," said Fleda, stitching away.

"Your hands are not strong enough for that work!"

Fleda again smiled at him, in the very dint of giving a hard push to her needle; a smile that would have witched him into good-humour if he had not been determinately in a cloud and proof against everything. It only admonished him that he could not safely remain in the region of sunbeams; and he walked up and down the room furiously again. The sudden ceasing of his footsteps presently made her look up.

"What have you got there?—Oh Charlton don't!—please put that down!—I didn't know I had left them there—They were a little wet and I laid them on the chair to dry."

"What do you call this?" said he, not minding her request.

"They are only my gardening gloves—I thought I had put them away."

"Gloves!" said he, pulling at them disdainfully,—"why here are two—one within the other—what's that for?"

"It's an old-fashioned way of mending matters,—two friends covering each other's deficiencies. The inner pair are too thin alone, and the outer ones have holes that are past cobbling."

"Are we going to have any breakfast to-day?" said he flinging the gloves down. "You are very late!"

"No," said Fleda quietly,—"it is not time for aunt Lucy to be down yet."

"Don't you have breakfast before nine o'clock?"

"Yes—by half-past eight generally."

"Strange way of getting along on a farm!—Well I can't wait—I promised Thorn I would meet him this morning—Barby!—I wish you would bring me my boots!—"

Fleda made two springs,—one to touch Charlton's mouth, the other to close the door of communication with the kitchen.

"Well!—what is the matter?—can't I have them?"

"Yes, yes, but ask me for what you want. You musn't call upon Barby in that fashion."

"Why not? is she too good to be spoken to? What is she in the kitchen for?"

"She wouldn't be in the kitchen long if we were to speak to her in that way," said Fleda. "I suppose she would as soon put your boots on for you as fetch and carry them. I'll see about it."

"It seems to me Fleda rules the house," remarked Capt. Rossitur when she had left the room.

"Well who should rule it?" said Hugh.

"Not she!"

"I don't think she does," said Hugh; "but if she did, I am sure it could not be in better hands."

"It shouldn't be in her hands at all. But I have noticed since I have been here that she takes the arrangement of almost everything. My mother seems to have nothing to do in her own family."

"I wonder what the family or anybody in it would do without Fleda!" said Hugh, his gentle eyes quite firing with indignation. "You had better know more before you speak, Charlton."

"What is there for me to know?"

"Fleda does everything."

"So I say; and that is what I don't like."

"How little you know what you are talking about!" said Hugh. "I can tell you she is the life of the house, almost literally; we should have had little enough to live upon this summer if it had not been for her."

"What do you mean?"—impatiently enough.

"Fleda—if it had not been for her gardening and management. She has taken care of the garden these two years and sold I can't tell you how much from it. Mr. Sweet, the hotel-man at the Pool, takes all we can give him."

"How much does her 'taking care of the garden' amount to?"

"It amounts to all the planting and nearly all the other work, after the first digging,—by far the greater part of it."

Charlton walked up and down a few turns in most unsatisfied silence.

"How does she get the things to Montepoole?"

"I take them."

"You!—When?"

"I ride with them there before breakfast. Fleda is up very early to gather them."

"You have not been there this morning?"

"Yes."

"With what?"

"Peas and strawberries."

"And Fleda picked them?"

"Yes—with some help from Barby and me."

"That glove of hers was wringing wet."

"Yes, with the pea-vines, and strawberries too; you know they get so loaded with dew. O Fleda gets more than her gloves wet. But she does not mind anything she does for father and mother."

"Humph!—And does she get enough when all is done to pay for the trouble?"

"I don't know," said Hugh rather sadly. "*She* thinks so. It is no trifle."

"Which?—the pay or the trouble?"

"Both. But I meant the pay. Why she made ten dollars last year from the asparagus beds alone, and I don't know how much more this year."

"Ten dollars!—The devil!"

"Why?"

"Have you come to counting your dollars by the tens?"

"We have counted our sixpences so a good while," said Hugh quietly.

Charlton strode about the room again in much perturbation. Then came in Fleda, looking as bright as if dollars had been counted by the thousand, and bearing his boots.

"What on earth did you do that for?" said he angrily. "I could have gone for them myself."

"No harm done," said Fleda lightly,—"only I have got something else instead of the thanks I expected."

"I can't conceive," said he, sitting down and sulkily drawing on his foot-gear, "why this piece of punctiliousness should have made any more difficulty about bringing me my boots than about blacking them."

A sly glance of intelligence, which Charlton was quick enough to detect, passed between Fleda and Hugh. His eye carried its question from one to the other. Fleda's gravity gave way.

"Don't look at me so, Charlton," said she laughing;—"I can't help it, you are so excessively comical!—I recommend that you go out upon the grass-plat before the door and turn round two or three times."

"Will you have the goodness to explain yourself? Who *did* black these boots?"

"Never pry into the secrets of families," said Fleda. "Hugh and I have a couple of convenient little fairies in our service that do things *unknownst*."

"I blacked them, Charlton," said Hugh.

Capt. Rossitur gave his slippers a fling that carried them clean into the corner of the room.

"I will see," he said rising, "whether some other service cannot be had more satisfactory than that of fairies!"

"Now Charlton," said Fleda with a sudden change of manner, coming to him and laying her hand most gently on his arm,—"please don't speak about these things before uncle Rolf or your mother—Please do not!—Charlton?—It would only do a great deal of harm and do no good."

She looked up in his face, but he would not meet her pleading eye, and shook off her hand.

"I don't need to be instructed how to speak to my father and mother; and I am not one of the household that has submitted itself to your direction."

Fleda sat down on her bench and was quiet, but with a lip that trembled a little and eyes that let fall one or two witnesses against him. Charlton did not see them, and he knew better than to meet Hugh's look of reproach. But for all that there was a certain consciousness that hung about the neck of his purpose and kept it down in spite of him; and it was not till breakfast was half over that his ill-humour could make head against this gentle thwarting and cast it off. For so long the meal was excessively dull. Hugh and Fleda had their own thoughts; Charlton was biting his resolution into every slice of bread and butter that occupied him; and Mr. Rossitur's face looked like anything but encouraging an inquiry into his affairs. Since his son's arrival he had been most uncommonly gloomy; and Mrs. Rossitur's face was never in sunshine when his was in shade.

"You'll have a warm day of it at the mill, Hugh," said Fleda, by way of saying something to break the dismal monotony of knives and forks.

"Does that mill make much?" suddenly inquired Charlton.

"It has made a new bridge to the brook, literally," said Fleda gayly; "for it has sawn out the boards; and you know you mustn't speak evil of what carries you over the water."

"Does that mill pay for the working?" said Charlton, turning with the dryest disregard from her interference and addressing himself determinately to his father.

"What do you mean? It does not work gratuitously," answered Mr. Rossitur, with at least equal dryness.

"But, I mean, are the profits of it enough to pay for the loss of Hugh's time?"

"If Hugh judges they are not, he is at liberty to let it alone."

"My time is not lost," said Hugh; "I don't know what I should do with it."

"I don't know what we should do without the mill," said Mrs. Rossitur.

That gave Charlton an unlucky opening.

"Has the prospect of farming disappointed you, father?"

"What is the prospect of your company?" said Mr. Rossitur, swallowing half an egg before he replied.

"A very limited prospect!" said Charlton,—"if you mean the one that went with me. Not a fifth part of them left."

"What have you done with them?"

"Shewed them where the balls were flying, sir, and did my best to shew them the thickest of it."

"Is it necessary to shew it to us too?" said Fleda.

"I believe there are not twenty living that followed me into Mexico," he went on, as if he had not heard her.

"Was all that havoc made in one engagement?" said Mrs. Rossitur, whose cheek had turned pale.

"Yes mother—in the course of a few minutes."

"I wonder what would pay for *that* loss!" said Fleda indignantly.

"Why, the point was gained! and it did not signify what the cost was so we did that. My poor boys were a small part of it."

"What point do you mean?"

"I mean the point we had in view, which was taking the place."

"And what was the advantage of gaining the place."

"Pshaw!—The advantage of doing one's duty."

"But what made it duty?" said Hugh.

"Orders."

"I grant you," said Fleda,—"I understand that—but bear with me, Charlton,—what was the advantage to the army or the country?"

"The advantage of great honour if we succeeded, and avoiding the shame of failure."

"Is that all?" said Hugh.

"All!" said Charlton.

"Glory must be a precious thing when other men's lives are so cheap to buy it," said Fleda.

"We did not risk theirs without our own," said Charlton colouring.

"No,—but still theirs were risked for you."

"Not at all;—why this is absurd! you are saying that the whole war was for nothing."

"What better than nothing was the end of it? We paid Mexico for the territory she yielded to us, didn't we, uncle Rolf?"

"Yes."

"How much?"

"Twenty millions, I believe."

"And what do you suppose the war has cost?"

"Hum—I don't know,—a hundred."

"A hundred million! besides—how much besides!—And don't you suppose, uncle Rolf, that for half of that sum Mexico would have sold us peaceably what she did in the end?"

"It is possible—I think it is very likely."

"What was the fruit of the war, Capt. Rossitur?"

"Why, a great deal of honour to the army and the nation at large."

"Honour again! But granting that the army gained it,

which they certainly did, for one I do not feel very proud of the nation's share."

"Why they are one," said Charlton impatiently.

"In an unjust war?"

"It was *not* an unjust war!"

"That's what you call a knock-downer," said Fleda laughing. "But I confess myself so simple as to have agreed with Seth Plumfield, when I heard him and Lucas disputing about it last winter, that it was a shame to a great and strong nation like ours to display its might in crushing a weak one."

"But they drew it upon themselves. *They* began hostilities."

"There is a diversity of opinion about that."

"Not in heads that have two grains of information."

"I beg your pardon. Mrs. Evelyn and Judge Sensible were talking over that very question the other day at Montepoole; and he made it quite clear to my mind that we were the aggressors."

"Judge Sensible is a fool!" said Mr. Rossitur.

"Very well!" said Fleda laughing;—"but as I do not wish to be comprehended in the same class, will you shew me how he was wrong, uncle?"

This drew on a discussion of some length, to which Fleda listened with profound attention, long after her aunt had ceased to listen at all, and Hugh was thoughtful, and Charlton disgusted. At the end of it Mr. Rossitur left the table and the room, and Fleda subsiding turned to her cold coffee-cup.

"I didn't know you ever cared anything about politics before," said Hugh.

"Didn't you?" said Fleda smiling. "You do me injustice."

Their eyes met for a second, with a most appreciating smile on his part; and then he too went off to his work. There was a few minutes' silent pause after that.

"Mother," said Charlton looking up and bursting forth, "what is all this about the mill and the farm?—Is not the farm doing well?"

"I am afraid not very well," said Mrs. Rossitur gently.

"What is the difficulty?"

"Why, your father has let it to a man by the name of Didenhover, and I am afraid he is not faithful; it does not seem to bring us in what it ought."

"What did he do that for?"

"He was wearied with the annoyances he had to endure before, and thought it would be better and more profitable to have somebody else take the whole charge and management. He did not know Didenhover's character at the time."

"Engaged him without knowing him!"

Fleda was the only third party present, and Charlton unwittingly allowing himself to meet her eye received a look of keen displeasure that he was not prepared for.

"That is not like him," he said in a much moderated tone. "But you must be changed too, mother, or you would not endure such anomalous service in your kitchen."

"There are a great many changes, dear Charlton," said his mother, looking at him with such a face of sorrowful sweetness and patience that his mouth was stopped. Fleda left the room.

"And have you really nothing to depend upon but that child's strawberries and Hugh's wood-saw?" he said in the tone he ought to have used from the beginning.

"Little else."

Charlton stifled two or three sentences that rose to his lips, and began to walk up and down the room again. His mother sat musing by the tea-board still, softly clinking her spoon against the edge of her tea-cup.

"She has grown up very pretty," he remarked after a pause.

"Pretty!" said Mrs. Rossitur.

"Why?"

"No one that has seen much of Fleda would ever describe her by that name."

Charlton had the candour to think he had seen something of her that morning.

"Poor child!" said Mrs. Rossitur sadly,—"I can't bear to think of her spending her life as she is doing—wearing herself out, I know, sometimes—and buried alive."

"Buried!" said Charlton in his turn.

"Yes—without any of the advantages and opportunities

she ought to have. I can't bear to think of it. And yet how should I ever live without her!"—said Mrs. Rossitur, leaning her face upon her hands. "And if she were known she would not be mine long. But it grieves me to have her go without her music, that she is so fond of, and the books she wants—she and Hugh have gone from end to end of every volume there is in the house, I believe, in every language, except Greek."

"Well she looks pretty happy and contented, mother."

"I don't know!" said Mrs. Rossitur shaking her head.

"Isn't she happy?"

"I don't know," said Mrs. Rossitur again;—"she has a spirit that is happy in doing her duty, or anything for those she loves; but I see her sometimes wearing a look that pains me exceedingly. I am afraid the way she lives and the changes in our affairs have worn upon her more than we know of—she feels doubly everything that touches me, or Hugh, or your father. She is a gentle spirit!—"

"She seems to me not to want character," said Charlton.

"Character! I don't know who has so much. She has at least fifty times as much character as I have. And energy. She is admirable at managing people—she knows how to influence them somehow so that everybody does what she wants."

"And who influences her?" said Charlton.

"Who influences her? Everybody that she loves. Who has the most influence over her, do you mean?—I am sure I don't know—Hugh, if anybody,—but *she* is rather the moving spirit of the household."

Capt. Rossitur resolved that he would be an exception to her rule.

He forgot however, for some reason or other, to sound his father any more on the subject of mismanagement. His thoughts indeed were more pleasantly taken up.

CHAPTER XXIV.

My lord Sebastian,
The truth you speak doth lack some gentleness
And time to speak it in: you rub the sore,
When you should bring the plaster.
TEMPEST.

THE Evelyns spent several weeks at the Pool; and both mother and daughters conceiving a great affection for Fleda kept her in their company as much as possible. For those weeks Fleda had enough of gayety. She was constantly spending the day with them at the Pool, or going on some party of pleasure, or taking quiet sensible walks and rides with them alone or with only one or two more of the most rational and agreeable people that the place could command. And even Mrs. Rossitur was persuaded, more times than one, to put herself in her plainest remaining French silk and entertain the whole party, with the addition of one or two of Charlton's friends, at her Queechy farm-house.

Fleda enjoyed it all with the quick spring of a mind habitually bent to the patient fulfilment of duty and habitually under the pressure of rather sobering thoughts. It was a needed and very useful refreshment. Charlton's being at home gave her the full good of the opportunity more than would else have been possible. He was her constant attendant, driving her to and from the Pool, and finding as much to call him there as she had; for besides the Evelyns his friend Thorn abode there all this time. The only drawback to Fleda's pleasure as she drove off from Queechy would be the leaving Hugh plodding away at his saw-mill. She used to nod and wave to him as they went by, and almost feel that she ought not to go on and enjoy herself while he was tending that wearisome machinery all day long. Still she went on and enjoyed herself; but the mere thought of his patient smile as she passed would have kept her from too much elation of spirits, if there had been any danger. There never was any.

"That's a lovely little cousin of yours," said Thorn one evening, when he and Rossitur, on horseback, were leisurely making their way along the up and down road between Montepoole and Queechy.

"She is not particularly little," said Rossitur with a dryness that somehow lacked any savour of gratification.

"She is of a most fair stature," said Thorn ;—"I did not mean anything against that,—but there are characters to which one gives instinctively a softening appellative."

"Are there?" said Charlton.

"Yes. She is a lovely little creature."

"She is not to compare to one of those girls we have left behind us at Montepoole," said Charlton.

"Hum—well perhaps you are right; but which girl do you mean?—for I profess I don't know."

"The second of Mrs. Evelyn's daughters—the auburn-haired one."

"Miss Constance, eh?" said Thorn. "In what isn't the other one to be compared to her?"

"In anything! Nobody would ever think of looking at her in the same room?"

"Why not?" said Thorn coolly.

"I don't know why not," said Charlton, "except that she has not a tithe of her beauty. That's a superb girl!"

For a matter of twenty yards Mr. Thorn went softly humming a tune to himself and leisurely switching the flies off his horse.

"Well"—said he,—"there's no accounting for tastes—

'I ask no red and white
To make up my delight,
No odd becoming graces,
Black eyes, or little know-not-what in faces.'"

"What *do* you want then?" said Charlton, half laughing at him, though his friend was perfectly grave.

"A cool eye, and a mind in it."

"A cool eye!" said Rossitur.

"Yes. Those we have left behind us are arrant will-o'the-wisps—dancing fires—no more."

"I can tell you there is fire sometimes in the other eyes," said Charlton.

"Very likely," said his friend composedly,—"I could have guessed as much; but that is a fire you may warm yourself at; no eternal phosphorescence; it is the leaping up of an internal fire, that only shews itself upon occasion."

"I suppose you know what you are talking about," said Charlton, "but I can't follow you into the region of volcanos. Constance Evelyn has superb eyes. It is uncommon to see a light blue so brilliant."

"I would rather trust a sick head to the handling of the lovely lady than the superb one, at a venture."

"I thought you never had a sick head," said Charlton.

"That is lucky for me, as the hands do not happen to be at my service. But no imagination could put Miss Constance in Desdemona's place, when Othello complained of his headache,—you remember, Charlton,—

> 'Faith, that's with watching—'twill away again—
> Let me but bind this handkerchief about it hard.' "

Thorn gave the intonation truly and admirably.

"Fleda never said anything so soft as that," said Charlton.

"No?"

"No."

"You speak—well, but *soft!*—do you know what you are talking about there?"

"Not very well," said Charlton. "I only remember there was nothing soft about Othello,—what you quoted of his wife just now seemed to me to smack of that quality."

"I forgive your memory," said Thorn, "or else I certainly would not forgive you. If there is a fair creation in all Shakspeare it is Desdemona; and if there is a pretty combination on earth that nearly matches it, I believe it is that one."

"What one?"

"Your pretty cousin."

Charlton was silent.

"It is generous in me to undertake her defence," Thorn went on, "for she bestows as little of her fair countenance upon me as she can well help. But try as she will, she cannot be so repellant as she is attractive."

Charlton pushed his horse into a brisker pace not favourable to conversation; and they rode forward in silence, till in descending the hill below Deepwater they came within view of Hugh's work-place, the saw-mill. Charlton suddenly drew bridle.

"There she is."

"And who is with her?" said Thorn. "As I live!—our friend—what's his name?—who has lost all his ancestors.—And who is the other?"

"My brother," said Charlton.

"I don't mean your brother, Capt. Rossitur," said Thorn throwing himself off his horse.

He joined the party, who were just leaving the mill to go down towards the house. Very much at his leisure Charlton dismounted and came after him.

"I have brought Charlton safe home, Miss Ringgan," said Thorn, who leading his horse had quietly secured a position at her side.

"What's the matter?" said Fleda laughing. "Couldn't he bring himself home?"

"I don't know what's the matter, but he's been uncommonly dumpish—we've been as near as possible to quarrelling for half a dozen miles back."

"We have been—a—more agreeably employed," said Dr. Quackenboss looking round at him with a face that was a concentration of affability.

"I make no doubt of it, sir; I trust we shall bring no unharmonious interruption.—If I may change somebody else's words," he added more low to Fleda,—"disdain itself must convert to courtesy in your presence.'"

"I am sorry disdain should live to pay me a compliment," said Fleda. "Mr. Thorn, may I introduce to you Mr. Olmney."

Mr. Thorn honoured the introduction with perfect civility, but then fell back to his former position and slightly lowered tone.

"Are you then a sworn foe to compliments?"

"I was never so fiercely attacked by them as to give me any occasion."

"I should be very sorry to furnish the occasion,—but what's the harm in them, Miss Ringgan?"

"Chiefly a want of agreeableness."

"Of agreeableness!—Pardon me—I hope you will be so good as to give me the rationale of that?"

"I am of Miss Edgeworth's opinion, sir," said Fleda blushing, "that a lady may always judge of the estimation in which she is held by the conversation which is addressed to her."

"And you judge compliments to be a doubtful indication of esteem?"

"I am sure you do not need information on that point, sir."

"As to your opinion, or the matter of fact?" said he somewhat keenly.

"As to the matter of fact," said Fleda, with a glance both simple and acute in its expression.

"I will not venture to say a word," said Thorn smiling. "Protestations would certainly fall flat at the gates where *les douces paroles* cannot enter. But do you know this is picking a man's pocket of all his silver pennies and obliging him to produce his gold."

"That *would* be a hard measure upon a good many people," said Fleda laughing. "But they're not driven to that. There's plenty of small change left."

"You certainly do not deal in the coin you condemn," said Thorn bowing. "But you will remember that none call for gold but those who can exchange it, and the number of them is few. In a world where cowrie passes current a man may be excused for not throwing about his guineas."

"I wish you'd throw about a few for our entertainment," said Charlton who was close behind. "I haven't seen a yellow-boy in a good while."

"A proof that your eyes are not jaundiced," said his friend without turning his head, "whatever may be the case with you otherwise. Is he out of humour with the country life you like so well, Miss Ringgan, or has he left his domestic tastes in Mexico? How do you think he likes Queechy?"

"You might as well ask myself," said Charlton.

"How do you think he likes Queechy, Miss Ringgan?"

"I am afraid, something after the fashion of Touchstone," said Fleda laughing;—"he thinks that 'in respect of itself it is a good life; but in respect that it is a shepherd's life it is naught. In respect that it is solitary, he likes it very well; but in respect that it is private, it is a very vile life. Now in respect it is in the fields, it pleaseth him well; but in respect it is not in the court, it is tedious.'"

"There's a guinea for you, Capt. Rossitur," said his friend. "Do you know out of what mint?"

"It doesn't bear the head of Socrates," said Charlton.

"'Hast no philosophy in thee,' Charlton?" said Fleda laughing back at him.

"Has not Queechy—a—the honour of your approbation, Capt. Rossitur?" said the doctor.

"Certainly sir—I have no doubt of its being a very fine country."

"Only he has imbibed some doubts whether happiness be an indigenous crop," said Thorn.

"Undoubtedly," said the doctor blandly,—"to one who has roamed over the plains of Mexico, Queechy must seem rather—a—a rather flat place."

"If he could lose sight of the hills," said Thorn.

"Undoubtedly, sir, undoubtedly," said the doctor; "they are a marked feature in the landscape, and do much to relieve—a—the charge of sameness."

"Luckily," said Mr. Olmney smiling, "happiness is not a thing of circumstance; it depends on a man's self."

"I used to think so," said Thorn;—"that is what I have always subscribed to; but I am afraid I could not live in this region and find it so long."

"What an evening!" said Fleda. "Queechy is doing its best to deserve our regards under this light. Mr. Olmney, did you ever notice the beautiful curve of the hills in that hollow where the sun sets?"

"I do notice it now," he said.

"It is exquisite!" said the doctor. "Capt. Rossitur, do you observe, sir?—in that hollow where the sun sets?—"

Capt. Rossitur's eye made a very speedy transition from the hills to Fleda, who had fallen back a little to take

Hugh's arm and placing herself between him and Mr. Olmney was giving her attention undividedly to the latter. And to him she talked perseveringly, of the mountains, the country, and the people, till they reached the courtyard gate. Mr. Olmney then passed on. So did the doctor, though invited to tarry, averring that the sun had gone down behind the firmament and he had something to attend to at home.

"You will come in, Thorn," said Charlton.

"Why—I had intended returning,—but the sun has gone down indeed, and as our friend says there is no chance of our seeing him again I may as well go in and take what comfort is to be had in the circumstances. Gentle Euphrosyne, doth it not become the Graces to laugh?"

"They always ask leave, sir," said Fleda hesitating.

"A most Grace-ful answer, though it does not smile upon me," said Thorn.

"I am sorry, sir," said Fleda, smiling now, "that you have so many silver pennies to dispose of we shall never get at the gold."

"I will do my very best," said he.

So he did, and made himself agreeable that evening to every one of the circle; though Fleda's sole reason for liking to see him come in had been that she was glad of everything that served to keep Charlton's attention from home subjects. She saw sometimes the threatening of a cloud that troubled her.

But the Evelyns and Thorn and everybody else whom they knew left the Pool at last, before Charlton, who was sufficiently well again, had near run out his furlough; and then the cloud which had only shewed itself by turns during all those weeks gathered and settled determinately upon his brow.

He had long ago supplied the want of a newspaper. One evening in September the family were sitting in the room where they had had tea, for the benefit of the fire, when Barby pushed open the kitchen door and came in.

"Fleda will you let me have one of the last papers? I've a notion to look at it."

Fleda rose and went to rummaging in the cupboards.

"You can have it again in a little while," said Barby considerately.

The paper was found and Miss Elster went out with it.

"What an unendurable piece of ill-manners that woman is!" said Charlton.

"She has no idea of being ill-mannered, I assure you," said Fleda.

His voice was like a brewing storm—hers was so clear and soft that it made a lull in spite of him. But he began again.

"There is no necessity for submitting to impertinence. I never would do it."

"I have no doubt you never will," said his father. "Unless you can't help yourself."

"Is there any good reason, sir, why you should not have proper servants in the house?"

"A very good reason," said Mr. Rossitur. "Fleda would be in despair."

"Is there none beside that?" said Charlton dryly.

"None—except a trifling one," Mr. Rossitur answered in the same tone.

"We cannot afford it, dear Charlton," said his mother softly.

There was a silence, during which Fleda moralized on the ways people take to make themselves uncomfortable.

"Does that man—to whom you let the farm—does he do his duty?"

"I am not the keeper of his conscience."

"I am afraid it would be a small charge to any one," said Fleda.

"But are you the keeper of the gains you ought to have from him? does he deal fairly by you?"

"May I ask first what interest it is of yours?"

"It is my interest, sir, because I come home and find the family living upon the exertions of Hugh and Fleda, and find them growing thin and pale under it."

"You, at least, are free from all pains of the kind, Capt. Rossitur."

"Don't listen to him, uncle Rolf!" said Fleda going round to her uncle, and making as she passed a most warning impression upon Charlton's arm,—"don't mind what he says—that young gentleman has been among the Mexican ladies till he has lost an eye for a really proper complexion. Look at me!—do I look pale and thin?—I was paid a most brilliant compliment the other day upon my roses—Uncle, don't listen to him!—he hasn't been in a decent humour since the Evelyns went away."

She knelt down before him and laid her hands upon his and looked up in his face to bring all her plea; the plea of most winning sweetness of entreaty in features yet flushed and trembling. His own did not unbend as he gazed at her, but he gave her a silent answer in a pressure of the hands that went straight from his heart to hers. Fleda's eye turned to Charlton appealingly.

"Is it necessary," he repeated, "that that child and this boy should spend their days in labour to keep the family alive?"

"If it were," replied Mr. Rossitur, "I am very willing that their exertions should cease. For my own part I would quite as lief be out of the world as in it."

"Charlton!—how can you!—" said Fleda, half beside herself,—"you should know of what you speak or be silent!—Uncle don't mind him! he is talking wildly—my work does me good."

"You do not understand yourself," said Charlton obstinately;—"it is more than you ought to do, and I know my mother thinks so too."

"Well!" said Mr. Rossitur,—"it seems there is an agreement in my own family to bring me to the bar—get up Fleda,—let us hear all the charges to be brought against me, at once, and then pass sentence. What have your mother and you agreed upon, Charlton?—go on!"

Mrs. Rossitur, now beyond speech, left the room, weeping even aloud. Hugh followed her. Fleda wrestled with her agitation for a minute or two, and than got up and put both arms round her uncle's neck.

"Don't talk so, dear uncle Rolf!—you make us very unhappy—aunt Lucy did not mean any such thing—it is only Charlton's nonsense. Do go and tell her you don't think so,—you have broken her heart by what you said;—do go, uncle Rolf!—do go and make her happy again! Forget it all!—Charlton did not know what he was saying—won't you go, dear uncle Rolf?—"

The words were spoken between bursts of tears that

utterly overcame her, though they did not hinder the utmost caressingness of manner. It seemed at first spent upon a rock. Mr. Rossitur stood like a man that did not care what happened or what became of him; dumb and unrelenting; suffering her sweet words and imploring tears, with no attempt to answer the one or stay the other. But he could not hold out against her beseeching. He was no match for it. He returned at last heartily the pressure of her arms, and unable to give her any other answer kissed her two or three times, such kisses as are charged with the heart's whole message; and disengaging himself left the room.

For a minute after he was gone Fleda cried excessively; and Charlton, now alone with her, felt as if he had not a particle of self-respect left to stand upon. One such agony would do her more harm than whole weeks of labour and weariness. He was too vexed and ashamed of himself to be able to utter a word, but when she recovered a little and was leaving the room he stood still by the door in an attitude that seemed to ask her to speak a word to him.

"I am sure, Charlton," she said gently, "you will be sorry to-morrow for what you have done."

"I am sorry now," he said. But she passed out without saying anything more.

Capt. Rossitur passed the night in unmitigated vexation with himself. But his repentance could not have been very genuine, since his most painful thought was, what Fleda must think of him!

He was somewhat reassured at breakfast to find no traces of the evening's storm; indeed the moral atmosphere seemed rather clearer and purer than common. His own face was the only one which had an unusual shade upon it. There was no difference in anybody's manner towards himself; and there was even a particularly gentle and kind pleasantness about Fleda, intended, he knew, to sooth and put to rest any movings of self-reproach he might feel. It somehow missed of its aim and made him feel worse; and after on his part a very silent meal he quitted the house and took himself and his discontent to the woods.

Whatever effect they had upon him, it was the middle

of the morning before he came back again. He found Fleda alone in the breakfast-room, sewing; and for the first time noticed the look his mother had spoken of; a look not of sadness, but rather of settled patient gravity; the more painful to see because it could only have been wrought by long-acting causes, and might be as slow to do away as it must have been to bring. Charlton's displeasure with the existing state of things had revived as his remorse died away, and that quiet face did not have a quieting effect upon him.

"What on earth is going on!" he began rather abruptly as soon as he entered the room. "What horrible cookery is on foot?"

"I venture to recommend that you do not inquire," said Fleda. "It was set on foot in the kitchen and it has walked in here. If you open the window it will walk out."

"But you will be cold?"

"Never mind—in that case I will walk out too, into the kitchen."

"Into the thick of it! No—I will try some other way of relief. This is unendurable!"

Fleda looked, but made no other remonstrance, and not heeding the look Mr. Charlton walked out into the kitchen, shutting the door behind him.

"Barby," said he, "you have got something cooking here that is very disagreeable in the other room."

"Is it?" said Barby. "I reckoned it would all fly up chimney. I guess the draught ain't so strong as I thought it was."

"But I tell you it fills the house!"

"Well, it'll have to a spell yet," said Barby, "'cause if it didn't, you see, Capt. Rossitur, there'd be nothing to fill Fleda's chickens with."

"Chickens!—where's all the corn in the land?"

"It's some place besides in our barn," said Barby. "All last year's is out, and Mr. Didenhover ha'n't fetched any of this year's home; so I made a bargain with 'em they shouldn't starve as long as they'd eat boiled pursley."

"What do you give them?"

"'Most everything—they ain't particler now-a-days—

chunks o' cabbage, and scarcity, and pun'kin and that—all the sass that ain't wanted."

"And do they eat that?"

"Eat it!" said Barby. "They don't know how to thank me for't!"

"But it ought to be done out of doors," said Charlton, coming back from a kind of maze in which he had been listening to her. "It is unendurable!"

"Then I guess you'll have to go some place where you won't know it," said Barby;—"that's the most likely plan I can hit upon; for it'll have to stay on till it's ready."

Charlton went back into the other room really downhearted, and stood watching the play of Fleda's fingers.

"Is it come to this!" he said at length. "Is it possible that you are obliged to go without such a trifle as the miserable supply of food your fowls want!"

"That's a small matter!" said Fleda, speaking lightly though she smothered a sigh. "We have been obliged to do without more than that."

"What is the reason?"

"Why this man Didenhover is a rogue I suspect, and he manages to spirit away all the profits that should come to uncle Rolf's hands—I don't know how. We have lived almost entirely upon the mill for some time."

"And has my father been doing nothing all this while?"

"Nothing on the farm."

"And what of anything else?"

"I don't know," said Fleda, speaking with evident unwillingness. "But surely, Charlton, he knows his own business best. It is not our affair."

"He is mad!" said Charlton, violently striding up and down the floor.

"No," said Fleda with equal gentleness and sadness,—"he is only unhappy;—I understand it all—he has had no spirit to take hold of anything ever since we came here."

"Spirit!" said Charlton;—"he ought to have worked off his fingers to their joints before he let you do as you have been doing!"

"Don't say so!" said Fleda, looking even pale in her eagerness—"don't think so Charlton! it isn't right. We cannot tell what he may have had to trouble him—I know he has suffered and does suffer a great deal.—Do not speak again about anything as you did last night!—Oh," said Fleda, now shedding bitter tears,—"this is the worst of growing poor! the difficulty of keeping up the old kindness and sympathy and care for each other!—"

"I am sure it does not work so upon you," said Charlton in an altered voice.

"Promise me, dear Charlton," said Fleda looking up after a moment and drying her eyes again, "promise me you will not say any more about these things! I am sure it pains uncle Rolf more than you think. Say you will not,—for your mother's sake!"

"I will not, Fleda—for your sake. I would not give *you* any more trouble to bear. Promise me; that you will be more careful of yourself in future."

"O there is no danger about me," said Fleda with a faint smile and taking up her work again.

"Who are you making shirts for?" said Charlton after a pause.

"Hugh."

"You do everything for Hugh, don't you?"

"Little enough. Not half so much as he does for me."

"Is he up at the mill to-day?"

"He is always there," said Fleda sighing.

There was another silence.

"Charlton," said Fleda looking up with a face of the loveliest insinuation,—"isn't there something *you* might do to help us a little?"

"I will help you garden, Fleda, with pleasure."

"I would rather you should help somebody else," said she, still looking at him.

"What, Hugh?—You would have me go and work at the mill for him, I suppose!"

"Don't be angry with me, Charlton, for suggesting it," said Fleda looking down again.

"Angry!"—said he. "But is that what you would have me do?"

"Not unless you like,—I didn't know but you might take his place once in a while for a little, to give him a rest,—"

"And suppose some of the people from Montepoole that know me should come by? What are you thinking of?"

said he in a tone that certainly justified Fleda's deprecation.

"Well!"—said Fleda in a kind of choked voice,—"there is a strange rule of honour in vogue in the world!"

"Why should I help Hugh rather than anybody else?"

"He is killing himself!—" said Fleda, letting her work fall and hardly speaking the words through thick tears. Her head was down and they came fast. Charlton stood abashed for a minute.

"You sha'n't do so, Fleda," said he gently, endeavouring to raise her,—"you have tired yourself with this miserable work!—Come to the window—you have got low-spirited, but I am sure without reason about Hugh,—but you shall set me about what you will—You are right, I dare say, and I am wrong; but don't make me think myself a brute, and I will do anything you please."

He had raised her up and made her lean upon him. Fleda wiped her eyes and tried to smile.

"I will do anything that will please you, Fleda."

"It is not to please *me*,—" she answered meekly.

"I would not have spoken a word last night if I had known it would have grieved you so."

"I am sorry you should have none but so poor a reason for doing right," said Fleda gently.

"Upon my word, I think you are about as good reason as anybody need have," said Charlton.

She put her hand upon his arm and looked up,—such a look of pure rebuke as carried to his mind the full force of the words she did not speak,—'Who art thou that carest for a worm which shall die, and forgettest the Lord thy Maker!'—Charlton's eyes fell. Fleda turned gently away and began to mend the fire. He stood watching her for a little.

"What do you think of me, Fleda?" he said at length.

"A little wrong-headed," answered Fleda, giving him a glance and a smile. "I don't think you are very bad."

"If you will go with me, Fleda, you shall make what you please of me!"

He spoke half in jest, half in earnest, and did not himself know at the moment which way he wished Fleda to take it. But she had no notion of any depth in his words.

"A hopeless task!" she answered lightly, shaking her head, as she got down on her knees to blow the fire;—"I am afraid it is too much for me. I have been trying to mend you ever since you came, and I cannot see the slightest change for the better!"

"Where is the bellows?" said Charlton in another tone.

"It has expired—its last breath," said Fleda. "In other words, it has lost its nose."

"Well, look here," said he laughing and pulling her away,—"you will stand a fair chance of losing your face if you put it in the fire. You sha'n't do it. Come and shew me where to find the scattered parts of that old wind instrument and I will see if it cannot be persuaded to play again."

CHAPTER XXV.

I dinna ken what I should want
If I could get but a man.

SCOTCH BALLAD.

CAPT. ROSSITUR did no work at the saw-mill. But Fleda's words had not fallen to the ground. He began to shew care for his fellow-creatures in getting the bellows mended; his next step was to look to his gun; and from that time so long as he staid the table was plentifully supplied with all kinds of game the season and the country could furnish. Wild ducks and partridges banished pork and bacon even from memory; and Fleda joyfully declared she would not see another omelette again till she was in distress.

While Charlton was still at home came a very urgent invitation from Mrs. Evelyn that Fleda should pay them a long visit in New York, bidding her care for no want of preparation but come and make it there. Fleda demurred however on that very score. But before her answer was written, another missive came from Dr. Gregory, not asking so much as demanding her presence, and enclosing a fifty dollar bill, for which he said he would hold her responsible till she had paid him with,—not her own hands,—but her own lips. There was no withstanding the manner of this entreaty. Fleda packed up some of Mrs. Rossitur's laid-by silks, to be refreshed with an air of fashion, and set off with Charlton at the end of his furlough.

To her simple spirit of enjoyment the weeks ran fast; and all manner of novelties and kindnesses helped them on. It was a time of cloudless pleasure. But those she had left thought it long. She wrote them how delightfully she kept house for the old doctor, whose wife had long been dead, and how joyously she and the Evelyns made time fly. And every pleasure she felt awoke almost as strong a throb in the hearts at home. But they missed her, as Barby said, "dreadfully;" and she was most dearly welcomed when she came back. It was just before New Year.

For half an hour there was most gladsome use of eyes and tongues. Fleda had a great deal to tell them.

"How well—how well you are looking, dear Fleda!" said her aunt for the third or fourth time.

"That's more than I can say for you and Hugh, aunt Lucy. What have you been doing to yourselves?"

"Nothing new," they said, as her eye went from one to the other.

"I guess you have wanted me!" said Fleda, shaking her head as she kissed them both again.

"I guess we have," said Hugh, "but don't fancy we have grown thin upon the want."

"But where's uncle Rolf? you didn't tell me."

"He is gone to look after those lands in Michigan."

"In Michigan!—When did he go?"

"Very soon after you."

"And you didn't let me know!—O why didn't you? How lonely you must have been."

"Let you know indeed!" said Mrs. Rossitur, wrapping her in her arms again;—"Hugh and I counted every week that you staid with more and pleasure each one."

"I understand!" said Fleda laughing under her aunt's kisses. "Well I am glad I am at home again to take care of you. I see you can't get along without me!"

"People have been very kind, Fleda," said Hugh.

"Have they?"

"Yes—thinking we were desolate I suppose. There has been no end to aunt Miriam's goodness and pleasantness."

"O aunt Miriam, always!" said Fleda. "And Seth."

"Catherine Douglass has been up twice to ask if her mother could do anything for us; and Mrs. Douglass sent us once a rabbit and once a quantity of wild pigeons that Earl had shot. Mother and I lived upon pigeons for I don't know how long. Barby wouldn't eat 'em—she said she liked pork better; but I believe she did it on purpose."

"Like enough," said Fleda smiling, from her aunt's arms where she still lay.

"And Seth has sent you plenty of your favourite hickory nuts, very fine ones; and I gathered butternuts enough for you near home."

"Everything is for me," said Fleda. "Well, the first thing I do shall be to make some butternut candy for *you*. You won't despise that, Mr. Hugh?"

Hugh smiled at her, and went on.

"And your friend Mr. Olmney has sent us a corn-basket full of the superbest apples you ever saw. He has one tree of the finest in Queechy, he says."

"*My* friend!" said Fleda, colouring a little.

"Well I don't know whose he is if he isn't yours," said Hugh. "And even the Finns sent us some fish that their brother had caught, because, they said, they had more than they wanted. And Dr. Quackenboss sent us a goose and a turkey. We didn't like to keep them, but we were afraid if we sent them back it would not be understood."

"Send them back!" said Fleda. "That would never do! All Queechy would have rung with it."

"Well we didn't," said Hugh. "But so we sent one of them to Barby's old mother for Christmas."

"Poor Dr. Quackenboss!" said Fleda. "That man has as near as possible killed me two or three times. As for the others, they are certainly the oddest of all the finny tribes. I must go out and see Barby for a minute."

It was a good many minutes, however, before she could get free to do any such thing.

"You ha'n't lost no flesh," said Barby shaking hands with her anew. "What did they think of Queechy keep, down in York?"

"I don't know—I didn't ask them," said Fleda. "How goes the world with you, Barby?"

"I'm mighty glad you are come home, Fleda," said Barby lowering her voice.

"Why?" said Fleda in a like tone.

"I guess I ain't all that's glad of it," Miss Elster went on, with a glance of her bright eye.

"I guess not," said Fleda reddening a little;—"but what is the matter?"

"There's two of our friends ha'n't made us but one visit a piece since—oh, ever since some time in October!"

"Well never mind the people," said Fleda. "Tell me what you were going to say."

"And Mr. Olmney," said Barby not minding her, "he's took and sent us a great basket chock full of apples. Now wa'n't that smart of him, when he knowed there wa'n't no one here that cared about 'em?"

"They are a particularly fine kind," said Fleda.

"Did you hear about the goose and turkey?"

"Yes," said Fleda laughing.

"The doctor thinks he has done the thing just about right this time, I s'pect. He had ought to take out a patent right for his invention. He'd feel spry if he knowed who eat one on 'em."

"Never mind the doctor, Barby. Was this what you wanted to see me for?"

"No," said Barby changing her tone. "I'd give something it was. I've been all but at my wit's end; for you know Mis' Rossitur ain't no hand about anything—I couldn't say a word to her—and ever since he went away we have been just winding ourselves up. I thought I should clear out, when Mis' Rossitur said maybe you wa'n't a coming till next week."

"But what is it Barby? what is wrong?"

"There ha'n't been anything right, to my notions, for a long spell," said Barby, wringing out her dishcloth hard and flinging it down to give herself uninterruptedly to talk;—"but now you see, Didenhover nor none of the men never comes near the house to do a chore; and there ain't wood to last three days; and Hugh ain't fit to cut it if it was piled up in the yard; and there ain't the first stick of it out of the woods yet."

Fleda sat down and looked very thoughtfully into the fire.

"He had ought to ha' seen to it afore he went away, but he ha'n't done it, and there it is."

"Why who takes care of the cows?" said Fleda.

"O never mind the cows," said Barby;—"they ain't suffering; I wish we was as well off as they be;—but I guess when he went away he made a hole in our pockets for to mend his'n. I don't say he hadn't ought to ha' done it, but we've been pretty short ever sen, Fleda—we're in the last bushel of flour, and there ain't but a handful of corn meal, and mighty little sugar, white or brown.—I did say something to Mis' Rossitur, but all the good it did was to spile her appetite, I s'pose; and if there's grain in the floor there ain't nobody to carry it to mill,—nor to thresh it,—nor a team to draw it, fur's I know."

"Hugh cannot cut wood!" said Fleda;—"nor drive to mill either, in this weather."

"I could go to mill," said Barby, "now you're to hum, but that's only the beginning; and it's no use to try to do everything—flesh and blood must stop somewhere.—"

"No indeed!" said Fleda. "We must have somebody immediately."

"That's what I had fixed upon," said Barby. "If you could get hold o' some young feller that wa'n't sot up with an idee that he was a grown man and too big to be told, I'd just clap to and fix that little room up stairs for him and give him his victuals here, and we'd have some good of him; instead o' having him streakin' off just at the minute when he'd ought to be along."

"Who is there we could get, Barby?"

"I don't know," said Barby; "but they say there is never a nick that there ain't a jog some place; so I guess it can be made out. I asked Mis' Plumfield, but she didn't know anybody that was out of work; nor Seth Plumfield. I'll tell you who does,—that is, if there *is* anybody,—Mis' Douglass. She keeps hold of one end of 'most everybody's affairs, I tell her. Anyhow she's a good hand to go to."

"I'll go there at once," said Fleda. "Do you know anything about making maple sugar, Barby?"

"That's the very thing!" exclaimed Barby ecstatically. "There's lots o' sugar maples on the farm and it's murder to let them go to loss; and they ha'n't done us a speck o' good ever since I come here. And in your grandfather's time they used to make barrels and barrels. You and me and Hugh, and somebody else we'll have, we could clap to and make as much sugar and molasses in a week as would last us till spring come round again. There's no sense into it! All we'd want would be to borrow a team some place.

I had all that in my head long ago. If we could see the last of that man Didenhover oncet, I'd take hold of the plough myself and see if I couldn't make a living out of it! I don't believe the world would go now, Fleda, if it wa'n't for women. I never see three men yet that didn't try me more than they were worth."

"Patience, Barby!" said Fleda smiling. "Let us take things quietly."

"Well I declare I'm beat, to see how you take 'em," said Barby, looking at her lovingly.

"Don't you know why, Barby?"

"I s'pose I do," said Barby her face softening still more, —"or I can guess."

"Because I know that all these troublesome things will be managed in the best way and by my best friend, and I know that he will let none of them hurt me. I am sure of it—isn't that enough to keep me quiet?"

Fleda's eyes were filling and Barby looked away from them.

"Well it beats me," she said taking up her dishcloth again, "why *you* should have anything to trouble you. I can understand wicked folks being plagued, but I can't see the sense of the good ones."

"Troubles are to make good people better, Barby."

"Well," said Barby with a very odd mixture of real feeling and seeming want of it,—"it's a wonder I never got religion, for I will say that all the decent people I ever see were of that kind!—Mis' Rossitur ain't though, is she?"

"No," said Fleda, a pang crossing her at the thought that all her aunt's loveliness must tell directly and heavily in this case to lighten religion's testimony. It was that thought and no other which saddened her brow as she went back into the other room.

"Troubles already!" said Mrs. Rossitur. "You will be sorry you have come back to them, dear."

"No indeed!" said Fleda brightly; "I am very glad I have come home. We will try and manage the troubles, aunt Lucy."

There was no doing anything that day, but the very next afternoon Fleda and Hugh walked down through the snow to Mrs. Douglass's. It was a long walk and a cold one, and the snow was heavy; but the pleasure of being together made up for it all. It was a bright walk too, in spite of everything.

In a most thrifty-looking well-painted farm-house lived Mrs. Douglass.

"Why 'tain't you, is it?" she said when she opened the door,—"Catharine said it was, and I said I guessed it wa'n't, for I reckoned you had made up your mind not to come and see me at all.—How do you do?"

The last sentence in the tone of hearty and earnest hospitality. Fleda made her excuses.

"Ay, ay,—I can understand all that just as well as if you said it. I know how much it means too. Take off your hat."

Fleda said she could not stay, and explained her business.

"So you ha'n't come to see me after all. Well now take off your hat, 'cause I won't have anything to say to you till you do. I'll give you supper right away."

"But I have left my aunt alone, Mrs. Douglass;—and the afternoons are so short now it would be dark before we could get home."

"Serve her right for not coming along! and you sha'n't walk home in the dark for Earl will harness the team and carry you home like a streak—the horses have nothing to do—Come, you sha'n't go."

And as Mrs. Douglass laid violent hands on her bonnet Fleda thought best to submit. She was presently rewarded with the promise of the very person she wanted—a boy, or young man, then in Earl Douglass's employ; but his wife said "she guessed he'd give him up to her;" and what his wife said, Fleda knew, Earl Douglass was in the habit of making good.

"There ain't enough to do to keep him busy," said Mrs. Douglass. "I told Earl he made me more work than he saved; but he's hung on till now."

"What sort of a boy is he, Mrs. Douglass?"

"He ain't a steel trap, I tell you beforehand," said the lady, with one of her sharp intelligent glances,—"he don't know which way to go till you shew him; but he's a clever enough kind of a chap—he don't mean no harm. I guess he'll do for what you want."

"Is he to be trusted?"

"Trust him with anything but a knife and fork," said she, with another look and shake of the head. "He has no idea but what everything on the supper-table is meant to be eaten straight off. I would keep two such men as my husband as soon as I would Philetus."

"Philetus!" said Fleda,—"the person that brought the chicken and thought he had brought two?"

"You've hit it," said Mrs. Douglass. "Now you know him. How do you like our new minister?"

"We are all very much pleased with him."

"He's very good-looking, don't you think so?"

"A very pleasant face."

"I ha'n't seen him much yet except in church; but those that know say he is very agreeable in the house."

"Truly, I dare say," answered Fleda, for Mrs. Douglass's face looked for her testimony.

"But I think he looks as if he was beating his brains out there among his books—I tell him he is getting the blues, living in that big house by himself."

"Do you manage to do all your work without help, Mrs. Douglass?" said Fleda, knowing that the question was "in order" and that the affirmative answer was not counted a thing to be ashamed of.

"Well I guess I'll know good reason," said Mrs. Douglass complacently, "before I'll have any help to spoil *my* work. Come along, and I'll let you see whether I want one."

Fleda went, very willingly, to be shewn all Mrs. Douglass's household arrangements and clever contrivances, of her own or her husband's devising, for lessening or facilitating labour. The lady was proud and had some reason to be, of the very superb order and neatness of each part and detail. No corner or closet that might not be laid open fearlessly to a visiter's inspection. Miss Catharine was then directed to open her piano and amuse Fleda with it while her mother performed her promise of getting an early supper; a command grateful to one or two of the party, for Catharine had been carrying on all this while a most stately tête-à-tête with Hugh which neither had any wish to prolong. So Fleda filled up the time good-naturedly with thrumming over the two or three bits of her childish music that she could recall, till Mr. Douglass came in and they were summoned to sit down to supper; which Mrs. Douglass introduced by telling her guests "they must take what they could get, for she had made fresh bread and cake and pies for them two or three times, and she wa'n't a going to do it again."

Her table was abundantly spread however, and with most exquisite neatness, and everything was of excellent quality, saving only certain matters which call for a free hand in the use of material. Fleda thought the pumpkin pies must have been made from that vaunted stock which is said to want no eggs nor sugar, and the cakes she told Mrs. Rossitur afterwards would have been good if half the flour had been left out and the other ingredients doubled. The deficiency in one kind however was made up by superabundance in another; the table was stocked with such wealth of crockery that one could not imagine any poverty in what was to go upon it. Fleda hardly knew how to marshal the confusion of plates which grouped themselves around her cup and saucer, and none of them might be dispensed with. There was one set of little glass dishes for one kind of sweetmeat, another set of ditto for another kind; an army of tiny plates to receive and shield the tablecloth from the dislodged cups of tea, saucers being the conventional drinking vessels; and there were the standard bread and butter plates, which be sides their proper charge of bread and butter and beef and cheese, were expected, Fleda knew, to receive a portion of every kind of cake that might happen to be on the table It was a very different thing however from Miss Anastasia's tea-table or that of Miss Flora Quackenboss. Fleda enjoyed the whole time without difficulty.

Mr. Douglass readily agreed to the transfer of Philetus's services.

"He's a good boy!" said Earl,—"he's a good boy; he's as good a kind of a boy as you need to have. He wants tellin'; most boys want tellin'; but he'll do when he *is* told, and he means to do right."

"How long do you expect your uncle will be gone?" said Mrs. Douglass.

"I do not know," said Fleda.

"Have you heard from him since he left?"

"Not since I came home," said Fleda. "Mr. Douglass, what is the first thing to be done about the maple trees in the sugar season?"

"Why, you calculate to try makin' sugar in the spring?"

"Perhaps—at any rate I should like to know about it."

"Well I should think you would," said Earl, "and it's easy done—there ain't nothin' easier, when you know the right way to set to work about it; and there's a fine lot of sugar trees on the old farm—I recollect of them sugar trees as long ago as when I was a boy—I've helped to work them afore now, but there's a good many years since—has made me a leetle older—but the first thing you want is a man and a team, to go about and empty the buckets—the buckets must be emptied every day, and then carry it down to the house."

"Yes, I know," said Fleda, "but what is the first thing to be done to the trees?"

"Why la! 'tain't much to do to the trees—all you've got to do is to take an axe and chip a bit out and stick a chip a leetle way into the cut for to dreen the sap, and set a trough under, and then go on to the next one, and so on;—you may make one or two cuts in the south side of the tree, and one or two cuts in the north side, if the tree's big enough, and if it ain't, only make one or two cuts in the south side of the tree; and for the sap to run good it had ought to be that kind o' weather when it freezes in the day and thaws by night;—I would say!—when it friz in the night and thaws in the day; the sap runs more bountifully in that kind o' weather."

It needed little from Fleda to keep Mr. Douglass at the maple trees till supper was ended; and then as it was already sundown he went to harness the sleigh.

It was a comfortable one, and the horses if not very handsome nor bright-curried were well fed and had good heart to their work. A two-mile drive was before them, and with no troublesome tongues or eyes to claim her attention Fleda enjoyed it fully. In the soft clear winter twilight when heaven and earth mingle so gently, and the stars look forth brighter and cheerfuller than ever at another time, they slid along over the fine roads, too swiftly, towards home; and Fleda's thoughts as easily and swiftly slipped away from Mr. Douglass and maple sugar and Philetus and an unfilled wood-yard and an empty flour-barrel, and revelled in the pure ether. A dark rising ground covered with wood sometimes rose between her and the western horizon; and then a long stretch of snow, only less pure, would leave free view of its unearthly white light, dimmed by no exhalation, a gentle, mute, but not the less eloquent, witness to Earth of what Heaven must be.

But the sleigh stopped at the gate, and Fleda's musings came home.

"Good-night!" said Earl, in reply to their thanks and adieus;—"'tain't anything to thank a body for—let me know when you're a goin' into the sugar making and I'll come and help you."

"How sweet a pleasant méssage may make an unmusical tongue," said Fleda, as she and Hugh made their way up to the house.

"We had a stupid enough afternoon," said Hugh.

"But the ride home was worth it all!"

CHAPTER XXVI.

'Tis merry, 'tis merry, in good green wood,
So blithe Lady Alice is singing;
On the beech's pride, and the oak's brown side,
Lord Richard's axe is ringing.
LADY OF THE LAKE.

PHILETUS came, and was inducted into office and the little room immediately; and Fleda felt herself eased of a burthen. Barby reported him stout and willing, and he proved it by what seemed a perverted inclination for bearing the most enormous logs of wood he could find into the kitchen.

"He will hurt himself!" said Fleda.

"I'll protect him!—against anything but buckwheat batter," said Barby with a grave shake of her head. "Lazy folks takes the most pains, I tell him. But it would be good to have some more ground, Fleda, for Philetus says he don't care for no dinner when he has griddles to breakfast, and there ain't anything much cheaper than that."

"Aunt Lucy, have you any change in the house?" said Fleda that same day.

"There isn't but three and sixpence," said Mrs. Rossitur with a pained conscious look. "What is wanting, dear?"

"Only candles—Barby has suddenly found we are out, and she won't have any more made before to-morrow. Never mind!"

"There is only that," repeated Mrs. Rossitur. "Hugh has a little money due to him from last summer, but he hasn't been able to get it yet. You may take that, dear."

"No," said Fleda,—"we mustn't. We might want it more."

"We can sit in the dark for once," said Hugh, "and try

to make an uncommon display of what Dr. Quackenboss calls 'sociality.'"

"No," said Fleda, who had stood busily thinking,—"I am going to send Philetus down to the post-office for the paper and when it comes I am not to be balked of reading it—I've made up my mind! We'll go right off into the woods and get some pine knots, Hugh—come! They make a lovely light. You get us a couple of baskets and the hatchet—I wish we had two—and I'll be ready in no time. That'll do!"

It is to be noticed that Charlton had provided against any future deficiency of news in his family. Fleda skipped away and in five minutes returned arrayed for the expedition, in her usual out-of-door working trim, namely,—an old dark merino cloak, almost black, the effect of which was continued by the edge of an old dark mousseline below, and rendered decidedly striking by the contrast of a large whitish yarn shawl worn over it; the whole crowned with a little close-fitting hood made of some old silver-grey silk, shaped tight to the head, without any bow or furbelow to break the outline. But such a face within side of it! She came almost dancing into the room.

"This is Miss Ringgan!—as she appeared when she was going to see the pine trees. Hugh, don't you wish you had a picture of me?"

"I have got a tolerable picture of you, somewhere," said Hugh.

"This is somebody very different from the Miss Ringgan that went to see Mrs. Evelyn, I can tell you," Fleda went on gayly. "Do you know, aunt Lucy, I have made up my mind that my visit to New York was a dream, and the dream is nicely folded away with my silk dresses. Now I must go tell that precious Philetus about the post-office—I am *so* comforted, aunt Lucy, whenever I see that fellow staggering into the house under a great log of wood! I have not heard anything in a long time so pleasant as the ringing strokes of his axe in the yard. Isn't life made up of little things!"

"Why don't you put a better pair of shoes on?"

"Can't afford it, Mrs. Rossitur! You are extravagant!"

"Go and put on my India-rubbers."

"No ma'am!—the rocks would cut them to pieces. I have brought my mind down to——my shoes."

"It isn't safe, Fleda; you might see somebody."

"Well ma'am!—But I tell you I am not going to see anybody but the chick-a-dees and the snow-birds, and there is great simplicity of manners prevailing among them."

The shoes were changed, and Hugh and Fleda set forth, lingering awhile however to give a new edge to their hatchet, Fleda turning the grindstone. They mounted then the apple-orchard hill and went a little distance along the edge of the table-land before striking off into the woods. They had stood still a minute to look over the little white valley to the snow-dressed woodland beyond.

"This is better than New York, Hugh," said Fleda.

"I am very glad to hear you say that," said another voice. Fleda turned and started a little to see Mr. Olmney at her side, and congratulated herself instantly on her shoes.

"Mrs. Rossitur told me where you had gone and gave me permission to follow you, but I hardly hoped to overtake you so soon."

"We stopped to sharpen our tools," said Fleda. "We are out on a foraging expedition."

"Will you let me help you?"

"Certainly!—if you understand the business. Do you know a pine knot when you see it?"

He laughed and shook his head, but avowed a wish to learn.

"Well, it would be a charity to teach you anything wholesome," said Fleda, "for I heard one of Mr. Olmney's friends lately saying that he looked like a person who was in danger of committing suicide."

"Suicide!—One of my friends!"—he exclaimed in the utmost astonishment.

"Yes," said Fleda laughing;—"and there is nothing like the open air for clearing away vapours."

"You cannot have known that by experience," said he looking at her.

Fleda shook her head and advising him to take nothing for granted, set off into the woods.

They were in a beautiful state. A light snow but an inch

or two deep had fallen the night before; the air had been perfectly still during the day; and though the sun was out, bright and mild, it had done little but glitter on the earth's white capping. The light dry flakes of snow had not stirred from their first resting-place. The long branches of the large pines were just tipped with snow at the ends; on the smaller evergreens every leaf and tuft had its separate crest. Stones and rocks were smoothly rounded over, little shrubs and sprays that lay along the ground were all doubled in white; and the hemlock branches, bending with their feathery burthen, stooped to the foreheads of the party and gave them the freshest of salutations as they brushed by. The whole wood-scene was particularly fair and graceful. A light veil of purity, no more, thrown over the wilderness of stones and stumps and bare ground,—like the blessing of charity, covering all roughnesses and unsightlinesses—like the innocent unsullied nature that places its light shield between the eye and whatever is unequal, unkindly, and unlovely in the world.

"What do you think of this for a misanthropical man, Mr. Olmney? there's a better tonic to be found in the woods than in any remedies of man's devising."

"Better than books?" said he.

"Certainly!—No comparison."

"I have to learn that yet."

"So I suppose," said Fleda. "The very danger to be apprehended, as I hear sir, is from your running a tilt into some of those thick folios of yours, head foremost.—There's no pitch there, Hugh—you may leave it alone. We must go on—there are more yellow pines higher up."

"But who could give such a strange character of me to you?" said Mr. Olmney.

"I am sure your wisdom would not advise me to tell you that, sir. You will find nothing there, Mr. Olmney."

They went gayly on, careering about in all directions and bearing down upon every promising stump or dead pine tree they saw in the distance. Hugh and Mr. Olmney took turns in the labour of hewing out the fat pine knots and splitting down the old stumps to get at the pitchy heart of the wood; and the baskets began to grow heavy. The whole party were in excellent spirits, and as happy as the birds that filled the woods and whose cheery "chick-a-dee-dee-dee," was heard whenever they paused to rest and let the hatchet be still.

"How one sees everything in the colour of one's own spectacles," said Fleda.

"May I ask what colour yours are to-day?" said Mr. Olmney.

"Rose, I think," said Hugh.

"No," said Fleda, "they are better than that—they are no worse colour than the snow's own—they shew me everything just as it is. It could not be lovelier."

"Then we may conclude, may we not," said Mr. Olmney, "that you are not sorry to find yourself in Queechy again?"

"I am not sorry to find myself in the woods again. That is not pitch, Mr. Olmney."

"It has the same colour,—and weight."

"No, it is only wet—see this and smell of it—do you see the difference? Isn't it pleasant?"

"Everything is pleasant to-day," said he smiling.

"I shall report you a cure. Come, I want to go a little higher and shew you a view. Leave that, Hugh,—we have got enough—"

But Hugh chose to finish an obstinate stump, and his companions went on without him. It was not very far up the mountain and they came to a fine look-out point; the same where Fleda and Mr. Carleton had paused long before on their quest after nuts. The wide spread of country was a white waste now; the delicate beauties of the snow were lost in the far view; and the distant Catskill shewed wintrily against the fair blue sky. The air was gentle enough to invite them to stand still, after the exercise they had taken, and as they both looked in silence Mr. Olmney observed that his companion's face settled into a gravity rather at variance with the expression it had worn.

"I should hardly think," said he softly, "that you were looking through white spectacles, if you had not told us so."

"O—a shade may come over what one is looking at, you know," said Fleda. But seeing that he still watched her inquiringly she added,

"I do not think a very wide landscape is ever gay in its effect upon the mind—do you?"

"Perhaps—I do not know," said he, his eyes turning to it again as if to try what the effect was.

"My thoughts had gone back," said Fleda, "to a time a good while ago, when I was a child and stood here in summer weather—and I was thinking that the change in the landscape is something like that which years make in the mind."

"But you have not, for a long time at least, known any very acute sorrow?"

"No—" said Fleda, "but that is not necessary. There is a gentle kind of discipline which does its work I think more surely."

"Thank God for *gentle* discipline!" said Mr. Olmney; "if you do not know what those griefs are that break down mind and body together."

"I am not unthankful, I hope, for anything," said Fleda gently; "but I have been apt to think that after a crushing sorrow the mind may rise up again, but that a long-continued though much lesser pressure in time breaks the spring."

He looked at her again with a mixture of incredulous and tender interest, but her face did not belie her words, strange as they sounded from so young and in general so bright-seeming a creature.

"'There shall no evil happen to the just,'" he said presently and with great sympathy.

Fleda flashed a look of gratitude at him—it was no more, for she felt her eyes watering and turned them away.

"You have not, I trust, heard any bad news?"

"No sir—not at all!"

"I beg pardon for asking, but Mrs. Rossitur seemed to be in less good spirits than usual."

He had some reason to say so, having found her in a violent fit of weeping.

"You do not need to be told," he went on, "of the need there is that a cloud should now and then come over this lower scene—the danger that if it did not our eyes would look nowhere else?"

There is something very touching in hearing a kind voice say what one has often struggled to say to oneself.

"I know it, sir," said Fleda, her words a little choked,—"and one may not wish the cloud away,—but it does not the less cast a shade upon the face. I guess Hugh has worked his way into the middle of that stump by this time, Mr. Olmney."

They rejoined him; and the baskets being now sufficiently heavy and arms pretty well tired they left the further riches of the pine woods unexplored and walked sagely homewards. At the brow of the table-land Mr. Olmney left them to take a shorter cut to the high-road, having a visit to make which the shortening day warned him not to defer.

"Put down your basket and rest a minute, Hugh," said Fleda. "I had a world of things to talk to you about, and this blessed man has driven them all out of my head."

"But you are not sorry he came along with us?"

"O no. We had a very good time. How lovely it is, Hugh! Look at the snow down there—without a track; and the woods have been dressed by the fairies. O look how the sun is glinting on the west side of that hillock!"

"It is twice as bright since you have come home," said Hugh.

"The snow is too beautiful to-day. O I was right! one may grow morbid over books—but I defy anybody in the company of those chick-a-dees. I should think it would be hard to keep quite sound in the city."

"You are glad to be here again, aren't you?" said Hugh.

"Very! O Hugh!—it is better to be poor and have one's feet on these hills, than to be rich and shut up to brick walls!"

"It is best as it is," said Hugh quietly.

"Once," Fleda went on,—"one fair day when I was out driving in New York, it did come over me with a kind of pang how pleasant it would be to have plenty of money again and be at ease; and then, as I was looking off over that pretty North river to the other shore, I bethought me,

'A little that a righteous man hath is better than the riches of many wicked.'"

Hugh did not answer, for the face she turned to him in its half tearful half bright submission took away his speech.

"Why you cannot have enjoyed yourself as much as we thought, Fleda, if you dislike the city so much?"

"Yes I did. O I enjoyed a great many things. I enjoyed being with the Evelyns. You don't know how much they made of me,—every one of them,—father and mother and all the three daughters—and uncle Orrin. I have been well petted, I can tell you, since I have been gone."

"I am glad they shewed so much discrimination," said Hugh; "they would be puzzled to make too much of you."

"I must have been in a remarkably discriminating society," said Fleda, "for everybody was very kind!"

"How do you like the Evelyns on a nearer view?"

"Very much indeed; and I believe they really love me. Nothing could possibly be kinder, in all ways of shewing kindness. I shall never forget it."

"Who were you driving with that day?" said Hugh.

"Mr. Thorn."

"Did you see much of him?"

"Quite as much as I wished. Hugh——I took your advice."

"About what?" said Hugh.

"I carried down some of my scribblings and sent them to a Magazine."

"Did you!" said Hugh looking delighted. "And will they publish them?"

"I don't know," said Fleda, "that's another matter. I sent them, or uncle Orrin did, when I first went down; and I have heard nothing of them yet."

"You shewed them to uncle Orrin?"

"Couldn't help it, you know. I had to."

"And what did he say to them?"

"Come!—I'm not going to be cross-questioned," said Fleda laughing. "He did not prevent my sending them."

"And if they take them, do you expect they will give anything for them?—the Magazine people?"

"I am sure if they don't they shall have no more—that

is my only possible inducement to let them be printed. For my own pleasure, I would far rather not."

"Did you sign with your own name?"

"My own name!—Yes, and desired it to be printed in large capitals. What are you thinking of? No—I hope you'll forgive me, but I signed myself what our friend the doctor calls 'Yugh.'"

"I'll forgive you if you'll do one thing for me."

"What?"

"Shew me all you have in your portfolio—Do, Fleda—to-night, by the light of the pitch-pine knots. Why shouldn't you give me that pleasure? And besides, you know Molière had an old woman?"

"Well," said Fleda with a face that to Hugh was extremely satisfactory,—"we'll see—I suppose you might as well read my productions in manuscript as in print. But they are in a terribly scratchy condition—they go sometimes for weeks in my head before I find time to put them down—you may guess polishing is pretty well out of the question. Suppose we try to get home with these baskets."

Which they did.

"Has Philetus got home?" was Fleda's first question.

"No," said Mrs. Rossitur, "but Dr. Quackenboss has been here and brought the paper—he was at the post-office this morning, he says. Did you see Mr. Olmney?"

"Yes ma'am, and I feel he has saved me from a lame arm—those pine knots are so heavy."

"He is a lovely young man!" said Mrs. Rossitur with uncommon emphasis.

"I should have been blind to the fact, aunt Lucy, if you had not made me change my shoes. At present, no disparagement to him, I feel as if a cup of tea would be rather more lovely than anything else."

"He sat with me some time," said Mrs. Rossitur; "I was afraid he would not overtake you."

Tea was ready, and only waiting for Mrs. Rossitur to come down stairs, when Fleda, whose eye was carelessly running along the columns of the paper, uttered a sudden shout and covered her face with it. Hugh looked up in astonishment, but Fleda was beyond anything but exclamations, laughing and flushing to the very roots of her hair.

"What *is* the matter, Fleda?"

"Why," said Fleda,—"how comical!—I was just looking over the list of articles in the January number of the 'Excelsior' "—

"The 'Excelsior'?" said Hugh.

"Yes—the Magazine I sent my things to—I was running over their advertisement here, where they give a special puff of the publication in general and of several things in particular, and I saw—here they speak of 'A tale of thrilling interest by Mrs. Eliza Lothbury, unsurpassed,' and so forth and so forth; 'another valuable communication from Mr. Charleston, whose first acute and discriminating paper all our readers will remember; the beginning of a new tale from the infallibly graceful pen of Miss Delia Lawriston; we are sure it will be' so and so; '*"The wind's voices," by our new correspondent "Hugh," has a delicate sweetness that would do no discredit to some of our most honoured names!*' —What do you think of that?"

What Hugh thought he did not say, but he looked delighted, and came to read the grateful words for himself.

"I did not know but they had declined it utterly," said Fleda,—"it was so long since I had sent it and they had taken no notice of it; but it seems they kept it for the beginning of a new volume."

"'Would do no discredit to some of our most honoured names'!" said Hugh. "Dear Fleda, I am very glad! But it is no more than I expected."

"Expected!" said Fleda. "When you had not seen a line! Hush—My dear Hugh, aren't you hungry?"

The tea, with this spice to their appetites, was wonderfully relished; and Hugh and Fleda kept making despatches of secret pleasure and sympathy to each other's eyes; though Fleda's face after the first flush had faded was perhaps rather quieter than usual. Hugh's was illuminated.

"Mr. Skillcorn is a smart man!" said Barby coming in with a package,—"he has made out to go two miles in two hours and get back again safe?"

"More from the post-office!" exclaimed Fleda pouncing

upon it,—" oh yes, there has been another mail. A letter for you, aunt Lucy! from uncle Rolf!—We'll forgive him, Barby—And here's a letter for me, from uncle Orrin, and —yes—the 'Excelsior.' Hugh, uncle Orrin said he would send it. Now for those blessed pine knots! Aunt Lucy, you shall be honoured with the one whole candle the house contains."

The table soon cleared away, the basket of fat fuel was brought in; and one or two splinters being delicately insinuated between the sticks on the fire a very brilliant illumination sprang out. Fleda sent a congratulatory look over to Hugh on the other side of the fireplace as she cosily established herself on her little bench at one corner with her letter; he had the Magazine. Mrs. Rossitur between them at the table with her one candle was already insensible to all outward things.

And soon the other two were as delightfully absorbed. The bright light of the fire shone upon three motionless and rapt figures, and getting no greeting from them went off and danced on the old cupboard doors and paper hangings, in a kindly hearty joviality that would have put any number of stately wax candles out of countenance. There was no poverty in the room that night. But the people were too busy to know how cosy they were; till Fleda was ready to look up from her note and Hugh had gone twice carefully over the new poem,—when there was a sudden giving out of the pine splinters. New ones were supplied in eager haste and silence, and Hugh was beginning "The wind's voices" for the third time when a soft-whispered "Hugh!" across the fire made him look over to Fleda's corner. She was holding up with both hands a five-dollar bank note and just shewing him her eyes over it.

"What's that?" said Hugh in an energetic whisper.

"I don't know!" said Fleda, shaking her head comically;—"I am told 'The wind's voices' have blown it here, but privately I am afraid it is a windfall of another kind."

"What?" said Hugh laughing.

"Uncle Orrin says it is the first fruits of what I sent to the 'Excelsior,' and that more will come; but I do not feel at all sure that it is entirely the growth of that soil."

"I dare say it is," said Hugh; "I am sure it is worth more than that. Dear Fleda, I like it so much!"

Fleda gave him such a smile of grateful affection!—not at all as if she deserved his praise but as if it was very pleasant to have.

"What put it into your head? anything in particular?"

"No—nothing—I was looking out of the window one day and seeing the willow tree blow; and that looked over my shoulder; as you know Hans Andersen says his stories did."

"It is just like you!—exactly as it can be."

"Things put themselves in my head," said Fleda, tucking another splinter into the fire. "Isn't this better than a chandelier?"

"Ten times!"

"And so much pleasanter for having got it ourselves. What a nice time we had, Hugh?"

"Very. Now for the portfolio, Fleda—come!—mother is fast; she won't see or hear anything. What does father say, mother?"

In answer to this they had the letter read, which indeed contained nothing remarkable beyond its strong expressions of affection to each one of the little family; a cordial which Mrs. Rossitur drank and grew strong upon in the very act of reading. It is pity the medicine of kind words is not more used in the world—it has so much power. Then, having folded up her treasure and talked a little while about it, Mrs. Rossitur caught up the Magazine like a person who had been famished in that kind; and soon she and it and her tallow candle formed a trio apart from all the world again. Fleda and Hugh were safe to pass most mysterious-looking little papers from hand to hand right before her, though they had the care to read them behind newspapers, and exchanges of thought and feeling went on more swiftly still, and softly, across the fire. Looks, and smiles, and whispers, and tears too, under cover of a Tribune and an Express. And the blaze would die down just when Hugh had got to the last verse of something, and then while impatiently waiting for the new pine splinters to catch he would tell Fleda how much he liked it, or how beautiful he thought it, and whisper enquiries and critical questions; till the fire reached the fat vein and leaped up in defiant emulation of gas-lights unknown, and then he would fall to again with renewed gusto. And Fleda hunted out in her portfolio what bits to give him first, and bade him as she gave them remember this and understand that, which was necessary to be borne in mind in the reading. And through all the brightening and fading blaze, and all the whispering, congratulating, explaining, and rejoicing going on at her side, Mrs. Rossitur and her tallow candle were devoted to each other, happily and engrossingly. At last however she flung the Magazine from her and turning from the table sat looking into the fire with a rather uncommonly careful and unsatisfied brow.

"What did you think of the second piece of poetry there, mother?" said Hugh;—"that ballad?—'The wind's voices' it is called."

"'The wind's voices'?—I don't know—I didn' tread it, I believe."

"Why mother! I liked it very much. Do read it—read it aloud."

Mrs. Rossitur took up the Magazine again abstractedly, and read—

"'Mamma, what makes your face so sad?
The sound of the wind makes me feel glad;
But whenever it blows, as grave you look,
As if you were reading a sorrowful book.'

"'A sorrowful book I am reading, dear,—
A book of weeping and pain and fear,—
A book deep printed on my heart,
Which I cannot read but the tears will start.

"'That breeze to my ear was soft and mild
Just so, when I was a little child;
But now I hear in its freshening breath
The voices of those that sleep in death.'

"'Mamma,' said the child with shaded brow,
'What is this book you are reading now?
And why do you read what makes you cry?'
'My child, it comes up before my eye.

"''Tis the memory, love, of a far-off day
When my life's best friend was taken away;—
Of the weeks and months that my eyes were dim,
Watching for tidings—watching for him.

"'Many a year has come and past
Since a ship sailed over the ocean fast,
Bound for a port on England's shore,—
She sailed—but was never heard of more.'

"'Mamma'—and she closer pressed her side,—
'Was that the time when my father died?—
Is it his ship you think you see?—
Dearest mamma—won't you speak to me?'

"The lady paused, but then calmly said,
'Yes Lucy—the sea was his dying bed.
And now whenever I hear the blast
I think again of that storm long past.

"'The winds' fierce howlings hurt not me,
But I think how they beat on the pathless sea,—
Of the breaking mast—of the parting rope,—
Of the anxious strife and the failing hope.'

"'Mamma,' said the child with streaming eyes,
'My father has gone above the skies;
And you tell me this world is mean and base
Compared with heaven—that blessed place.'

"'My daughter, I know—I believe it all,—
I would not his spirit to earth recal.
The blest one he—his storm was brief,—
Mine, a long tempest of tears and grief.

"'I have you my darling—I should not sigh.
I have one star more in my cloudy sky,—
The hope that we both shall join him there,
In that perfect rest from weeping and care.'"

"Well mother,—how do you like it?" said Hugh whose eyes gave tender witness to *his* liking for it.

"It is pretty—" said Mrs. Rossitur.

Hugh exclaimed, and Fleda laughing took it out of her hand.

"Why mother!" said Hugh,—"it is Fleda's."

"Fleda's!" exclaimed Mrs. Rossitur, snatching the Magazine again. "My dear child, I was not thinking in the least of what I was reading. Fleda's!—"

She read it over anew, with swimming eyes this time, and then clasped Fleda in her arms and gave her, not words, but the better reward of kisses and tears. They remained so a long time, even till Hugh left them; and then Fleda released from her aunt's embrace still crouched by her side with one arm in her lap.

They both sat thoughtfully looking into the fire till it had burnt itself out and nothing but a glowing bed of coals remained.

"That is an excellent young man!" said Mrs. Rossitur.

"Who?"

"Mr. Olmney. He sat with me some time after you had gone."

"So you said before," said Fleda, wondering at the troubled expression of her aunt's face.

"He made me wish," said Mrs. Rossitur hesitating,—"that I could be something different from what I am—I believe I should be a great deal happier"—

The last word was hardly spoken. Fleda rose to her knees and putting both arms about her aunt pressed face to face, with a clinging sympathy that told how very near her spirit was; while tears from the eyes of both fell without measure.

"Dear aunt Lucy—*dear* aunt Lucy—I wish you would! —I am sure you would be a great deal happier—"

But the mixture of feelings was too much for Fleda; her head sank lower on her aunt's bosom and she wept aloud.

"But I don't know anything about it!" said Mrs. Rossitur, as well as she could speak,—"I am as ignorant as a child!—"

"Dear aunty! that is nothing—God will teach you if you ask him; he has promised. Oh ask him, aunt Lucy! I know you would be happier!—I know it is better—a million times!—to be a child of God than to have everything in the world.—If they only brought us that, I would be very glad of all our troubles!—indeed I would!"

"But I don't think I ever did anything right in my life!" said poor Mrs. Rossitur.

"Dear aunt Lucy!" said Fleda, straining her closer and with her very heart gushing out at these words,—"*dear* aunty—Christ came for just such sinners!—for just such, as you and I."

"*You*,"—said Mrs. Rossitur, but speech failed utterly, and with a muttered prayer that Fleda would help her, she sunk her head upon her shoulder and sobbed herself into quietness, or into exhaustion. The glow of the firelight faded away till only a faint sparkle was left in the chimney.

There was not another word spoken, but when they rose up, with such kisses as gave and took unuttered affection, counsel and sympathy, they bade each other good-night.

Fleda went to her window, for the moon rode high and her childish habit had never been forgotten. But surely the face that looked out that night was as the face of an angel. In all the pouring moonbeams that filled the air, she could see nothing but the flood of God's goodness on a dark world. And her heart that night had nothing but an unbounded and unqualified thanksgiving for all the "gentle discipline" they had felt; for every sorrow and weariness and disappointment;—except besides the prayer, almost too deep to be put into words, that its due and hoped-for fruit might be brought forth unto perfection.

CHAPTER XXVII.

If I become not a cart as well as another man, a plague on my bringing up.
SHAKSPEARE.

EVERY day could not be as bright as the last, even by the help of pitch pine knots. They blazed indeed, many a time, but the blaze shone upon faces that it could not sometimes light up. Matters drew gradually within a smaller and smaller compass. Another five dollars came from uncle Orrin, and the hope of more; but these were carefully laid by to pay Philetus; and for all other wants of the household excepting those the farm supplied the family were dependent on mere driblets of sums. None came from Mr. Rossitur. Hugh managed to collect a very little. That kept them from absolute distress; that, and Fleda's delicate instrumentality. Regular dinners were given up, fresh meat being now unheard-of, unless when a kind neighbour made them a present; and appetite would have lagged sadly but for Fleda's untiring care. She thought no time nor pains ill-bestowed which could prevent her aunt and Hugh from feeling the want of old comforts; and her nicest skill was displayed in varying the combinations of their very few and simple stores. The diversity and deliciousness of her bread-stuffs, Barby said, was "beyond everything!" and a cup of rich coffee was found to cover all deficiencies of removes and entremêts; and this was always served, Barby said further, as if the President of the United States was expected. Fleda never permitted the least slackness in the manner of doing this or anything else that she could control.

Mr. Plumfield had sent down an opportune present of a fine porker. One cold day in the beginning of February Fleda was busy in the kitchen making something for dinner, and Hugh at another table was vigorously chopping sausage-meat.

"I should like to have some cake again," said Fleda.

"Well, why don't you?" said Hugh, chopping away.

"No eggs, Mr. Rossitur,—and can't afford 'em at two shillings a dozen. I believe I am getting discontented—I have a great desire to do something to distinguish myself—I would make a plum pudding if I had raisins, but there is not one in the house."

"You can get 'em up to Mr. Hemps's for sixpence a pound," said Barby.

But Fleda shook her head at the sixpence and went on moulding out her biscuits diligently.

"I wish Philetus would make his appearance with the cows—it is a very odd thing they should be gone since yesterday morning and no news of them."

"I only hope the snow ain't so bright it 'll blind his eyes," said Barby.

"There he is this minute," said Hugh. "It is impossible to tell from his countenance whether successful or not."

"Well where are the cows, Mr. Skillcorn?" said Barby as he came in.

"I have went all over town," said the person addressed, "and they ain't no place."

"Have you asked news of them, Philetus?"

"I have asked the hull town, and I have went all over, 'till I was a'most beat out with the cold,—and I ha'n't seen the first sight of 'em yet!"

Fleda and Hugh exchanged looks, while Barby and Mr. Skillcorn entered into an animated discussion of probabilities and impossibilities.

"If we should be driven from our coffee dinners to tea with no milk in it!"—said Hugh softly in mock dismay.

"Wouldn't!" said Fleda. "We'd beat up an egg and put it in the coffee."

"We couldn't afford it," said Hugh smiling.

"Could!—cheaper than to keep the cows. I'll have some sugar at any rate, I'm determined. Philetus!"

"Marm!"

"I wish, when you have got a good pile of wood chopped, you would make some troughs to put under the maple trees—you know how to make them, don't you?"

"I do!"

"I wish you would make some—you have pine logs out there large enough, haven't you?"

"They hadn't ought to want much of it—there's some 'gregious big ones!"

"I don't know how many we shall want, but a hundred or two at any rate; and the sooner the better. Do you know how much sugar they make from one tree?"

"Wall I don't," said Mr. Skillcorn, with the air of a person who was at fault on no other point;—"the big trees gives more than the little ones—"

Fleda's eyes flashed at Hugh, who took to chopping in sheer desperation; and the muscles of both gave them full occupation for five minutes. Philetus stood comfortably warming himself at the fire, looking first at one and then at the other, as if they were a show and he had paid for it. Barby grew impatient.

"I guess this cold weather makes lazy people of me!" she said bustling about her fire with an amount of energy that was significant. It seemed to signify nothing to Philetus. He only moved a little out of the way.

"Didenhover's cleared out," he burst forth at length abruptly.

"What!" said Fleda and Barby at once, the broom and the biscuits standing still.

"Mr. Didenhover."

"What of him?"

"He has tuk himself off out o' town."

"Where to?"

"I can't tell where teu—he ain't coming back, 'tain't likely."

"How do you know?"

"'Cause he's tuk all his traps and went, and he said farming didn't pay and he wa'n't a going to have nothin' more to deu with it;—he telled Mis' Simpson so—he lived to Mis' Simpson's; and she telled Mr. Ten Eyck."

"Are you sure, Philetus?"

"Sure as 'lection!—he telled Mis' Simpson so, and she telled Mr. Ten Eyck; and he's cleared out."

Fleda and Hugh again looked at each other. Mr. Skillcorn having now delivered himself of his news went out to the woodyard.

"I hope he ha'n't carried off our cows along with him," said Barby, as she too went out to some other part of her premises.

"He was to have made us quite a payment on the first of March," said Fleda.

"Yes, and that was to have gone to uncle Orrin," said Hugh.

"We shall not see a cent of it. And we wanted a little of it for ourselves.—I have that money from the Excelsior, but I can't touch a penny of it for it must go to Philetus's wages. What Barby does without hers I do not know—she has had but one five dollars in six months. Why she stays I cannot imagine; unless it is for pure love."

"As soon as the spring opens I can go to the mill again," said Hugh after a little pause. Fleda looked at him sorrowfully, and shook her head as she withdrew her eyes.

"I wish father would give up the farm," Hugh went on under his breath. "I cannot bear to live upon uncle Orrin so."

Fleda's answer was to clasp her hands. Her only words were, "Don't say anything to aunt Lucy."

"It is of no use to say anything to anybody," said Hugh. "But it weighs me to the ground, Fleda!"

"If uncle Rolf doesn't come home by spring—I hope, I hope he will!—but if he does not, I will take desperate measures. I will try farming myself, Hugh. I have thought of it, and I certainly will. I will get Earl Douglass or somebody else to play second fiddle, but I will have but one head on the farm and I will try what mine is worth."

"You could not do it, Fleda."

"One can do anything!—with a strong enough motive."

"I'm afraid you'd soon be tired, Fleda."

"Not if I succeeded—not so tired as I am now."

"Poor Fleda! I dare say you are tired!"

"It wasn't *that* I meant," said Fleda, slightly drawing her breath;—"I meant this feeling of everything going wrong, and uncle Orrin, and all—"

"But you *are* weary," said Hugh affectionately. "I see it in your face."

"Not so much body as mind, after all. Oh Hugh! this is the worst part of being poor!—the constant occupation of one's mind on a miserable succession of trifles. I am so weary sometimes!—If I only had a nice book to rest myself for a while and forget all these things—I would give so much for it!—"

"Dear Fleda! I wish you had!"

"That was one delight of being in New York—I forgot all about money from one end of it to the other—I put all that away;—and not having to think of meals till I came to eat them. You can't think how tired I get of ringing the changes on pork and flour and Indian meal and eggs and vegetables!—"

Fleda looked tired, and pale; and Hugh looked sadly conscious of it.

"Don't tell aunt Lucy I have said all this!" she exclaimed after a moment rousing herself,—"I don't always feel so—only once in a while I get such a fit—And now I have just troubled you by speaking of it!"

"You don't trouble any one in that way very often, dear Fleda," said Hugh kissing her.

"I ought not at all—you have enough else to think of—but it is a kind of relief sometimes. I like to do these things in general,—only now and then I get tired, as I was just now, I suppose, and then one sees everything through a different medium."

"I am afraid it would tire you more to have the charge of Earl Douglass and the farm upon your mind;—and mother could be no help to you,—nor I, if I am at the mill."

"But there's Seth Plumfield. O I've thought of it all. You don't know what I am up to, Mr. Rossitur. You shall see how I will manage—unless uncle Rolf comes home, in which case I will very gladly forego all my honours and responsibilities together."

"I hope he will come!" said Hugh.

But this hope was to be disappointed. Mr. Rossitur wrote again about the first of March, saying that he hoped to make something of his lands in Michigan, and that he had the prospect of being engaged in some land agencies which would make it worth his while to spend the summer there. He bade his wife let anybody take the farm that could manage it and would pay; and to remit to Dr. Gregory whatever she should receive and could spare. He hoped to do something where he was.

It was just then the beginning of the sugar season; and Mrs. Douglass having renewed and urged Earl's offer of help, Fleda sent Philetus down to ask him to come the next day with his team. Seth Plumfield's, which had drawn the wood in the winter, was now busy in his own sugar business. On Earl Douglass's ground there happened to be no maple trees. His lands were of moderate extent and almost entirely cultivated as a sheep farm; and Mr. Douglass himself though in very comfortable circumstances was in the habit of assisting, on advantageous terms, all the farmers in the neighbourhood.

Philetus came back again in a remarkably short time; and announced that he had met Dr. Quackenboss in the way, who had offered to come with *his* team for the desired service.

"Then you have not been to Mr. Douglass's?"

"I have not," said Philetus;—"I thought likely you wouldn't calculate to want him teu."

"How came the doctor to know what you were going for?"

"I told him."

"But how came you to tell him?"

"Wall I guess he had a mind to know," said Philetus, "so I didn't keep it no closer than I had teu."

"Well," said Fleda biting her lips, "you will have to go down to Mr. Douglass's nevertheless Philetus, and tell him the doctor is coming to-morrow but I should be very much obliged to him if he will be here next day. Will you?"

"Yes marm!"

"Now dear Hugh, will you make me those little spouts for the trees!—of some dry wood—you can get plenty out here. You want to split them up with a hollow chisel, about a quarter of an inch thick, and a little more than half an inch broad. Have you got a hollow chisel?"

"No, but I can get one up the hill. Why must it be hollow?"

"To make little spouts, you know,—for the sap to run in. And then, my dear Hugh! they must be sharpened at one end so as to fit where the chisel goes in—I am afraid I have given you a day's work of it. How sorry I am you must go to-morrow to the mill!—and yet I am glad too."

"Why need you go round yourself with these people?" said Hugh. "I don't see the sense of it."

"They don't know where the trees are," said Fleda.

"I am sure I do not. Do you?"

"Perfectly well. And besides," said Fleda laughing, "I should have great doubts of the discreetness of Philetus's auger if it were left to his simple direction. I have no notion the trees would yield their sap as kindly to him as to me. But I didn't bargain for Dr. Quackenboss."

Dr. Quackenboss arrived punctually the next morning with his oxen and sled; and by the time it was loaded with the sap-troughs, Fleda in her black cloak, yarn shawl, and grey little hood came out of the house to the wood-yard. Earl Douglass was there too, not with his team, but merely to see how matters stood and give advice.

"Good day, Mr. Douglass!" said the doctor. "You see I'm so fortunate as to have got the start of you."

"Very good," said Earl contentedly,—"you may have it;—the start's one thing and the pull's another. I'm willin' anybody should have the start, but it takes a pull to know whether a man's got stuff in him or no."

"What do you mean?" said the doctor.

"I don't mean nothin' at all. You make a start to-day and I'll come ahint and take the pull to-morrow. Ha' you got anythin' to boil down in, Fleda?—there's a potash kittle somewheres, ain't there? I guess there is. There is in most houses."

"There is a large kettle—I suppose large enough," said Fleda.

"That'll do, I guess. Well what do you calculate to put the syrup in?—ha' you got a good big cask, or plenty o' tubs and that? or will you sugar off the hull lot every night and fix it that way? You must do one thing or t'other, and it's good to know what you're a goin' to do afore you come to do it."

"I don't know, Mr. Douglass," said Fleda;—"whichever is the best way—we have no cask large enough, I am afraid."

"Well I tell you what I'll do—I know where there's a tub, and where they ain't usin' it nother, and I reckon I can get 'em to let me have it—I reckon I can—and I'll go round for't and fetch it here to-morrow mornin' when I come with the team. 'Twon't be much out of my way. It's more handier to leave the sugarin' off till the next day; and it had ought to have a settlin' besides. Where'll you have your fire built?—in doors or out?"

"Out—I would rather, if we can. But can we?"

"La, 'tain't nothin' easier—it's as easy out as in—all you've got to do is to take and roll a couple of pretty sized billets for your fireplace, and stick a couple o' crotched sticks for to hang the kittle over—I'd as lieve have it out as in, and if anythin' a leetle liever. If you'll lend me Philetus me and him'll fix it all ready agin you come back—'tain't no trouble at all—and if the sticks ain't here we'll go into the woods after 'em, and have it all sot up."

But Fleda represented that the services of Philetus were just then in requisition, and that there would be no sap brought home till to-morrow.

"Very good!" said Earl amicably,—"*very* good! it's just as easy done one day as another—it don't make no difference to me, and if it makes any difference to you, of course we'll leave it to-day, and there'll be time enough to do it to-morrow; me and him 'll knock it up in a whistle.—What's them little shingles for?"

Fleda explained the use and application of Hugh's mimic spouts. He turned one about, whistling, while he listened to her.

"That's some o' Seth Plumfield's new jigs, ain't it. I wonder if he thinks now the sap's a goin to run any sweeter out o' that 'ere than it would off the end of a chip that wa'n't quite so handsome!"

"No, Mr. Douglass," said Fleda smiling,—"he only thinks that this will catch a little more."

"His sugar won't never tell where it come from," remarked Earl, throwing the spout down. "Well,—you shall see more o' me to-morrow. Good-bye, Dr. Quackenboss!"

"Do you contemplate the refining process?" said the doctor, as they moved off.

"I have often contemplated the want of it," said Fleda; "but it is best not to try to do too much. I should like to make sure of something worth refining in the first place."

"Mr. Douglass and I," said the doctor,—"I hope—a—he's a very good-hearted man, Miss Fleda, but, ha! ha!—he wouldn't suffer loss from a little refining himself.—Haw! you rascal—where are you going! Haw! I tell ye—"

"I am very sorry, Dr. Quackenboss," said Fleda when she had the power and the chance to speak again,—"I am very sorry you should have to take this trouble; but unfortunately the art of driving oxen is not among Mr. Skillcorn's accomplishments."

"My dear Miss Ringgan!" said the doctor, "I—I—nothing I assure you could give me greater pleasure than to drive my oxen to any place where you would like to have them go."

Poor Fleda wished she could have despatched them and him in one direction while she took another; the art of driving oxen *quietly* was certainly not among the doctor's accomplishments. She was almost deafened. She tried to escape from the immediate din by running before to shew Philetus about tapping the trees and fixing the little spouts, but it was a longer operation than she had counted upon, and by the time they were ready to leave the tree the doctor was gee-hawing alongside of it; and then if the next maple was not within sight she could not in decent kindness leave him alone. The oxen went slowly, and though Fleda managed to have no delay longer than to throw down a trough as the sled came up with each tree which she and Philetus had tapped, the business promised to make a long day of it. It might have been a pleasant day in pleasant company; but Fleda's spirits were down to set out with, and Doctor Quackenboss was not the person to give them the needed spring; his long-winded complimentary speeches had not interest enough even to divert her. She felt that she was entering upon an untried and most weighty undertaking; charging her time and thoughts with a burthen they could well spare. Her energies did not flag, but the spirit that should have sustained them was not strong enough for the task.

It was a blustering day of early March; with that uncompromising brightness of sky and land which has no shadow of sympathy with a heart overcast. The snow still lay a foot thick over the ground, thawing a little in sunny spots; the trees quite bare and brown, the buds even of the early maples hardly shewing colour; the blessed evergreens alone doing their utmost to redeem the waste, and speaking of patience and fortitude that can brave the blast and outstand the long waiting and cheerfully bide the time when "the winter shall be over and gone." Poor Fleda thought they were like her in their circumstances, but she feared she was not like them in their strong endurance. She looked at the pines and hemlocks as she passed, as if they were curious preachers to her; and when she had a chance she prayed quietly that she might stand faithfully like them to cheer a desolation far worse and she feared far more abiding than snows could make or melt away. She thought of Hugh, alone in his mill-work that rough chilly day, when the wind stalked through the woods and over the country as if it had been the personification of March just come of age and taking possession of his domains. She thought of her uncle, doing what?—in Michigan,—leaving them to fight with difficulties as they might,—why?—why? and her gentle aunt at home sad and alone, pining for the want of them all, but most of him, and fading with their fortunes. And Fleda's thoughts travelled about from one to the other and dwelt with them all by turns till she was heart-sick; and tears, tears, fell hot on the snow many a time when her eyes had a moment's shield from the doctor and his somewhat more obtuse coadjutor. She felt half superstitiously as if with her taking the farm were beginning the last stage of their falling prospects, which would leave them with none of hope's colouring. Not that in the least she doubted her own ability and success; but her uncle did not deserve to have his affairs prosper under such a system and she had no faith that they would.

"It is most grateful," said the doctor with that sideway

twist of his jaw and his head at once, in harmony,—"it is a most grateful thing to see such a young lady—Haw! there now!—what are you about? haw,—haw then!—It is a most grateful thing to see"—

But Fleda was not at his side; she had bounded away and was standing under a great maple tree a little ahead, making sure that Philetus screwed his auger *up* into the tree instead of *down*, which he had several times shewed an unreasonable desire to do. The doctor had steered his oxen by her little grey hood and black cloak all the day. He made for it now.

"Have we arrived at the termination of our—a—adventure?" said he as he came up and threw down the last trough.

"Why no, sir," said Fleda, "for we have yet to get home again."

"'Tain't so fur going that way as it were this'n," said Philetus. "My! ain't I glad."

"Glad of what?" said the doctor. "Here's Miss Ringgan's walked the whole way, and she a lady—ain't you ashamed to speak of being tired?"

"I ha'n't said the first word o' being tired!" said Philetus in an injured tone of voice,—"but a man ha'n't no right to kill hisself, if he ain't a gal!"

"I'll qualify to your being safe enough," said the doctor. "But Miss Ringgan, my dear, you are—a—you have lost something since you came out—"

"What?" said Fleda laughing. "Not my patience?"

"No," said the doctor, "no,—you're—a—you're an angel! but your cheeks, my dear Miss Ringgan, shew that you have exceeded your—a—"

"Not my intentions, doctor," said Fleda lightly. "I am very well satisfied with our day's work, and with my share of it, and a cup of coffee will make me quite up again. Don't look at my cheeks till then."

"I shall disobey you constantly," said the doctor;—"but, my dear Miss Fleda, we must give you some felicities for reaching home, or Mrs. Rossitur will be—a—distressed when she sees them. Might I propose—that you should just bear your weight on this wood sled and let my oxen and me have the honour—The cup of coffee, I am confident, would be at your lips considerably earlier—"

"The sun won't be a great haighth by the time we get there," said Philetus in a cynical manner; "and I ha'n't took the first thing to-day!"

"Well who has?" said the doctor; "you ain't the only one. Follow your nose down hill, Mr. Skillcorn, and it'll smell supper directly. Now, my dear Miss Ringgan!—will you?"

Fleda hesitated, but her relaxed energies warned her not to despise a homely mode of relief. The wood-sled was pretty clean, and the road decently good over the snow. So Fleda gathered her cloak about her and sat down flat on the bottom of her rustic vehicle; too grateful for the rest to care if there had been a dozen people to laugh at her; but the doctor was only delighted, and Philetus regarded every social phenomenon as coolly and in the same business light as he would the butter to his bread, or any other infallible every-day matter.

Fleda was very glad presently that she had taken this plan, for besides the rest of body she was happily relieved from all necessity of speaking. The doctor though but a few paces off was perfectly given up to the care of his team, in the intense anxiety to shew his skill and gallantry in saving her harmless from every ugly place in the road that threatened a jar or a plunge. Why his oxen didn't go distracted was a question; but the very vehemence and iteration of his cries at last drowned itself in Fleda's ear and she could hear it like the wind's roaring, without thinking of it. She presently subsided to that. With a weary frame, and with that peculiar quietness of spirits that comes upon the ending of a day's work in which mind and body have both been busily engaged, and the sudden ceasing of any call upon either, fancy asked no leave and dreamily roved hither and thither between the material and the spirit world; the will too subdued to stir. Days gone by came marshalling their scenes and their actors before her; again she saw herself a little child under those same trees that stretched their great black arms over her head and swaying their tops in the wind seemed to beckon her back to the past. They talked of their old owner, whose steps had so often passed beneath them with her own light tread,—light now, but how dancing then!—by his side; and of her father, whose hand perhaps had long ago tapped those very trees where she had noticed the old closed-up scars of the axe. At any rate his boyhood had rejoiced there, and she could look back to one time at least in his manhood when she had taken a pleasant walk with him in summer weather among those same woods, in that very ox-track she believed. Gone—two generations that she had known there; hopes and fears and disappointments, akin to her own, at rest,—as hers would be; and how sedately the old trees stood telling her of it, and waving their arms in grave and gentle commenting on the folly of anxieties that came and went with the wind. Fleda agreed to it all; she heard all they said; and her own spirit was as sober and quiet as their quaint moralizing. She felt as if it would never dance again.

The wind had greatly abated of its violence; as if satisfied with the shew of strength it had given in the morning it seemed willing to make no more commotion that day. The sun was far on his way to the horizon, and many a broad hill-side slope was in shadow; the snow had blown or melted from off the stones and rocks leaving all their roughness and bareness unveiled; and the white crust of snow that lay between them looked a cheerless waste in the shade of the wood and the hill. But there were other spots where the sunbeams struck and bright streams of light ran between the trees, smiling and making them smile. And as Fleda's eye rested there another voice seemed to say, "At evening-time it shall be light,"—and "Sorrow may endure for a night, but joy cometh in the morning." She could have cried, but spirits were too absolutely at an ebb. She knew this was partly physical, because she was tired and faint, but it could not the better be overcome. Yet those streaks of sunlight were pleasant company, and Fleda watched them, thinking how bright they used to be once; till the oxen and sled came out from the woods, and she could see the evening colours on the hill-tops beyond the village, lighting up the whole landscape with promise of the morrow. She thought her day had seen its brightest; but she thought too that if she must know sorrows it was a very great blessing to know them at Queechy.

The smoke of the chimney-tops came in sight, and fancy went home,—a few minutes before her.

"I wonder what you'll take and do to yourself next!" said Barby in extreme vexation when she saw her come in. "You're as white as the wall,—and as cold, ain't you? I'd ha' let Philetus cut all the trees and drink all the sap afterwards. I wonder which you think is the worst, the want o' you or the want o' sugar."

A day's headache was pretty sure to visit Fleda after any over-exertion or exhaustion, and the next day justified Barby's fears. She was the quiet prisoner of pain. But Earl Douglass and Mr. Skillcorn could now do without her in the woods; and her own part of the trouble Fleda always took with speechless patience. She had the mixed comfort that love could bestow; Hugh's sorrowful kiss and look before setting off for the mill, Mrs. Rossitur's caress ing care, and Barby's softened voice, and sympathizing hand on her brow, and hearty heart-speaking kiss and poor little King lay all day with his head in her lap, casting grave wistful glances up at his mistress's face and licking her hand with intense affection when even in her distress it stole to his head to reward and comfort him. He never would budge from her side, or her feet, till she could move herself and he knew that she was well. As sure as King came trotting into the kitchen Barby used to look into the other room and say, "So you're better, ain't you, Fleda? I knowed it!"

After hours of suffering the fit was at last over; and in the evening, though looking and feeling racked, Fleda would go out to see the sap-boilers. Earl Douglass and Philetus had had a very good day of it, and now were in full blast with the evening part of the work. The weather was mild, and having the stay of Hugh's arm Fleda grew too amused to leave them.

It was a very pretty scene. The sap-boilers had planted themselves near the cellar door on the other side of the house from the kitchen door and the wood-yard; the casks and tubs for syrup being under cover there; and there they had made a most picturesque work-place. Two strong crotched sticks were stuck in the ground some six or eight feet apart, and a pole laid upon them, to which by the help of some very rustic hooks two enormous iron kettles were slung. Under them a fine fire of smallish split sticks was doing duty, kept in order by a couple of huge logs which walled it in on the one side and on the other. It was a dark night, and the fire painted all this in strong lights and shadows; threw a faint fading Aurora-like light over the snow, beyond the shade of its log barriers; glimmered by turns upon the paling of the garden fence, whenever the dark figures that were passing and repassing between gave it a chance; and invested the cellar-opening and the out-standing corner of the house with striking and unwonted dignity, in a light that revealed nothing except to the imagination. Nothing was more fancifully dignified or more quaintly travestied by that light than the figures around it, busy and flitting about and shewing themselves in every novel variety of grouping and colouring. There was Earl Douglass, not a hair different from what he was every day in reality, but with his dark skin and eyes, and a hat that like its master had concluded to abjure all fashions and perhaps for the same reason, he looked now like any bandit and now in a more pacific view could pass for nothing less than a Spanish shepherd at least, with an iron ladle in lieu of crook. There was Dr. Quackenboss, who had come too, determined as Earl said, "to keep his eend up," excessively bland and busy and important, the fire would throw his one-sidedness of feature into such aspects of gravity or sternness that Fleda could make nothing of him but a poor clergyman or a poor schoolmaster alternately. Philetus, who was kept handing about a bucket of sap or trudging off for wood, defied all comparison; he was Philetus still; but when Barby came once or twice and peered into the kettle her strong features with the handkerchief she always wore about her head were lit up into a very handsome gypsy. Fleda stood some time unseen in the shadow of the house to enjoy the sight, and then went forward on the same principle that a sovereign princess shews herself to her army, to grace and reward the labours of her servants. The doctor was profuse in enquiries after her health and Earl informed her of the success of the day.

"We've had first-rate weather," he said;—"I don't want to see no better weather for sugar-makin'; it's as good kind o' weather as you need to have. It friz everythin' up tight in the night, and it thew in the sun this mornin' as soon as the sun was anywhere; the trees couldn't do no better than they have done. I guess we ha'n't got much this side o' two hundred gallon—I ain't sure about it, but that's what I think; and there's nigh two hundred gallon we've fetched down; I'll qualify to better than a hundred and fifty, or a hundred and sixty either. We should ha' had more yet if Mr. Skillcorn hadn't managed to spill over one cask of it—I reckon he wanted it for sass for his chicken."

"Now, Mr. Douglass!"—said Philetus, in a comical tone of deprecation.

"It is an uncommonly fine lot of sugar trees," said the doctor, "and they stand so on the ground as to give great felicities to the oxen."

"Now Fleda," Earl went on, busy all the while with his iron ladle in dipping the boiling sap from one kettle into the other,—"you know how this is fixed when we've done all we've got to do with it?—it must be strained out o' this biler into a cask or a tub or somethin' 'nother,—anythin' that'll hold it,—and stand a day or so;—you may strain it through a cotton cloth, or through a woollen cloth, or through any kind of a cloth!—and let it stand to settle; and then when it's biled down—Barby knows about bilin' down—you can tell when it's comin' to the sugar when the yellow blobbers rises thick to the top and puffs off, and then it's time to try it in cold water,—it's best to be a leetle the right side o' the sugar and stop afore it's done too much, for the molasses will dreen off afterwards—"

"It must be clarified in the commencement," put in the doctor.

"O' course it must be clarified," said Earl,—"Barby knows about clarifyin'—that's when you first put it on—you had ought to throw in a teeny drop o' milk fur to clear it,—milk's as good as a'most anything,—or if you can get it calf's blood 's better"—

"Eggs would be a more preferable ingredient on the present occasion, I presume," said the doctor. "Miss Ringgan's delicacy would be—a—would shrink from—a—and the albumen of eggs will answer all the same purpose."

"Well anyhow you like to fix it," said Earl,—"eggs or calf's blood—I won't quarrel with you about the eggs, though I never heerd o' blue ones afore, 'cept the robin's and bluebird's—and I've heerd say the swamp black bird lays a handsome blue egg, but I never happened to see the nest myself;—and there 's the chippin' sparrow,—but you'd want to rob all the bird's nests in creation to get enough of 'em, and they ain't here in sugar time nother; but anyhow any eggs 'll do I s'pose if you can get 'em—or milk 'll do if you ha'n't nothin' else—and after it is turned out into the barrel you just let it stand still a spell till it begins to grain and look clean on top"—

"May I suggest an improvement?" said the doctor. "Many persons are of the opinion that if you take and stir it up well from the bottom for a length of time it will help the coagulation of the particles. I believe that is the practice of Mr. Plumfield and others."

"'Taint the practice of as good men as him and as good sugar-bilers besides," said Earl; though I don't mean to say nothin' agin Seth Plumfield nor agin his sugar, for the both is as good as you'd need to have; he's a good man and he's a good farmer—there ain't no better man in town than Seth Plumfield, nor no better farmer, nor no better sugar nother; but I hope there's *as* good; and I've seen as handsome sugar that wa'n't stirred as I'd want to see or eat either."

"It would lame a man's arms the worst kind!" said Philetus.

Fleda stood listening to the discussion and smiling, when Hugh suddenly wheeling about brought her face to face with Mr. Olmney.

"I have been sitting some time with Mrs. Rossitur," he said, "and she rewarded me with permission to come and look at you. I mean!—not that I wanted a reward, for I certainly did not—"

"Ah Mr. Olmney!" said Fleda laughing, "you are served right. You see how dangerous it is to meddle with such equivocal things as compliments. But we are worth looking at, aren't we? I have been standing here this half hour."

He did not say this time what he thought.

"Pretty, isn't it?" said Fleda. "Stand a little further

back Mr. Olmney—isn't it quite a wild-looking scene, in that peculiar light and with the snowy background? Look at Philetus now with that bundle of sticks—Hugh! isn't he exactly like some of the figures in the old pictures of the martyrdoms, bringing billets to feed the fire?—that old martyrdom of St. Lawrence—whose was it—Spagnoletto!—at Mrs. Decatur's—don't you recollect? It is fine, isn't it, Mr. Olmney?"

"I am afraid," said he shaking his head a little, "my eye wants training. I have not been once in your company I believe without your shewing me something I could not see."

"That young lady, sir," said Dr. Quackenboss from the far side of the fire, where he was busy giving it more wood,—"that young lady, sir, is a pattron to her—a—to all young ladies."

"A patron!" said Mr. Olmney.

"Passively, not actively, the doctor means," said Fleda softly.

"Well I won't say but she's a good girl," said Mr. Douglass in an abstracted manner, busy with his iron ladle,—"she means to be a good girl—she's as clever a girl as you need to have!"

Nobody's gravity stood this, excepting Philetus, in whom the principle of fun seemed not to be developed.

"Miss Ringgan, sir," Dr. Quackenboss went on with a most benign expression of countenance,—"Miss Ringgan, sir, Mr. Olmney, sets an example to all ladies who—a—have had elegant advantages. She gives her patronage to the agricultural interest in society."

"Not exclusively, I hope?" said Mr. Olmney smiling, and making the question with his eye of Fleda. But she did not meet it.

"You know," she said rather quickly, and drawing back from the fire, "I am of an agricultural turn perforce—in uncle Rolf's absence I am going to be a farmer myself."

"So I have heard—so Mrs. Rossitur told me,—but I fear—pardon me—you do not look fit to grapple with such a burden of care."

Hugh sighed, and Fleda's eyes gave Mr. Olmney a hint to be silent.

"I am not going to grapple with any thing, sir; I intend to take things easily."

"I wish I could take an agricultural turn too," said he smiling, "and be of some service to you."

"O I shall have no lack of service," said Fleda gayly;—"I am not going unprovided into the business. There is my cousin Seth Plumfield, who has engaged himself to be my counsellor and instructor in general; I could not have a better; and Mr. Douglass is to be my right hand; I occupying only the quiet and unassuming post of the will, to convey the orders of the head to the hand. And for the rest, sir, there is Philetus!"

Mr. Olmney looked, half laughing, at Mr. Skillcorn, who was at that moment standing with his hands on his sides, eying with concentrated gravity the movements of Earl Douglass and the doctor.

"Don't shake your head at him!" said Fleda. "I wish you had come an hour earlier, Mr. Olmney."

"Why?"

"I was just thinking of coming out here," said Fleda, her eyes flashing with hidden fun,—"and Hugh and I were both standing in the kitchen, when we heard a tremendous shout from the wood-yard. Don't laugh, or I can't go on. We all ran out, towards the lantern which we saw standing there, and so soon as we got near we heard Philetus singing out, 'Ho Miss Elster!—I'm dreadfully on't!'—Why he called upon Barby I don't know, unless from some notion of her general efficiency, though to be sure he was nearer her than the sap-boilers and perhaps thought her aid would come quickest. And he was in a hurry, for the cries came thick,—'Miss Elster!—here!—I'm dreadfully on't'—"

"I don't understand—"

"No," said Fleda, whose amusement seemed to be increased by the gentleman's want of understanding,—"and neither did we till we came up to him. The silly fellow had been sent up for more wood, and splitting a log he had put his hand in to keep the cleft, instead of a wedge, and when he took out the axe the wood pinched him; and he had the fate of Milo before his eyes, I suppose, and could do nothing but roar. You should have seen the supreme indignation with which Barby took the axe, and released him with 'You're a smart man, Mr. Skillcorn!' "—

"What was the fate of Milo?" said Mr. Olmney presently.

"Don't you remember,—the famous wrestler that in his old age trying to break open a tree found himself not strong enough; and the wood closing upon his hands held him fast till the wild beasts came and made an end of him. The figure of our unfortunate wood-cutter though, was hardly so dignified as that of the old athlete in the statue.—Dr. Quackenboss, and Mr. Douglass,—you will come in and see us when this troublesome business is done?"

"It'll be a pretty spell yet," said Earl;—"but the doctor, he can go in,—he ha'n't nothin' to do. It don't take more'n half a dozen men to keep one pot a bilin'."

"Ain't there ten on 'em, Mr. Douglass?" said Philetus.

END OF VOL. I.

PUTNAM'S

HOME CYCLOPÆDIA

IN SIX VOLUMES;

COMPRISING THE FOLLOWING:—EACH SOLD SEPARATELY.

HAND-BOOK OF LITERATURE AND FINE ARTS,

By GEORGE RIPLEY, Esq., and BAYARD TAYLOR, Esq. 1 vol. 8vo., cloth, $2 00.

HAND-BOOK OF BIOGRAPHY,

By PARKE GODWIN, Esq. 1 vol. 8vo., cloth, $2 00.

HAND-BOOK OF THE USEFUL ARTS, &c.,

By Dr. ANTISELL. 1 vol. 8vo., $2 00.

HAND-BOOK OF THE SCIENCES,

By Prof. ST. JOHN, of Western Reserve College. 1 vol. 8vo., cloth, $2 00.

HAND-BOOK OF GEOGRAPHY,

Or, UNIVERSAL GAZETTEER.

HAND-BOOK OF HISTORY AND CHRONOLOGY,

Or, THE WORLD'S PROGRESS: A Dictionary of Dates.

In all 6 Vols., small 8vo., each containing from 600 to 800 pages, double columns, with Engravings.

In issuing the above works, the publisher flatters himself that he shall meet a literary and educational want which has long been urgently felt by families and schools, no less than by the general reader. The present active circulation of intelligence in all classes of society, demands the constant use of authentic and convenient books of reference. Labor-saving machinery has become as essential in the acquisition of knowledge, as in the application of the practical arts.

Most of the encyclopædias in popular use are on an extensive scale, contain a large quantity of matter which is seldom referred to, and can only be obtained at considerable expense. Indispensable to public libraries, and to the student whose researches embrace a wide field, they often exceed the demands, no less than the means of the intelligent reader, who wishes merely to take a rapid survey of the general branches of knowledge.

The present series of popular manuals is intended not for professional scholars, but for the great mass of American readers. No labor nor expense has been spared in this preparation which could more perfectly adapt them to their intended purpose. They have been edited with great care by able scientific and literary men. The materials have been drawn from a great variety of sources. In a small compass, they contain the essence of many large and valuable works. The subjects are brought down to the latest dates, and presented with all the completeness and accuracy which could be secured by the experience and industry of the editors.

The whole series furnishes a collection of manuals adapted both for the use of classes and for general reference, presenting a lucid and comprehensive view of general History and Geography, Literature and the Fine Arts, Biography, and the Sciences and Useful Arts.

The Hand-Book of Literature and the Fine Arts

Embraces all terms of Logic and Rhetoric, Criticism, Style, and Language; sketches of works which stand as types of their age or tongue; reviews of all systems of philosophy and theology, both of ancient and modern times; and a complete series of the history of literature among all nations, made up wholly from original sources. All the most important terms of common and international law, all technical words and phrases employed in theology and philosophy, and a number of scientific and historical phrases which have become familiarized in Literature have been included. The explanations are not confined to mere definitions; whenever it has been found necessary, illustrative woodcuts have been introduced, which will greatly assist the reader in his knowledge of architectural terms. In Art, the departments of Painting, Sculpture, and Architecture have been treated as fully and carefully as the nature and limits of the work would permit. While a mere technical array of terms has been avoided, care has been taken to explain all the words, and phrases of art-criticism have been defined at some length, as of interest and value to the general reader, especially since criticism has been recognized as a distinct department of literature. All words relating to the art and practice of music have been likewise retained.

The Hand-Book of Biography

Is founded on Maunder's excellent work, the compiler having endeavored to preserve the compactness, while he has improved upon the fidelity and comprehensiveness of his original. He has re-written most of the articles, either to enlarge or condense them ; and has added a vast number of names, especially of American men of eminence, and those who have died since former works were prepared. In all cases he has consulted the most reliable authorities, and given as much authentic information under each head as could be condensed into the allotted space.

The Hand-Book of the Useful Arts

Includes a description of the improvements and discoveries of the present advanced state of science, as well as a history of their gradual development. It will convey as far as the limits of the volume will permit, the greatest possible amount of information concerning the subjects treated of, that could be combined in a work at once intended for popular use and private reference. Very many of the publications issued in this country have added little to the knowledge previously existing in regard to its products, manufactures, or capabilities. Based, as all such works necessarily are, upon contemporaneous English productions, reference to the statistics and local peculiarities of this country is rarely found in their pages. It is hoped that in this Hand-Book of the Useful Arts, a step in advance has been made in chronicling the progress in Art to which the United States so rapidly and with such excellence have attained

The Hand-Book of the Sciences

Contains a brief explanation of scientific and technical terms, together with historical notices, descriptions of machinery, and other information requisite to enable the reader to gain an intelligent view of the nomenclature of the sciences, and their successive discoveries.

The Hand-Book of Geography

Is a complete, universal Gazetteer, showing the present relations of the different countries of the world, with the numerous changes that are constantly occurring carefully noted to the present moment.

The Hand-Book of History and Chronology

Has already appeared under the title of the "World's Progress," and has met with signal favor from the public. Whatever errors have crept into the previous edition will be carefully corrected, and the latest intelligence embodied in its pages.

It will be perceived from the above slight description, that the present series forms an encyclopædia of the most comprehensive character, easy of consultation, authentic in its statements, and afforded at a moderate price. The publisher is persuaded that he is greatly promoting the interests of sound knowledge in this country by its issue, and he confidently anticipates for it a wide circulation, and a long career of utility.

Notices of the "World's Progress."

"The World's Progress presents an immense mass of information, historical, biographical, geographical, mythological, literary and scientific, which can be found in no other single volume."—*So. Lit. Gaz.*

"The world's whole history—its chronologies, races, battles, eras, great men, wonderful events; indeed, every thing worth recording is compressed in alphabetical manner within the cover of this rare volume. It is a little library in itself—an Encyclopædia full of the right kind of data, in the briefest possible shape. Mr. Putnam has published many noble works, but few more useful than "The World's Progress."—*New Yorker.*

"This unique contribution to our literature is a library in itself, and we would rather enjoy the reputation of making and compiling this really extraordinary book than almost any other work of the season.

"Every young man should get it at once, and keep it close at hand, and he will soon find that his education is going on. No parent can give a better present to his child than this most useful moral manual of history."—*Christian Times.*

"This is about the most remarkable book we have seen. It is a monument of industry and research—an unparalleled embodiment of statistical knowledge, and a paragon of methodical arrangement. It is a volume of 700 pages of historical facts, dates, and memoranda, condensed almost beyond precedent, and compressed with so much skill and judgment as to afford a complete and thoroughly intelligible index of events. Prefixed to this treasury of knowledge is a chart of history. We would not be without this volume for many times its cost."—*Commercial Advertiser.*

"No book of reference has appeared of late years with greater claims to a place on every library table than the '*World's Progress.*' The work is a large volume of about 700 pages, full of facts, so arranged and classified as to be always easily found. It commends itself to all, who like ourselves, find the need of every sort of time-saving help in literary labor."—*Meth. Quarterly Rev.*

The Alhambra, Illustrated.

The Alhambra. By WASHINGTON IRVING. New edition, with large additions. Illustrated by 14 beautiful engravings on wood, by the best engravers, from designs by F. O. C. DARLEY. 8vo. Dark cloth, extra gilt, $3 50; extra blue, gilt edges, $4; morocco extra, very elegant richly gilt edges, $6.

This elegant volume is the last of the Illustrated Series. The subject, and the graceful mode of handling it, combine to render this a peculiarly attractive volume for presentation.

"The Alhambra is one of the most finished and fascinating of Mr. Irving's works. It possesses the elaborate polish of the Sketch Book. The splendor of diction, and musical flow of words, are, at times, perfectly charming.—*Southern Lit. Messenger.*

"This is one of Irving's most poetical and beautiful works, abounding in those exquisite pictures, which, although mere word-paintings, have all the fascination and impressiveness of the living, breathing canvas." *Southern Lit. Gazette.*

"The Alhambra is one of the most finished and fascinating of Irving's works."—*Western Lit. Messenger.*

Irving's Works, Illustrated.

New editions, in new and uniform style, viz., "KNICKERBOCKER," "TRAVELLER," "SKETCH-BOOK," and "ALHAMBRA." Square 8vo. Extra cloth, gilt edges, $16; morocco extra, best style, $24.

"DARLEY'S IRVING.—Putnam has published a most beautiful edition of the Sketch-Book, illustrated inimitably well by the racy pencil of Darley. It is this embalming of works of genius in the amber of art, which makes a library a luxury as well for the eye as the imagination. Sunny, genial, original, and tasteful Irving, worthily graced with fair print and appreciative illustration! It is indeed a completion of fitness, in which these days of haste and imperfectness should rejoice, as a bright spot of exception."—*Home Journal.*

New Portrait of Washington Irving.

Sketched from life, in crayons, by CHARLES MARTIN, Esq., and engraved in the finest style, on Steel, by F. HALPIN. Single copies, 50 cts.; proofs on large paper, $1 50.

As this is probably the last portrait that will be taken of Mr. Irving, this circumstance will consequently tend to enhance its value, apart from the fact of its acknowledged fidelity of expression.

"PORTRAIT OF IRVING.—There has seldom been a more felicitous piece of work. It is not only like Irving, but like his books: and though he looks as his books read, (which is true of few authors)—and looks like the name of his cottage, Sunnyside—and looks like what the world thinks of him—yet a painter might have missed this look, and still have made what many would consider a likeness. He sits, leaning his head on his hand, with the genial, unconscious, courtly composure of expression that he habitually wears, and still there is visible the couchant humor and philosophic inevitableness of perception, which form the strong under-current of his genius. The happy temper and strong intellect of Irving—the joyously indolent man, and the arousably brilliant author—are both there. As a picture, it is a fine specimen of art."—*Home Journal.*

Uniform with the above:

New Portrait of William Cullen Bryant.

Sketched from life, in crayons, by CHARLES MARTIN, Esq.; engraved on Steel in the best style, by ILLMAN. Single copies, 50 cts.; proofs, $1 50.

"No better likness will ever be made of Bryant and Bancroft than Martin's two portraits of these ante-mortem immortals. Bryant's true, though occasional look, is there—thanatopsically expansive and liberal."—*Home Journal.*

Letters of a Traveller. By W. C. Bryant. Illustrated

With numerous fine engravings on Steel. 1 vol. square 8vo. Cloth extra, $4; morocco extra, $6.

"Full of lively and picturesque sketches, acute observations, and nice discrimination. These notes possess peculiar interest."—*Christian Inquirer.*

The Shakspeare Gift-Book.

Tales of the Girlhood of Shakspeare's Heroines. By Mrs. COWDEN CLARKE, Author of the "Concordance to Shakspeare," with 10 fine Illustrations on steel, consisting of the following subjects:—Portia—View of Cawdor Castle—Portrait of Helena—View of Venice—Windsor Castle—Portrait of Isabella—The Town-Hall, Padua—Elsinore, and the Forest of Ardennes—A View of Verona. Fine edition, on large paper. First and Second Series. 8vo., elegantly bound, cloth, $4.

This is a charming Gift-Book for young persons, while it is not at all unsuited for the most fastidious and cultivated lady.

"Let everybody buy these Tales. From mothers and daughters we bespeak a hearty reception."—*Christian Inquirer.*

"Mrs. Cowden Clarke, whose 'Concordance of Shakspeare' shows such mastery of the letter of the poet's works, now evinces her appreciation of their spirit in a series of fictions, entitled the 'The Girlhood of Shakspeare's Heroines.'"—*Dickens's Household Narrative.*

"The design is one that would afford ample play to a lively and sympathetic imagination; and we are bound to say that the ingenious thought is admirably carried out."—*London Mor. Chron.*

The New Literary Gift-Book.

The Memorial: a Souvenir of Genius and Virtue.

Edited by MARY E. HEWITT. With splendid Illustrations on steel. 1 vol. 8vo. Elegantly bound in muslin, gilt, $3 50; morocco, extra, $5 00.

Among the contributors to this beautiful volume are the following:—

N. HAWTHORNE,	N. P. WILLIS,	MRS. SIGOURNEY,
A. B. STREET,	R. H. WALWORTH,	JOHN NEAL,
S. G. GOODRICH,	MRS. HEWITT,	G. LUNT,
R. W. GRISWOLD,	R. H. STODDARD,	E. L. MAGOON,
BISHOP OF JAMAICA,	J. R. THOMPSON,	G. P. R. JAMES,
A. DUGANNE,	MRS. HARRINGTON,	J. T. FIELDS,
MRS. E. A. LEWIS,	MRS. OAKES SMITH,	MARY E. BROOKS,
EMMA C. EMBURY,	ALICE R. NEAL,	DR. MAYO,
GEO. P. MORRIS,	R. B. KIMBALL,	BISHOP DOANE,
PROF. GILLESPIE,	ANNE C. LYNCH,	W. G. SIMMS.

"The extreme beauty of this interesting volume, and the high literary character of its contents, amply compensate for the delay which has attended its publication. It contains so many contributions of a superior order, that it may justly claim a less ephemeral interest than is usually attached to holiday offerings. Beside her own contributions in prose and verse, which are among the most pleasing productions of her pen, Mrs. Hewitt has gathered a delightful variety of original articles, many of which are from eminent writers, and which, taken as a whole, possess an unusual degree of excellence. The typography, paper, and binding of the volume. are in a style of refined and tasteful elegance, in a high degree appropriate to the object for which it was designed. We cannot doubt that it will meet with the cheering welcome to which it is so richly entitled." —*Tribune.*

"As a literary production, no work has been issued in this country containing such a list of contributors, distinguished by reputation and ability. The volume will sustain the reputation of being at the head of its class."—*Newark Advertiser.*

"For the literary merits of the volume, we will only say that most of the ablest writers in our country in this department of literature, are represented. Many of their articles are in their happiest vein. In its mechanical execution, however, the work has no superior in anything which has issued from the American press."—*Albany State Register.*

Rural Hours. By Miss Cooper.

Illustrated by a series of finely colored Illustrations. 1 vol. square 8vo. Cloth extra, $5; morocco extra, $7.

"A very pleasant book—the result of the combined effort of good sense and good feeling, an observant mind, and a real, honest, unaffected appreciation of the countless minor beauties that nature exhibits to her assiduous lovers."—*Albion.*

"This is one of the most delightful books we have lately taken up."—*Evening Post.*

"This is a delightful book, containing, in the form of a diary or journal, the reflections of a person of cultivation and refinement; of one who had an eye to see. and powers to appreciate the real meaning, the natural objects and phenomena around her. The reader is constantly reminded of Gilbert Whites 'National History of Selborne.' 'Rural Hours' is just the book for the drawing-room. Open where you will, you may find something of interest."—*Cambridge Chronicle.*

Poems. By Samuel G. Goodrich

Illustrated with a series of Original Designs, beautifully engraved on Wood. One volume, 8vo. Cloth extra.

"A collection of short pieces in verse, happy in their choice of subjects, and showing poetic fancy,—the cadences particularly are musical. It is very nicely embellished."—*Album.*

"One of the most beautiful works, in typographical appearance, that has issued from the American press. Adorned with sixty wood cuts, and vignettes, and arrayed in scarlet and gold, its appearance at this season of the year is most opportune. All those whose youth has been made happy by the ever pleasing stories of Peter Parley, will find that the old gentleman, having dropped his assumed name, is still catering for their pleasure. They will buy this book on the strength of the past, and will find that its melodious strains will charm the educated ear, as well as his tales delight the young heart."—*Newark Advertiser.*

The Girlhood of Shakspeare's Heroines.

By MARY COWDEN CLARKE, Author of "The Concordance to Shakspeare." Illustrated with fine Engravings on Steel. Price, 25 cents each part. Also in two volumes, cloth, gilt, $2 50.

I.—PORTIA, with Portrait on Steel.

II.—THE THANE'S DAUGHTER, with a View of Cawdor Castle.

III.—HELENA; the Physician's Daughter. With Portrait.

IV.—DESDEMONA; the Magnifico's Child. With fine View of Venice.

V.—MEG AND ALICE; the Merry Maids of Windsor. With a View of Windsor.

VI.—ISABELLA; the Votaress. With Portrait.

VII.—KATHARINE AND BIANCA; the Shrew and the Demure. With a View of Padua.

VIII.—OPHELIA; the Rose of Elsinore. With a View of Elsinore.

IX.—ROSALIND AND CELIA; the Friends. With a View of the Forest of Ardennes.

X.—JULIET; the White Dove of Verona. With a View of Verona.

"An original and felicitous idea, well executed, and very sweetly written."—*Home Journal.*

"Extremely well done."—*Evening Post.*

"Worthy to rank beside the delightful '*Tales*' by *Lamb.*"—*Scotsman.*

"Mrs. Cowden Clarke, whose "Concordance of Shakspeare" shows such mastery of the letter of the poet's works, now evinces her appreciation of their spirit in a series of fictions entitled 'The Girlhood of Shakspeare's Heroines.'"—*Dickens's Household Narrative.*

"The design is one that would afford ample play to a lively and sympathetic imagination, and we are bound to say that the ingenious thought is admirably carried out."—*London Morning Chronicle.*

Swallow Barn.

A Sojourn in the Old Dominion. By the Hon. J. P. KENNEDY. Illustrated with Twenty Fine Engravings on Wood, from Original Designs by Strother. In one large volume, 12mo., cloth, $2 00.

"Swallow Barn is one of the few American classics. It is for Virginia life what the Sketch-book or Bracebridge Hall is for that of England not less vivid, not less true. The illustrations of this edition are by a Virginian of remarkable abilities as a mere artist, and deserving of an eminent rank also as a humorist. The book cannot fail of being one of the most popular illustrated volumes that has appeared in America."—*R. W. Griswold, D. D.*

"We have always regarded "Swallow Barn" as one of the very highest efforts of American mind. It is exquisitely written, and the scenes are vividly described. Its features of Virginia life and manners are the best ever drawn. The work is eminently a splendid edition,—it is a most excellent and interesting production."—*Louisville Journal.*

American Historical and Literary Curiosities.

Comprising *fac-similes* of Autographs and Historical Documents of great interest and value. An entirely New Edition, greatly improved, with Additions. Large 4to., half morocco, gilt edges, $7 00.

The same. Large paper, Imperial folio, antique morocco, very elegant. Only 50 Copies printed, $16 00.

"Among the numerous books from the American press in which art and taste is combined, none seems to fill the place to which the volume before us is appropriated.

"The volume before us is entirely different from any thing we have seen. It consists of sixty-six folio engravings on stone, all fac-similes of curious letters, documents and autographs; together with portraits and drawings of interesting objects connected with old customs."—*Providence Journal.*

United States Exploring Expedition Round the World.

By CHARLES WILKES. The complete Edition, with all the Illustrations on Wood and on Steel, and all the Maps. 5 vols. Imperial 8vo., cloth, $15; do., half calf, extra, $20 00.

Wilkes' Voyage Round the World.

Comprising all the Essential Incidents of the Exploring Expedition. With numerous Wood Cuts. 8vo. Cloth, $3 00.

The Men of Manhattan; or, Social History of the City of New-York.

By FENIMORE COOPER. With Illustrations. 1 vol. 8vo.

The Shield. A Narrative.

By MISS COOPER, Author of "Rural Hours." (*A new work.*) 1 vol. 12mo.

"The deep and ancient night that threw its shroud
O'er the green land of graves, the beautiful waste."

Five Years in an English University.

By CHARLES ASTOR BRISTED, late Foundation Scholar of Trinity College, Cambridge. 1 vol. 12mo. Cloth. (In October.)

The Monuments of Central and Western America.

By FRANCIS L. HAWKS, D. D. 1 vol. 8vo. With numerous Illustrations. (In preparation.)

Dickens' Household Words.

In numbers, published weekly. Price, 6 cents each. Also First, Second and Third volumes. 8vo. Cloth, $1 75 each.

"From the time of the Spectator down to the present era of periodical publications, there has never appeared a literary magazine of so excellent a character as the Household Words."—*S. Courier.*

Para: Scenes and Adventures on the Banks of the Amazon.

By J. E. WARREN, Esq. A new and popular work. 12mo. Cloth, 75 cts.

"A well written and quiet entertaining narrative of travels, given in so pleasant a style as to charm while it informs the reader."—*Home Journal.*

"This book has given us great pleasure, and we shall be thanked by our readers for commending it to their attention."—*New-York Tribune.*

"A very interesting narrative of adventures—the author excels in descriptive ability."—*New-York Courier & Enquirer.*

Trenton Falls, Picturesque and Romantic.

By N. P. WILLIS, Esq. Wood Cuts. 18mo. Cloth, 50 cts.

"This is a beautiful little volume, descriptive of one of the most delightful spots and some of the most picturesque and romantic scenery in all our country. It is written in Mr. Willis's peculiarly agreeable style, and though local in its description, is of universal interest. Its principal illustrations, nine in number, are finely executed by Orr."—*Eclectic.*

The Wide, Wide World.

By ELIZABETH WETHERELL. Fifth Edition. 2 vols. 12mo. Cloth, $1 50.

"This is a tale depending for its interest on lively and truthful pictures of domestic and country life. Its portraiture of character is striking and true to nature, and the whole work is prevaded by a healthy religious and moral tone."—*Recorder.*

"It is the most valuable work of the kind I ever read. It is capable of doing more good than any other book—other than the Bible."—*Newark Advertiser.*

Mosses from an Old Manse.

By NATHANIEL HAWTHORNE. New Revised Edition. 12mo. Cloth, $1 25.

"Hawthorne is a man of quaint fancy, of considerable powers of description, holds a quiet but humorous pen, sometimes tinctured with wit and sly sarcasm."—*Newark Advertiser.*

The Home; or, Family Cares and Family Joys.

By FREDERIKA BREMER. Translated by MARY HOWITT. Author's Revised Edition. Cloth, $1 00.

"The world-wide popularity of "The Home" renders it unnecessary to speak of its merits. It is one of the most sterling novels which will outlive change; and in its present form is an ornament to the drawing room as well as the library."—*Home Journal.*

"Miss Bremer's warm affections, shrewd observation, and pictorial fancy, are visible on every page. The poetical power of her mind is exhibited in "The Home" to better advantage than in any of her other works."—*Graham's Magazine.*

The Berber; or, The Mountaineer of the Atlas. A Tale of Morocco.

By WILLIAM STARBUCK MAYO, Author of "Kaloolah." 12mo. $1 25.

"A romance of the highest class, replete with character, plot, and incident, and occupying ground entirely new. It is a much higher effort than "Kaloolah."—*Home Journal.*

"Dr. Mayo's new work has astonished us. It is an advance on his "Kaloolah," showing far greater resources of imagination than were evinced in his previous work. It is the book of the season."—*Newark Advertiser.*

Bayard Taylor's Eldorado; or, Adventures in the Path of Empire.

Second edition, with colored Illustrations. 2 vols. 12mo. Cloth, $2 00.

A cheap edition of the above work. Two volumes in one, without plates. 12mo. Cloth, $1 25.

"These volumes relate most striking and novel adventures, and cannot fail to be eminently popular."—*Commercial Advertiser.*

"They contain the most authentic, sparkling, and best printed information and adventure yet published."—*Literary World.*

Borrow's Autobiography: Lavengro.

By GEORGE BORROW, Author of "The Gipsies in Spain," "The Bible in Spain," &c. With fine Portrait.

NEW AUTHORIZED EDITION, LARGE TYPE. *Complete in one volume. Reduced to 75 cts. in cloth.* Paper covers, 50 cts.

"He colors like Rembrandt, and draws like Spagnoletti."—*Edinburgh Review.*

"The pictures are so new, that those best acquainted with England will find it hard to recognize the land they may have travelled over."—*National Intelligencer.*

"Not for years have our eyes lighted on a more fascinating or mysterious title. We could hardly sleep at night for thinking of Lavengro."—*Blackwood.*

The Conquest of Florida.

By Prof. THEODORE IRVING. Author's Revised Edition. One volume, 12mo. Cloth, $1 25. (Uniform with *Washington Irving's Complete Works.*)

"It is like reading an old romantic chronicle to pass these pages in review, so full are they of chivalric feeling and gallantry, so strange the adventures, and so beautiful the scenes which surrounded the adventurers. The whole career of the brave De Soto is one of romance, and would prove a great theme for the light fancy of the poet and novelist. Mr. Irving has given us a book which will be enduring, which, in fact, is proven by its present re-appearance, it having been originally published some years ago. It is finely written, and is an accession to American historical literature."—*Albany Atlas.*

The Optimist.

By H. T. TUCKERMAN, Esq. In one volume, 12mo., cloth, 75 cents.

"Among the Essayists in America, Mr. Tuckerman perhaps deserves the highest distinction. The "Optimist" is marked by nice analysis, delicate discrimination, a gentle taste, harmonious style, and a pleasant discursive vein of thought."—*Southern Quarterly Review.*

Sleep Psychologically Considered,

With Reference to Sensation and Memory. By BLANCHARD FOSGATE, M. D. One volume, 12mo. Cloth, 75 cents.

"A subject treated with much acuteness and grateful interest. It is discussed psychologically, illustrated by anecdotes, and attempts to explain and systematize a class of phenomena but little observed and less understood. The work is attractive and suggestive, not only to the professional man, but to the general reader."—*Home Journal.*

Mental Hygiene.

Or an examination of the Intellect and Passions, designed to show how they affect and are affected by the bodily functions, and their influence on health and longevity. By WILLIAM SWEETSER, M. D. Second edition, rewritten and enlarged. 12mo. Cloth, $1 00.

"We shall close our notice of this excellent and truly intellectual performance, not without urgently recommending its attentive perusal to all who desire the meus sana in corpore sano."—*London Medico Chirurgical Review.*

University Education.

By HENRY P. TAPPAN, D. D. 12mo. Cloth, 75 cents.

"This is the production of a skilful hand, and exhibits a very perfect analysis of the higher institutions of learning in this country, in England, and on the continent. We know of no work comprising in a small compass so much interesting and valuable information upon the subject."—*Evening Post.*

Treatise on Banking.

Revised Edition. By J. W. GILBART. 1 vol. 8vo. Cloth, $2 50.

"The work is judiciously arranged, and the instructions are clear and decisive.

"The work, in its present form, is far more comprehensive than any of the previous editions, and embraces a great variety of topics of great interest to bankers."—*London Bankers' Magazine.*

The Artist.

By MRS. TUTHILL. Being the fourth of the Series entitled "*Success in Life.*" One volume, 12mo. Half-bound. (In press.)

"Mrs. Tuthill's plan would seem to be—inciting to the noblest deeds in the profession or pursuit which she discusses, by first mapping out, as it were, what is necessary to success, and filling out the outline by practical common sense advice, enforced by illustrious biographical examples."—*Philadelphia Saturday Gazette.*

"Just the little book that a hundred thousand boys in this country ought to read."—*Christian Inquirer.*

American Genealogies.

Being a History of some of the early Settlers of North America and their Descendants, with Anecdotes, Personal Sketches, and Geneological Tables, &c. By J. B. HOLGATE, A. M. 4to., paper covers, $5 00.

"The plan of this work is new; it furnishes a key to American history heretofore neglected." —*Utica Contributor.*

The Smithsonian Contributions to Knowledge.

A new volume. Just out. 4to., cloth, $5 00.

This new volume formed the Second of a Series, composed of Original Memories on different branches of Knowledge, by S. C. WALKER, FRANCIS LEIBER, C. ELLET, Jr., R. B. GIBBES, L. AGASSIZ, J. W. BAILEY, E. G. SQUIER, &c.; published under the direction of the Smithsonian Institution.